The cool fingers that caressed her neck nearly caused her to skid off the road as she hammered the brake, jerking the wheel hard to throw "it" off of her. After some fancy maneuvering that the vehicle was never meant to execute, the car slid to a stop as she leaped out. The engine was still running, but she'd shoved the gear shift into neutral and yanked the emergency brake on. Instantly, she was grabbed and spun around to face a monstrosity. The Vampire had her by her shoulder and her throat, his dark eyes inches from her own, black hair falling over his shoulders like obsidian sheets.

Gillian gasped. He was handsome, of course. Most Vampires were breathtaking. He'd have been perfect, if you didn't count the horrible scarring visible on his throat, jaw, and chest where his antique shirt gaped open.

Holy water. That or direct exposure to some other holy item was the only explanation for why a Vampire would permanently scar. Although his face had been spared, it would have been an agonizing injury. He'd had it thrown on him or applied to him from close range. Probably right before he ripped out the hapless person's throat, she thought. Like what was about to happen to her if she wasn't lucky.

Gill leaned back reflexively, away from the gleaming fangs that snapped together an inch from her neck before the Vampire pulled back and smiled as her fingers tightened on the ruined skin of his throat.

"Prince Dracula sends his regards, Dr. Key. Consider this a warning as to how vulnerable you really are."

He spoke in a hollow but oddly compelling voice, then abruptly released her, dissolving into mist ＿＿＿ eaking away into the dark.

Key to Conflict

TALIA GRYPHON

ACE BOOKS, NEW YORK

THE BERKLEY PUBLISHING GROUP
Published by the Penguin Group
Penguin Group (USA) Inc.
375 Hudson Street, New York, New York 10014, USA
Penguin Group (Canada), 90 Eglinton Avenue East, Suite 700, Toronto, Ontario M4P 2Y3, Canada
(a division of Pearson Penguin Canada Inc.)
Penguin Books Ltd., 80 Strand, London WC2R 0RL, England
Penguin Group Ireland, 25 St. Stephen's Green, Dublin 2, Ireland (a division of Penguin Books Ltd.)
Penguin Group (Australia), 250 Camberwell Road, Camberwell, Victoria 3124, Australia
(a division of Pearson Australia Group Pty. Ltd.)
Penguin Books India Pvt. Ltd., 11 Community Centre, Panchsheel Park, New Delhi—110 017, India
Penguin Group (NZ), 67 Apollo Drive, Rosedale, North Shore 0745, Auckland, New Zealand
(a division of Pearson New Zealand Ltd.)
Penguin Books (South Africa) (Pty.) Ltd., 24 Sturdee Avenue, Rosebank, Johannesburg 2196,
South Africa

Penguin Books Ltd., Registered Offices: 80 Strand, London WC2R 0RL, England

This is a work of fiction. Names, characters, places, and incidents either are the product of the author's imagination or are used fictitiously, and any resemblance to actual persons, living or dead, business establishments, events, or locales is entirely coincidental. The publisher does not have any control over and does not assume any responsibility for author or third-party websites or their content.

KEY TO CONFLICT

An Ace Book / published by arrangement with the author

PRINTING HISTORY
Ace mass-market edition / June 2007

Copyright © 2007 by Talia Gryphon.
Cover art by Judy York.
Cover design by Annette Fiore.
Interior text design by Kristin del Rosario.

ISBN: 978-0-441-01503-0

ACE®
Ace Books are published by The Berkley Publishing Group,
a division of Penguin Group (USA) Inc.,
375 Hudson Street, New York, New York 10014.
ACE and the "A" design are trademarks belonging to Penguin Group (USA) Inc.

PRINTED IN THE UNITED STATES OF AMERICA

10   9   8   7   6   5   4   3   2   1

On the chance that anyone else reads this page, those mentioned are indeed deserving of dedications, medals, awards, canonization and significant hoopla.

For my mother, Eleanor, who told me I should write and didn't criticize my choice of genre; my remarkable sons, Justin and Forrest, whose unending patience about my time on the computer and unswerving love allowed this book to be written, and for just being great kids who are proud of their mother.

Laurell K. Hamilton, Christine Feehan, Stephanie Burke, Robin Owens, Sheila English and Rosemary Laurey. I am so grateful for their encouragement, friendship and being invaluable mentors to an unknown aspiring writer.

Ginjer Buchanan, my wonderful editor. A simple, heart-felt "Thank you" for believing in me.

Joe Veltre, my agent extraordinaire. Joe, I don't know how to thank you. You are amazing.

Darla Cook, my incomparable line editor and dear friend, without your help this truly would not have gotten off the ground. Also, to Ann Tredway, thank you. You started this. I blame you. *Wink*.

Special thanks to: Charles Randolph, Sgt. U.S. Army Special Operations Command; Jon Eppler, Sgt. U.S. Army Reserves Intelligence Analyst; Steven Mills, Sgt. USMC, Retired, for their invaluable help with technical consultation, military influence and approval.

And especially, to my best friend, Ali Houghton-Garrett. Your enthusiasm, loyalty, friendship and encouragement have been invaluable every single day.

Talia Gryphon

CHAPTER

1

GILLIAN Key, United States Marine Corps Captain, Special Forces Operative, former flower child, wiseass extraordinaire, also legitimately known as Dr. Gillian Key, Paramortal psychologist, was at the moment . . . lost. Swearing, she pulled her little rented Opal off to the side of the narrow road to study her map by the overhead light.

It had been a long day driving deep into the Carpathian Mountains of Romania from Bucharest. She was heading toward the village of Sacele. It lay off the main roads, not far from Brasov, deep in the mountains. Now it was getting dark and the town marked on the map was nowhere in sight.

The road was edged by dense forest. Tall pines and thick deciduous trees blanketed the landscape, dense but lacking undergrowth from the lack of light due to the forest canopy. There were no discernable landmarks, no lights on the roadway and the encroaching utter blackness was only grudgingly giving way to her headlights. The day was just getting better and better.

Gillian clamped a firm lid on her seething emotions, turned off the engine, lit a cigarette while rolling down her window, then leaned back in her seat to think. It would have been so much easier to fly into Brasov, but some fuckwit at headquarters had deemed it less obvious for her to land in Bucharest for the drive to Sacele. Probably some little desk jockey with no field experience.

She'd find out who it was and make damn sure they got field experience—under her command. A light smirk crossed her lovely mouth, followed by the ghost of a frown. Easy, girlfriend. Just a flunky following orders. Don't shoot the messenger or the scheduler.

"Goddess help me control my temper," she thought to herself absently as she exhaled the bluish-gray smoke. It wasn't exactly a prayer, but it was enough to bring her thoughts back into proper perspective. This was not a good time to unravel. She was early, as was her typical practice when going into a new assignment.

There was plenty of time even if she was a bit directionally challenged. Stop. Think. Act. Okay, fine, she'd stopped. Now she was thinking. Bully for her.

As she watched the sky darken overhead, Gillian thought about the beginning of her career in Paramortal psychology and as an operative. It all started with a Vampire: her lab partner in a college psychology class. Lovely girl . . .

Through her fanged friend, Gill had developed an appreciation for the inner workings of a person of Paramortal persuasion. Lupe was a fairly new Vampire, but was managing to keep it well hidden. This had been before the Human-Paramortal Wars of a few years back when Vampires were still creatures of legend and Werewolves, Fairies, Goblins and Ghosts still only stories to frighten each other with around a campfire or on Halloween.

No one but Gillian knew what her friend was. It was a night class with a late lab. Gill was taking it because it coincided with her schedule in officer training with the Marines. They were paying for her education as promised, but it was on their time frame. Lupe was her assigned partner and a total bitch. Gillian finally got pissed off enough to confront her after lab one night. Her inherent empathy began flaring to beat hell when Lupe turned at her sharp command of "Hold up, bitch!" Instead of wanting to break the woman's nose, Gillian found herself wanting to help her.

It must have shown in her face, because the Vampire softened and burst into bloody tears as Gillian neared. They'd spent the next several hours sitting in a tree on campus with Gillian learning that even immortals get the blues, have problems, experience heartbreak, are dissatisfied with the direction their prolonged lives took them. The next day, Gillian had switched her major from criminal justice to a double major with clinical Paramortal psychology added as her primary focus. Lupe's problems and needs fascinated her in a way no Human client ever could.

That had been eight years ago. Now a clinical psychologist with the Marines' Special Forces, Gillian had never regretted her decision. She'd done well. First as a Lieutenant at the Pentagon assigned as security during the first official Summit between Human and Paramortal delegations. That obligation had forced her directly into a field assignment that had turned out the best for all concerned. It earned her a fast promotion and recognition in both the military and Paramortal psychology hierarchy.

After her promotion to captain she had been field commander of a crack unit of commandos specializing in black operations: assassination and reconnaissance missions. Now she was an individual operative at present being utilized to infiltrate and report on the activities of small factions of Romanian Vampires who were potentially allied with the Vampire Lord, Dracula.

The legendary Vampire was rumored to not be content with the current peaceful dealings of the Human-Paramortal world and was trying to stir things up. To what extent and purpose, no one could seem to gather any information on. Hence why she was now on a darkening Romanian road in the very heart of his domain. Probably with a huge target painted on her ass, she thought to herself wryly.

Her cover for the mission had come as a request from the local Master Vampire. It seemed after four hundred years he had decided that he could use a bit of mental help. Gillian was surreptitiously working for the International Paramortal Psychology Association (IPPA), but was still a special operative. It was a fact unknown to all but one of her closest colleagues in the organization.

Absently she pushed her thick, long, blonde hair back over her shoulder, thinking she should have tied it up. Expertly removing another cigarette from a pack, putting it in her mouth and lighting it one-handed, she snapped the map flat. Sharp green eyes raked over the lines and contours indicated on the map. It was chilly in the Carpathians this time of year and her exhalation of smoke combined with the breath cloud formed by cold air from the open car window.

Coming to Romania to counsel this particular Vampire, Count Aleksei Rachlav, seemed like the best way to get the inside track on Dracula's plans. That was, if the Count knew anything.

Gillian's very public persona, bolstered by the Marine Corps and her membership in IPPA had brought her to Count Rachlav's attention. He had placed an ad in one of the IPPA's trade journals requesting therapy. He preferred a psychologist to come to him, all expenses paid.

There was an additional ad from Romania, placed by another family, the Boganskayas, requesting help for a bothersome Ghost. Gillian wanted both clients, as they were in close proximity to each other. There was no telling what a Ghost might know, so she'd requested this assignment. The IPPA had assigned them to her and she'd left at the earliest opportunity after informing her contact, Dr. Helmut Gerhardt, where she was off to.

At the moment, as she continued driving down the darkened roadway, surrounded by thick, foreboding forest, she wondered if this was one of her brighter ideas.

"Sacele should be just a little up ahead" she thought crossly as she studied the map, which unfortunately was in Romanian. Who the hell knew? She tossed the map into the passenger side, where it fluttered to the floor. Starting the engine again, she released the brake, shifted into gear and rolled on down the road.

Ahead on the left, after a short jaunt around some hairpin curves, she could see lights from a rather large area where the road abruptly forked. Straight on was darkness, so she veered onto the left fork, throwing gravel as she downshifted and gunned the engine, rivaling an Indy driver in skill.

Pulling into what looked like a gravel parking lot, she angled the car toward a cottage with the porch light lit and lights on within the structure. It looked like she was on a large estate rather than anywhere near a town. Unlike any of her male counterparts, Gillian was not opposed to asking for directions. She turned sharply, then backed up, parking with the nose of the car toward the exit. Never hurt to be too careful.

She stubbed the cigarette out, yanked the handbrake and killed the engine while she opened the door. Eight years in the Corps had taught her efficiency of movement, to combine several motions into one. Sometimes it kept you from getting killed. It only took a moment for her to flare her empathy around and determine that nothing with talons or fangs lurked in the immediate area around the cabin. It was a habit, but a habit that had saved her life on more than one occasion.

Visibly relaxing, she cast Nile-green eyes up to the cloudless sky. Her breath fogged out of her mouth, part cigarette smoke, part exhalation. It was chilly, but the snows had not yet come and the sky was velvet black, the stars glittering on the obsidian field.

She took a brief moment to admire the magnitude of stars before booting the door shut and walking purposefully toward the structure, which looked like a very large quaint cottage. As her eyes adjusted to the darkness, she could see what appeared to be a castle farther up the drive, but it looked dark and foreboding. There were lights here, and her empathy wasn't flaring . . . yet.

Hearing noises within, she knocked on the door and waited while footsteps headed her way. The light on the porch helped not to blind her as the door opened to a brightly lit room, but the man who opened the door made her reflexively reach for the gun she no longer wore openly at her side.

She stood her ground but inwardly flinched. He was tall, very tall. Ebony black hair fell in waves over his broad shoulders and silvery gray eyes appraised her from beneath elegantly arched brows placed on a harshly beautiful face.

The supernatural power radiating from him raised the hair on her arms and her nerves screamed at her to run. Vampire. No doubt in her mind. No Human ever looked like *that*. Probably one of the Count's entourage.

The sensuous mouth opened and a deeply toned, liquid-velvet voice, beautifully accented, caressed her. "How may I help you, Miss . . . ?"

The fact that he spoke English was interesting but not surprising. If he were an older Vampire, he was probably fully fluent in several languages. Vampires could read Humans like books, generally. The older and really powerful ones could get uncomfortably inside your mind if you weren't paying attention.

He had assessed her completely within a heartbeat of opening that door, she had no doubt. It was something fanged folk just did automatically without thinking, like breathing . . . *Oh, wait.*

Gillian found her voice and nerve at the same time. It would not do to look scared or broadcast nervousness. She snapped her metaphysical shields down firmly, flashed a winning smile, then answered him.

"For starters, I need to know where the hell I've gotten myself lost to so I can find my way back."

Her spontaneous grin struck a chord in the male as he felt her fatigue and irritation but also her warmth and authenticity. She was genuinely lost, honestly perturbed, but she was polite.

"Please do come in," came the rich voice again, sending a shiver up her spine.

Gillian entered cautiously, keeping the male in the periphery of her visual range by turning her head almost imperceptibly. She knew absolutely that if he chose to attack her in the enclosed walls of the cabin, there was absolutely nothing she could do against Vampire reflexes, strength and speed to stop him.

Unfortunately she could see no way around letting him be this close. *Grin and bear it . . . just smile, smile, smile.* Nerves of steel, that was the ticket. Right.

The room was large and brightly lit but the dark wood paneling and heavy gothic furniture toned it down for a comfortable, homespun feel. A massive fireplace occupied almost the entirety of one wall with an enormous carved mantelpiece and ornate tapestry over it. Her brief glance picked out the silvery furred wolf set prominently in the woven threads. It was depicted lying on an ivy-covered mound watching over a hunting scene and a village far below it.

The furniture was heavy, solid carved oak with both the couch and chairs overstuffed and upholstered with expensive tapestry-like fabric. The scenes on the material were of a countryside, with wolves running through the forest, mirroring the tapestry over the fireplace in theme.

Nice, she thought. *Obvious but nice.*

"Gillian Key." She offered her hand to the tall, dark and stunning door-opener. Being polite never hurt, especially to someone who was offering to help.

An elegant ebony brow rose in quizzical amusement. "Dr. Key? I am Count Rachlav. I had thought that we would meet in town, then come back here, but thankfully you are here now."

The hand that enclosed hers was large, warm and firm. He'd already fed that evening apparently. His eyes held questions, his gaze warm and inviting; his demeanor suggested that she relax and trust him. Not a chance in hell.

Gillian nodded and swallowed, feeling her irritation dissolve under his quiet, nonthreatening perusal. "Then I have inadvertently found you, and please call me Gillian."

"Aleksei, then, Gillian, if we are dispensing with formality."

His smile was more than friendly as she moved around him into the room. It was suggestive. Oh boy.

She could feel the weight of the Vampire's presence behind her, but she'd be damned if she'd be intimidated by him. He had already fed; he was about to be her client. There was nothing to be nervous about.

Like hell there isn't was her unbidden thought before she could squelch it.

Aleksei could feel her too. A Vampire for the last four hundred years, his power growing by the decade, he was sensitive to all life-forms, their needs and feelings. She was an empath he was certain, and he was betting she knew it or was aware of her own sensitivity.

He gently probed her mind and was a bit astonished by the roll of emotions near the surface. He'd never encountered a Human woman with her sensitivity, yet also with a deeply ingrained penchant for real violence. For a Human, she might actually be dangerous, a realization that surprised him and snapped his own predatory instincts to attention automatically.

Walking past him, Gillian felt the unspoken threat. Aleksei had made no move, given no signal, but she felt the shift in him.

Predator! screamed her mind, and she fought her instinct to turn and deck him before he pounced. It wouldn't do to knock the teeth out of one's host and client immediately upon arrival.

Instead, she turned slowly, looked directly into those metallic, silvery gray eyes. "I'm sorry, I'm a little jumpy and a little frazzled right now, and it is distracting to have someone directly behind me."

There, that was honest. A Master Vampire of Count Rachlav's age would be able to ascertain the truth from a lie in the space of a breath, likely before a thought was even completed.

Realizing that she'd reacted to him, embarrassed that he'd been so obvious, Aleksei moved. "I am sorry, *signorina*; please come in and relax. Perhaps we can begin right away."

An elegant hand indicated the pair of overstuffed chairs. "Please sit. Allow me to get you some tea."

Gillian sank gratefully into the proffered chair, pulling out her pad and pen, preparing to start with whatever Aleksei wanted as her client vanished behind a swinging door on the opposite side of the room.

Waiting for his return, she collected her thoughts. For now, she needed to do her job honestly. As a legitimate PhD, she really was there to help him and the local Ghost with their issues.

Her only instructions from the brief dossier she'd received were to find out if Count Rachlav knew anything about Dracula or any of the Vampire Lord's plans, and report her findings. Since any Vampire who was either Master-level caliber or a full Lord would be able to ascertain any hidden agenda she might harbor, the less she knew about the entire situation the better it was for her cover and, ultimately, her survival.

There would be no breaking of his personal confidentiality. His sessions with her and what transpired during them would remain private. For the next thirty days, she was his therapist and the nearby Ghost's counselor. After that, if she found nothing amiss, she would most likely be reassigned. If she found something . . . well, she'd cross that bridge if and when she came to it.

Aleksei returned with a platter that held a single cup and saucer, sugar, milk, lemon, spoon and the tea, setting it on the low table between them. Elegant, aristocratic hands poured the tea for her and handed her the cup. He consciously avoided brushing her fingers with his own as she took the cup. She was here to help him, not be seduced by him.

⸻

As he took the chair angled across from her, he dropped into it with the casual inherent grace all Vampires possessed, watching as she added sugar and lemon to the tea. Long, lean, muscled legs encased in knee-length black suede boots and tight black pants were casually crossed, giving the illusion of ease, though he felt coiled as tightly as a watch spring.

The lace cuff of his ivory lawn shirt softly folded back over his thick wrist as he brought elegant fingertips to his temple, resting a muscled arm on the padded chair. He was completely aware of the effect he had on her. Vampiric senses were registering all of it with alarming alacrity as he studied her reaction to his proximity: heightened pulse, faster and shallower breathing, blood pressure rising, eyes slightly dilated, genitalia becoming turgid and moist—a sensual perfume to his supernaturally heightened senses in the quiet cottage.

———◆———

Gillian and he regarded each other. With her mouth going dry and other parts of her body below her waist growing damp, she couldn't help thinking that he looked as if he'd fallen out of a Romanian Studs "R" Us, catalog. Masculine, virile looking, sensually stimulating and stunning as he was, she'd dealt with Vampires before and squelched any attraction she might have had.

Radiating testosterone, sex and sensuality was just an element of what he was. It wasn't intentional and he couldn't help it. Vampires just exuded sex. It was part and parcel of the magic that inhabited them, plus it made finding and feeding from their prey easier. Your meal tended to be extremely cooperative if it was experiencing the ecstasy of intense foreplay while you sank your teeth into its neck and the throes of a monumental orgasm while you drank your fill.

It wasn't that Vampires couldn't or didn't have sex; they did. Frequently. Generally though, unless they were emotionally involved with their donor in some manner, having sex together with blood-taking was strictly avoided.

Whether that was a Vampire rule, taboo or just common practice wasn't quite clear to non-Vampires. Vampires drank blood. They had sex. They just by and large didn't do both at the same time unless they intended a permanent attachment to the other party. Feeding without sex was efficient, impersonal— at least for the Vampires—and kept the prey happy. It was also less messy, faster and didn't involve removing anyone's clothing.

Their ability to bring mind-blowing ecstasy during feeding and sex was one of the reasons that Vampires rarely had any Human posse after them since their recognition as real and sentient beings. Satisfied prey rarely bitched. Presently, any Vampire alive could make it known they were short on donors and instantly have a full dance card.

There were an alarming number of Humans and other beings who craved the savage bliss they could find only in a Vampire's heated embrace. Addiction with purpose was what some of them called it.

The small blonde in front of him had Aleksei's mind in turmoil. She wasn't particularly young in Human years, about twenty-five, perhaps a bit older, he guessed, but a mere fledgling in Vampire terms. Young, short, but with a presence about her that suggested she was more treacherous than she looked. He shook off the thought immediately.

Dangerous maybe, but not to him. He could break her in half or tear out her throat before she drew a breath or a gun. Something about her was evoking all sorts of interesting instinctual feelings within him, not all of them unpleasant.

He was six feet, seven inches tall, his frame was large, but he was lean and muscular. She was over a foot shorter and her delicate appearance masked a body put together with feminine curves supported by hard muscle. The way she moved suggested a graceful strength and a certain amount of coiled power ready to explode.

Not exactly beautiful, she was extremely pretty, except when she smiled. When she'd smiled at him in the doorway, his heart had slammed in his chest from her sheer loveliness.

Therapy, he'd thought idly, when he'd seen her. She was the spitting image of someone he'd known. Someone who had been dead for over four hundred years.

Plunging right in, Gillian began their session to keep from drooling all over her lap. Aleksei Rachlav was easily the hottest male of any species she had ever seen in her life. *Focus. Focus and do the job. Forget how he looks or what he would feel like rolling around in bed. Do the job. Just the job. Clinical. Think clinical.*

"The report I got from you said that you were suffering from what we would term *fangxiety*. That is, you've never totally adjusted to your . . ."—she hesitated over the word—"reborn state."

"That would be correct." Aleksei's voice was one of unparalleled beauty. Gillian thought she could definitely get used to his voice, not to mention the rest of the package.

Shaking off her unprofessional thoughts, she continued. "In what way, specifically, Count . . . um, sorry . . . Aleksei, do you feel you have not made the adjustment? You are functioning rather well from what I have observed, and four hundred years is a long time to not be used to your circumstances."

Vampires who suffered fangxiety tended to be pale, shy, almost shriveled-looking and be far younger than the man seated before her who exuded the strength, health and sexual prowess of an older, powerful Vampire. Aleksei seemed to be more depressed than anxiety-ridden, but appearances could be, and often were, deceiving. She needed more information.

"I have adjusted to the lifestyle, Gillian, but not to the circumstance. I feed because I want to survive. I sleep in the earth or with the earth in my tomb because I want to survive. I am not suicidal by any means, but I am having trouble looking at an endless eternity of being alone.

"The circumstances of my life have been difficult. I lost someone very dear to me over four hundred years ago because I failed to see what was before my eyes. Coupling that with the realization that anyone I do begin to care for will eventually age and die a natural death, you begin to see my dilemma. I am lonely, Gillian. Eternity is very long indeed if there is no one to truly share it with."

Taking notes and glancing up to study his face and body language, Gillian caught the flicker of pain in his voice. He wasn't broadcasting emotions, but then he'd had centuries of practice.

"So what you are saying is that you are looking for some deeper meaning in your existence beyond simply being one of the more powerful supernatural beings with eternity to kill."

Aleksei smiled a wondrous smile and ignored her unintentional pun. "That is as close to the truth as we may get for a while, Doctor."

Easing him into his own solution was Gillian's job. Like any good therapist, it wasn't her place to tell him what she thought, it was to lead him around to what he thought. He'd already made the decision to make the changes in his life; Gillian just had to get him to a mental place where he could make them. Vampires were notoriously stubborn about changing age-old thought patterns and habits. She'd have her work cut out for her.

CHAPTER

2

AFTER some time, Gillian called a halt to the session. Scanning her notes, she felt she had a firmer grasp of Aleksei's problem. It wasn't unique by any means; she met conflicted and unwilling Vampires almost weekly. Aleksei was indeed depressed as well.

He'd spent four hundred years harboring guilt over a lost love and mourning his lost Humanity. The love had been lost because he'd refused to make her into what he was. He'd let her die, and still he mourned her loss. Four hundred years was a long time to embrace guilt.

She'd happened upon the very place she was supposed to be by chance. The inn and the village of Sacele, which she was looking for when she turned in here, had been around the next bend. Aleksei's manor home was indeed the castle she'd seen up the drive in the night's shadows.

The guesthouse where she currently sat was part of his vast property. After saying goodnight, Aleksei left to do whatever it was Aleksei did—Gill didn't want to dwell on that thought—so she finished his intake file before going to bed.

Deliberately staying up late since she would be working late afternoon into the late night with these two particular patients, Gillian took a moment to read over her other file. This one was for an Italian Ghost who was haunting a castle near where she was presently located.

She'd brought it along hoping she'd have an opportunity to meet with "him"—it was a male Ghost—while she was working with Aleksei. Staying permanently in Romania wasn't on her agenda, but she'd be at least a month with Count Rachlav. Depending on the Ghost's issues and knowledge base, she would be working with him as well.

She slept deeply and peacefully. Aleksei had assured her that the house was well protected and that none would disturb her while she was under his protection. Gillian knew Vampires well. There were good Vampires and bad Vampires. Her natural empathy stood her in good stead with her Paramortal clientele. Instinct and her empathy had kept her from being hurt or killed on more than one occasion—she was generally right in her assessments.

If someone were a decent Human being in life, they became a decent Vampire in their "rebirth." Vampires definitely didn't like the term "undead." That was reserved for Revenants, sort of the mentally challenged of the Vampire world, who were not much more than animated corpses with the intellects of tennis balls.

However, if someone were a murdering psychopath in life and managed to be reborn into a Vampire, you could bet lock, stock and silver bullets that they would maintain their original sadistic personality traits, which would be coupled with an extremely attractive package. Those were the dangerous ones.

Gillian had one or two dealings with a "Dracula," as they were called. Neither of them pleasant. One had almost gotten her because she'd guessed wrong. Once. Aleksei didn't seem to be the sort, at least not that she could tell this early in their therapeutic relationship.

Awakening early enough the next afternoon, Gillian made it down to Sacele and sought out the local magistrate. Buying supplies for the cabin and getting directions to the Ghost's castle took up most of the afternoon. By the time she got back, cooked, ate dinner, cleaned up and got her thoughts organized, it was time to meet with Aleksei.

His insurance had approved her as a provider for daily, intensive therapy for thirty days. Gillian was encouraged when, precisely at eight o'clock, Aleksei knocked on the door.

"Enter and be welcome, Count Rachlav." Gillian recited the

appropriate words for granting a Vampire access. She could re-
voke her invitation at any time, which lent her a small sense of
security. He'd been in the home the night before because it was
his cabin, his property. When he turned the keys over to Gill, it
had become hers and he needed her permission to enter. Of
course the rule only applied to a privately owned, personally
occupied structure. Buildings, churches, abandoned homes and
empty offices did not apply.

"Thank you, Dr. Key." Aleksei's black-velvet voice washed
over her, tightening her insides, making her blush slightly. *Gah!
Bad Gillian. Very bad.*

Mentally kicking herself as her own personal humidity in-
dex tipped into the red zone, she turned away to sit down. She
was going to have to watch her responses. Vampires were very
sensitive to physical reactions. She was betting Aleksei knew
she was attracted to him, though there was no help for it, given
what he was. He probably had females of all flavors and persua-
sions falling down in front of him in precoital . . . er . . . prefeed-
ing excitement.

What she wanted him to notice was that she was squashing
her reaction with determined effort and remaining as clinical as
possible. Even in the unlikely possibility of a mutual interest,
their relationship could be nothing but totally professional for at
least one year after his discharge from her care. Thinking about
him as anything but a client would undermine their relationship.
Gillian had no intention of letting that happen.

Aleksei had to admit that he was enjoying being able to speak
freely with a trained professional. Gillian listened intently and
he had no doubt he had her full attention. He knew she was attracted to him; any Human female would have been affected, he
recognized without a trace of egotism. The fact that she cen-
sored it in favor of his mental health needs, endeared her to him
in a way blatant flirtation or easy conquest never could.

Her comments were insightful, thought-provoking and politely stated. Thinking, truly thinking about how he had felt all
those long lifetimes ago in the manner in which she suggested,
opened up new realizations to him. Watching her as she listened
and took notes, he was struck by the depth of her personality.

He knew she'd been a Captain in the United States Marine
Corps from her curriculum vitae that he'd reviewed when the

IPPA had sent him her qualifications as a potential therapist. She was used to standing out and being in command. Now, she was seated quietly, keeping her own dynamic personality tamped down, listening to his problems, apparently content in her more subdued role.

She was dressed almost unobtrusively in olive drab cargo pants, a black turtleneck and hiking boots; she wore no makeup. As short as she was, she had curled up in the large chair, balancing her notepad on her leg as she wrote. Right-handed, he noted. Her nails were short and without polish, hands small and only a Gaelic *claddagh* ring adorned the little finger of her right hand.

Watching her tuck her golden hair absently behind her ear, he saw the small diamond studs she word as earrings. Multifaceted, like their owner. Sparkling. His mind drifted.

Aleksei wondered if there was anyone in her life, then snapped back to focus at her question. "This woman, Elizabeta, wanted to be reborn, but you refused because you thought she wasn't serious about her feelings for you, is that what I heard you say?"

He nodded slowly. Elizabeta had been his fiancée, strikingly similar in looks to the good Dr. Key. She'd been warm and silly and fun, but when he'd faced his greatest trial, dying and being reborn, she hadn't "felt" serious about him any longer, though she continued to profess her undying love.

His heightened perceptions had found that Elizabeta had a gold-digging little heart. She'd been a commoner; the Rachlavs were low-rung nobility, but the highest rung on the ascending rank ladder of royalty she'd ever be able to obtain.

Aleksei wound up breaking the engagement and letting her go her own way. When she died two years later in childbirth while married to another minor noble, he'd been distraught at her loss. When he learned she'd died calling for him, his guilt had racked him through the centuries. Now was the time to face the truth of the situation.

"Yes. Elizabeta didn't want me, she wanted new experiences, new challenges, new worlds. She'd hated being trapped in the role women were confined to in those days. She wanted what I could offer her, Doctor, but not in the manner in which a true love wants something from their fiancée."

"You were a means to an end," she softly noted. It wasn't said in anger or in an accusatory fashion, but Aleksei's temper stirred.

"A Vampire sugar daddy, yes. That's what she would have made me."

Gillian looked up; iron was in that velvet voice. He was blaming himself because he'd had an emotionally immature woman for a fiancée. He'd been honorable, not wanting to condemn her to his new dark life, and she'd looked to him for nothing but the freedom such a transition would afford her. Not the life they could have had together, even as Vampires.

Aleksei suddenly stiffened almost imperceptibly. Gillian's senses came on, full alert, her empathy flaring in response to his uneasiness and warning her of a potential threat. They both rose as one, her eyes on Aleksei and his eyes on the door. Ascertaining that he wasn't the threat, she instinctively moved in front of him as combat training and experience switched to autopilot.

Immediately she morphed from Dr. Key the psychologist and became all soldier once more. Though her mission was foremost in her mind, he was her client, and if there was something outside that made him nervous, blowing her cover was the least of her worries.

Incredulous, Aleksei stared down at her, noting the subtle shifts in her demeanor, body chemistry and bearing as she stepped between him and the door. She was going to protect him? The reflexive gesture on her part struck a tender chord inside him. This would not do. It was his privilege to stand between her and harm and his duty as Master of this place. Soldier she might have been, but she was female, Human and in his domain, under his protection.

Gently, he put his hands on her shoulders, intending to move her behind him and out of harm's way. What he sensed outside was powerful, cloaked to his mental probe, almost surely Vampire and headed directly to the cottage.

Gillian shook his hands off without looking at him. "I'm still a soldier, Aleksei," she informed him in a quiet but authoritative tone. "If something outside is causing you concern, I am probably not even on its radar. That makes you the potential target. Please stay back. I will not allow you to be harmed."

Her hand went to a spine sheath where she kept a long stiletto blade made of sterling silver and drew it, automatically distributing her weight evenly on the balls of her feet. The silver would seriously injure any Lycanthrope and do enough damage to a Vampire to buy them a few seconds of time for Aleksei to get clear.

The stunning Count's eyebrows rose; he hadn't known she was armed. It intrigued him that she had masked something from him. Curious, he asked her softly, "What do you sense?"

"There's something out there; you feel it and I feel it too, mostly through your perceptions."

Any further discussion would have to wait as the door drifted ethereally open. There in a swirl of mist, a tall, cloaked stranger materialized on the porch, radiating power and menace. Vampire. Shit. Gill would ask "what the hell?" later. She threw the knife with deadly accuracy and purpose.

"My brother," came from a deep, melodious, beautiful voice, a heartbeat before Gillian snapped the knife toward him.

"No!" Aleksei's voice thundered in the room.

She checked her throw literally as she was letting go of the stiletto. The action threw her off balance, so she dipped her head and flipped forward instead of staggering into the new being. Regaining her feet like a cat, she found herself past the threshold, on the porch and nearly in the stranger's arms.

The surprise of a small Human female flipping nearly under his chin brought the stranger's black-gloved hands out to steady her from slamming into his chest. Fingertips barely grazed her arms when she brought her own hands up violently, knocking his grip away and managing not to impale him on a silvery stiletto.

"Back. Off!" Gillian barked, resuming a fighting stance, knife gleaming and blood in her eye. The first thing she noticed was that he was now between her and the door. Fabulous.

The new male moved, nearly blurring with speed, to grasp the knife. Gillian noticed, chambered her leg and power kicked him in the chest as he enclosed her knife-wielding arm in a firm, vise-like grip. The impact threw him toward the doorway, but he took her with him, jerking her toward him as he fell. Stupid Vampire reflexes.

He seemed to bounce off the open doorway, stopped by an invisible barrier, the hood on his cloak falling back. Gill wound up on her stomach, halfway across the thigh and hip of another Vampire male who rivaled Aleksei in pure, stunning male beauty. In fact, they looked quite a bit alike, as she discovered when she turned her head and looked up at a fabulously attractive face, which also looked extremely pissed.

Damn, he was attractive. Dressed in retro-noble like Aleksei, the new arrival was a vision of the Old World. Black cloak, gleaming boots, tight black pants and a silk shirt of a lovely soft copper color clung to his tall frame.

"Hello, Tanis," Aleksei stated flatly before anything else could happen. "Dr. Key, may I introduce my brother, Count Tanis Rachlav, also a Vampire."

Lovely, thought Gillian. *Just fucking lovely*. But she fluttered the fingers of her knife hand at him from her position across his thigh. "Pleased to meet you."

CHAPTER
3

O H yeah, Tanis definitely looked pissed. Gorgeous but pissed, Gillian thought as she tried to contrive a way off him that just might resemble something in the dignified range. Shit, he really smelled good too, like pine forest and sandalwood.

Aleksei discreetly covered his mouth with his hand, hiding the smile that suddenly widened on his face. He didn't think Tanis had ever experienced being knocked on his rear end by anyone, let alone a small Human female.

Gillian was watching him warily. She bet when Tanis was vertical he was as tall as Aleksei. He had the same stunning good looks, same raven black hair, but his eyes were golden, almost like a lion's, and they were full of fire, leveled on her. He still held her wrist captive and had placed his other large, gloved hand over the small of her back. Uh-oh. What to do, what to do? Getting angry back seemed like a good idea if he wouldn't let her up.

Aleksei saw what was coming and reached down to pluck Gillian off his brother's lap and out of his grasp, taking the knife as a precaution. Setting her on her feet, he gave Tanis his hand, pulling the furious Vampire to his matching height. Both pairs of eyes oriented on the small blonde.

"Dr. Key, may my brother enter your home?"

Having some level of control unexpectedly put back in her

hands, Gillian recovered instantly, now realizing why Tanis had hit that invisible wall when she kicked him.

"Enter and be welcome, Count Rachlav, if you truly mean me no harm." There. She knew Vampire protocol. Let him answer honestly.

Those gold eyes should have been warm, but they were chilly. Tanis regarded her for a moment, "I mean you no harm, but you are sorely in need of manners, *piccola*."

Damn, his voice was as good as Aleksei's. Too bad he'd just pissed her off. Gillian liked anger. It was better than being scared, except that it dropped her IQ by several points. It was times like this that her inner Marine Corps hardass went head to head with her inner Gandhi. Today the marine won.

Fueled by adrenaline, her professional demeanor was shot to hell. "I beg your pardon, you ignorant ass, don't lecture me about needing manners when you tried to barrel in here uninvited during a session with my client and scaring everyone half to death."

Gillian's voice was hard and clipped. Her drill instructor would have laughed her ass off. Dr. Gerhardt, her IPPA contact, would have killed her on the spot. Major Daedelus Aristophenes, her commanding officer, would have laughed his ass off, then killed her. Oops. Her cover. Right. Dammit.

Twin ebony eyebrows lifted at her audacity. Tanis had been around for the same four hundred years Aleksei had, but he had never met a woman as cheeky as this one. Certainly not a combat vet marine with a low tolerance for snarky chauvinists of any variety.

"The women I am used to, Dr. Key, are less sarcastic to guests in their home."

"Obviously you've been hanging around with the wrong women," Gillian snapped back.

Silence reigned for an interminable amount of time. Nobody moved and Gillian started feeling slightly idiotic standing there with two very large Vampires between her and inside. Aleksei silently handed her back the knife, hoping that she would put it away before Tanis's temper got the better of him.

———⊷◉⊶———

Aleksei's familiar thoughts came to Tanis softly. *"You are scaring my therapist, brother. Could you manage to look a little less threatening at the moment?"*

"She needs to be scared. You should have left her where she was: bent over my knee for a lesson in manners. You picked her up too quickly." Tanis's heated thought came through just as clearly.

This was not going well. Aleksei thought that Gillian might punch a hole in Tanis with her shiny blade if he tried to make good on his threat. He did not want to think about what Tanis might do to the lovely Dr. Key if it came to that.

Gillian resheathed the blade, then glanced at Aleksei and took a private vote on how to handle this. It wouldn't do to skewer her client's brother, not on the first meeting anyway. Swallowing her irritation—thank goodness for those anger management classes—she offered him her hand and went for polite.

"Look, we've started off badly. I'm Dr. Gillian Key. Please come in, Count Rachlav." There. That was so polite it made her teeth hurt. Stupid Vampire Rules.

Tanis's expression never changed and the lovely voice was chilly. He ignored her proffered hand. "Doctor, is it? Let us hope that your professional skills far exceed your social abilities or you will find yourself placed across my knee once more for a rectification of your appalling conduct."

He swept past her into the room, stopping by the massive fireplace to turn and look expectantly at Aleksei, still standing by the door.

O . . . kay. Domination Dracula was just running his fanged mouth, so she'd let that go. *Diplomacy*, Gill reminded herself, blushing at his implication. Yup. Diplomacy. The art of saying "nice Vampire" before you found a stake and a mallet.

She gritted her teeth and waited for the next glass coffin to shatter. Aleksei came to her rescue. "What do you need, Tanis? I am in the middle of a session with my therapist. And why were you cloaking yourself so completely?"

Tanis's golden gaze raked over Gillian then swept up to his brother's eyes. "We need to talk, Aleksei. There are some things you should be aware of. Immediately."

Gillian thought that she might make herself scarce before decorum became any more broken. "Listen, Aleksei, why don't you and your brother talk. We were about done for the evening anyway. I think I'll just trot on down to the village. You did say there was a nice pub there, didn't you?"

Aleksei looked at her. In relation to himself and Tanis, she looked impossibly young and vulnerable, but that was illusion. She would be up to any problem she might encounter in the small village. He reminded himself that she was a successful combat veteran and would not be easily daunted or intimdated.

He nodded. "Yes, the innkeeper, Radu, is a friend. Please tell him to charge your expenses to me."

Gillian gathered her things quickly as Aleksei stepped back from the door. "Thank you, Dr. Key. I will see you later then."

"Thank you, Aleksei. I'll be back in a couple of hours." She nodded to Tanis. "Tanis, I hope you and your brother have a nice chat."

"Despite your shitty attitude," she added under her breath and hustled out the door before he could reply.

As she got into the small Opal, she saw that Aleksei left the porch light on for when she should return. Nice Vampire. Too bad his brother was a shithead.

Soon she rolled into the town, which looked like a picture postcard from a fantasy movie like *The Tenth Kingdom*. Even at night it was lovely. She pulled up to what looked like an inn, judging by the rectangular sign that hung from the side of the building. It was a painted woodcut featuring a sleek, well-fed wolf lying on a hill overlooking a flock of fluffy white sheep. The sheep were positioned so that a couple were looking up, aware of the wolf as they continued to graze happily under its watchful eye. There was no sheepdog nor shepherd in sight. The wolf was the guardian of the contented flock.

The carved letters were in Romanian, but Gillian got the gist of the meaning. Something big and bad watched over this village and its people and the gods help any who would interfere. She was betting it was referring to Aleksei and his family.

After she freshened up, she went down to the pub and ordered food and plenty to drink. The owner/bartender came to sit at her table. He was attractive, like most of the men in the area seemed to be, and anxious to make sure of her comfort.

"What else we can do for you, miss, to make you happiest?" His voice was heavily accented Romanian and his eyes were kind.

"Who owns that compound back down the road?" she asked, wrapping her mouth around a delicious smoked sausage.

"Ah, that is Count Aleksei's guest home. You have met him, then?"

"Oh yes, I met him. Him and his brother. Who are they?"

The owner, Radu, grinned widely. "They are wealthy landowners. All of us in Sacele, in this province, owe them much. Their family for centuries have been here. You are fortunate to have turned there for help. You will be safe from the Nosferatu if you are their friend."

"Nosferatu? Vampire?" Gillian looked at his face, his eyes. He was serious, despite the grin.

"Yes. Outsiders think these are legends only but they are real, miss. Too real."

Gillian settled back, lit a cigarette and let him pour her drinks while she listened to some very strange tales. She took no notes, relying on a steel-trap memory. In her room, later, she would enter it all on her laptop. Radu confirmed her guess about the sign. The direct translation was "watchful shepherd." Well, it was fitting.

Back at the Rachlav compound, agitation reigned. Tanis had started to go after her for her whispered comment when she'd fled but Aleksei had stopped him.

"What is so important that you unexpectedly come here after being gone for the last twenty years and arbitrarily reveal yourself to a Human, Tanis? Oh, and welcome home."

His younger brother regarded him. "Our beloved Lord, Prince Dracula." Five words. But it was enough. Aleksei's expression couldn't have been more shocked if Tanis had suddenly told him he'd figured out how to regain his Humanity.

"How? He couldn't have entered the Country without one of us being aware of him." Aleksei's voice was calm as ever, but inside his gut was churning with anger.

"He has to have a plant, an accomplice in Immigration," Tanis said flatly, starting to pace in agitation.

Aleksei regarded his brother's figure as he roamed the cabin like a caged tiger. Tanis was seething with barely controlled fury. Infinitely dangerous and an unpredictable predator, he was still the one person Aleksei trusted above all others. Neither had forgiven the Prince for decimating their family, for making them what they were. They hadn't seen the warlord in over three hundred years. No one had, that they knew of. It had been assumed that he'd been killed by one of his many vengeful victims or by some miracle, had Faced The Sun.

Raking a hand through his long, raven-black hair, Aleksei stated the obvious, "What are we going to do?"

———◦———

Tanis stared at him. "We are going to gather whatever reinforcements we can, brother, and defeat this ancient evil. Now, collect your little spitfire therapist and let us formulate a plan."

"What does Gillian have to do with it?" Aleksei wasn't following Tanis's thoughts; he was still reeling with the knowledge that Prince Dracula, the bane of all the Rachlav family's and of most Vampires' existence was back in the Country.

"She is residing here, in your home, for a start. That alone makes her a target. Every soul in this village we protect and hold dear is a target. Gillian is also a combat-experienced soldier, Aleksei. I read that clearly in your mind. She can advise us tactically, help protect these people if it comes to open conflict on our doorstep. We will need every ally we can get."

Tanis never was one to mince words. Aleksei glowered at him, but he continued. "Aleksei, like it or not, her life and the lives of our village are now in mortal danger. Aside from direct assassination, she could be used as a means to manipulate you if she is captured.

"If Dracula is here, if he has operatives in the area, then he already knows of her acquaintance with you. It is in her best interest and ours if we attempt to utilize her knowledge and she agrees to accept our protection."

"And will you personally guarantee her safety?" Aleksei had been an honorable man in life; being a Vampire hadn't changed his basic nature.

"She did not come here to be a soldier, Tanis; that is in her past. She is a clinical psychologist now, here at my behest, to help me with what has plagued me these long years."

Tanis stepped up close to his brother, gently laying his hands on Aleksei's shoulders. "No true practicing psychologist would have lost her temper with me as she did. No one but a veteran soldier would have stepped in front of you with nothing but a ten-inch silver blade between her and death to face whatever was coming through that door. Gillian Key is not what she seems."

"And how did you come to this particular conclusion, Tanis?" Aleksei crossed his arms over his impressive chest, looking intently into his brother's golden eyes. He did not want to believe that Gillian had deceived him or was something more than what she had represented herself.

Tanis smirked. "I am not so far removed from the world as you would believe, dear brother. I do read the occasional magazine or watch an occasional television program or newscast. The professional standards of her field would prohibit her from behaving in such a manner in the first place. She would have been behind you or a table at the first sign of trouble and she never would have started an antagonistic dialogue with me. Demonstrations of logical behavior and thought are important to those in her profession. Blatant aggression is not.

"Her purpose here is clandestine, Aleksei, mark my words. We need to ascertain what her true purpose is for being in Romania and taking you on as a patient. Meanwhile, we will keep her safe. I swear I will give her my protection as well. The good doctor will have to put aside her idiotic Human feminist principles and allow us to look after her." He smiled, and it wasn't a friendly smile, but rather toothy.

"Tanis . . ." Aleksei's tone said it all. Having Tanis and Gillian in a confrontational situation so soon after their disastrous meeting did not seem like a wise course of action.

"I give you my word, Aleksei. I will try to curtail any unreasonable, outdated and chauvinistic male instincts I harbor. However, if she lies to us about her purpose here, or if she accosts me again gratuitously, you may expect repercussions," Tanis said resolutely. "Now go get her, and let us see if we can discuss this with civility."

———

Leaving to get Gillian from the pub, Aleksei wasn't sure about the two of them having the capability for a civil discussion.

Tanis was only five years younger than he, but he'd never gotten around to conforming to modern ideals and thoughts, mostly due to his solitary predisposition. Even as a Daywalker, Tanis had not been the most sociable of creatures. As a Vampire, he was positively reclusive.

Aleksei had tried to make it a point to keep up with current trends through the ages, but Tanis seemed stuck in ground zero of the sixteen hundreds. He rarely had lengthy contact with any of his prey, though he enjoyed brief female companionship when he desired a taste of flesh, but never allowed himself a deeper involvement. Aleksei suspected that was partly due to Tanis's insistence on maintaining an arrogance and attitude that was out of place in the current century.

Tanis was stunningly attractive and had no trouble finding a woman for company. Keeping her was quite another matter when she found out how overtly chauvinistic and domineering he could be.

Tanis hadn't had a serious relationship of any kind in centuries, Aleksei was certain. Neither had he, for that matter, Aleksei thought wryly, even if for different reasons. Having Gillian under foot was bound to create some serious fireworks at some point.

The situation with Dracula aside, Aleksei wasn't looking forward to spending time with his younger brother and thoroughly liberated therapist. He was already struggling to keep his own interest in her locked down beneath an iron will. The fact that she may have lied to him and gotten away with it displeased him to no end. If that were true, he needed to have a little chat with her.

He found Gillian in the pub, teaching Peter, Paul and Mary songs to a rapt audience of locals. The interior of dark Gothic paneling, heavy carved tables, chairs, booths and paneling gave the pub an Old World charm and presence. The bar was on one side, the wall behind it lined with bottles of various alcoholic concoctions. All the lighting was from candles or oil lamps. Sacele was proud of its ancient Romanian heritage and kept to the old ways in many aspects outsiders could not fathom.

Gillian was at the other end of the room, strumming a guitar while Radu accompanied her on a fiddle. Her enthusiastic audience applauded when she finished, calling for more. Laughing, she crushed out her cigarette, waving merrily to Aleksei.

Telling the crowd, "Later," she handed Radu the guitar, and joined Aleksei at his table in a darkened corner of the bar. Sighing, he tried to explain what was about to transpire and eventually what he was concerned with about her.

Gillian listened without interrupting. This was very bad. This was very, very bad. Some of her prior patients had told her about the real Prince Dracula. It was a name spoken of in whispers if it was spoken at all. All Vampires that she'd had contact with feared him, even those of his direct line.

He'd risen out of obscurity in Transylvania in the fourteen

hundreds, a warlord who had loved and freed his people from the Turks, by unorthodox methods to be sure. Dracula had been a national hero, beloved, almost worshipped—the Romanian King Arthur of his time.

Somewhere, somehow, something dark and evil had gotten to him, turned him, changed him. The hero he had been was transformed into a bloodthirsty psychopath who stopped at nothing to inspire fear and intimidation in his enemies and in his own people. The only other plausible explanation was that he had always been inherently evil and, like a good sociopath, he'd hidden it well for a time before revealing himself.

Dracula had started a reign of terror among mortals and Paramortals alike. He'd taken only the most beautiful, the most desirable, most wealthy and most morally bereft men and women that he could find.

There were rival Vampire lineages but Dracula's were the most feared, since a large percentage of them were as psychotic as their Liege Lord. Gillian had met at least two of his line in her practice, she recalled grimly. At least one of which she'd been sure of. He'd been consumed by guilt and wanted to assimilate what was his fault and what was in response to his Lord's direction.

The second had been very skilled at cloaking himself from her empathy. By the time she discovered how psychotic he truly was, she had been alone, on a visit to a kill site with him when his true nature and fangs had come out.

He'd almost killed her because she had let her guard down trying to establish some kind of compassionate contact. It was only pure luck that she had killed him first. He'd only been a fledgling Vampire and not very powerful. That experience left her with a definite uneasiness about her abilities for awhile.

Time and exorcising her own personal fears had allowed her to overcome them. Hearing Aleksei's explanations of the danger they were all in sent real fear coursing through her veins. She so did not sign on for this. A centuries-old Vampire like Dracula who was a true sociopath was not something she was prepared to deal with.

Aleksei's lovely voice continued on, telling her about his own family history. She felt a twinge of unease when he revealed to her that he and Tanis were also of the pathological Prince's lineage.

One of Dracula's Vampires, a female named Nadia, had

managed to seduce Tanis first. It had been a calculated move, the equivalent of a Mafia hit. Tanis had been thirty, young, volatile, arrogant and adventuresome. While Human, was a vocal opponent of Dracula's influence and crimes, following the opinion of the rest of the Rachlav family.

Nadia had been beautiful, seductive and single-minded on orders that were never proven to come from Dracula himself. She'd bedded Tanis, turned him and left him in the space of two weeks, barely fulfilling her obligation as his Maker. Aleksei was left with a temperamental and incredibly dangerous younger brother to protect from his own family, most of whom wanted to end Tanis's suffering on the end of a sharpened stake.

Tanis was way ahead of them on that idea. He had tried to end his life at first. Frightened of what he'd become, he tried intimidation tactics without actually killing anyone and placing himself at the mercy of a bloodthirsty mob of peasants armed with pitchforks and torches.

When Aleksei intervened, literally stepping in front of that enraged mob to protect his younger brother, Tanis had fled. It was months before they saw him again. The younger Rachlav returned to ask his brother to witness his suicide: Facing The Sun the following morning. It seemed that he'd learned a few things during his absence about Vampire culture and tradition.

Aleksei surprised him by bringing a number of family members to the event and making an impassioned plea for Tanis's life. He convinced the family and Tanis that they were better off with a reborn, live brother than a truly dead one. The suicide was called off, Tanis was welcomed home by brother, family and the village, who hadn't quite been ready to destroy the second son of their benevolent local Count.

Soon after that, in another preemptive strike, Aleksei had been taken. This time there was no question that it was a deliberate act on Dracula's part to wipe out his vocal opponent's family.

There was no seduction; Aleksei had been attacked one night by one or more Vampires—he still could not clearly remember—drained and left for dead. Tanis had found him breathing his last by the side of the road. Giving his brother his own powerful blood and keeping him hidden during the transformation, Tanis brought his sibling over into rebirth without a moment's hesitation. Aleksei hadn't forgiven him for the first fifty years, hadn't spoken to him either except for the first few critical weeks as a fledgling when Tanis had to teach him how to hunt and to survive.

Going from a thirty-five-year-old noble to a reborn Count took some getting used to. Strangely, it had been Aleksei who had made a better adjustment eventually, even with all his angst.

Tanis remained angry. Nadia had been the last woman he'd actually trusted in four hundred years. He had no use for Human females except for food and the occasional sex partner when the interminable loneliness became too much to bear.

That particular indulgence he had not pursued in over a century. He fed almost exclusively on men or women he did not find particularly attractive. He had no desire to share a blood-and-sex bond with anyone.

Aleksei felt badly for Tanis's reclusive tendencies but he always returned to touch base and reconnect with his older brother after disappearing for years at a time. Tanis was the older Vampire by a few months but Aleksei was more powerful and more stable from the onset of their Shadowed Rebirth.

Tanis had traveled the world, mostly keeping to uninhabited areas, focusing on a career in archeology, where he could work alone and undisturbed. It kept him isolated and kept his highly intelligent mind focused and active. Aleksei remained in his homeland, looking after the people of Sacele and the lands around his castle, bound by a code of honor that was as old as the Country itself. The two didn't always get along, but whenever Aleksei had needed him, Tanis had been there.

Facts, suppositions and strategies were all forming in Gillian's mind. She was stuck there. She'd agreed to see Aleksei and she would honor that commitment. Now she was forced into another role of self-preservation and of consorting with not only her client but his family and the villagers as well.

When Aleksei pointed out that he and Tanis suspected her of being a bit more than a psychologist, Gillian slammed her shields down with a force that almost hurt. He was attuned to her, she'd been open and receptive. That kind of reaction to his assertion was all the confirmation he needed that she was there with another agenda.

Blushing furiously under his intense silvery gaze and pissed off that she'd been so obvious, Gillian hadn't actually admitted to anything but she had confirmed that she was still able to operate legally in soldier mode and lend whatever assistance she could. She also assured him that she genuinely was a doctoral-level clinical psychologist and that everything that transpired between them would remain confidential. She was still legitimately his therapist for as long as he wanted her.

Aleksei didn't press her for further disclosure right then. He did let her know he was rather annoyed and disappointed that she'd used him for her cover and had deceived him, but right now they had bigger fish to fry.

Gillian realized several things. One, she was totally screwed. Leaving was out, even if she could have convinced the oh-so-studly Count Rachlavs to let her leave. Two, whether they knew her cover was blown or not, she wasn't done ferreting out what the hell was going on in Romania with the burgeoning fanged turf war.

If she left, Dracula would be sure to have her killed. He did not believe in the mixing of Vampire and Human, according to what Aleksei told her at the pub. A belief not shared by most Vampires or other Paramortals and certainly not by the Rachlav clan. Aleksei was quick to point out that while he and Tanis were of Dracula's direct lineage through the Vampire virus, they were allied elsewhere, in direct opposition to the Line of their ultimate creator and Master.

An important fact she learned was that Dracula's subordinates generally believed that Humans were cattle to be fed upon, used and controlled. Vampires did not need to be out in the open, subjecting themselves to Human laws. Humans who tried to mix in with Vampires for any sort of relationship other than as a prey animal should not be allowed to live. Such was Prince Dracula's decree.

The occasional "appropriate" Human may be turned for expansion of Big D's empire or to subvert his enemies, but for the most part they were amusing sustenance only. Humans were not to be nurtured, brought into any Vampire's affairs, cared for or done business with. They were food. You do not make friends with your food.

Aleksei went a long way to reassure Gillian that she was under his and Tanis's protection. He would be her patient but she must trust them in matters of her safety. The prospect of dealing with Tanis on a nightly basis set her teeth on edge, but Gillian was practical. Survival skills had always been her strong suit. She'd comply. She just didn't have to comply happily.

"All right. I'm not happy about it but I'll do it. Now I need to let the IPPA and my superiors know what the hell is going on."

And won't they just be thrilled shitless, she thought as she went to make the call, mentally bracing herself in preparation of telling them that there definitely was a slight problem in "Fangland" and who was behind it.

Gillian made her call and got special dispensation from the grand pooh-bahs at the IPPA to remain and act as she saw fit. Fortunately they had a twenty-four-hour emergency line, she had a calling card and both Major Aristophenes and Dr. Gerhardt were in.

Her license would have been on the line if she had blurred the boundary lines too drastically between client and counselor as she might have to do to keep all them alive, without express permission. The Marine Corps and the IPPA gave her their full support and blessing since Aleksei was wise to her anyway. She was on her own tactically. They couldn't send anyone in to help her just yet. Act with discretion, complete her mission, take care of her patients and stay alive were her orders.

The IPPA was used to dealing with crazy shit, but a full Vampire turf war was a new one. The Human conflict with the Paramortal world had left everyone a little obsequious and suspicious with each other. Having one of their highly trained therapist/operatives caught in the middle of such a conflict required desperate actions and a writing of new policy jointly with Gillian's division of the USMC.

By the time Gillian had gotten off the phone, there was already paperwork in place to protect her against any malpractice or court martial in the course of her duties with this situation. Covering her ass was a specialty that she was proud of.

Riding back with her to the cottage, Aleksei watched her driving. Outwardly, she was cool, calm, although she'd consumed a large amount of alcohol during their discussion. She was chain-smoking, however, drawing the smoke deep into her lungs and almost sighing it out. Inwardly, from what he could read on the surface of her mind, there was chaos. She felt trapped, insecure about the enemy she was going to face and vastly irritated at being discovered.

Used to being in command of her life and, in military situations, of her troops, it grated on Gillian to have to rely on the Rachlavs. She knew, however, that the situations in which she might find herself would be wholly alien to her. This was their world and what it harbored could kill her . . . or worse.

Guns and Human thinking were irrelevant. Silver bullets, flamethrowers, a crossbow, her own psychic sensitivity, a large amount of Paramortal ability and protection from Aleksei, Tanis and their allies would be what would keep her alive. She needed them. It pissed her off and made her knee-jerk response of getting the hell out of there seem paramount.

Aleksei's amused voice was low but full of power as he caught her surface thought without trying. "You are a soldier, Doctor. A warrior, trained to be a weapon for your own people. I know you will not run. You may fight, but you will never run."

He felt a swelling of admiration and desire for this woman he barely knew. She hadn't run screaming from the pub and onto the next flight out of the Country. Not that it would have done her any good. It would prolong the inevitable attack by a Dracula-allied Vampire in her home or office or out on the job some dark night. She would be dead. Here or in the United States, she would be just as dead simply because of her open association with him.

"I admire your fortitude, Gillian. I hope that you understand that I would not bring any of this up if your life were not directly in danger." Gillian glanced at him as she drove. His lovely face was full of concern but also admiration.

Gillian laughed harshly. "I have a bad feeling that I am not nearly as frightened as I should be Aleksei, but I really hate bullies. Dracula sounds like a first-class bully."

"Bully? No Gillian, he is not a bully. He is your worst nightmare come to life."

His words held a dark finality that Gillian didn't want to contemplate right then as she turned into the estate. The tires crunched on the gravel as they left the paved road and entered between the open iron gate. Iron wolves stood guard on top of the stone gateposts on either side as the car drove through. The cabin itself looked almost picturesque, framed by the mountains and the thick forest.

"I'd put that out if I were you, and let me do the talking." Aleksei indicated the cigarette as he exited the car.

"Because . . . ?" Gillian's eyes were cold. The alcohol was making her edgier and more reactionary than usual.

"Tanis does not have a liking for inordinately liberated women, Gillian, nor ones who are deceitful. He's not a bad man, just an opinionated, backward one on occasion." Aleksei was grinning from ear to ear.

"Well, I tell you," Gillian took a long drag on her cigarette, "if I gave a shit what Tanis thought, that might concern me just a tad, but seeing how I don't, I won't worry about it."

Kicking the car door shut, she turned to see Aleksei staring at the porch, part of which was cast in shadow, despite the outside light still being on. She took a shot at the possibility. "He's standing on the porch and he just heard everything I said, right?"

Aleksei nodded, then started for the house, keeping his smile turned away from the little blonde courting danger.

"Fuck." Gillian swore under her breath. She didn't want to start out fighting with Tanis again. It was late, she was tired and she was a little muddled from at least two bottles of wine. Alcohol had a tendency to subdue the therapist in her and bring out the Marine. Unfortunately, the Marine had an attitude with bossy men as did the actual woman. *Screw it*, she thought, Tanis wasn't her client and she didn't owe him shit.

This was not going to go well, she could tell already, and it was about to get a lot worse when she heard his deep velvet voice,

"Apparently someone needs to put a stop to the damage you are doing to your body from your smoking and drinking and to your inclination for deception, Dr. Key." He could smell the alcohol and nicotine from where he was, even if he hadn't seen the smoke streaming from her mouth and nose.

His statement was accompanied by the light crunch of his boots on the gravel. Tanis stepped off the porch and was moving up to her. For a big man, he moved with the grace of a panther, softly and ominously, broad shoulders and lean hips all in alignment, his step buoyant on the crushed pebbles of cement.

Gillian shifted her backpack to her left hand, walked directly up to him, effectively stopping him in his path. Her temper started to skyrocket. She was torqued up from everything that had happened, the alcohol fueling her attitude, squashing all cautionary warnings from her senses, which were screaming at her to shut up.

Deliberately, she took another drag on the cigarette while

staring straight up into those shimmering golden eyes, and blew the smoke into Tanis's surprised face. Snarling audibly, she crossed the professional etiquette line without another thought. Hell with it.

"You pretentious prick, who do you think you're talking to?"

CHAPTER

4

EVERYONE froze. Aleksei had just opened the door to the house, thinking Gillian would be following even if Tanis tried to intervene. Obviously she wasn't right behind him. And what she just said . . . oh hell. That was a mistake.

"Tanis!" Aleksei's telepathic shout to his brother was both a warning and a plea.

The last thing he needed was Tanis losing his temper with the lovely doctor. They were supposed to sort this out together, the three of them. He hadn't taken Gillian's blood so he couldn't issue the same mental warning to her, but he turned, trying to catch her eyes in his icy gray glare. Trouble was, she wasn't looking at him. Her attention was focused on his tall, dark and deadly brother. The porch light illuminated the disaster in progress.

Tanis's eyes narrowed and his voice was low but full of black fury. "What did you say to me?" He stared at Gillian, golden eyes literally shooting sparks, menace radiating from him. He stepped forward, aggressive, male and very dominant.

That did it. Gillian did not take to being bullied by anyone. Not even exceptionally handsome Romanian men, whose beautiful voices and eyes would normally intrigue her. She threw caution completely to the wind, uncaring at the moment about what disciplinary actions the IPPA and the Marine Corps might take for her blowing her stack with a patient's brother.

"Pretentious prick!" she bellowed at him, less than two feet away. "I called you a pretentious prick! Are you deaf as well as undead?"

She used the insult *undead* deliberately, and because he was blocking her path, she strong-armed him in the shoulder to push past. A fully sober Gillian would have gone around him and avoided purposely insulting someone who was twice her size and about twelve times stronger physically. Then again, an entirely sober Gillian would not have started this line of rudeness to begin with, but she was unconsciously spoiling for a fight as a tension release. At least that would be the rationale she used when she thought this through tomorrow. If she survived.

There was a sharp intake of breath from Aleksei. Whatever happened, no matter that he had preternatural speed, he was not going to get to Gillian in time for Tanis not to rip her head off. He moved as quickly as he could while the veins in Tanis's neck became instantly visible, and a black cloud of rage seemed to extend out, with him in the center. Aleksei felt his brother's anger swell, but curiously, not that the woman was in any real danger.

Two steps. Gillian made it exactly two steps when her right arm was grabbed by a steel band—correction, Tanis's hand. She dropped the backpack instantly, cocked a fist back and whirled, throwing her strength and weight into the punch. He was faster, much faster. Unnatural speed. Preternatural speed. Vampire speed.

His arm blurred and caught her small fist before she connected with his jaw. *Shit and double shit.* Now he had both of her arms and he pulled them together to capture them with one hand. First thing she noticed was that he wasn't really hurting her, just holding her. Second thing was that he still had the cigarette in her mouth and that the ash hadn't fallen off. She pulled on it, squinting in the smoke that billowed around her face and puffed it out. "Well, fuckadoodle doo," she muttered as he hauled her arms up over her head and reached a hand out to cup her chin.

"You are definitely in need of a lesson in manners, my dear lady." Tanis spoke every word softly and through his teeth, staring down into surprised green eyes through the smoke from her cigarette.

He plucked the cigarette from her lips, dropped it and ground it out, without looking, with his foot. In response, she jackknifed her hips upward and two-footed him in the stomach. He doubled over momentarily in astonished reflex, but that was all. Vampires do not require air in their lungs to function so the blow to his diaphragm did little except surprise him and make him angrier.

Lowering his arm when she kicked him, Tanis inadvertently set her feet on the ground. Gillian twisted her wrists and jerked backward, but her legs were quivery from the alcohol and from kicking Tanis's rock hard, amazing abs. The jolt to her legs was like kicking a concrete pylon. She was free of his grasp but more off balance than she had anticipated. Her knee buckled and she stumbled away from him, toward the tall stone gatepost directly behind her.

When she staggered and nearly fell, Tanis moved with blurring speed. If he had been Human, she would have fractured her skull or broken her neck on the stone obstruction. Unnatural speed, unnatural strength, preternatural reflexes were what saved her from serious injury or death. Not that she would be grateful.

He grabbed her leg in midair and flipped her all the way over, catching her in his arms bridal-style. Gillian wound up cradled in his arms, balanced on his thigh. Tanis had gone down on one knee as he caught her to cushion her fall and not jolt her fragile-looking body. Aleksei had stopped where he was, seeing that his brother had everything under control. Sort of.

Gillian was horrified as she stared up from her vantage point in Tanis's lap into a pair of golden eyes that held amusement and quite a bit of residual fire. Good Goddess, this was just getting better and better. She knew she was blushing under that amber gaze.

"Are you all right, sweetheart?" Tanis said in a patronizing tone, a smirk curling his lip. He shifted her a little on his leg and patted her bottom lightly. "Nothing damaged, I hope?"

Aleksei nearly moaned aloud. It was like a train wreck about to happen. He could see it coming and was helpless to prevent it. To Tanis, he fired off, *"No! Do not provoke her further!"*

Gillian went from horrified to pissed in a heartbeat. Intellectually, she knew that going head to head with a Vampire was not bright, but she wasn't at her level-headed best at the moment.

She spit out a string of expletives that would have made her drill instructor proud, finishing with, "You cocksucking corpse, let go of me right now!"

To her abject horror, she did the utmost girly thing she could have. She was very inebriated and a whole lot scared, and when he didn't immediately release her, she reached up and slapped Tanis across the face. It shocked him more than inflicted damage, but it served as a goad to push him over an edge he didn't know he had.

Later, Tanis would not be able to recall what had come over him, but he had never encountered a female of any species with so much audaciousness and so little common sense. Before the slap and her last scathing comment, he had been prepared to let her up and lecture her as soon as she calmed down, but not now. He rolled her over in his arms, draping her face down across his bent knee, pinning her pelvis against his leg.

"Not just yet, *piccola guerriera.*" The words were ground out between clenched teeth, beautiful in tone but filled with dark menace.

The crack of his palm connecting to her butt was sharp and loud. Aleksei started forward but the look in his brother's gleaming golden eyes stopped him. In four hundred years Tanis had never raised his hand to any female. He wouldn't injure her, not really, but the tanning he was giving her backside was surely going to leave a mark.

Gillian was beyond mortified. She was a twenty-eight-year-old adult. In the past two minutes, she'd lost her temper, nearly started a fight and was now bent over the knee of a very angry Vampire, being spanked like a kid. She nearly bit her lip through not to shriek. It was obvious he was tempering his hand or he would have broken her pelvis, but it still stung like hell. Too bad she'd left her gun in the car. She could have shot herself and spared everyone embarrassment.

Determined that this young female learn some manners, Tanis was swift and resolute. It was obvious no one had ever cared about her enough to take her to task for her insufferable insolence and inclination toward physical aggression. Rectifying that situation was his pleasure this evening. When he stopped and lifted her to her feet, he was prepared to finish this incident off with a firm lecture on her behavior. To his surprise, she straightened up and, with furious tears sparkling in her eyes, she belted him in the mouth, rocking him back.

Aleksei leapt forward, inserting his body between Gillian

and Tanis, who was now rising to his feet, pressing a hand to his bleeding lip. Gillian looked up at Aleksei to survey if he were a new threat. She saw amusement and admiration in the nearly metallic gray eyes. Blushing furiously, she whirled and stomped off into the nearby dark forest to collect her thoughts.

"Assault and battery. That's what I'll charge him with." She was fuming. Her alcohol-sodden thoughts were scattered and disordered.

More mad at herself than Tanis, Gillian took herself to task more than he had. She was a professional. She dealt with Paramortal people and their problems for a living, yet she'd just let a Vampire piss her off to the point of losing her temper, something she couldn't remember doing since her early days in the Marine Corps.

Chauvinistic bastard spanked me. Shit and double shit, she couldn't even go home. Finding her way into a clearing about halfway up the mountain, Gillian sat on a fallen log, wincing a little, and cursed the day that she decided to come to Romania. In the quiet among the immense pine trees she tried to collect her thoughts and her dignity.

Hathor's hells, Daedelus was going to laugh his ass off when she relayed this little tidbit of trivia to him. Helmut would be mortified and probably sanction her ass for losing her mind . . . *temper* like she did. Daed would say she had provoked it and give Tanis a medal. Bastards. All of them.

When was she going to learn? Psychology was an even playing field for men and women, but the military was something else. It had been her temper that had gotten her into the Special Forces in the first place. Well, her temper and her empathy, to be fair. It had been during her assignment at the Pentagon. She was head of the security detail for the Vampire delegation during the Human-Vampire Peace Talks. Her mind flicked unwittingly to that unpleasant incident.

One of the Vampire delegation, Baron Von Essen, had propositioned her more than once, not realizing she was an inherently powerful empath and knew immediately that all he wanted was bragging rights about bagging a Human female. Gill had refused because he was an insincere prick. The insincere prick was insulted by her refusal and had given her a gift, publicly, which was designed to humiliate her.

Gill had opened the box and found a heavy gold cross on a very long chain. The Vampire had suggested that she wear it as her chastity belt to avoid any sort of Vampiric penetration. It was a bad enough idea to give a Jewish-Pagan girl a Christian cross with intent to insult, but it was a worse idea to piss off a United States Marine for any reason, at least in public.

She'd taken the object out of the box and surreptitiously admired the shining gold ornament, then flicked it into the Baron's surprised face with a smile and a hearty, "Go fuck yourself, *sir*."

Crosses and other religious artifacts only work if they're wielded by a true believer against a Vampire who is also a believer. Gillian, being non-Christian, knew she didn't believe, but being pissed off, didn't stop to think that Baron von Essen was most likely Catholic during his Daywalker life.

The cross had spun through the air like a *shuriken* and embedded itself like a hot knife in the butter of His Excellency's jaw before Gillian's horrified eyes and his great dismay.

Probably the only reason Gill was still in one piece was that the other members of the Vampire delegation hated the Baron's creaky ass and intervened before he could tear into her. One in particular, Cassiopeia Delphi, PhD, was rather impressed by the little blonde's chutzpah and utter lack of fear. She was busy surreptitiously working with Daedelus to recruit Gillian for a project she was working on at the Miller and Jackson Clinic for Paramortal Understanding and Intimacy, where she was clinical director.

Once Daed heard Gillian's side of the story, he was impressed that she hadn't killed the Baron outright. The fact that she hadn't even shot him was amazing of itself. Hell, he had new recruits and diplomatic liaisons who would have killed the Austrian Vampire just for making a pass in the first place.

If it were only up to him he'd have let the incident go with no report on her record. Regrettably, although Gillian was currently the flavor of the month for the brass, these Summit meetings were too important to ignore her actions. The Baron had been replaced, sent home from the delegation by one of the Vampire Lords, Daed wasn't sure which one or how anyone could tell who had allegiance with whom. Gillian would have to be punished in some manner.

Gill watched the wheels turning behind Daedelus's icy black eyes. She saw the myriad of emotions flicker across his face. Her highly functional empathy told her that he believed her even if he didn't condone how she'd handled it. He wouldn't allow any severe action to be taken against her, of that she was certain given his current feelings. But there was a pensive look to Captain Aristophenes and a warning niggle in his psyche that she wasn't sure she liked.

Daed was frantically thinking of a solution that would please the brass, get them off his ass and hers, yet send a message to the Vampires and anyone else that a marine is not to be trifled with, ever.

Aha! He had just the thing.

"Tell you what," he said wryly, his eyes narrowing a little as he looked down at her. "Our unit got orders this morning to collect a team for a recon mission. It's in Austria, near a little village called Badgastein. Interested?"

Shit. Gillian knew what he had in mind. Send her on a dangerous combat search-and-seizure mission and all would be forgiven. No mark on her record, no one the wiser. Gill knew that Daed was trying to help her out of her predicament. It wasn't a palatable way out but it was a way. She also reasoned it would send a clear message to all the delegates that she was being entrusted with further responsibility rather than being officially reprimanded.

"I'll do it." She'd said without hesitation and never looked backward.

Yup. That had been the start of her field operative career. That mission had been the first of many successful endeavors with her handpicked team. It had given her a promotion to Captain and a place of unshakable faith within the USMC. Now she was on a mountainside in Romania, nursing her wounded pride and tingling butt. Oh how the mighty will fall.

CHAPTER
5

DOWN at the cabin, while Gillian made her way up the mountain and had her little chat with herself, Tanis was laughing, dabbing at his split lip with the back of his hand. He couldn't help it. She was so delicate, so Human, so completely helpless in the face of his outraged fury but so fearless to even take him on. Even now, she had no idea of the danger she had been in.

Aleksei was glaring at him, arms folded over his chest. "I hope you are satisfied, Tanis. If she sues you for assault, I will not lift a finger to help you."

That made Tanis laugh harder. "That is the most complicated, infuriating, beautiful woman I have ever met. I confess, Aleksei, I have to admire her spirit. And you know perfectly well that if she had been that cheeky with you, you might have reacted the same way." His smile was maddening. Male ego at it's finest.

"I would not have spanked her," Aleksei said flatly.

"Oh yes you would have, brother. She may be your therapist, but you are attracted to her, admit it. I could feel your protective outrage in her defense and your wish to punish her when you learned of her deception.

"The first time that little spitfire puts herself in danger or the next time she lies to you, will be the time we see the calm Aleksei come apart with fury. I look forward to it." His brother could be a real pain in the ass sometimes. Aleksei had forgotten just how much.

"You had better go straighten this out with her, Tanis. Whatever your feelings are, she is my therapist and is helping me come to grips with a few things. Not to mention the fact that we are asking her for her assistance to keep our villagers alive." Aleksei's voice held a note of finality that Tanis knew not to argue with.

"As you wish, Aleksei. I will make sure she is not devoured by any of the beasts which roam our mountains."

Chuckling, Tanis made off in the direction Gillian had taken. After a moment's thought, Aleksei followed, wanting to make sure their discussion was a peaceful one and not trusting Tanis's temper to remain so jovial.

Gillian was in a tranquil setting. The moon was full, the air clean and crisp, the forest a dark and comforting haven surrounding her little clearing. But she was still fuming.

"Terrific, I'm out in the middle of this fucking backward Country with guys who think they fell out of a John Wayne movie." Gillian's hand involuntarily went to her butt and she rubbed it ruefully. "If those knuckle-dragging troglodytes think they can get away with this, they have got another thing coming."

She looked beautiful there in the moonlight, talking to herself, the blush of embarrassment still on her cheeks, eyes flashing emerald fire. Tanis had located her easily on the mountain. Vampire hearing and scent perception was outstanding. It had been easy to track her to where she sat alone in the moonlight, looking like a lost fairy queen: small, blonde, magical.

He watched her for a few moments silently from the shadows, admiring her, even admitting that as ill-mannered as she was, he was very attracted to the little Human. Aleksei had ordered him to make peace and make up. Admitting that he had been wrong in his treatment of her was going to be difficult. They needed her right now, needed her expertise, needed to keep her safe, and he could swallow his pride. He hoped.

Gillian felt his raw power before he said anything. It was strong, like nothing she'd ever encountered, and it made her cautious. When Aleksei's voice startled her from a different direction than where she was looking and expecting Tanis's arrival, she spun, hand going toward the knife in the spine sheath. "What?" she barked.

The gray-eyed Master Vampire approached her, hands held out. "Gillian, please accept my apology for Tanis's actions and please accept Tanis's apology as well. He overstepped his rights and boundaries with you. He does realize that."

Aleksei had followed Tanis, wanting to make sure neither of them killed each other. He watched Gillian's response; she was angry, that he could tell. Whether or not she would listen, was another story. If she wanted to leave, he would have to let her go. Keeping her prisoner was not typical of the man he had been nor the Vampire he now was.

Aleksei spoke softly but with a commanding push in his low, velvet voice. "You have nothing to fear, Gillian. We are not Dracula's Vampires." He reached a hand out toward her and started forward but stopped when she brandished the knife.

"You stay the hell away from me, Count Rachlav. You already told me at the inn that you and your brother certainly are Dracula's spawn. I'm not *that* drunk."

Cold anger was taking over as her calculating mind clicked through their prior conversation and tried to make it mesh with what he was telling her. Gillian felt her mind going to that very empty place it went whenever she was faced with the very real possibility of killing or being killed. He was lying . . . sort of. No matter. Come hell or these Vampires, she wasn't going down without taking somebody with her. A breath later, her arms were pinned, the knife was on the ground and she was pulled back into a hard masculine chest. She didn't need to turn around to figure out who held her.

"Tanis, either you let me go right now, or you kill me right now. I've had enough." She spat the words out but didn't struggle in his iron grip. It would have been futile anyway. She wasn't moving unless he wanted her to.

"I have no intention of killing you, Gillian. Neither of us do." His voice was hauntingly beautiful and full of concern. She turned slightly in his grasp and looked up into his golden eyes. She believed him; she could feel truth in his words and aura.

"You want me to listen? Fine. I'll listen. I just love having conferences with Machiavellian undead in the middle of the fucking forest in the middle of the fucking night." She was, however, still pissed off.

Tanis's face darkened. "Perhaps the lesson we began back at the gate needs to be reinforced, *piccola*, if you are going to begin with ill-advised and derogatory statements." Somehow she knew *piccola* wasn't meant an insult.

Anger began to build into rage again but she was now sober enough to realize that this line of conversation was getting her nowhere, so she changed tactics. Plus he was telling the truth. About all of it. He wouldn't kill her but he would tan her ass again, given half a chance. She could feel him seething.

"All right. You win. For now. Let me go, Tanis, I mean it. I will listen because if you two had meant to kill me, you would have done it by now." He released her cautiously and stepped back, watching her warily.

Aleksei stepped up, towering over her. "You are not afraid of me, are you?"

"No, I'm not. I'm not afraid of either of you, I just don't want to wind up as an indentured servant to Count Dracula."

She was lying through her teeth. She knew it, they knew it. She was more scared than she'd ever been in her life with the magnitude of what she'd learned from Aleksei back at the inn. In fact, if the worst thing that would happen to her had been Tanis's enthusiastic spanking, she was still ahead. Embarrassed, but ahead.

Aleksei came closer slowly. "If you will allow me to, I can enter your mind and give you more of a basic understanding, but it must be with your consent. I will not force you, nor will Tanis." Hearing his beautiful voice with no compulsion behind it fortified her trust in him. He felt safe. It went against all her logic, but he felt safe to her.

Aleksei stood in front of her. "I don't need to touch you for this but it will help since you are Human. Will you permit this and not attempt to hurt me?"

He cocked an elegant eyebrow at her and a slight smile crept over his mouth. Gillian stared hard at him, then started to grin.

"All right Aleksei, you do whatever you need to do. I give you my word that I will not kick you in the face while you're doing it."

A strong elegant hand reached toward her face. Gillian had a brief *Star Trek* flashback, envisioning Mr. Spock about to mind meld with her and started to giggle. Aleksei, already attuned to her, said softly, "I am not a green-blooded, pointy-eared Vulcan, Gillian."

"A what?" Tanis questioned in response to the vision of Spock superimposed over his brother's face through their link.

"Later," Aleksei replied, focusing on Gillian, who giggled, opening her mind to his; then he touched her lightly and they fell into a rapport.

Swiftly she gained the information he wanted her to read. Tentatively she pressed further and he allowed it. Dropping his shields, Aleksei gave her complete access to whatever she wanted to see within his powerful mind. He wanted her to know beyond any doubt that he would never harm her, that he and Tanis were wholly and completely opposed to Dracula and his plans.

Gillian unexpectedly shied away from going deeper, puzzling Aleksei a little. She had an inbred sense of what would make him uncomfortable and avoided it. Since she was in his thoughts, she knew there was nothing of portent about their situation that lurked in the shadows of Aleksei's mind. The mere fact that he had offered to literally bare his soul to her won her trust in this circumstance.

He did notice that she had a deep-seated fear of getting too involved on a personal level with anyone. Either of her jobs practically insured that she would remain alone. He knew that wasn't by accident, but couldn't dwell on it just now.

After a few minutes, Aleksei dropped his hand and Gillian opened her eyes. "As I expected," the Vampire began. "A true empath, but you knew that didn't you?"

At Gillian's nod, he continued. "How is it that you have been able to kill? To open yourself to another's internal pain, and then take a life?"

"It's hard to explain, really. I just isolate myself in a 'quiet place' and allow my survival skills to take over, just like a good sociopath." Gillian's grin crept over her face but he felt her metaphysical dodge. It was painful for her. She killed only when ordered to and even then only when absolutely necessary.

"Sociopath?" Aleksei's lovely voice washed over her. "I would hardly call you a sociopath. With your sensitivity it must have been agony for you growing up as you did. You must understand that to us, even at twenty-eight years, you are still very young. Young and female to us, Gillian, inspires a deep protective instinct that is difficult for an older male Vampire to overcome."

She blushed and looked away, not wanting to delve too deeply into the idea of someone looking after her. He took a deep breath to explain to her what must now be explained.

"Dracula will be aware that you are here and able to attune to you. Do you understand why?"

Gillian looked back and forth between the two Vampires with her. Both of them were magnificent. Equally lovely. Aleksei's dark majesty and silvery gray eyes sparkled with power in the moonlight. Tanis's noble bearing was unconscious. His eyes glowed gold and his face was calm, but warring underneath there was something dark, dangerous and mysterious.

"No, I don't. He's your enemy, not mine. I'm just here as an observer."

"He has a network of spies, some of them are Human. Anyone could have noticed you at the inn, anyone could have learned you had come through Immigration," Aleksei stated, as if that would explain everything. "And it would not be hard to track you to my home. To Dracula, it does not matter why you are under my roof, only that you are or have been.

"You are a noted professional, you give solace to Paramortal beings. You are also apparently a decorated soldier. You have fought for the peaceful existence of Paramortals and Humans. Drawing attention to Human-Vampire camaraderie is absolutely against everything Dracula believes in. Humans are cattle to him. Nothing more." His voice held bitterness and shame for his Lord's outmoded and prejudicial beliefs.

Tanis moved to the log and sat, patting the space next to him. Gillian hesitated a moment, then sat beside him, a thousand questions in her eyes. He put an arm behind her carefully in a protective gesture, unconsciously sheltering her with his larger frame.

"In our culture," he began, taking his cue from Aleksei, "all Vampires are descended from three main Lines: Dracula's, which is the Eastern European Line, the Egyptian and the Greek. Dracula's Line, unfortunately, is the one Aleksei and I were reborn from.

"Our allegiance, however, is to the Egyptian Line of Osiris. He has been a staunch supporter and friend to Aleksei and myself over the centuries. Dionysus, who is the Sire or Font of the Greek line, is a wild and chaotic collaborator, but an ally nonetheless.

"There are other Vampiric types in the world. China and India have their own variations, but they are more like our Revenants: mindless, damaged, self-directed corpses who chew more than they drink and who are the true horrors in our culture."

Gillian thought about what he said for a moment. The enormity of what she'd learned in snatches from Aleksei's mind made sense with what Tanis was telling her.

Finding her voice she asked, "So how did I get a target painted on my ass, and how do you suppose that I can help you?"

The entire idea of a Vampire turf war over the intellectual properties of Humans suddenly struck her as ridiculous. She'd been asked to swallow a lot of things this evening but sitting here, having a discussion about metaphysical lineages with Vampires in the moonlight, was a bit much for even her open mind to grasp all at once.

From beside her right shoulder, Aleksei's voice came as he sat next to her, trapping her between himself and Tanis.

"You are unfortunately in the wrong place at the wrong time, Gillian. If Dracula has truly returned, it is because he thinks to carry out this war by causing dissention between the Bloodlines and perhaps even other Paramortals.

"I suspect that he believes he is now powerful enough to win with whatever allegiances he has formed. There is no other explanation for his return at this time. He would never be welcomed back in this Country, not by me, nor any of the other local Master Vampires who were once loyal to him. He has simply become too mad."

Watching her face, he found it impassive, her eyes widening slightly at his statement was her only reaction.

He continued. "Dracula had vanished for three hundred years, Gillian. If he is back, that can only mean that he has spent a good deal of that time formulating a plan, a network of allies and an army.

"Knowledge like that would be very hard to keep secret. Dionysus and Osiris are probably aware of it by now. We will need to meet with them or their representatives soon to find out how to fortify our allegiances to each other."

He paused for a moment, unconsciously tucking a strand of Gillian's shining blonde hair behind her ear.

"Tanis and I are out of the loop, so to speak. Dracula is the Sire of our Line, but we give him no loyalty and his minions get no quarter here. We have no access to his knowledge base. Osiris and Dionysus will not volunteer information outside of their lineage, but now we must become informed, and quickly."

"To keep you safe, *piccola guerriera*, we must keep you

close to us. There are horrors in Dracula's mind and army that you cannot imagine."

That was from Tanis, and he watched her closely. "Thoughts flow across your face, Gillian, but I wonder, what thoughts?"

"All right." She rose and walked away from the log before turning and looking at the two Vampires, waiting expectantly. "I'll stay. *But*, I'm only here for a few weeks. I need you to know two things: One, there will be no blood play involving me at all. In other words, nobody takes my blood nor gives me theirs.

"Two, let's all try to keep this from being as unnerving as possible for me, okay? I'm a little out of my depth. When I figure it out, I'll be less edgy. But for now, let's all try to keep a lid on our tempers."

She stared pointedly at Tanis. "Can we get along without killing each other?" But she smiled when she said it.

Surprisingly, Tanis smiled. He couldn't help it; she was just cute . . . and brave. "I think we might be able to manage that, *piccola*."

"What . . . exactly does that mean? And the other one you just said," Gillian asked Tanis, then looked to Aleksei.

"'*Piccola*'? It means 'little one' in Italian. '*Piccola guerriera*' is 'little warrior'," Tanis provided for her, smiling as she became flustered.

"Shit. Nicknames. I feel like a fraternity mascot," she groused, kicking at a clump of sod.

Both the males laughed, making her jump. It was warm, rich laughter, like a bubbling hot tub filled with chocolate or honey, but frothy and light. It filled her with extraordinary feelings, making her giggle along with the two pantie-drenching males. Oh yeah, she was way sober now.

Tanis began thinking of ways to make amends with the little hellion. She was appealing to him in more ways than just a professional interest for her military skills and as someone to protect. His blood was stirring as it had not stirred for decades.

A deep chuckle bubbled up from Aleksei's chest, interrupting his thinking. "That is good to hear. I do not want to have to intervene between the two of you."

"I do not think your intervention will be necessary, Aleksei," Tanis rumbled in a bet-I-can-get-you-wet timbre, staring directly into Gillian's eyes.

Her chin jerked up a notch and her smile faded as their eyes locked. Pure sex was radiating from his gaze but he wasn't looking at her like she was Prey. The other thing she noticed was that he wasn't trying to bespell her, though he certainly could have. Tanis was looking at her in open invitation, pure and simple.

She had sensed a measure of his power and Aleksei's. She knew power and they had it in buckets. If Tanis wanted her, willing or not, he could make her his and she would have no idea the thought wasn't her own. The fact that he was obviously offering but allowing her a chance and a choice said something about his inherent character. A true Dracula Vampire would have no qualms about enforcing his will on a Human. Maybe he and Aleksei could be trusted with her life.

Tanis was a powerful, virile, dominant male Vampire. He was a backwater chauvinist, irritating as hell, and as breathtakingly attractive as his brother. The instant antagonism between them could be the basis for something more . . . interesting, if his character really was as sterling as he was projecting.

CHAPTER
6

"No, I don't think you will have to intervene, Aleksei," Gillian said in a breathy voice while staring into Tanis's molten eyes that had her kicking herself mentally. What the hell? Marilyn Monroe? For fuck's sake. She tried again.

"What I mean is that I'm sure Tanis and I can get along just fine. You don't have to worry about us killing each other." There, that was better. That was almost command-grade normal.

Before Aleksei could respond, Tanis rose, striding forward taking Gillian's hand and kissing it. Gillian couldn't have been more shocked if he'd bitten her. She would have pulled back automatically, but he had her wrist too and she couldn't extract herself from his light grip without appearing obvious.

Gazing directly into her lovely green eyes, Tanis spoke to his brother. "Would you mind if I walked Dr. Key down the mountain, Aleksei? Surely she is off duty by now."

Aleksei's eyebrows lifted in surprise. "Gillian?"

She eyed Tanis warily. Tanis couldn't resist a quip. "Scared, *piccola*?"

"Not hardly, Count Rachlav."

Smiling but seething inwardly, Gillian reached a delicate but strong hand up and ran a fingertip down the side of Tanis's face, continuing down his neck and onto his powerful chest. He watched her warily but shivered under her touch as she swayed closer, his eyes alive with hunger that wasn't about food.

Without warning, she hooked a booted foot behind his ankle and shoved. Tanis fell rather ungracefully onto his beautiful butt. This time, having learned from the prior situation, she backed up out of range and grinned wickedly. "I have no reason to be afraid of you," she said, then turned to Aleksei. "I'll be fine, Aleksei. I'm sure Tanis will take extraordinarily good care of me."

Aleksei regarded her and the tall, dark, infinitely dangerous Vampire climbing menacingly to his feet behind her. Their sexually charged horseplay was beginning to wear very thin. If Gillian wanted to provoke his volatile brother, or vice versa, he was staying well out of it.

"I believe I will let Tanis bring you back down the mountain, Gillian," he said in a chilly voice. "Perhaps you two need time alone to work out your issues."

With that, he turned to leave, then paused, glancing back over his shoulder at the little blonde. "And Gillian? I understand your reason for subterfuge in coming here, though if you had simply asked, I would have offered whatever information Tanis and I had.

"For future reference, however, since you will be staying with us on our lands, do not lie or attempt to deceive me again. I will not tolerate it." Aleksei's black velvet voice lashed across her psyche in gentle reprimand as he vanished into the thick forest, leaving Gillian to deal with Tanis, alone.

She turned back toward Tanis, a little flustered by Aleksei's parting shot. Her intention to help him to his feet was stalled as she collided with his very solid chest. Looking up into his handsome angry face, she noticed the split in his lip, barely visible now due to his Preternatural healing ability. She felt a brief stirring of fear, dismissed it, then took a moment and admired him. Goddess, he was extraordinary.

"Well?" she said finally, cocking her head to one side.

Tanis gripped her upper arms gently yet firmly. His voice was beautiful, soft and low, but carried a wealth of reprimand. "Playing with fire, *piccola*, will get your lovely backside warmed again."

Gillian yanked her arms out of his grip, backing away from him. He allowed it, then began stalking her with deliberate slowness, male arrogance in every step.

"I am well aware of your superior physical strength, Tanis. You can drain me, tear me apart or rip out my throat before I could get a knife or gun drawn. Better yet, you could fuck me and leave with absolutely no affect on your conscience." Her voice was cold and deliberate.

He raised an eyebrow at the abrupt change in her tone and demeanor, his face achieving a harsh beauty as he regarded her with a chilly glare. Eyes that were alight with golden flame from the beast within him held hers captive. The voice when it came from deep in his chest was low and full of anger.

"Yes, I could take your blood, claim you in every way. I might even kill you, Gillian, or decide merely to put you across my knee again. Is that what you want, *piccola*? Do you enjoy this continual antagonism between us?

"We may be in the same proximity for quite a long time. Would you rather I left you strictly alone? Not express my desire for you? Tell me, Gillian. I will respect your wishes but *do not play with me*." His volume had increased until he roared the last at her. When she flinched from his tone, he fell silent and waited, aggravated that he had let her provoke him.

Watching his steady, deliberate movements and really listening to him, she heard then felt the hurt beneath the anger in his voice. Studying his face, which was raw with need and obvious confusion as he approached her, twisted something inside of her.

Playing? Yeah, playing. When the hell had she become so cruel? Ouch. That stung a bit. Tanis was right; she was playing with him. Self-defense mechanism on overdrive. Why? Why, indeed. He scared her, that's why. His attraction to her scared her but not because he wanted her in bed. He scared her because she saw things in him that she liked and admired, though she couldn't put her finger on any of it. He disconcerted her. She didn't like the feeling.

Aleksei had harbored the same look in his eyes, so different from Tanis's in color, so similar in the way they hid nothing from her. Need. Pure, primal need that had nothing and everything to do with sex. If it were Aleksei standing before her now, if he weren't her patient . . . Stop it. That was dangerous thinking. She stopped backing up and thought before she answered.

"I don't know, Tanis, one minute you're chastising me, then tanning my butt, then being almost respectful; now you're looking at me like I'm the main course on your personal sexual buffet table. I'm having a little trouble keeping up."

He had to smile slightly as she ticked off her thoughts on her little fingers. At her next words though, he felt his temper galvanize his body.

"Are you simply being an ass because you are unused to a grown woman who can take care of herself? I've commanded men on the battlefield, Tanis. I am not going to suddenly become agreeable and submit to whatever you want to do. I am not going to be one of those wide-eyed Humans who will worship you because you're a Vampire and lower yourself to have sex with me. If you want a fan club, you've got the wrong girl. I need a better reason for going to bed with you than you being bigger and badder than me." There. That was an adult conversation. Let him deal with that first.

That made him mad. He snarled and blurred forward, grabbing her before she could breathe. Shaking her a little, he pulled her to him and spoke slowly, emphasizing every word. "Worship? Is that what you think I want? For the love of Isis, Gillian, do you believe myself or even Aleksei to be so Human as to need obsequiousness from anyone?"

Now fear warred with the naked anger on his face. Fear for her perception of herself, fear that she was afraid he wanted her; fear that she might believe . . .

"Lower myself, Gillian? You believe I am settling for some sort of sexual consolation prize by wanting to bed you?" Tanis searched her eyes, her face. Yes, that was exactly what she thought. That she was merely available and that was the reason he was attracted to her.

"You need to learn a few things, *piccola*, like why a man might desire you and want to take care of you; or why I might find you attractive in ways that have nothing to do with sexual need. It is not an insult, Gillian, to be under my protection.

"No matter what your choice here tonight, I will never withdraw that, or the offer of my friendship, if that is what you wish."

She thought about that for a moment. Like it or not, she needed his protection and Aleksei's. Dammit. It all just went so completely against her grain. Still, it was not her intent to hurt him or toy with him. Aleksei had said they both were usually alone.

"I'm sorry, Tanis, I was judging you and Aleksei . . . by Human standards and that was unfair." She looked straight into his eyes, not flinching, not giving an inch, just stating a new-found fact that she'd discovered. He looked into her guileless eyes, which stared levelly into his. She meant it and relief flooded him.

Unexpectedly he folded her into his arms, drawing her close so that she could hear his heart, his breathing, feel the security he was offering. Burying his face in her hair, he pressed her against the full length of him.

"*Piccola*, you do not know what it means to me to hear you say that. You have had a lot to handle these last few hours and I am sure that I have been a difficult man to deal with."

Gillian fought him for a moment, totally confused by his abrupt turn of behavior, struggling against the steel bands of his arms, then relaxed, feeling no direct threat from him.

"You've been a royal pain in the ass, Tanis." Her voice was muffled against his broad chest. They were highly attracted to each other despite their initial animosity, there was no getting around that fact. Hell with it. She put her arms around his slender waist and hugged him back lightly.

Totally unrepentant, she was. He had to laugh. She jumped as the laughter rolled from deep within him and he reached around her to gently slap her bottom. "In so many ways, as well." His voice full of male amusement.

Shoving him back, her eyes blazed green. "In very many ways," she snarled.

Still laughing, he moved closer and put an arm over her shoulder, pulling her beneath the safety of his. "I apologize for spanking you, *piccola*. I truly do. It is not like me to lose control like that, but you needed it."

She turned and glared up at him. "Oh, really? I suppose it escaped your notice that I'm an adult. If I'd had a gun, I'd have shot you for pulling that shit."

"I will make sure you are not heavily armed the next time I take you over my knee."

He grabbed her fist as she swung it at him and kissed her knuckles, laughing. Tanis was amazed at the intensity of his attraction to her. He'd been furious with her only awhile ago, now all he wanted to do was kiss her, hold her, make sure she didn't get killed in the coming melee.

He picked her up and held her above him, bringing her down into the warmth of his embrace. His mouth claimed hers hungrily and his arms were unbreakable bands around her back.

Gillian surprised herself by returning his kiss. Vampire attraction and sex too? Real attraction? Too early to tell, so she'd just enjoy the moment. Despite their rocky meeting, there were definite sparks igniting between them. She was an adult. If this was a temporary fling, she could handle it.

Sliding down his body as he lowered her, she felt the thick length of him, hardening in response to her. He slid a hand down her back before her feet touched the ground and pulled her groin into his tightly. When he pressed his hand onto her rear, she flinched. Instantly, he broke off the kiss and stood her in front of him.

"I have hurt you?"

"Look, it's nothing. I've had worse."

"It is not nothing, Gillian. You will let me examine any bruises." He took her shoulder and started to turn her, when she knocked his hand away.

"Oh no, I will not! I am not dropping trou out here in the middle of nowhere! What is *wrong* with you?" she yelled, incredulous that he would ask such a thing.

Tanis's anger boiled close to the surface again, but remembering their earlier conversation, he also thought before he spoke.

"All right, *piccola*, I won't look at your lovely backside. You're right, it is unreasonable of me to ask at this point. However, I would mention that I have seen the female form before."

He ruffled her hair for emphasis, chuckling at her irritation with him.

Exasperated, she turned and stomped off downhill. In a flash, Tanis was at her side, capturing her hand and bringing it to his lips. He slowed his long stride to match hers and was encouraged when she didn't immediately pull away.

Watching her walk beside him, he was amazed by the smallest details about her. The way her hair shimmered in the moonlight, the memory of the flash in her beautiful eyes in her rage toward him, the strength and courage she had to challenge an ancient Vampire.

Her walk was electric. Muscles flexed beneath the cargo pants she wore. She walked like a woman, but there was the promise of deadly violence in her. He'd never met anyone like her.

Totally secure and unafraid, she had relied upon herself in

the worst of situations as a combat veteran. It could be a definite problem, that kind of confidence here, in his world. He wanted to say something to her, something about how impressed he was with her, but he settled for holding her hand and matching her stride as they walked through the moonlight together.

The slope started to slant sharply and Gillian shook free of his hand to balance herself. Tanis was in front of her instantly to catch her should she start to slide.

"Oh, for Hell's sake, Tanis, I won't break." Her head was down, watching her footing, so she didn't see him stop and ran into him again.

He caught her easily and kissed her nose. "Dammit, Tanis, stop going immobile in front of me. I'm going to break my nose on your chest, you grabastic snotwad!"

She'd picked up a few original phrases in the Marines and that was one Tanis had never heard. He doubled over in laughter, and she shoved him. Problem was, he was backward on a steep slope, one leg hooked over a fallen tree. He toppled over, rolling partway down the embankment. Gillian bolted after him in horror, afraid he'd bash his stupid head open on a rock. Aleksei would fire her for sure if she broke his brother.

He stopped rolling and she skidded to a halt, tangling her foot in a root and falling partly across his lap. Tanis caught her so her face didn't hit the ground. She turned and braced herself up on an elbow, glaring at him.

"What *is* it with you? Every other minute you're either trying to fondle me or you've got me over your lap." She grinned at the perplexed look on his face.

Tanis lightly popped her on the butt, then started running his hand over the shapely curve. "It's karma, *piccola*. The universe knows you need a guiding hand."

Gillian raised up with a murderous look, then found his arms around her again, this time cradling her back on his lap and pulling her against him. His mouth was hot and demanding on hers, his hand sliding over her butt, lightly rubbing her, sliding over her hip and dipping down between her thighs to urge her legs apart, pressing his palm to her feminine heat.

A four-hundred-year-old sensual Vampire gains a lot of experience kissing, stimulating, tantalizing; Tanis wasn't holding back. He wanted her; he wanted her to want him with the same ferocity. Gillian was responding to his ministrations with her own level of skill, leaning her breasts against him, lightly rubbing her nipples over the hardness of his chest.

She could feel the length and width of his straining erection under her hip. He swung around so that his legs faced downhill, pulling Gillian up with him. She straddled him and pressed herself against his hard need. No stranger to lovemaking herself, she knew his mood mirrored her own.

All the fire and fury between them was erupting in that kiss. Their tongues dueled as Tanis ran his hand up her chest to cup a firm, full breast, rubbing his thumb over her nipple. He moaned softly as she ground her warmth over him and ran her arm around her hips to pull her in tighter. Her natural sensuality tightened his body into a painful ache. He could smell her hot, damp warmth and feel her responding to him.

Small, delicate hands ran up his chest and over his shoulders, one continuing down his back and over his hip, down his thigh to massage him through his pants. He shuddered with repressed desire. Right now, he wanted to be deep inside her; to feel her quaking with pleasure, pulling him in and riding him to heaven.

Gently, he slid his hand under her tunic and snapped open her bra, letting her full breasts free for his examination, kissing down her jawline to her neck. His large hand cupped her, kneading gently, her nipple hardening against his palm.

Gill arched into his touch, enjoying the velvet luxury of his soft, warm mouth against her neck. The scrape of his fangs along her fragile skin was soothed by his silky tongue as he fought not to bite her. Empathy flared as she pulled back, breathing hard. He wanted sex, but his body wanted blood too.

Her eyes were dilated, dark emerald with desire, her lips full and swollen from his kiss. Not stopping his investigation of her breast, Tanis brought his free hand up to caress her face.

"What is wrong, *cara*? Am I going too fast for you?"

She stared hard at him to see if he was joking, but there was only tenderness, respect and need in his eyes. It was a look she would never have expected to find in Tanis's eyes while she was sitting against his hardened shaft, only their clothing separating them.

"Okay, Tanis, if we do this, there is to be no teeth, no blood. You understand? I mean it. One canine shows itself and we're done."

She held her hand against his chest, holding him back from kissing her again. The other hand came up to her own mouth. "And don't nick me when we're kissing either. I'm not used to French kissing a Vampire." She smiled.

"Are you sure this is what you want to do, *cara mia*? I am trying very hard to play the Human suitor, but I am not sure what the rules are." Tanis's voice was thick with sex, but her sense told her he was confused with the dark needs he felt for her.

"Tanis," she sighed, leaning her forehead to his. "I am a grown woman. If I want to have sex with you, or any other available male, I'm capable of making my own decisions. This isn't rape, you know. In fact, I'm practically raping you."

She leaned in and kissed him, surprised when he jerked back. Amber eyes roamed her face and his brows rose at her words. "Gillian, what kind of monster do you take me for? I would never force you. Rape? *Caressima*, do not ever joke about such a thing.

"It is unbelievably difficult for me to stop right now. I want to strip our clothes off, roll you under me and drive into you hard and deep." His voice was shaking with his effort to remain rational. "I will not deny that I want to sink my teeth into you and taste your blood. I also want to dip my tongue into you, sweetheart, to spread you open and taste every part of you. I want to bring you pleasure that you will never forget. But Gillian, you have only to say stop and I will stop. You have nothing to fear from me, now or ever." He held her face gently and made her look at him.

Gillian blushed under the intensity of his gaze and from his explicit description of what he wanted to do to her. She stayed quiet and patiently waited for him to finish, very aware of how wet he'd gotten her and that he realized it too.

When it seemed he was through speaking, she tried her own voice. Taking a deep breath, she answered him. "I apologize for my choice of words then, Tanis. I want you too but I want it understood that I do not intend to be a snack. Even if this is just to alleviate the tension of the moment, I'd like to think that despite our initial hatred of each other, there is a solid attraction too."

She searched his face as he did hers. "Do you hear me, Tanis? I need to know that you're still in there and that you understand what I'm telling you, or I get off and this stops here."

To her surprise, he laughed softly. "*Piccola*, I have not paid a lot of attention to the needs of Human females. I will not take your blood, nor ask you to take mine. I will not use my teeth in any way on you until you give me leave to do so."

His eyes were still full of passion, but his voice was serious and she could feel the honesty.

"I will give you my protection freely and keep you absolutely safe while you are here; both Aleksei and I will. The thought of you being harmed sends me into a blind rage, *cara*, you need to know that. If I am arrogant, overprotective or chauvinistic, it is not because I do not respect you. It is because I know no other way to be."

"Then you need to remember that I have been taking care of myself on the battlefield, in snipers' nests and with your Paramortal friends for a long time. I do not need a keeper," she reminded him, a delicate eyebrow lifting.

"No, *piccola guerriera,* I suppose you do not," Tanis agreed grudgingly. "But do not forget, you are squarely in my world now. Mine and Aleksei's. You may have Vampires and the lot for patients, but I assure you, here, in our world, you can be killed before you draw a full breath. I ask you to remember that before you fight us over your safety."

Gillian thought about that for a moment. He was right about one thing. All her training, combat experience and psychology weren't going to help her here. She would have to rely on the Rachlav brothers to keep her from being slaughtered. Dammit.

"All right, Tanis. I won't fight you. But you keep a lid on your caveman bullshit."

Tanis laughed at that and pulled her back into his embrace. Gillian kissed him again. Tanis melted into her arms, pulling her tighter and pushing up against the V in her legs. He felt constricted in his clothing, and feeling the dampness of her through her pants was not helping. They had to either stop or make love very soon, or he'd explode.

Gillian reached between them and deftly unfastened her pants. Taking Tanis's hand off her butt, she brought it around to the front and placed his fingers on the band of her panties. His kiss deepened as he gently slid his fingers lower, gliding through the soft down and over the small button to find her wide open and wet.

Moaning audibly, he slid two fingers into her as she rose on her knees, straddling him. Her hands were already busy with his belt and fastenings, letting him spring free of the clothing, huge, hot and hard.

Grasping his thick shaft, she began to move her hand up and down, in time with Tanis's in and out motion.

"*Dio, piccola*, this is not helping," Tanis managed between his teeth.

In response, she moved her hand faster, nipping at his neck and flexing on his hand. His breath was harsh and ragged. When she started moaning and pressing down harder on his hand, gripping his fingers tighter, Tanis thought he'd lose it.

She was watching his eyes glow even more with desire as she rode his fingers and pressed into his palm. Tanis's growl was all she needed to increase her pace on his member, now pulsing and growing even harder in her hand.

"*Piccola*, I have to be inside you." Tanis's voice hit her low and deep, so she raised up and slid her cargo pants down her thighs. Gillian turned and leaned back against his chest, letting him brace her bottom as she lowered herself onto his shaft, guiding him into her.

As she slid over him, a deep guttural sound came from his throat. "Gillian, *Dio, piccola* . . ." He started thrusting up immediately, hands on her hips, holding her tight to him.

Gillian pressed back, lifting up a little, then sliding down in time with his movement. Tanis was trembling. He'd never been with a woman as uninhibited as she was. The ridges of her canal were gripping him and creating a delicious friction. The angle of his cock was pressing right on her g-spot.

Tanis didn't think about the anatomical name, but he felt it, the smoothness beyond the ridges. He kept pressing it as he buried himself deeper in her. He could feel her breathing quicken and felt her getting wetter with each stroke. He moved his hand between her legs and gently rubbed her small bud, bringing a gasp and more wetness to cover him.

"Oh yeah, Tanis, that's it . . ." Gillian wasn't shy about letting him know he was doing a good thing. Goddess, he was big enough to be stretching her, making her wetter than she'd ever been, moaning in her hair.

"*Cara mia*, I can't hold on. I need a release, and so do you."

He didn't need Vampiric senses to know she was climbing a high precipice with him and they needed to go over. Alpha instincts took him then as he pressed deep. Holding her tightly against him, a powerful arm around her pelvis, he rolled them both to their knees, facing her downhill. She complied and went on all fours following his lead, relishing the sensation of him locked deep inside her.

Tanis took her hips and slammed home, stroking deeper and harder as she cried out with pleasure. His body moved without thought, seeking only one thing, her release to bring him relief from the tightness in his groin. She pushed back against him, her channel hot and silken, closing tightly on him as she started to climax.

"Relax, *caressima*, relax and come for me. Let go, *mio amore*. I am here to catch you."

Tanis couldn't breathe for a moment as electricity ran through him when her powerful contractions started. She clenched around him and her one word—"Tanis!"—took him over.

The orgasm pulled him from the base of his spine outward. Jets of his seed erupted, pouring into her as her body pulled him in deeper. Both of them cried out, pushing against each other. When they could breathe again, he stroked his hand down her back, making her shiver.

"*Piccola*, I can't tell you how good it felt to be joined with you like this." His voice was husky and low.

"You aren't so bad yourself, Tanis." Her voice was soft and still ragged.

Reluctantly, he pulled out of her, helped her up and fastened her clothing for her. He would have preferred to prolong the moment but cuddling in the dark of night on a mountainside wasn't practical. She assisted in tucking him all away and, looking up into his fathomless gold eyes, she saw him smile. Tanis gathered her into his arms and held her tightly.

"Tanis! I need to breathe here!"

He loosened his grip but leaned down to kiss her. "*Piccola*, I will take tonight to my grave."

Gently, he kissed her hair, her face and her lips. She would have normally made a smart-ass remark about Vampires and graves, but the look on his face and his absolute tenderness stopped her.

"Tanis, I don't know what just happened between us or why, and I'm a very intelligent woman. I can't believe we were just fighting a while ago. But you are special and I do like you. We would not have just had sex if I didn't."

"You may have had sex, *piccola*, but for me, it was making love." His eyes were tender on her face, his voice low and gentle and she had to touch his cheek.

"All right, making love, then. It was great, but remember, I'm only here for a short time."

That brought a dark look to his eyes. "Yes, *piccola*, I remember." His voice held a wealth of hurt.

Gillian looked at him and turned his face to hers. "Tanis, I'm not staying."

"I know, Gillian. It has been a long time since I have been really attracted to a woman. Believe me, I did not go in search of a lover tonight, nor have I for a long time." He sounded sad.

"What's wrong then? It's not like you haven't had girlfriends before. Whatever happens, Tanis, you're gorgeous and very good in the lovemaking department. You won't lack for partners, I assure you." Gillian forced her smile to be overly bright.

Getting involved with her patient's brother wasn't the smartest thing she'd ever done, but she didn't know if she was going to survive the next few weeks. Having Tanis to take the edge off looked like it might be a good thing.

Gold eyes roamed over her face. "Gillian, I have not made love to a woman in over a century. Just let this be special to me, can you?"

"*What?!* You can't be serious! You're telling me that you haven't had sex in over a hundred years?" Gillian was incredulous.

She knew Tanis and Aleksei were four hundred years old. She was also a healthy woman with healthy needs and tended to measure sex by her own yardstick.

"That is simply impossible."

Tanis laughed softly, stroking her cheek. "We are not Human, *cherie*. We are not subject to Human passions and need for sex. There has to be something else that is intriguing or else it is just about the blood. I find your spirit, your bravery, even your nasty temper, extraordinarily attractive."

He kissed her forehead, a completely different person from the arrogant bastard who had walked into Aleksei's home several hours before. "I hope you do not regret this moment, Gillian."

"I'll deal with it. Ye gods, Tanis, it's not like this relationship was permanent." She regretted that instantly when she saw insecurity in his eyes for the first time. His feelings shifted. He was unsure, vulnerable. The inborn empathy flared and she wanted to comfort him.

Her voice was gentle, almost musical. "If I'd known it had been so long for you, Tanis, I would have tried to make it more special for you."

Amazed by her sudden turn to gentleness, he pulled her closer to him. "*Piccola*, it will always be special, because it was with you."

The deep howl of a hunting wolf shattered the night air. Gillian stiffened in his arms. Tanis pulled back instantly, scanning the area for any threat. He looked down at her to find her smiling and looking around into the depths of the black forest in excitement.

"That is so cool! I haven't heard a real wolf howl for a long time. Come on, let's track him."

Tanis took her hand, and with difficulty began to follow her into the forest. Emotions were roiling in him and he didn't think he could stand a protracted run in the woods with her at that moment. He pulled up short and she turned with questions in her eyes. "What's wrong?"

Smiling wryly, he said, "I need to take you to the cabin right now, Gillian, and bid you *addio*—farewell. After what we just did, I cannot be with you any longer tonight. I did not fully feed earlier this evening and I find my desire for you has not fully been sated. To remain close to you, a woman I am very attracted to sexually . . . it simply would not be safe for you."

"Tanis, I'm not afraid of you." She snorted derisively, dismissing his concern.

Fangs exploded in his mouth and fire blazed in his eyes as his temper flared with his protective instincts. Dammit, she was going to take him seriously. This was her life she was potentially risking.

He jerked her to him and opened his mouth wide enough for her to see what she was dealing with. "You should be," came the deep rumble from his chest.

Vampire. Fear flickered for an instant in her eyes, then cold resolve replaced it, turning her eyes into icy chips of frozen emerald. Bastard. He made her flinch.

"I see. Then please take me back to the estate, it'll be light in an hour or two and I'd like to be asleep by dawn." She didn't fight him, but stood passively in his hard embrace, realizing that to struggle or fight would trigger something Tanis might not be able to control. He was trying to warn her, to protect her. Gillian choked on the thought, but realized she had to accept his judgment.

The Vampire's emotions had been long suppressed. He was very attracted to her. Her easy antagonism earlier and his reaction to her should have been a warning to himself that he was dangerous. After their passionate lovemaking, he was taut as a piano wire, his control tenuous. It was all he could do not to crush her to him for another round of wild sex and more than one type of penetration.

He wanted to taste her blood, to take her inside himself as she had accepted him within her body. Just being near her was a strain at the moment. Above everything he wanted her to remember that he was a predator. Her passivity did nothing to inflame him further and he was able to hold his inner beast in check.

Tanis stroked a hand over her hair, regaining control with relief. To take her unwilling was completely against the nature of the man he had been and the Vampire he now was. He wasn't a rapist. To force his fangs into her would be the same as rape, reducing her to merely an object to meet his needs. He didn't want that. He wanted her. If they could be together, he wanted her to come to him with open arms. Tanis could only wait, be patient and not scare Gillian to death while they were sorting through all this.

"Allow me to escort you, my lady." He bowed formally at the waist, tucking her hand into his arm. Gillian had to laugh. She was walking casually with a Romanian nobleman who looked like he'd fallen out of a storybook. A nobleman she'd had a fight with and who'd busted her ass; a man she'd had sex with only moments ago. It was too ridiculous. Letting Tanis lead, she walked beside him back to the compound, listening to his glorious voice as he told her of the coming attractions.

All too soon, the lights of the compound glared ahead. Arm in arm, they walked to the house to find Aleksei leaning against one of the pillars on the porch. His metallic gray eyes raked over her, checking her for any injuries or rumpled clothing. She could feel his surging emotions from where she stood with Tanis: irritation, worry, jealousy? What? He was her patient. There could be no jealousy about this.

She needed to sleep. She'd had enough of Vampire emotionality for the night. Still, Aleksei was blameless in all that had happened and she needed to retain a good relationship with him. Wanting to reassure him in her characteristic manner, she released Tanis's arm and went toward him.

Tanis watched her carefully as she approached the house and Aleksei. Even to his expectant eye, Aleksei made no sign, no move. There was no mental push or command. Gillian stopped in front of his brother, turned to him briefly and waved.

"Thank you, Tanis. It has been most enlightening."

Turning to Aleksei, she spoke to him. "Thank you, Aleksei. I gratefully accept yours and Tanis's protection. I have a full day tomorrow so I think I'll be off to bed."

"Are you all right, Gillian?" The other Vampire's voice washed over her. She knew what he meant. He could smell Tanis's scent on her. Nosy, are we?

"Yes, Aleksei. I am just absolutely terrific. Thanks for asking." There. That was honest.

She swept into the house and locked the door so they both heard it. It wouldn't have stopped either of them had they wanted inside—they both had been invited. All she had to count on was their honor. At the moment, it was the only safety she had.

Aleksei had checked out the area surrounding the house before the two returned, making sure that none of Dracula's Vampires were about. He also checked the house. Dracula had more under his command than just Vampires—Ghouls, Werewolves, Revenants and the occasional Human slave were not bound by the "no entry until invited" rule and Aleksei didn't want any unpleasant surprises.

He and Tanis took the time to set wards around the perimeter. Nothing would get in that wouldn't alert them. Now, they needed to find a Daywalking fait accompli. Someone who would watch over her during the day. They had no idea of her plans for tomorrow.

"You are not going to rob me of my therapist, are you, Tanis?" Aleksei's voice was warm with the stirrings of irritation. It was a distinct warning.

"Of course not, brother. You cannot expect her to see you as anything but a patient at this time. To do so, for her would be unethical."

At Aleksei's raised brow, Tanis continued. "I did not expect to find her attractive nor for her to find me worth her interest.

I do find her worth my most diligent attention, Aleksei, but I have pledged to keep her safe."

"See that you do, Tanis." Aleksei's voice held a note of command and he left Tanis staring at him as he went to find prey.

CHAPTER
7

THE next day, Gillian went off in search of the castle that held her other client, leaving Aleksei and Tanis a note as to where she'd gone since she didn't know how long this would take. The history on the case said that an Italian mercenary swordsman named Dante Montefiore had met his end due to ambush in the castle.

The Ghost was very melancholy and vengeful, but also shy. Frightening the castle occupants and visitors alike with images of his murdered form, Dante was able to transubstantiate his blood and his physical body for brief periods. He'd been a bane of the existence of the Boganskaya family for six hundred years. No one had been able to exorcise him, so he remained a landlocked spirit, bound to the castle, its grounds and his hallway of death, deep in his world of weary sadness and boredom.

Arriving at the rambling dark-stoned hulk of Boganskaya Castle, Gillian was greeted by Arkady Boganskaya, the count whose family had lived there for hundreds of years. Arkady was an attractive man just under six feet tall with long, dark brown hair and dark, compelling hazel eyes, he would have been really imposing had he been taller and had she not just experienced the Rachlav charm. Gillian still had to look up to speak to him.

Arkady showed her in. Between his bad English and Gillian's

lousy Romanian, she got it across that she wanted to be where Dante had died and she wanted to be alone. He brought her to a little-used hallway, blocked by a tapestry hanging over its width.

"Here," he said, ominously. "This where Italian die."

Gill thanked him and sent him on his way. She needed to be able to concentrate on her task. Simple spells of summoning and protection were standard training for any field operative or Paramortal psychologist. She needed quiet and privacy without Arkady's curious eyes.

She'd read the file. Dante Montefiore had been an expert swordsman, minor noble and sometime highwayman. Handsome, charming and debonair, he'd traveled Europe, looking for adventure, ladies and the occasional duel, which was how he earned his living, as a hired sword.

Basically a professional "second," Dante had fought duels for whomever had the greatest amount of coin. He'd come to Romania to champion a Boganskaya who was accused of dallying with another family's daughter. The fact that it was a true accusation meant nothing to Dante. They were paying him well and that was all that concerned him.

The duel had taken place; Dante had slain the defender. In true jovial Boganskaya fashion, the family held a victory party, inviting the rest of the dead man's family to attend. Late that night, well into his cups and uncharacteristically without his sword, Dante had been set upon in that hallway and slaughtered.

No witnesses, no one who would talk, a shoddy investigation and the matter was dropped by the Boganskaya family. The death of a mercenary swordsman, even one who had just successfully defended the family name, was a small matter and life would have returned to normal except for one thing: Dante.

Dante had never received so much as a scratch from a blade during his tenure as a swordsman. He was lethal with any light blade, from foil to rapier, to epeé and would have been an insufferable ass except for his dynamic personality. Always smiling and supremely confident, not to mention devastatingly handsome, he was a ladies' man and a true gentleman. People liked Dante, even after hearing about his profession. Fame has its disadvantages too, and Dante was challenged far and wide to prove his prowess both in and out of the bedroom and on and off the dueling field.

Never before receiving an injury, Dante was mostly shocked while traversing that shadowy hallway when the first dagger slid between his ribcage and kidney. The blows that followed were not meant to bring immediate death. The goal had been to bleed him out, and that is what happened.

There had been more than one assailant, but it was too dim and Dante's eyesight was failing too fast from blood loss and shock to make out any of the faces. Nauseated and dying, he'd cursed the Boganskayas with his afterlife. Fear had entered his world for the first time in those last few moments of life. Dante was supremely offended at the dishonorable act of his own murder and terrorized by the event so badly that when his spirit claimed the castle late the next night, he could hardly force himself back into that hallway.

Haunting became an adventure. He'd always made the best out of bad circumstances and he made the most of this one. The Boganskaya family had tried wards, spells and even an exorcism, but Dante held firm. The local priest said it was because the Boganskaya family was responsible for Dante's death and therefore could not be absolved until the Ghost gave them absolution. They'd called Gillian when they found out there was such a thing as a Paramortal psychologist, hoping that she could help Dante with some anger management and get him the hell out of their castle.

Gillian knew Dante had a tendency to transubstantiate for periods of time. That is, he could take solid, material form; either as a whole being, or as merely blood and gobbets of flesh, such as had been flung around the hall during his murder. She was prepared for horror. Time on the battlefield had toughened her against sights that most people wouldn't have been able to bear.

She set up a chair and a small table left for her by Arkady or one of his servants. On the table she placed her white cloth, a copper plate and some sandalwood incense in the center. Taking a small vial from her pocket, she dripped white willow oil onto the cone of the incense. Lighting it, she sat, closed her eyes, concentrated her empathy and began to chant Dante's name. Ideally this would have been done on the night of a full moon, but she didn't have time. Dante was not a spirit who would be hard to find, and she needed to exercise some control over the situation.

It didn't take long. Gillian smelled the blood before she opened her eyes. Eyeing the incense, she saw it hadn't burned but halfway down. The hall had transformed into the semblance of a slaughterhouse. Blood spatter and trails were everywhere. Little shreds of flesh and bits of internal organs littered the floor. From the wall to her right, the apparition appeared. Gill was ready for him. Ghosts with Dante's problem typically projected fear and terror. This one was no exception.

Dante Montefiore had been a breathtakingly handsome man in life. Long, wavy auburn hair brushed his shoulders. Creamy skin, offset by black eyebrows and lashes. His eyes were the clearest turquoise that Gillian had ever seen. A full, sensual mouth and perfect teeth, above which an aristocratic nose was poised. He wasn't particularly tall, just about six feet, but he was well built: graceful and slender, almost like a dancer, she thought as he emerged from the ancient stone. She steeled herself against the wave of fear he projected, and when it came, it chilled her to the bone.

"Who calls me?" His voice was deep and cavernous.

He began to bleed. Stepping close enough so that the blood splashed onto her boots, he loomed over her. Gillian's teeth were chattering from sheer terror and the chill he was manifesting. She kept her eyes firmly fixed on his, not wanting to watch the full glory of the multitude of bleeding wounds, through which white bone and raw muscle showed. The worst was a slash from his lower abdomen to his groin. The original cut had severed the femoral artery, which spurted in an endless stream, a loop of perforated intestine bulging from the ghastly wound.

Dante looked like a Human who had been put through an ancient Vegematic. Stopping inches from her, she could hear the bubbling of his breath through the punctured lungs that had drowned him in his own blood. The smell of a slaughterhouse, blood and bowel, was in her nostrils and her stomach roiled. It took every ounce of Marine Corps grit and discipline not to run screaming from the hall.

"You. Why do you call me?" Dante's voice was grating and unpleasant, thick with blood and anger.

Gillian breathed through her mouth and was instantly sorry. The taste of blood was heavy on her tongue as she spoke. "I have called you, Dante Montefiore, to ease your pain, to help your suffering end. I have called you, Dante Montefiore, to bring you a measure of peace, the hope for an end to your torment. I have called you, Dante Montefiore, to be your guide and your counselor."

The words and the manner she spoke them were from a colleague who specialized in disheartened and angry spirits. Saying his name three times, combined with the scents of sandalwood and willow that were battling the blood and offal for supreme odor of the hallway, bound him to her for this conversation. He had to stay and listen, like it or not. What form he took was his choice. She could tolerate it or not.

The Ghost hissed with anger, spattering her with blood from his ruptured lungs and torn throat. "You cannot give me back my life, woman."

This was overdoing it. There was more than one way to handle him and Gill chose one. She'd tried "polite"; now she went for "bitch." Feeling the first stirrings of anger, she affixed him with green eyes that were as cold as his aura when she replied.

"No, I can't, but what I can do, you dumb son of a bitch, is help you over your issues so you can be a nice Ghost instead of a grotesque, drippy, bleeding one with a pissy attitude."

Her nose wrinkled in open disgust as the royal blue velvet of his tunic and pants grew dark and wet with the continual outpouring of body fluids.

The long-dead swordsman stared at her incredulously. "What are you, *signorina*, that you come into my hall and insult me?"

"I am a Paramortal psychologist. The owners of this house hired me to help you with your pain, Dante, if you will accept my help. It is up to you. If you refuse, then I will leave and not bother you again."

Gillian concentrated on the odor of the sandalwood and willow and pushed her nausea firmly back. She prayed that Dante would have something of value to contribute to the general information pool. This was so not worth it otherwise.

Dante regarded her. He could tell she was shaking with terror, but she didn't run. In fact, she was angry. Angry enough to fight him. It was so ludicrous that he laughed, spraying blood from his torn throat again and completely grossing Gillian out.

"Goddammit, stop it!! I know the blood will vanish when you do, but that is just fucking disgusting!" She rose from the chair and turned away. Even she could only take so much.

A low, lovely, melodious voice accented with Italian answered her. "My apologies, *caressima*. I have been rude."

Gillian spun at the change in his vocal intonation to face an amazingly attractive man who was now free from blood, injuries and spatter. Even the hallway was clean. Looking down at her boots and clothing, she saw they were clean too. Even the blood smell was gone, leaving the sandalwood and willow wafting through the hall.

"Well, thank you very much. Yes, you were rude, but that doesn't take away from the fact that I am still here to help you." She glared at him.

The Ghost, fully solid for the moment, reached out and took her hand. It took all of Gillian's nerve not to jerk back from the icy touch. He leaned over it, his eyes locked with hers and brushed his lips across her knuckles. His breath was warm. She did jerk back then. *What. The. Hell?!*

"You're not a Ghost. Ghosts can't touch, and they sure don't have warm breath," she snapped accusingly.

"I assure you, *signorina*, that I am a Ghost. There are a great many things that the living do not realize about the dead."

His clear blue eyes sparkled at her and a boyish grin lit his face.

"Isn't that special," Gillian groused. "Now do you want to hear about how I can help you or not?"

Were all the men in this country advertisements for Lust Is Us? This was ridiculous. Dante wasn't even Romanian, but he was a stunning advertisement for wet-pantie syndrome.

"Please sit back down, *cara*. I will listen to what you have to say." He leaned against the wall casually, one shoulder on the stones, folded his arms, crossed his legs and waited.

Gillian explained to him that she was not there to perform an exorcism or to recommend one. Her purpose was to help the Ghost over whatever horror was holding him to Earth. Afterward, if he were better, he could stay or leave the castle as he liked. The owners didn't object to him, per se; it was his terrorizing of the tourists they tried to attract to their bed-and-breakfast, and his frequent bleeding everywhere.

Dante listened carefully. It was an intriguing thought. He hadn't liked dying, and he could imagine that "up" was not the destination he would be headed if he were ever truly exorcised. The more Gillian spoke, the more impressed he was with her.

She was pretty and intelligent; finding out she was a former soldier only added to her charm. She'd questioned him about his favorite sword and he'd asked her why she wanted to know. Gillian had explained about the Marine Corps, being a Captain, being on the fencing team in college. Dante offered to spar with her, in complete seriousness. It was just goofy enough of an idea to make her smile.

When she smiled, Dante was smitten. He was overcome as her face transformed from merely pretty to lovely when her lips turned up in a genuine grin. Even to his jaded eyes, the transformation was amazing.

Now that she had his undivided attention, Gillian got to work. Unconsciously adjusting her empathy, she became at once receptive to him and a calming, comforting presence. Feeling her extended warmth and acceptance, Dante had to admit that she was skilled at her profession. Once he had relaxed into the feelings she brought out in him, he found himself telling her things about his life that he'd never shared with anyone.

He'd enjoyed being a rake, never committing to anyone or any particular cause. Being an expert swordsman, being in demand, being popular, pleased him immensely. That was why his murder was more than a shock to him. Nowhere had he ever encountered animosity no matter whose side he had fought on. With natural charisma and charm in abundance, Dante easily compensated for the bad or harsh feelings his duels produced. Winning over enemies as easily as he won over friends, he couldn't imagine why someone would want to kill him, especially in such an unchivalrous, dishonorable manner.

Gillian listened intently, interjecting when needed, asking him gentle questions at first, then intensifying the exchange and focusing on the pain and betrayal he had felt. She dialed up the comfort, keeping him in an emotional cradle where he could feel safe during his disclosure to her.

A natural empath, Gillian was tapping into the whorl of emotions Dante was emanating. Carefully compartmentalizing his emotions from her own as she'd done all her life, the level of his anguish was truly shattering. Perhaps his emotions being able to simmer for six hundred years intensified them. Gill hadn't met too many individuals, Paramortal or not, with this level of emotional turmoil. Finally, she called a halt.

Dante looked at her, surprised. "So soon, Doctor?"

She smiled gently. "It's been over three hours, Dante. That's more than enough time for the first session."

Rising she gathered her things, turning back to the Ghost and offering her hand. "I'm glad we were able to work this out. I will be back in a couple days to continue. May I send word through the Boganskaya family?"

Dante took her hand and bent over it formally, brushing his lips across her knuckles. "Of course, my lady." His voice shifted into a timbre that was as warm as his breath. Gillian's eyebrows rose.

"Dante . . . *Signore* Montefiore, please remember this is a professional relationship. I can't help you if you take a personal interest in me." The edge in her voice made him pay attention.

"I will remember, *signorina.* Even if it is difficult in more ways than one." He backed away from her slowly, still smiling beautifully, and melted into the wall.

Gillian went down to find Arkady Boganskaya and report to him that Dante was willing to cooperate. Arkady was more than pleased and immediately wrote her a sizable check. Gillian tried to dissuade him but he insisted.

"No, *signora,* it is worth every penny if the swordsman can be a proper house Ghost—a little fright to visitors is fine, but making them run screaming from my household is not. If you can help him to be content, it will all be worth it."

CHAPTER

8

DRIVING back to the cottage, Gillian was turning over Dante's potential knowledge base in her mind. Allowing herself time to ruminate over each case was a habit with her whether or not she was working as a field operative. It was too soon to find out how much he might know about the regional Vampire volatility. This had been a session to establish her credibility with him, to make him at ease with her, hopefully setting the stage for further information gathering and to honestly help him with his problem.

Ethically she couldn't do any less, nor would she want to. She was legitimately a licensed psychologist and enjoyed that part of her career as much as being a special operative for the Marine Corps. Having Paramortal clients made her job more interesting. They were never typical and she often needed the extra reflection to sort things out. As distracted as she was, she didn't notice the shadows in the backseat of her car, moving, undulating.

The cool fingers that caressed her neck nearly caused her to skid off the road as she hammered the brake, jerking the wheel hard to throw "it" off of her. After some fancy maneuvering that the vehicle was never meant to execute, the car slid to a stop as she leaped out. The engine was still running, but she'd shoved the gear shift into neutral and yanked the emergency brake on.

Instantly, she was grabbed and spun around to face a monstrosity. The Vampire had her by her shoulder and her throat, his dark eyes inches from her own, black hair falling over his shoulders like obsidian sheets.

Gillian gasped. He was handsome, of course. Most Vampires were breathtaking. He'd have been perfect, if you didn't count the horrible scarring visible on his throat, jaw and chest where his antique shirt gaped open.

Holy water. That or direct exposure to some other holy item was the only explanation for why a Vampire would permanently scar. Although his face had been spared, it would have been an agonizing injury. He'd had it thrown on him or applied to him from close range. Probably right before he ripped out the hapless person's throat, she mused. Like what was about to happen to her if she wasn't lucky.

Gill leaned back reflexively, away from the gleaming fangs that snapped together an inch from her neck before he pulled back and smiled as her fingers tightened on the ruined skin of his throat.

"Prince Dracula sends his regards, Dr. Key. Consider this a warning as to how vulnerable you really are."

He spoke in a hollow but oddly compelling voice, then abruptly released her, dissolving into mist and streaking away into the dark.

Shaking, nearly in shock from her newest near-death experience, Gillian went to her knees in the deserted road, not caring at the moment that there might be more of them around; only that she was definitely a target. It was Dracula's way to toy with people first, Aleksei had told her. If the order had been to kill her, she would be dead in her car right now, instead of kneeling on tarmac and trying not to cry. Furious, trembling from her own sudden unaccustomed vulnerability, she waited until she had herself firmly under control before reentering the vehicle and driving back to the cottage.

Pulling into the gravel parking lot, she saw Aleksei waiting respectfully outside the building, casually leaning on one of the pillars. Gillian put on what she hoped was her professional face and went to greet him, smiling.

Aleksei's eyebrows lifted. She was far too pale. From where he was he could discern physiological differences in her: elevated blood pressure, eyes calm but respiration more rapid than it should have been. Her walk lacked the unconscious power normally displayed. Something had happened. His heart nearly stopped as he caught her scent, which was thick with recent fear. Dracula had announced his presence.

"Tanis, something's happened to Gillian." The thought went out to his brother without hesitation.

Aleksei desperately wanted to comfort her himself, his arms ached to hold her. He was protective by nature; the centuries had not dimmed any part of the original man. As her client, he was not in a position to offer comfort to her, nor would it be accepted. Since the little doctor needed consoling, through Tanis, Aleksei would see that she got it.

Powerful arms unexpectedly surrounded her from behind. Gillian would have screamed but for the familiar feeling filtering through her overly heightened empathy. The black velvet voice that accompanied their solid embrace confirmed her gut feeling.

Tanis. Materializing as he pulled her close.

"What has happened, *piccola*?"

Feeling her body coil, ready to fight, Tanis scooped her up, carried her over to the porch and sat her on it in front of him. It didn't quite bring her up to the level of his eyes; he was still much taller. His arms walled her in on either side, his hips were against her knees, not crowding her, but she wasn't going anywhere.

A chilly glance at Aleksei from Gillian told him she didn't appreciate his interference. It didn't take a genius to know that he'd called his brother. His smug smile confirmed it. He knew what she needed as Tanis did and would make sure she got it one way or another.

Looking up at Tanis's lovely face, Gillian nearly cracked. It had been a long time, like never, since she'd been able to lean on anyone, and it was nearly impossible for her to open up. Even when the source of comfort was wrapped in a six foot, six inch package that looked like a case study in Vampire virtues.

"Stop it, dammit!" Gillian's voice was harsh as she shoved at the immovable chest in front of her.

"Do not be nice to me right now. I need to handle this. If you start with the tea and sympathy, I will fall apart." Her voice was thick with emotion and sounded nervous even to her own ears.

It broke Aleksei's heart and cut Tanis like a knife. This would not do. Being strong did not mean she could not be in need as well. Time for a little lesson in relationships for both of them.

Tanis frowned, then pulled her closer against her vehemently uttered protests, wrapping his arms around her, holding her in the shelter of his large frame. She didn't want comfort but she needed it. That was his only motivation.

"Let it out, *piccola*. You are scared to death. I can hear your heart pounding and feel your body trembling. You do not have to speak, Gillian; just let me help you."

The gentleness in his amazing voice with the feeling of his arms securely around her made her eyes sting. She bit her lip not to bawl on his shoulder.

Tanis felt her shaking with unshed tears. "It is all right, Gillian. Aleksei and I will keep you safe." He brushed his lips over her hair. "Let go, *piccola guerriera*; let the tears come."

A wracking sob tore from her as tears, violent and brief, poured. Tanis pressed her against his chest gently, murmuring to her in Italian and French, letting her hear the steady rhythm of his own heart.

Aleksei gazed at him in amazement. His younger brother normally had no patience for any overt emotional outbursts. Yet here he was, holding their new little blonde accompaniment almost tenderly, soothing away the terror she felt. Gillian had gotten under his brother's skin. Aleksei wasn't sure he was happy about it.

Tanis just held her, let her cry it out. He was grateful her position on the porch kept her away from his lower body. Her nearness, her scent, her vulnerability . . . her need called to him and his body was hardening into a painful ache. He was amazed that his Vampiric sexuality was surfacing when all he wanted to do was comfort her. Firmly pushing down his need to join with her and chase all doubts of her safety from his mind, he materialized a handkerchief from somewhere and held it out to her.

Gillian smiled through the tears. "I told you not to be nice to me, you king-size pain in the ass."

She took the handkerchief, wiped her eyes and blew her nose. Her voice was shaky, but Tanis was glad to see her rally. He chuckled and patted her back.

"You needed to cry, *piccola*. It was a release of tension, nothing more. Aleksei and I do not think less of you because you were frightened. It is a normal thing to need comfort, Gillian."

There was a wealth of reprimand in his voice. He wasn't

pleased that she hadn't asked for help, but his anger was for whatever had happened to her. He expected an answer, and so did Aleksei. She looked up at him. The golden eyes were warm with budding affection and a little anger.

"Now," he continued, "tell us what has happened."

Gillian related only the drive home; they didn't need to know about Dante's case. They knew she'd been to see a client, but his problem was confidential. When she finished, she could feel Tanis's great body trembling with fury. Aleksei looked positively murderous.

"Now what happens?" she asked.

Aleksei swore eloquently and reached for Tanis through their familiar link. *"We have no way to monitor her when she is away. Unless we bind her to us, how can we keep her safe?"*

"I do not know, Aleksei. It must be discussed, but she will not like it." Tanis countered. Neither of them knew Gillian well, but given her basic personality, it was a good bet she wouldn't take kindly to the suggestion of a blood bond.

"No, she will not, but I do not know how else to protect her fully. We need a Daywalker ally to be with her when we cannot. Dracula evidently has spies who can function in full sunlight."

"You should broach this topic, Aleksei, as overseer of this realm. If I suggest it, she will choose to believe that I seek to bind her to me, and me alone, for ulterior motives. There is real fear about being in any sort of permanent relationship within her. Her commitment phobia is quite strong." Tanis's voice in his mind was amused. Aleksei found it interesting that his brother had developed a sudden interest in psychology.

"And when did you determine this, Dr. Freud?"

"I merely took the time to speculate on our good doctor's personality quirks," Tanis said smugly. *"I did some research."*

"You really are full of shit. You are trying to ingratiate yourself further with her and we both know it," Aleksei groused.

Turning to Gillian before Tanis had a chance to snarl at him, Aleksei introduced the topic. "Gillian, there is a way we may better be able to monitor you when we cannot be at your side. I do not know how to present this in a way that will not offend you, however."

Gillian knew they were "talking" about her. She'd watched their silent exchange and could feel the surges of emotion between them in response to whatever the topic was. She was equally sure she wasn't going to like it.

Looking into Aleksei's pale eyes, so silvery in the moonlight that they glowed, Gillian felt a deep shiver go through her, responding to his overwhelming "maleness," his overt sexuality, and to his need to help her. Tanis's arms tightened around her instantly, offering reassurance.

Aleksei continued. "We cannot be with you during the day, that is obvious and a matter which we will try to resolve by providing you with a Daywalker guardian. However, if we had a tie to you, we would have felt the danger to you with the Vampire and perhaps acted before he got so close."

"What kind of a tie to me are you referring to?" Gillian's voice was low and angry. She had an idea what he was getting at and she didn't like it one damn bit.

"Yes, a blood tie," Aleksei relayed softly, easily reading her thoughts and fears.

"Hell no," Gillian said fiercely, shoving at Tanis's chest. "Absolutely *not*."

Tanis didn't move, but he lifted his head to stare at her from the intensity of the anger in her voice. She was seething, that he could see. She would refuse the offer out of hand, whether it would keep her alive or not, simply because she wanted no permanent attachment to them or anyone else. So she was stubborn as well as volatile. That irritated him. Personal preferences were one thing; simply refusing because she hadn't thought of it first was not an option.

"Gillian . . . ," he began, a warning note in his voice.

"Don't even say it, Tanis. I mean it." Despite her anger, her voice quavered a little. "I am a soldier, a psychologist. I am capable and competent in what I do. Don't you think it absolutely scares the hell out of me to know that I am *that* vulnerable, that a lesser Vampire like that one can have the opportunity to rip my throat out? That if he had been a Master or a Lord, I wouldn't have even known he was in the car with me before he bled me dry? Don't you know how it goes against my grain to have to depend on anyone, including you, for protection?"

Gillian hopped off the porch, successfully divesting herself of Tanis's embrace and began pacing. "I have led men on the battlefield, faced down sociopaths and murderers. I have dealt with Vampires many times before. I've had a whole host of

Paramortal clientele over the years, including Werewolves, Ghosts, Sidhe and been in combat situations that would give nightmares to most people." She paused to take a breath and look at the two of them.

"But I have never felt so completely and utterly helpless and vulnerable as I did tonight when that Vamp appeared in my car." Her shoulders slumped in defeat, voice dropping to a softer register. She sounded so vulnerable that both men ached to hold her.

Aleksei went to her, exchanging a look with Tanis as he moved to lock her between them, embracing her. "The Paramortals, up till now, were your patients or opponents where you had full backup. This is our world. Your training, your knowledge of battle, will assist you, but you will still need us and the protection we can offer. No one doubts your courage, Gillian. It will stand you in good stead, but we will still shield you from what is to come."

Gillian struggled a little, then looped her arms around both of them, wondering how many more rules she was breaking. As Tanis had said, needing comfort was natural and right now she could use it. Besides, they were certainly impressive teddy bears. Fanged, enigmatic and dangerous, but sweet nonetheless.

"I appreciate it, truly I do. I just can't let you . . ." Her voice trailed off.

"I know, Gillian." Tanis's voice rumbled in his chest. "We will find another way."

"For now." Aleksei's statement held a note of finality, and they both looked at him.

He returned their gazes, all aristocratic and commanding once again. "We will find an alternative for now, but if it becomes necessary, we will have to seriously consider a blood bond."

At Gillian's hardening gaze, he held up a hand and shook his head. "No, we will not argue this point until it becomes necessary. Your agency has given you authority to act as you see fit. It will not penalize you for staying alive, Gillian."

They argued into the night about the best way to approach the problem of Gillian's continued safety. Her clients' wellbeing was her first concern and Tanis's. Aleksei and his brother were conveniently on site, but Dante required a small amount of travel. She was able to summon him during the day, so that wasn't an issue. They were fighting about Gillian's need to not have a large, stunningly handsome Vampire on her heels from dusk till dawn. Aleksei angrily called a halt finally, and said he would find someone to shadow her. His dynamic, prevailing personality making an appearance when Gillian tried to protest.

"There is no argument in this matter, Gillian." Aleksei's silvery eyes were positively sparking. "If you neglect your safety, I will contact the IPPA and demand the right to reprimand you professionally for causing me, your client, undue stress."

Where no other threat could move her, this one did. Gillian was on her feet and in his face instantly. "You wouldn't dare!"

"Try me, *piccola guerriera*." Aleksei spoke softly but there was iron in his beautiful voice.

Gillian was furious. *Antiquated son of a bitch* . . . "I am here to take care of you, you overgrown fossil! How dare you threaten me professionally!"

Aleksei's eyebrows shot up, then lowered into a scowl. He was beginning to have sympathy for his brother's initial reaction to her temper. He moved forward so quickly that she didn't have time to breathe before he was towering over her, eyes blazing.

"I am your patient, that is true, but you are on my land, at my behest, with your government's orders. You are now in the middle of the war you were investigating. That makes you my responsibility, will it or no."

He reached out a hand, using his fingertips to tip her chin up with exquisite gentleness. "You will do as I tell you in terms of your safety or you will cause me undue stress and potentially degrade the progress I have made in therapy under your skilled care. That is the last I will say on the subject . . . Doctor."

His voice was beautiful, but filled with censure. He swept past her and out the door before she could respond.

Tanis was staring at her as he leaned casually against the mantelpiece. His look wasn't friendly when she turned back to him.

"Do not cross Aleksei, Gillian. He is fond of you, both as a therapist and as a woman." Tanis didn't move but she could feel his anger from where she stood.

"Don't tell me that, Tanis. I have to keep our relationship professional. If he's crossing the line, I'll have to terminate our therapeutic relationship." She flopped down into a nearby overstuffed chair.

"Terminate it if you will, but you cannot leave either Sacele or Romania until this is over."

Tanis went to her when she averted her eyes from him: tall, masculine, domineering and breathtaking, kneeling in front of her chair and trapping her between his arms. "Do not judge him or me by Human standards, Gillian. Vampires are territorial and protective with those we care for. Aleksei is perfectly capable of keeping you in perspective, for the moment. But do not trigger a protective reaction in him by being foolhardy. I do not want to have to protect *you* from my brother's wrath."

Gillian looked up at his warm, golden eyes. He was absolutely serious. Frustrated, she dropped her eyes, squirming under his direct gaze and powerful presence. Then her jaw was stroked by a strong, large hand and she looked up to watch his mouth close on hers. She sat passively, allowing the kiss, not wanting to enflame him. His need beat at her as she slowly moved a hand up to cup his head, tangling her fingers in his long, silken hair. Tanis pulled back soon after. She needed comfort, not seduction.

"Let me stay with you, *piccola*. You need only comfort tonight and that is what I am offering."

Without waiting for her response, he stood and swept her up in his arms, carrying her to the bedroom. There, he lay her gently on the bed, then curled his large frame around hers, just offering comfort and security. Gillian relaxed after a bit when it was clear to her that he really wasn't trying to seduce her tonight. Lying there with Tanis stroking her hair and whispering softly to her in a mixture of Italian and Romanian, she fell asleep in the Vampire's arms. Tanis made sure she had no nightmares.

CHAPTER
9

ALEKSEI left the cottage after Tanis made off with Gillian, his emotions in an uproar. Furious with Tanis, furious with Gillian, more furious with himself for allowing his own iron control to slip where she was concerned. He really couldn't blame either of them; he'd practically thrown them together, but it still hurt more than he cared to acknowledge. Knowing that Gillian would terminate their professional relationship in an instant if he showed interest in her outside of counseling didn't help his mood. The truth was, he was becoming more interested in her in many ways.

Vampire society was complex and multilayered. Any Human who became important or necessary was respected and guarded with a ferocity unmatched in Human society. If Gillian were to have a blood tie to him or Tanis, she would be marked as a friend to Osiris and Dionysus and cement her position as an enemy to Dracula even if she wasn't already on his hit list. It would give her protection like she'd never known, but at what cost? She wasn't quite in the *enemy* category yet, Aleksei thought wryly, but she was certainly a target. For what, he didn't want to contemplate.

His blood chilled as he thought of what might have happened to her tonight. The idea of her delicate body being shredded by

Dracula's soldiers nearly stopped his heart; not that it needed to beat constantly, but the pain was still very real. Instinct and need warred with his intellect.

Finding that he was deeply attracted to Gillian, in more ways than professional ones, was disturbing to say the least. Aleksei ached for answers to his dilemma. He moved blindly, without purpose, striding through the forest in the night, his thoughts chaotic and intense. So intense, he failed to recognize the deft probe into his mind that only a very powerful being with a direct blood tie could generate, until a mocking chuckle stopped him in his tracks.

"Interesting, Rachlav," came the voice he had not heard in over three hundred years.

Aleksei froze, slamming barriers down, his insides feeling as though worms were suddenly crawling through him. His own power overrode Dracula's probe but not before the Dark Prince made it clear what his intentions were.

"Dead, reborn or alive, she will be useful to me when my coup is complete. She will assist you in adjusting to my authority."

Gathering his own impressive power and cursing himself for allowing his guard to slip, Aleksei sent out a call. It was a plea for assistance, a calling in of an old favor, and it was answered from thousands of miles away in Egypt.

"Come to me, my friend and ally, for answers and aid. Bring her. We will sort this out together."

Aleksei's entire being vibrated with the force of the mind behind that response. The tentative link Dracula had established vaporized as if it had never been, the mental door locked and barricaded by a mind and intellect of the highest order of his kind.

Osiris was the oldest of the Vampire Lords, the most knowledgeable, most powerful of them all. One-on-one, face-to-face, he could obliterate Dracula with a single thought, command him to destroy himself, make him his slave. Osiris, however, was honorable and benevolent. A civilized ruler, he had kept his own sect peaceable and as secret as possible.

When Dionysus sprang forth centuries later in Greece, powerful and wild, yet another honorable being, the two of them had formed a tenuous alliance. The two Lines rarely interacted. Osiris's bloodline being more focused on magic and mysticism, while those of Dionysus's lineage were watchers of the physical earth. There was, however, mutual respect.

Dionysus proved himself time and again to Osiris as a scrupulous if chaotic leader, his inherent wildness contrasting sharply with Osiris's orderly thoughts and manner of governing.

Dracula was a tyrant in any world. Mortals and immortals alike feared him. He ruled through fear and blood, slicing through whoever stood in his way or crossed his path. A sociopath in any society, twisted beyond comprehension, his goal was not title or even acknowledgment. He enjoyed power.

The giving of quarter or the taking of life was incidental. It didn't matter how he got there, power was what he coveted and power would be what he would obtain. The Vampire world and then the Human one would feel the tightening of his mailed fist. And soon.

Centuries before, his megalomania had made him reach out for power and control. Young and impetuous, he had unleashed his inner beast, trying to obtain alliances with Osiris and Dionysus in hopes of enslaving Humanity into a world of endless night. A world ruled by the superior race of the Vampire. Reading his twisted vision, the two opposing rulers had forced his compliance, sending their own legions to deal with the upstart.

Calculating and clever, Dracula had avoided assassination, but just barely. Osiris issued a command: go to ground and learn the error of his ways, or the Egyptian Lord would deal with him personally. Preferring banishment to true death, Dracula had gone to ground, but outside Romania, in the frozen north. Decades, then centuries, passed. He rose briefly from time to time, formulating a plan, drawing others desirous of power or as bigoted in their beliefs as he was, to his cause though his charismatic personality.

The army he quietly formed was impressive. A direct blood link kept those in his inner circle close to his powerful but cruel mind. He sent them out to the four corners of the world and in between. With the exception of Greece, Romania and Egypt, not an area was spared the infestation. Being of his Line tied him to their collective crimes, but he stayed out of the limelight, preferring subterfuge to direct attack until he was ready.

Dracula finally judged that he had amassed enough allies. The revolution of the Goth culture worldwide, the fascination with Vampires, the seductive lure of the power of the blood brought converts to him in droves. Minor Vampire Masters who believed in his vision were assimilated, Humans possessing the right amount of cruelty, beauty and desire were turned and brought into the fold.

He didn't stop there. Other Paramortals joined him. Werebeasts, Ghouls, Ghosts, even some of both the darker and light Fey, combined their loyalty. They didn't necessarily like Dracula as much as they hated Humans. Most of them had been treated poorly by Humanity and its biased laws and most were eager for a change of status quo.

Now was the time. Dracula could feel it. The time for a shift of power was near. The army of darkness was moving like a cancer over the world. Minor pockets of resistance like Rachlav's Romania, Osiris's Egypt and Dionysus's Greece would soon fall. The coup was about to begin.

Still tingling from Osiris's brief touch on his mind, Aleksei created his resting place, opening the ground away from his castle and gave himself over to the healing earth. It was too close to dawn to secure himself within the family tomb. He needed the embrace of the earth itself this sunrise. When he rose that evening, he would need only a brief amount of time to prepare for his journey to his sworn liege.

———

Tanis also felt the touch of the phenomenal power of the Egyptian God, through his brother's link to him. Resting with Gillian in his arms, merely enjoying her nearness and warmth, he was jolted by the tingle that ran through Aleksei's mind.

Osiris. He would be their only safety in this war. Dionysus was an ally but a wild card. Tanis knew where they would be going. He'd spent decades in Egypt and knew Osiris and his people well. If anywhere on Earth could be considered safe, it was within the Egyptian Lord's domain.

Years after their rebirth and after learning, painfully at times, the intricacies and subterfuge of Vampiric politics, the brothers had learned of the other bloodlines. Finding Dionysus incommunicative and unresponsive to their requests, they'd turned to the great Egyptian deity. Osiris did not consider himself a supernatural being to Vampire or Human worshippers, but the early Egyptians, marveling at his ability to rise from the dead, cure illness, grant some prayers—abilities that exceeded anything their primitive minds could comprehend—had made him into a god. Osiris, Lord of the afterlife.

He took it all with humility and grace. A pantheon of his

closest and most trusted comrades and advisers was set. They
accepted the Human worship and gifts, giving comfort to those
who sought them with honest motives and never interfering in
Human advancement or evolution.

Dawn was cresting and Tanis needed to seek shelter. Kissing
Gillian's head tenderly, he withdrew from her even as his body
clenched in painful need. Shimmering into mist, he left the
home and sought shelter not far from Aleksei. Plans needed to
be made and quickly. The next night would be soon enough.

The next afternoon, Gillian woke alone. Tanis was gone, of
course, and she felt curiously bereft. She placed a call to the
IPPA with the latest news and developments. They reiterated
that extreme circumstances call for extreme measures and that
she had carte blanche to do what she needed to do to stay alive
and to pull her client through, since he was apparently a main
stumbling block in Dracula's plan. There was at least one other
Paramortal psychologist and special operative caught in the
midst of this as well, but he was in the States and hopefully safe
from Dracula's reach.

One other festive piece of information the IPPA shared with
her was that Count Aleksei Rachlav was sort of the unofficial
major domo over the Vampires in Romania and that she needed
to play nicely with her new client in hopes of garnering more
respectability and clientele from Rachlav's potential referrals.
More clients, more informational possibilities.

Gillian sweetly informed them that her cover was blown and
that she really could move on rather than staying there in the
middle of nowhere. They suggested, just as sweetly, that her opportunities for knowledge not found on the current highways of
information would imply that she stay there, continue to learn
what she could and report back.

Swearing profusely about being all but ordered to be cooperative, but feeling a little better after the phone call, Gillian prepared to visit Dante. She needed to keep her mind busy, and
dealing with Dante's issues would be a good focus for her at
this point.

Driving over in the bright light of day erased a lot of the cold
fear she'd felt the night before. Gill had never been prone to
anxiety of any kind. She was calm, cold and calculating on the
battlefield. Her firm resolve and hypersensitive empathy had

saved her troops many times over. With her ability to divide her mind and emotions so sharply, she rarely was sucked into the void of emotion that a good many natural empaths found to be their logistical downfall.

She was a genuine, decorated, blooded hero, and she hated with a passion that a random Vampire threat could rattle her so badly. Mentally shaking herself, she was determined to get on top of this. Aleksei and Tanis did not need to "*piccola*-sit" her. If she let herself wallow in their protection, she was sure to get them or herself killed, and not pleasantly.

Although, Aleksei's voice filtered through her memory of their conversation at the inn: *"There are a good many things worse than death, Dr. Key. You must believe me."* She shuddered at the thought of what he might have meant.

As soon as she entered Boganskaya Castle, she could feel Dante's presence. They were attuned to each other. Good. Sort of. Gillian had no wish to encourage the flirtatious Ghost, but they needed the tenuous link with each other. She hoped he'd not make her job harder by trying to insinuate himself in her life. Ghosts did that sometimes, particularly with gifted empaths like herself. Hungry for feeling and purpose, Ghosts latched on to places, people or things, hoping to fill the cavernous hole in their spirit that their absence of life had left.

Going in unguarded was foolish. She took a moment in the great hall to prepare herself, closing down barriers and erecting safeguards to prevent him from following her out of his earthly prison. It took only moments, as the practice of years took over. Waving to Arkady as she mounted the stairs, she made her way to Dante's hallway. The chair and table she'd used were exactly as she left them, the owners apparently deciding to leave well enough alone after her apparent success of the first encounter.

Dante materialized almost as soon as she stepped into the hall. "Greetings, *dolcezza*." His voice was deep and musical, completely unlike the empty, echoing vibration he used to terrorize people with. Gillian realized he was lonely and happy to see her. Courteously, she offered her hand, steeling herself against the warmth-stealing cold of his touch.

"Dolcezza?" she asked, raising a brow.

Bending over her hand, Dante allowed his lips to linger on her knuckles, gazing up at her with longing in his crystal turquoise eyes and smiling what he hoped was a seductive smile. She brought back warmth and light to his barren existence. The counseling discussions were tedious, but if it meant her visiting, he would endure it.

"*Si*, it means 'sweetness'," he murmured softly.

Extracting her hand from his lingering hold, Gillian smiled and seated herself. "And how fare you today, *Signor* Montefiore?"

He *tsk tsk*'d her. "Dante, please, Dr. Key. And may I address you as Gillian?" The smile was breathtaking. Gillian nearly rolled her eyes at him and his light scolding.

"You may . . . Dante. Now, let's get busy. Tell me about the feelings of helplessness you experienced during your murder." Her voice wasn't quite as clipped as she meant it to be, but it got her point across. She was here for business.

Dante sighed. She was not going to be easy to seduce, but he couldn't deny that she had his best interests at heart, so he collected his thoughts and began to share. During the session, Gillian explained to him about why he was experiencing flashbacks of his murder, why his personality was so mercurial: charming one moment, then switching to hostile and distrustful. Ghosts didn't dream per se but their thoughts did drift and often he found himself replaying the moment, over and over again.

Post-traumatic stress disorder was not a familiar term to him, but as she gently explained how the trauma of his murder could have affected him, Dante began to understand his own pathology. He stared in amazement at the little blonde seated before him. Raised in a time period where women were looked upon as a means to an end, Dante had never really taken a female seriously. Until now.

Watching his eyes and face change, feeling the difference in his spirit, Gillian felt the rush of satisfaction she always got when a client made a breakthrough of understanding. Dante wasn't "cured" by any means. But now he had a tool, a key. Knowledge was a powerful thing. Understanding why he had harbored feelings of betrayal, knowing what held him forcefully on this plane, was the beginning of wisdom for him. Dante could not regain his life, but he could choose to either transition or to stay, albeit more peacefully, when he came to terms with his fear and hatred.

Abruptly, Dante fell to one knee before her, taking her hand in a grasp that was far less icy than before. Shocked, Gillian's eyes widened as he spoke. "*Caressima*, I do not know how to thank you for making this clear to me." Lips that were smooth, silky and *warm*, kissed the back of her hand and Gill jerked away.

"What are you doing?" she demanded.

"Forgive me, *cara*. I know no other way to thank a lady." Dante's frosty turquoise eyes raked over her, full of glowing blue fire. His sensual mouth curved in a magical smile. Shivering suddenly, but not from cold, Gillian rose, putting the chair between them, instantly wary, and backed away. Ghosts weren't supposed to have warm lips; they also weren't supposed to project sex either. Sex was the Vampire's realm; Ghosts were about scaring the shit out of you. Okay, he was doing that too. Point for Dante. Gads.

"Stop it, Dante."

"Stop what, *dolcezza*?" That smile alone, on Dante's generous mouth, was lethal. Gillian felt the projection of desire from him, as it tightened her body, dampened her palms . . . and other areas, sped up her pulse. Her breathing sounded ragged, even to her own ears, and she knew he heard.

Dante watched her eyes dilate with desire and his own transubstantiated form responded, heaviness growing between his legs. Death had not affected his ability to read a woman. Seconds passed. He made no move and she backed up no further. There were many things the lady did not know about the dead, it seemed. Seeing that she was on the verge of bolting, he acquiesced, rising and dipping his head to her respectfully.

"Forgive me, Gillian." Dante was at his most charming, pushing calm and security toward her gently. "It has been so long since I have truly spoken to an intelligent, lovely woman; I forgot myself."

Swallowing heavily, the molten desire that she'd felt evaporating like dew, Gillian regained her composure. Dante wasn't threatening her. She felt comfortable with him. It must have been a misunderstanding. He couldn't help looking like that. Hell, he was an attractive man . . . *was* . . . he was a dead man. A *Ghost*. A *Ghost* with a very prominent erection.

What?! she thought, real fear starting to creep into her mind. There shouldn't be any attraction or any erection. He was dead. Ghosts didn't have blood, blood pressure or arteries with which to fill a penis. He wasn't real, he shouldn't *have* a penis, or lips or hands, or those damned turquoise eyes, either.

Metaphysical theories and postulations filled her mind, trying to remember all that she'd learned about what Ghosts could and couldn't do. None of this made sense. Dante simply shouldn't be able to do any of this. Frowning, she regarded him.

Dante watched back, his expression growing more quizzical. "Are you all right, Gillian?" He strengthened the glamour on her, watching her relax a little. Control, he had to remember his own control.

"Fine. What the hell just happened?" *Careful*, she thought. Getting angry with a Ghost was an exercise in futility. Dante, like most Ghosts, wouldn't give a shit if he made her angry; anger was just another emotion to feed on. He was also her client and she needed to get a grip. She fought to control her fluctuating emotions.

———◆———

Feeling her anger charged him more. He hadn't felt this level of desire in ages. It enflamed his senses, warmed him to the core. She was bringing life back to him, energizing his empty existence; he couldn't afford to tip his hand too soon. Dante wanted her. All of her. Living or dead didn't matter to him but he made up his mind in that moment that she would be his. Now was not the time. He had eternity on Earth if he wished. He could afford to show decorum and wait.

"Unforgivable of me, Dr. Key." Using her formal title would take her mind off the fact that he'd just tried to seduce her, he hoped. "I was merely so enthralled by the simple explanation that you have given me . . . so happy to know that I do not have to exist in hate and remorse, that I quite forgot myself."

Bowing low, he swept his arm across his chest in a courtly gesture. "It was my nature in life to express my happiness, my joy, in a more physical manner. I apologize if I have overstepped."

"Don't do it again." Gillian said flatly. "This is a professional relationship, Dante. I know you're lonely. I know you're attracted to my level of empathy, but the reality is that you are my patient, first and only."

"Again, I apologize. It was unforgivable of me." Dante's silken voice warmed her and she felt a deep understanding of his predicament flow through her.

"Accepted. Now I must go." Gathering her things, she tried not to look at him for the moment. "I do hope you will think on the issues we discussed. I will return tomorrow and we can determine if you've had any further revelations."

Straightening, she spared him a glance and found his hand outstretched. There was a pregnant pause as she looked at his hand, then back to him, then down at his hand again. Mentally kicking herself for being silly, Gillian took his hand, steeling herself against the chill of the grave that his touch afforded. Dante made no provision for his grip not to be cold. He wanted her off guard and unsure of her senses after his near mistake. It wouldn't do for her to think him anything but a trapped spirit. At least not right now. Releasing her hand first, Dante touched his fingers to his lips and backed into his hallway, shimmering out of existence again. There was nothing he left behind. No sense of his presence, his warmth, nothing. Just like the Ghost was supposed to be.

A little uneasy, Gillian made her way back downstairs, to her car. It was still an hour or two before sunset and she knew she needed to return to the estate. Looking briefly for Arkady but not finding him, she left via the heavy front door. Grateful to be in the bright sunshine again, Gillian took stock. Dante either was one of the most powerful Ghosts she'd ever encountered, or most of the knowledge that had been accumulated and written on them was woefully incomplete.

Spirits could transubstantiate, that was a given, she mused as she got into her car. They could project fear, terror, cold, heat, even calm and acceptance. Why not sex? Dante had been a notorious ladies' man and flirt when he was alive. His sexuality was as much a part of him as his expertise with a sword. Perhaps they did take it with them when they died. She would do some searching on the Internet with her laptop later and see what else she could ascertain.

Attaching to a person, place or object was clearly within their realm of possibility, as was influencing the atmosphere of an area. Ghosts tended to be either very shy or very bold. Dante was clearly not shy. The information in his file had been erroneous. He had been aloof from the Boganskaya family but not shy.

Ghosts also tended to be either very hostile or very accepting of the living. Dante had been hostile as hell until she'd established her connection with him. She'd better get through the session with Aleksei early tonight and do some research before she stepped back into that hallway again. Ignorance of a subject in her line of work tended to be fatal, or at the very least, injury-inducing or permanently inconvenient.

CHAPTER
10

ALEKSEI would be on time as always. Vampires generally were punctual. Their reborn lives were orderly. Hunt, stalk, seduce, feed—sometimes kill. The stronger, more intelligent ones fared better, having other intellectual and personal pursuits besides the thrill of the hunt. Contrary to prior public belief, the "good" Vampires rarely killed their prey. Generally, they took only enough blood to satisfy their immediate hunger, though they could feed lightly several times during an evening if a situation warranted it.

Gillian wasn't worried about Aleksei or Tanis forcing themselves on her. Now that she had an established professional relationship with Aleksei and a somewhat established personal one with Tanis and knew who their allies were, she knew neither man was capable of rape or a forced seduction. Still suffering some of the aftereffects of Dante's sexual projection, she braced herself mentally for the seductive allure Aleksei would project, as she heard his soft footsteps on her porch when the sun had barely left the sky.

He entered the cottage at her assent, tall, gorgeous as ever, graceful, sensual and dangerous. Gillian felt her body react to him as always, but at a deeper, gut-wrenching level, thanks to Dante. Clamping an iron will over it and thinking about hacked up bodies to distract her from the mouthwatering Vampire, she seated herself as he closed the door. Following her into the room, Aleksei took his usual position across from her, dropping into a chair with fluid ease.

"Shall we begin?" Gillian's voice broke the silence.

Aleksei regarded her, his metallic gray eyes missing nothing. She was uptight about something. Her blood pressure was elevated, there was tension in her back and shoulders and she smelled of past arousal, but not of Tanis or any other male. Interesting. He wouldn't pry . . . just yet.

"I would like to talk about our upcoming trip to Egypt." Deep and pure, his voice washed over her.

Gillian's head snapped up. "Egypt? Why Egypt?" Leaning slightly forward, she looked at him intently.

"Osiris. We need him."

"Aleksei, I am only here for a month. I'd like to finish your therapy before you go gallivanting off to visit mummies."

"I intend to take you with me—as my guest, of course."

"What?" To say that she was surprised was an understatement. "I can't go with you to Egypt. I have another patient here. Your own issues are getting resolved, but interrupting your therapy at this time would . . ."

"Gillian," Aleksei interjected. "I am well aware of how well my therapy is progressing. However, Osiris has offered aid. He is in Egypt, so to Egypt we will travel. You have the permission of your organization and I have an obligation to keep you safe at all times. I cannot be assured of your safety if you are not with me."

"Tanis will be here."

"Tanis will be in Egypt with me, as will you. I cannot be wholly assured of your safety if you are not with me. We will leave later tonight. I have arranged for suitable travel and accommodations for us all."

When she opened her mouth to argue with him, he cut her off. Shaking his head, he continued. "No, Gillian. Unless your other patient is an immediate danger to him or herself or others, you do not need to remain here. I do know something of your professional code of conduct." Damn. Smart Vampire.

His tone was forceful and commanding, but even delivered in that magical voice it pissed her off. Gillian sat back in her chair, irritated, frustrated and blindsided. She could tell him that Dante was suicidal—they knew nothing of her other case, but lying to Aleksei, or any other Vampire was not an option. They could smell a lie before the words left your lips and tended to react in a very negative manner. She hadn't seen this development coming. She didn't see a way out, either, but she'd deal with it. She needed to get word to Dante that she'd be gone for a few days.

"Fine. I'm between a rock and a hard place, so I will have to accompany you." Then smiling slightly, her sudden sheer loveliness causing Aleksei's body to tighten, she added, "I've always wanted to see Egypt."

After a brief discussion about what she should take, Aleksei left to make final arrangements and to organize with Tanis. Gillian quickly packed a few things, then called Boganskaya Castle to tell them she'd been called out of town on an emergency and would return soon. She asked that they announce to Dante the reason for her absence so he wouldn't be angry.

Standing in the shower, letting the warm water relax her, Gillian thought about what was coming. So far, except for the Vampire attack in her car, there had been little evidence of Dracula, his troops, or the danger they were all in. She wondered about that. Vampires could exercise mind control of the highest order. It was possible Aleksei and Tanis were planting fear in her mind, enhancing a minor situation to seem out of control. *No.* she refused to believe it. For one thing, the IPPA had confirmed the severity of the situation during her subsequent phone calls to them.

Their information was gathered from a multitude of diverse sources and there was no way an entire organization could fall under the lure of two Vampires, no matter how powerful they were. Gillian forced herself to relax, exiting the shower and wrapping herself in a towel to stretch out on the bed. She wanted to grab a quick nap before their travels. Aleksei had a private helicopter and jet—*Of course he did!*—and it would be a short flight to Egypt. There the Vampires would sleep for the day, and Gillian intended to explore.

Floating clouds, a sunlit meadow. The air was alive with the scent of clover. Fragrant. Warm. Enticing. She was alone, but there was a distinct heat pooling between her legs. Gillian knew vaguely that she was dreaming, but the sensations were very real. Laying down in the fragrant grass of her dream, she discovered she was naked. Of their own volition, her legs parted, opening her like a flower to the rays of the sun. Her breasts ached for a warm male hand. Her arms rose above her head, lengthening her line, leaving no part of her covered.

Somehow, in the dream, it made perfect sense that she could feel the sensation of strong, male hands covering her, teasing her breasts and body to greater arousal. Firm lips closed over hers and a velvet tongue plundered her mouth. Moaning, she wanted to reach for him, but there was nothing over her but a brilliant sky. The sensations continued. A large, masculine form seemed to blanket hers. She felt the hard arousal of erect male sex against her thigh. Again, her legs moved further apart and she gasped as she felt the phantom erection enter her in a smooth, deep stroke.

Arching her hips toward the sky, she felt the penetration go deeper and begin to move. Gliding. She was wet and hot, her hips moving restlessly against the imagined pelvis pressing her down into the grass and clover. It was the most erotic dream she'd ever experienced.

Warm and gentle, the sun's rays made her tingle. The pleasure was growing, winding her body tighter and tighter as the movement within her continued. Slowly, inexorably, it was bringing her closer and closer toward orgasm. Her arms felt leaden. They were still high above her head, held there by gentle pressure. Needing release, Gillian writhed, pressing upward against the full, stretching feeling. At once, the pressure increased, seeming to swell harder and thicker within her. Suddenly, she was crying out, the ripple of her climax bringing her inner muscles tight around nothing. She felt the heavy wetness of a lover's orgasm against her core. Wide open, she lay beneath the sky, drifting on aftershocks, feeling empty.

Tanis sucked in his breath sharply from the doorway. He'd come into the cabin to help Gillian with any last minute preparations and had heard noises from the bedroom. Walking in, he was stunned to see Gillian, naked and asleep, spread open before him. She was in the deep grip of a dream, moaning, flexing her hips, opening her deep pink sex to his hungry gaze. Her hands were tangled in the wooden slats of the headboard. No one was touching her, but she reached a shattering orgasm before his eyes.

Need slammed into him and Tanis moved to the bed, unable to stop himself, the tangy scent of her orgasm hardening him to a painful ache. Easing himself over her as he loosened his pants and fit his hips into the cradle of hers, he took her mouth in a deep kiss as he pressed inside her.

Gillian came to slowly, smelling Tanis's familiar scent and the taste of him in her mouth. Her arms wrapped around him and her thighs moved to encircle his hips as he pushed his rigid, aching flesh into her. Groaning with need, Tanis began to move. Gliding in and out of her tight canal, his large hand caught her bottom, pulling her against him as his strokes became deeper, harder, faster. Gill arched up into him, needing everything he could give her. The dream had been too erotic, too real, and she needed sex. Hard, rough, mind-blowing sex. Tanis was eager to comply.

"*Piccola* . . . my God . . . you are so wet . . . so ready." His whispered voice faltered, becoming an inarticulate growl as she tightened her muscles around him, her small hands moved over his muscular buttocks as he rocked into her.

The silken ridges of her canal were like tight, wet bands around his thick erection. The feeling during each thrust and backstroke was so intense that Tanis thought he might pass out. It seemed all the blood in his body was filling his already tight organ. He had needed to be inside her so badly, he hadn't even removed his clothing.

"Shut up, Tanis," Gillian panted. "Just shut up." She took his mouth in a blistering kiss and held him tightly.

Their tongues dueled, his hand moved downward, cupping a full breast and teasing her nipple into a hard peak. The other was lifting her bottom, lengthening her line so he could bury himself deeper inside her. Gillian was moaning against his mouth, matching him thrust for deep thrust. His mind inadvertently entering hers due to their closeness and sheer proximity, he read her needs. Gripping her hips to hold her, Tanis increased his pace and the delicious friction between them. Having her open and wet beneath him, triggered his dominancy. His fangs found her shoulder, nipping her, pinning her under him. Gillian opened her legs wider, knowing he wanted it, her neck arched back, offering her throat unconsciously.

Tanis snarled at the temptation, his fangs scraping over the ramifying pulse of her artery, fighting to retain control, his body tight and heavy, an unrelenting ache that grew stronger with each thrust.

"Do it!" Gillian ordered breathlessly, a strangled scream of need in her throat. She was past thinking. Her body was on the edge of a shattering release, held there by Tanis's powerful mind. He needed blood. Her blood.

Tanis nipped her shoulder again, the barest of cuts, but enough to make blood well to the surface. He would not violate her trust in a vulnerable moment. Blood he would have, but not from a sexual feeding. His mouth fastened on her, but his teeth didn't penetrate. The flavor of her blood burned on his tongue. Spicy, sweet, tangy and light. He drove deep and Gillian came. She cried out, a sound so uniquely feminine and erotic that it brought him over the edge with her as her body clenched over his.

Arching back, his body exploded, delivering his seed deep against her womb. Tanis's deep voice echoed in the small bedroom as he emptied into her, pulling her tight against him, filling her completely. Gillian pressed up, needing every fraction of him inside her. Her arms and legs wrapped tightly around his body, her channel pulling him in as they rode out the aftershocks together.

As their heartbeats returned to normal, Tanis held her. He was still nestled between her thighs, still buried to the hilt inside her. Neither wanted to move. Gillian stroked his hair and he leaned in to kiss her with such tenderness that she nearly cried.

Seeing the sudden tears, Tanis was alarmed. "Did I hurt you, *piccola*?" He stroked her hair gently, his golden eyes full of concern, cradling her to his body protectively.

She shook her head, unable to speak for the moment. When she could talk, her voice sounded vulnerable, even to her own ears.

"No, you're just so sweet to me, Tanis. It's a little disconcerting, that's all. I offered you my blood and you didn't take it. Why?"

He heard the softness enter her voice and smiled. A deep chuckle vibrated up from his chest, warming her to the core. "You deserve tenderness and caring, Gillian." His voice was so magical, so warm, that she felt stirrings of desire again. "I could not take advantage of the situation, *piccola*. Perhaps another time you will offer again."

Tanis pulled her tighter against his heavily muscled chest, enjoying the moment of being allowed to witness her momentary vulnerability.

"I will take care of you if you let me, *cara*."

Gillian reflexively bristled, then relaxed. "Tanis, I really don't need to be taken care of, but I appreciate your protection and I can always use a friend."

He'd felt her stiffen, then relax. Tanis felt warmth suffuse him. She was stubborn, strong, brave and beautiful. She didn't need him, but she wanted him. At least as a friend. He would do his best to court her properly. She deserved that at the very least. Gillian was a remarkable woman. Just how remarkable, he was beginning to see very clearly. Kissing her, he withdrew, then rolled away to let her rise and dress as he straightened his clothing and gathered her bags for their journey.

———

The helicopter and plane flights were uneventful. Gillian did little more than read up on ancient Egyptian beliefs and customs. Aleksei had told her that Osiris wasn't a stickler for protocol, but being polite never hurt, particularly when they were going to the Egyptian Vampire with their hands out, asking for protection.

They arrived very late in the night, the sky velvety black and spangled with stars in the clear air. Getting into the airport from the tarmac, they were met by Osiris's envoy, Sekhmet. Gillian was floored by the woman's beauty and poise. Also the power radiating from her was immense, the mark of a very ancient Master Vampire.

Sekhmet was the goddess of vengeance in the Egyptian pantheon, and was one in Osiris's inner circle of power. She wore a lion-head pendant and a light, cream-colored linen dress with matching heels. Although taller than Gillian by several inches, with a slighter build, Sekhmet was grace personified. Sleek and elegant, her muscles rippled under the linen, belying her delicate appearance.

Her hair was so black it had a blue sheen to it and her eyes so dark they seemed to be cut from polished obsidian. Sekhmet wore no makeup except around her eyes in the Egyptian manner. Truth was, she didn't need any. Gillian had never seen a more beautiful woman in her life.

Extending her hand, she introduced herself. "Gillian Key."

Sekhmet responded with a blinding smile, taking Gill's hand in a firm grip. "I am Sekhmet. Osiris will be pleased to meet you, as am I."

Nodding to Aleksei and Tanis in a mental exchange of greetings, the "goddess" guided them smoothly through the crowded airport. It was four in the morning and yet people were clamoring everywhere. It wasn't until they were halfway through the airport that Gillian noticed that no one seemed to see them.

Cloaking spell or glamour of some kind, she mused. Sekhmet turned to her, smiling, and motioned that she stay close to her. Gillian increased her stride to keep pace with the taller woman. She didn't bother looking for Aleksei and Tanis; even if she hadn't known they were behind her, she would have felt the power emanating from them.

Sekhmet took them out to a waiting vehicle. Dawn was already threatening the sky, and the driver made haste through Cairo's already busy streets to a small hotel across from the pyramids. They entered the building and the woman turned abruptly to open a door to what looked like a small maintenance closet. The back wall pushed inward, opening a space that she slipped through.

Gill followed, wary and wishing she had her gun with her. As she angled around the edge of the wall, Sekhmet's form was moving silently down a ramped hallway. The hallway slanted back, under the street. Gillian could hear the traffic noises faintly as they made their way through what was becoming a long, sloping tunnel.

There were occasional doors and passageways off to each side, but they continued straight on. The walls were decorated with stenciled art deco lotus and papyrus blooms in gold paint, lit from incandescent lights near the ceiling. The floor appeared to be bare concrete, echoing the slight noise she was making as they proceeded. The Vampire made no sound whatsoever.

Finally, after walking for what seemed like a mile, they turned off down a passage that was more richly decorated than the previous hall. The floor changed from concrete to marble, muffling the slight sounds of their footsteps. Reaching a set of doors decorated with hieroglyphs of the gods and goddesses, a majestic-looking seal held the handles of the doors together. The seal fell, the doors swung open at a wave of Sekhmet's hand. She stood aside to let them enter before her.

A large chamber lined with lapis lazuli, lit by torches, was before them. Deeper blue than a late evening sky and shot with gold, the lapis reflected in the torch light, making the room seem warmer. Bas-relief scenes of ancient Egypt were carved into the semiprecious stone. The furnishings were sparse but ornate. Gilded benches and chaise lounges were placed here and there on a floor of polished black marble. Scents of frankincense and other exotic oils filled the air. It looked and smelled like an ancient ballroom of Cleopatra's.

"Aleksei, you and Tanis will go to rest. I will see to your lady." Sekhmet's voice was pure and lovely.

Gillian shivered as the black eyes of the stunning goddess turned to her. "Come with me, little doctor. I will see to your safety while we Vampires sleep."

A hand on her shoulder made Gillian pause. She turned to see Tanis's concerned and lovely face. "You will be all right, Gillian. You are safer here than anywhere else on the planet."

His voice was deep and full of concern and affection. Bending quickly, Tanis pressed a gentle kiss on her lips, then stood back as Sekhmet led her away. Gillian waved to the two handsome men who watched after her with worry etched on their ageless faces. Aleksei watched Gillian's departure, tension written on his body.

"She is intriguing, your guest." A deep, echoing voice startled Tanis and Aleksei and they spun toward the sound. Anubis, Lord of the Underworld and Osiris's right-hand Vampire, came to them across the polished floor, his arms open in welcome.

He glided, floated, strode purposely, a contradiction in physics, a dream, a solid presence . . . astonishing even to the eyes of other Vampires; Anubis was breathtaking in his sheer beauty. His hair was long and plaited, black, luminous, brushing his shoulders with the glitter of tiny golden beads. A heavy golden collar encircled his neck, resting on his bare but massive chest. Like the figures in the bas-relief carvings on the walls, Anubis wore a linen kilt, belted with heavy gold and jewels. His feet were bare. Reaching Aleksei, he offered his arms in greeting, palm to elbow, a gesture of good will. The raw energy flowed from him, raising the hair on Aleksei's arms. Anubis's fathomless black eyes missed nothing.

"It has been long since you have come to us, Aleksei. You have forgotten the power of our companionship. I am sorry it is under circumstances such as these."

The voice was so like Osiris's. It held the wisdom of ages in those deep echoing tones. Anubis's power radiated from him, energizing both the men. "You need an infusion of our Lord's strength; you are both drained from worry."

Turning to Tanis, he held out his arms in a duplicate gesture. "Welcome, my friend." His smile and greeting was genuine as he dropped all pretense of formality, pulling the other Vampire into a brotherly embrace. Anubis and Tanis had formed a close friendship during Tanis's stay in Egypt.

Returning the greeting and the hug, Tanis replied, "I have been too long away. I have missed the monuments and the colors."

Anubis smiled. "Come. Let us retire; you are not used to being awake so long after dawn. This evening, we will talk."

He took them to opulent chambers lined with obsidian and semiprecious gems, lit by torches, smelling of incense. There were golden beds styled after those of the pharaohs. Flat, hard daises with elevated headrests. The exception was that sandwiched between the structure of the beds' flat surfaces was an inch of earth; rich, black earth. Enough to keep a Vampire at full strength, but not entirely necessary for their survival. Direct contact with earth wasn't obligatory for them, nor was earth essential for each and every rest period, yet with the threat of Dracula's presence hanging over all of them, no chances would be taken. Day was now hard upon all of them, Aleksei and Tanis being more affected than the ancient Anubis. They settled in to let the torpor take them.

Gillian spoke with Sekhmet briefly after getting to her room. The female Vampire was lovely and enigmatic and she answered Gillian's questions politely. The power radiating from her was immense. She was one of the ancients, one of the original pantheon of Osiris's advisors and friends. It made Gillian wary of just what she'd face when they finally stood before Osiris. She thought she'd rest for a bit, then go explore the pyramids.

Sekhmet gave her a golden scarab key, with which she could freely leave and reenter the underground complex. In a soft, compelling voice, she explained that Gillian was a guest, not a prisoner, and could come and go as she liked. If Aleksei and Tanis had brought her there, she was a trusted and valued Human and would be treated with the utmost respect and care.

There was a warning too. Sekhmet assured her that while in Cairo, throughout all of Egypt in fact, she was safe from Dracula and his lot. There was, however, always the possibility of a rogue Vampire or another less-than-savory entity seeking her out. She was to take care when she went exploring and let them know where she went and when she went out. Sekhmet added that an appropriate Daywalking guide and escort would be found by the next rise, but for now, Gillian was free to do as she liked within the complex or immediate vicinity, just to be careful doing it. Sekhmet accepted Gillian's assurances that she would be careful and departed.

Settling in, Gillian was in awe of the chamber she occupied, actually in the entire structure itself. It was a phenomenal feat of architecture to have this building below Cairo's busy streets. She had no idea how large it was, based on what she'd seen. The entrance through which they'd come wasn't the only way in or out; she was sure of that.

Her tactician's mind was sorting through what she knew and what could be speculated. As a captain in the Marine Corps and a special operative, she'd had to wrap her mind and logic around both the known and the unknown. It had saved her life and the lives of those under her command more than once. She knew she'd sort everything out. It would just take time.

The room was lovely. Painted traditionally with hieroglyphics and stylized drawings, it rivaled anything she'd ever seen in a documentary of ancient Egypt. The floors throughout the areas she knew were polished black marble. The walls inlaid with lapis, coral, turquoise and other semiprecious stones. The bed was raised on a platform, covered with linen. There was the traditional Egyptian headrest as well as pillows, the choice left up to her.

A linen throw was laid across a chair, dyed a deep indigo blue. Gillian was sure it was authentic dye. Picking it up, she discovered it was a gown. Lightweight, very sheer and perfect for the heat of the desert; however, it wasn't hot down in the chambers. It was delightfully cool. Shrugging, she took off her own clothes and slipped the garment on. A polished mirror gave her the reflection of a small but determined-looking woman. The indigo color enhanced the yellow in her hair, toning down the reddish cast it generally had and making her green eyes glow with a blue undertone. She looked delicate. Shit. This would *not* do. Irritably, she peeled it off and grabbed an oversized T-shirt from her bag, dragging it over her head. Now she looked like herself. Tough and capable. *Much better*, she thought as she lay on the hard but extremely comfortable bed, put the headrest aside in favor of the pillows and drifted off to sleep.

When she woke hours later, she was relieved to find that nothing in her room had been disturbed. Apparently the Egyptian Vampires weren't concerned with invading her privacy. It gave her some solace. Intuitively, she'd realized she could trust Tanis and Aleksei. They would never deliberately lead her into harm's way. Trusting Sekhmet so completely within seconds of meeting her both scared and impressed her. The Vampire was enormously powerful, much more so than Aleksei or Tanis. She could have used mind control, compulsion, any manner of things to control Gillian's thoughts and emotions without her awareness, make her trust them, make her into food. Yet she hadn't. Apparently absolute power did not necessarily corrupt absolutely. Osiris indeed must be either an honorable or a scary fucking leader if his people had opportunities to misuse their gifts but did not.

Feeling secure, she dressed, checked her watch, found it was still daytime and prepared to explore. Surely she would find food from a street vendor. Opening her door, she found a tray with chilled fruit, cheese and icy cold water in a gold pitcher. Pleasantly surprised, Gillian brought it in, setting it on an ornately carved table with a little stool beside it. She ate lightly, then, feeling refreshed, set off to discover Cairo while the sun still shone.

Sekhmet had told her which passageways to take, and showed her how to read the hieroglyphs that decorated every wall. The bright paintings and bas-relief carvings were actually a map, directing anyone who knew how to interpret them through the honeycombed maze of corridors. The figures changed, but it was the background that subtly indicated direction. The pyramids were represented as tiny triangles farther away. The closer you got to where they were located aboveground, the bigger they became until they dominated the background behind a picture of the Pharaoh Khefre and his slaves. There was a door a few feet beyond.

Gillian pressed her scarab key into the depression in the middle of the door and it slid back noiselessly. Up a long incline that curved slightly so that no sunlight could accidentally penetrate, then to another door. Again, Gillian used her key and again, the door slid open, shutting noiselessly behind her as she climbed out into an archeologist's hut at the feet of the Sphinx. A kneeling man brushing sand out of pottery pieces glanced up at her, smiled and went back to work. Apparently he was used to his hut being utilized as a exit ramp.

Gillian moved out, awed by the gigantic figure of the Sphinx and the monumental pyramids. It was autumn in Egypt, hot but not entirely unpleasant in the late afternoon sun. Gillian was dressed for the weather—white tank top, long khaki cargo pants, desert boots and a hat. She had a Thermos she'd brought with her full of the icy cold water that had been left in her chamber, her Glock 22C semiautomatic pistol, a flashlight, a knife and a lightweight fifty-foot cord with rappelling equipment, in case she wanted to climb. Once a marine, always a marine, Gill thought. She was used to efficiently packing for whatever need should arise.

There were soldiers here and there, guns shouldered and ready. Gillian unconsciously patted the pistol she had in her pocket. It wouldn't do a damn thing against a Vampire, but it would take down anything short of an elephant. Buying a guidebook at a vendor's tent, she went to the pyramids. Entering the smaller two, Khefre and Menkaure, was out of the question. They were closed to the public. Khufu, the Great Pyramid, was still open. Or at least parts of it were.

Following the line of the structure, Gillian was impressed by the sheer size of the thing. The huge limestone blocks were as tall as she was. Each had been cut and fit so precisely that a sheet of paper wouldn't fit between them. No mortar had been used. It had endured due to exact calculations and measurements of placement and balance. She climbed the steps to the entrance, already lightly sweating from the dry heat. Upon entry, the passage went up into the center, to the very top where the King's chamber lay.

The Queen's chamber—or so it was called—lay to the left and down. The corridor roped off against visitors' entry with a "Danger" sign in English, French and Arabic. Turning back to the upward slope, Gillian climbed to the top. The corridor was steep and had little ventilation. She was bathed in sweat by the time she reached the top. It opened into a large room, bare, unadorned. Off center from the middle of the room was a mammoth sarcophagus, also unadorned. The lid had been pushed back and was broken in one corner. Air moved freely around her here. The ingenuity of the ancient Egyptians resulted in ventilation shafts in the stone behemoth.

Opening her Thermos, she drank, letting the breeze cool her and the fluid replenish her. She was able to stand on tiptoe and look out one of the openings, enjoying the full view of Cairo. There were few tourists out, and Gillian was able to enjoy the peace and serenity of the ancient chamber for awhile before a

French couple slogged up the incline. She left them to their own enjoyment and traipsed back down to the entrance. Some internal devil made her slip under the guard rope and hurry downward, taking out her flashlight and flicking it on. "Just a quick look," she thought.

Slipping and stumbling down into the growing darkness, Gillian pulled her flashlight out and snapped it on. The lower chambers had been open for years but the air remained stale and still. She was below the earth, and there was no wind here. Lower she went, but it became cooler as she went down, the layers of sand insulating and protecting from the sweltering heat. Gillian looked carefully at the walls as she entered the lower chamber. Devoid of any artwork, they still had interesting grooves that looked carved. She brushed at the embedded sand, looking for what, she didn't know, only that it fed a secret desire of hers for archeology.

The chamber was dark save for her flashlight beam. An opening in the floor was a black forbidding hole and she had no desire to crawl down into something she wasn't assured of getting out of. Straining, sweating and swearing, she went back up the way she came, emerging into the late-afternoon sunlight and still air.

There wasn't time to do much else, so she decided on a brisk walk around the other two pyramids. There were fewer people here, no soldiers with guns. The smaller pyramids were still monumental, farther away from each other than they appeared in photographs and movies she had seen. Khefre's monument, built for the son of Khufu was closest; Gillian went around it, noting its dimensions and height, impressive even near the larger Khufu. Khefre stood taller. The section of desert where it rested was mounded higher, making it appear larger than it was. The Sphinx, silent, massive and mysterious was in a direct line with it. The recent excavation of a mortuary temple yawned before her.

Once, thousands of years ago, the Nile had run right by the pyramids. Scholars figured that the mortuary temple and the lower levels of the pyramid would be flooded, via a trench, with the sacred water of the Nile once the mummified body was placed within its sarcophagus, then sealed for eternity. Unfortunately, over the course of time, the Nile had shifted and the lower levels dried up, affording an opportunity by less scrupulous individuals to profit from the deceased ruler's tomb.

Gill wandered into the excavation, fascinated by the setup. Embalming platforms carved from granite, a deep bathtub-shaped receptacle for holding the body in its natron bed. Natron, a naturally occurring salt-like substance also known as bitumen, was readily found in the desert country. It had been used by the ancient Egyptians to desiccate and preserve the bodies of their more affluent dead.

As Pharaoh, Khefre's body would have been wrapped in the finest linen. Amulets, jewelry and religious symbols would have been placed among the endless wrapping, ensuring that the body was protected and blessed. He would have been placed in his inner coffin, arms crossed over his chest, hands holding the crook and flail of his rank, symbolizing shepherd and master of his people. A mask or crown would have been placed over his face or on his head, and the inner coffin sealed. The entire container would have been placed within the granite sarcophagus, his treasures assembled around him when the tomb was sealed and flooded. Khefre was supposed to remain undisturbed for eternity. Obviously that hadn't happened. There were no known royal tombs in Egypt, with the exception of the boy king, Tutankhamen, that had remained unplundered.

Easily picking her way through the rubble, Gillian found the back of the mortuary temple connected directly to the pyramid. *Makes sense*, she thought. Less chance of anyone viewing the king's body being moved, or what exactly went into the tomb. Not that it mattered. A royal tomb was simply too much temptation. Deeper within the ancient structure, she noted the wall carvings telling the story of the king's life, accomplishments and death. It was fascinating to see the precision with which the ancient artisans had worked. The flashlight beam illuminated key areas as she traveled under the sands and finally under the pyramid itself. Khefre's pyramid had two entrances, one literally on top of the other. Gill was in the lower passage, traveling at a fair pace. She needed to get in and get out. This might be her only chance to look at some of the renowned wall paintings some of the tombs had as she had no idea how long they would remain in Egypt.

Angling down steeply, the passage opened into a burial chamber, dark and foreboding. Gillian swept the flashlight beam around to assure herself that nothing was there. Her empathy clicked on suddenly and crawled over her nerves relentlessly. Uneasiness increased as she made her way forward. At the opposite end of the chamber was an opening. Stepping through, she discovered it went up at the same grade as the last had gone down. Practically sprinting up the incline, she found herself at a junction. Right or left? Both passages looked equally unappealing at the moment but she couldn't force herself back through that lower room right at the moment. There had been nothing that she had seen, but her senses were on full alert. Some "thing" was either there, or had been there recently. Gillian didn't want to find out what it was.

Reaching into the deep pocket of her cargo pants, she extracted the pistol, slapped the magazine in, automatically chambering a round. She was being ridiculous, she knew, but there was a crawly feeling between her shoulder blades that wouldn't go away. Even if she had to put the gun back, there was no danger of it going off. The Glock 22C had three safety features built in, plus antirecoil. It wasn't standard military issue but she preferred its sleek design and felt more comfortable with its weight in her hand.

Taking the left-hand passage, she moved on. The incline smoothed, becoming level, and she went cautiously. She walked as quietly as she could, trying not to imagine additional footfalls. The ceiling lowered abruptly but she was short enough to pass beneath it. Still, it made her feel slightly claustrophobic and she hurried. It opened into another burial chamber, this one holding a sarcophagus. The feeling of dread behind her increased and Gill bolted around the granite burial box, her light and gun locked on the opening she had just come through.

Undead, reborn, raised, reanimated, transformed or transubstantiated, all creatures who rose again after death had an aura. It was different than the auras of the living; the soul's vibration shifted a little after the death of the physical body but it was still an indicator of a presence. Gillian had experience with how most of them felt. Whatever was in that tomb was not in her realm of experience. She had no illusions about the gun in her hand. It would stop living flesh, but generally each and every type of Paramortal required a specific method to ensure true and permanent death.

Silver bullets would take out a Lycanthrope but were useless against anything else unless you emptied a clip and blew heads off. Cold iron was the bane of a Sidhe of any Court. Even the Sluagh could be killed with an iron weapon. Wooden stakes, wood-shafted arrows or wood bullets would turn a Vampire to dust, providing you were close enough and fast enough and the

Vampire was injured or in torpor enough, but did nothing against a Zombie, Ghost or Revenant.

Zombies needed a *houngan* or *mambo*, a *voudoun* priest or priestess, to lay them permanently to rest. Ghosts required an exorcism and numerous potent blessings, but nothing really bothered a Revenant. Self-directed instead of mindless, and externally controlled like a Zombie, Revenants were incredibly stupid but a hell of a lot faster than a Zombie, and nothing fazed them. They just kept coming until you found something to incinerate them with or moved beyond their immediate attention span.

Shuffling. Slow, heavy shuffling. Gillian's heart jackhammered in her chest. Fear projection. Whatever it was was fueling fear like a Ghost. She never moved, she never blinked. The passage was too narrow for her to run past it, though she doubted it could have caught her by the sound of its gait. Her world narrowed in focus to the dark rectangle across from her. All of her prior experience had not prepared her for the horror that shambled out of that frame of darkness and into the glare of her flashlight.

CHAPTER
11

DARK, discolored linen hung in tattered strips from the tall lanky form. Mouth agape in a soundless scream, hands outstretched, feet shuffling, the Mummy came. Where in hell it had come from Gillian had no idea, unless it had come from one of the side passages in the mortuary temple or somehow from the royal cemetery just being excavated nearby, but she had no time to worry about its origins.

Slowly, inexorably, it moved toward her, snuffling as it scented the air through dry sinus cavities in its ruined nose. She tried to move around the sarcophagus but it moved with her. Whether it responded to movement, scent or visual clues, she couldn't tell. Unnatural light flickered in the sunken eye sockets like points of yellow flames. It wasn't extremely fast, but it was persistent. When she moved, it mirrored her.

"Shit, hell and damn," she muttered.

Bullets would have absolutely no effect. It was tall, its arms and legs long and lean despite being moldy, and the room wasn't that big. The smell hit her next. It wasn't the rotting corpse stench that came with Zombies; it was a smell of ancient rigid death and it added to its projection of fear.

A Revenant was the only thing she could think to compare it too. She had no fire with her, and it was ludicrous to think that the spark from a fired bullet might catch the ancient pitch that sealed its bandages. It couldn't reach her over the expanse of the sarcophagus, which Gillian fervently hoped was unoccupied. She didn't need two inquisitive, hungry Mummies after her just now. The Mummy lurched, trying to snatch at her as she ducked behind the solid granite. It couldn't get to her, but she couldn't get past. Stalemate. Shit.

Time passed. Irritation built. Thoroughly disgusted with being pinned down by this one denizen of the dead, her teeth chattering with fear, Gillian's mind was in overdrive. Revenants had a taste for both blood and flesh. They were also enormously strong. Somewhat of a cross between a Vampire and a Zombie, they could rend and tear with their teeth, holding the luckless person while they chewed, slurped and crunched their way through to a vital spot while their prey screamed.

She had no intention of being food. Her temper was soaring, she was scared and her arms were getting tired from holding the gun and flashlight on her shambling assailant. That was the bad thing about the undead— they had seemingly endless energy and could wait you out. When you were too tired to run or fight, they pounced on you. Trying to negotiate with it was pointless. The Mummy, like a true Revenant, would have little cerebral cortex left to process vocabulary words, so talking with it was out.

Finally, completely out of patience, Gillian decided her best defense was a good offense. Hungry, angry and scared made for an explosive combination. Feinting to the right, she held her ground as the shuffling, snuffling horror moved around the edge of the sarcophagus. Quaking with fright while every nerve in her body fired in the flight-or-fight sequence, Gillian held her ground.

The grasping fingers reached and the Mummy's foot cleared the corner. She moved, but not fast enough. Lurching suddenly, the long-dead fingers caught her shirt, the fist closing with an unnerving creak. Gillian had no problem with false modesty versus survival.

Yanking the shirt up, out of her pants, she ducked her head, momentarily putting her arms, gun and flashlight within reach of the creature, who was too stupid to notice. The shirt peeled off her like a layer of an onion and she bolted for the door around the other side of the sarcophagus. The Mummy, not being bright, brought the shirt to its open mouth, tasting and chewing as Gill hauled ass up the passageway, praying that she wouldn't run into any more surprise linen packages.

To her right lay the lower burial chamber, at the bottom of an incline. She couldn't bring herself to go back through that lower room. Something was down there, she was certain of it; maybe hidden in the walls or the floor, but she had no intention of finding out what it was. The forward passage went up, and that's where she wanted to be. Up. Out. Into the fresh air. Ahead were double doors and she poured on the speed, vaguely realizing that her haste was unnecessary. It would take the Mummy several minutes to get to her after it discovered the shirt was empty.

Instinct is a wonderful thing. Seconds before she would have collided with the doors, her head down and shoulder out, she skidded to a halt . . . sort of . . . and bounced off the chained doors.

Shit and double shit!

Booting her foot against the door and pushing so that a crack appeared, exposing the locked chain, she took aim and fired. The noise ricocheted in the tight hallway, nearly deafening her in the enclosed area, but the chain parted and fell open. A moment of frantic pushing as the chain untangled from the handles and she was out and running away from the pyramid, only then noticing that it was full dark. Great. Just lovely. She needed to get back to the underground and fast.

Feeling somewhat silly in just her bra and cargo pants but cranked on adrenaline, thankful there were no people anywhere in sight, she jogged toward the front of Khufu, looking for the hut where the door lay. Finding it, she pushed through the door flap, and snapped the scarab key into place. The door slid obediently, Gill grabbed the key and tore down the curving incline. Reaching the second door, again placing the key in, she moved as soon as it started to slide and collided with a very solid, bare, male chest. Her eyes snapped up to lock onto Anubis's amused face.

"Your companions are most distressed that you were out after dark, little one. They are all waiting for you in the council room."

Anubis's deep echoing voice rumbled from his chest. He was smiling, but his smile faded as he caught the scent of where she'd been on her.

"I am Anubis. Tanis is one whom I call friend. You are all right?"

He looked her up and down, turning her in front of him, concern written on his spectacular features. "Osiris would be most unhappy if you were to come to harm. You are an honored guest and to be treated with the utmost care."

Gillian rolled her eyes. "Yes, yes, I understand that. I know I'm protected and I know Aleksei and Tanis are pissed off. Please just tell me what to wear if I have to be in that meeting." Unthinking, she grasped his arms, her voice full of urgency.

Anubis's eyebrows rose at her unexpected touch and he smiled but made no move to touch her. "Proper attire awaits you in your chambers, little warrior. I will take you there, then escort you to the council room." He led the way to her room, then waited while she changed.

Gillian was embarrassed that she'd grabbed him like that. She was getting too damn comfortable around Vampires and that could get her very, very dead if she wasn't careful.

Discovering an opulent bathroom hidden by a strategically placed decorative screen, she raced through a shower to get the grit and sweat off. She opted for braiding her wet hair, then shrugged into the sage linen pants and tunic lying on her bed.

At least it wasn't a dress, she thought as she regarded herself for a moment in the mirror. Her dusty hiking boots would have to do, though she brushed her towel over them to dispense with most of the sand. The top was a tunic-like vest, the pants tapered with a drawstring waist. The color looked good on her, warming her skin and making her hair glow. At least she didn't look delicate in it, she mused.

Joining Anubis in the hall, she swiftly walked to the council room, a few hallways away from her own. The doorway was open and Gillian swept in, Anubis at her side. Tanis and Aleksei were seated on opposite sides of a large circular table and rose when she entered. Old-World manners at their finest, except both looked ready to strangle her. She detected the undercurrent of anger from both the men and an amused feeling from Osiris, who also rose, sweeping his arm to indicate a chair near Tanis. Anubis remained by the door, a silent guardian.

"Please, Gillian. Do sit."

Osiris's smile was perfection. His voice was deep, rich, delightful, like melting sugar. He was beyond breathtaking. It was easy to believe he actually was a god. Humans simply did not look like that. Vampires didn't either, for that matter. Osiris was more than a cut above the rest—he was a standard unto himself that could never be matched in this world.

Heartstopping, pantie-liquifying, divinely perfect; dressed simply in the belted linen kilt of an Egyptian pharaoh, Osiris was royalty, nobility and omnipotence rolled into a very tall, coppery-skinned package. He was Egyptian through and through. His thick blue-black hair was cut short, obsidian-shiny and wavy, stubbornly curling at his neckline and around perfect ears. No crown adorned his brow. He didn't need one. The power radiating from him made Gillian's skin crawl, but in a most pleasant manner.

She appraised him openly, trying to keep her lower jaw shut, since it kept wanting to drop to the floor. Pure, raw sensuality was carved into the very structure of his face. Where Tanis's eyes were golden, the tawny amber of a great cat, Osiris's eyes were literally gold. Metallic, shimmering and triangular-shaped, they missed nothing—no detail in the room, no detail about his guests.

He knew their every thought, felt every heartbeat, heard every breath, and Gillian knew that he knew, which was good, because she had one hell of a question list.

This was where innate telepathy was a phenomenal time-saver. Up until five seconds ago, Tanis, Aleksei and Anubis had been the most spectacular men she'd ever seen. Osiris made them all look nearly average. Palms sweating, pulse accelerating, she moved toward the table.

Osiris watched her as she strode into the room. Small, compact, she walked like a warrior; confident and aggressive. He admired her but she was not his type, could never be. Isis, his companion and lover for the last four thousand years, held his heart securely. He appreciated Tanis's affection for her, could see why his friend was nearly frantic with worry and why even Aleksei was quietly furious with her for being absent these few hours. The little thing looked positively delicate, and he bet she hated that.

Tanis held her chair and Gillian afforded him a glancing smile. He was not happy. That much she could tell. Dropping into the chair with less grace than she would have liked, she glanced around the table as the men also sat, all eyes on her.

"Well? What?" They were staring at her, and she fidgeted.

Osiris laughed, startling Gillian and bringing incredulous looks from Tanis and Aleksei. She trembled as the rich voice poured over her.

"You have caused your friends great distress, young one. They feared for your safety, and yet you march in as if nothing has happened, no apologies whatsoever." He chuckled. "I admire courage, Gillian. You are a brave warrior and an honorable woman. However, you must remember that you are under threat, much as these two are, but they are far more capable of avoiding harm than you. You frightened them and should apologize."

Blushing under his gentle scolding, Gillian lowered her eyes and bit back a sharp retort. "I am sorry it got so late, I was . . ."—now was not the time to share her recent linen-wrapped adventures in geometric structures—". . . sightseeing, and lost track of the time."

Eyebrows shot up on the aristocratic face as Osiris caught the blatant lie. From the sharp intake of breath from the other two Vampires, they did too. However, he could afford to be magnanimous. The little Human would learn soon enough the truth of his words.

"I also admire loyalty, Gillian. You understand as much as we do the meaning of that word. I would like for your loyalty to be with me and mine, but I do not demand an oath of allegiance. Your word will be enough."

Gillian thought about that for a moment, since he had basically read her surface thoughts back to her. Carefully avoiding Aleksei's cold stare and Tanis's heated gaze, she spoke cautiously. "From what I've been told, I can trust you, and from what I feel from you and yours, I know I can. However, I hope you can appreciate that I am very much out of my element here and be patient when I ask questions or take my own risks for my own reasons."

Admiring her honesty and forthrightness, Osiris regarded her. "Fair enough, little warrior, but there are many things that you do not know, and we cannot spend months educating you in every nuance of Vampire society and infrastructure."

Her eyebrows shot up at that, until she remembered Aleksei telling her that Osiris was thorough and deliberate. He kept abreast of the modern world; he simply chose not to live in it.

"I understand that," she replied, carefully keeping her voice level, but she knew he felt her irritation. "I am just not accustomed to obeying without question."

Osiris managed an almost inelegant snort. "You are a soldier, madam. You most certainly are accustomed to instant obedience. Whether or not you are at the head of the army or merely a cog in the wheel, discipline and obedience are part of every soldier's life. Do not insult my intelligence nor try my patience on this matter."

Ouch. That stung. Osiris's voice never varied from the beautiful, deep, level pitch, but the reprimand snapped like a whip across her conscience. It took all her control not to squirm in her chair. Feeling like a child who'd been caught in a lie, Gillian could do nothing but acknowledge his truth.

"You are right. I apologize. I will try to remember that I am over my head and that I have to rely on you . . . on all of you, to stay alive and in one piece."

"Apologies and promises mean nothing without actions, little warrior. See to it that you remain alive. I will then consider your promise fulfilled and believe your apology sincere."

Gillian blushed again at that. Dammit, those little arrows of truth were starting to sting. Not to mention the fact that his power flared briefly during his anger, making her gasp. She remembered that he was probably only a couple of years younger than the Gods, so he probably had picked up a few things in the last few millennium, like wisdom. Real ancient wisdom. Didn't mean she had to like it.

"All right" was the only thing she could think of to say.

Pathetic. Absolutely pathetic. Hell, he would make anybody quake in their boots. She hoped Dracula would come face-to-face with Osiris.

Tanis felt the tremor of fear in her. *Good*, he thought. It would do her good to face a little reality tonight.

Aleksei's thoughts were on par with his. *"When we are through with this meeting, I intend to interject more harsh reality upon the* piccola guerriera's *backside. For lying, if nothing else."*

"I believe that since she is my lover, Aleksei, that it should be my pleasure to do so. You are still her patient. I am not bound by professional protocol."

"You had your chance already, Tanis. I did not agree with your method at the time, but I am beginning to believe that it may be the only way to get her attention."

Not missing the fact that a silent exchange between the Rachlavs had just occurred, but not understanding it, Gillian's brow furrowed. They were up to no good and it involved her, she was sure of it.

Osiris laughed again, reading every thought in the room.

"Gillian, you could not have chosen two more difficult men to intertwine yourself with. They are hopelessly old fashioned and absolutely determined to provide for your safety whether you wish it or not."

The Egyptian Lord rose and straightened to his full height, noble and imposing. "I have already spoken to them of this, but I understand that you have questions about how we will proceed. I respect you enough from Aleksei and Tanis's glowing reports to relay it directly so there is no chance of you not trusting what they may tell you."

He paused a moment to make sure he had her full attention. He did. He also noticed her surprise in hearing about "glowing reports."

"I could destroy Dracula outright in a face-to-face confrontation, that is true, but I cannot destroy all the thoughts and feelings of those involved with him. They serve him because they share the same attitudes and beliefs. We must fight and win this war openly. Only then will those who serve him and follow the path he has set them on, be willing to come fully under the banner of either myself or Dionysus.

"I am not a tyrant. I do not simply take what I am able to take. That is not what encompasses being a ruler of my people or any people. Prince Dracula is evil and twisted, yes. But if I insinuate my force, use my abilities to manipulate and control this situation, demand that the defeated swear allegiance to me, then I am no better than he is.

"While he would be brought to heel, the threat from those who would follow him and make him a martyr, will forever remain. I will have committed the coup instead of Dracula and this process will begin again with another Vampire of his line or belief at the helm of his followers."

Pausing again, he looked at her carefully. Comprehension was flaring in her eyes. Yes, she was understanding. Good. Now to do what he was able to do.

"I am sending Anubis and a small contingent of my personal guard with you back to Romania. Dionysus will send a few of his own as well. Do not be seduced into a false sense of security, Gillian. Aleksei will be required to generate his own protection for his country and his Human contingent. That will take time and time is one thing you do not have."

Her thoughts were clear on the surface and he gave her chills when he answered what she did not even think to ask.

"I know you have seen very little evidence of a war. I understand that you have little reason to believe in the seriousness of this situation based on your own knowledge of what you have seen thus far.

"Wars among us are not fought in a Human manner, Gillian. There will be no bombs, no clash of troops. Subterfuge and subversion is how we destroy each other or win allegiances. Dionysus and I intend to win. We shall win, but we will do it honorably, or all Vampire kind will be as much at his mercy as the Human world. Do you understand?"

He waited. His gold eyes, like discs from the sun, probed her. Finally she nodded. "Yes, I do. I will place my loyalty on this table. I know what you stand for much better now and can honestly say that I do trust you in this situation."

Truth was in her voice and he acknowledged it. "I am glad of that." He turned, nodding to Aleksei and Tanis. "I will do what I can to protect you, but you must take your own precautions."

Gill, Aleksei and Tanis also rose as Osiris padded silently from the room. At the door he paused and turned back, pinning Gillian with his eyes. Being food to the good guys was almost as bad as being food to the bad guys in her opinion, but she'd thrown her hat in the ring and she'd stand by it. She wondered how most Humans would see the situation—not having the experience and viewpoint of someone used to dealing with Paramortals.

"Gillian." His voice was soft and caressing. "You are not food to be used. Humans are our sustenance, that is true, but our lives would be empty without the glory of Humanity, with all its developments and changes. Humans are nourishment to the soul of the Vampire. We have no reason or need to enslave you. Do not forget that."

With a wink to Aleksei and another nod to Tanis, the Egyptian God swept from the room.

CHAPTER
12

AWESTRUCK, Gillian didn't notice Aleksei and Tanis flanking her until it was far too late. Damn Vampire glamour anyway. Both her upper arms were gripped firmly, a Vampire on either side.

Aleksei's low and angry voice was spoken at a pitch only for her to hear. "I want an explanation, Gillian. Why did you lie a few minutes ago?"

Jeez, Gillian thought. *It's like being caught sneaking in after curfew by your parents.*

Anubis had the audacity to snicker. Gillian leveled a hard stare at him, but he only smiled from his place at the doorway. Leaning against it, he crossed his arms, enjoying the interplay.

Tanis interjected, but he wasn't masking his words or his displeasure. "Aleksei asked you a question, Gillian. I also am very interested in the answer."

She tried to shake free of them, but it was an ineffectual gesture. "Fine. You want to know where I was? I was trapped in Khefre's pyramid with a fucking Mummy who was trying to eat me. And I lied because I knew you both would flip out if I told you the truth."

Turning her head so she could glare at both of them, she concluded. "Happy now?"

"Not quite," Tanis ground out between his teeth. The look on his face said he wasn't through with her yet.

"Anubis?" Aleksei looked toward his friend, then back down at Gillian, who was looking uncomfortable and angry. "What the hell were you doing inside that pyramid?"

"Exploring!" Gillian was vastly annoyed. "What the hell else do you think you do inside a pyramid if you're not dead?"

"What I think is, if you ever lie to me again, therapist or not, grown woman or not, I will resort to my 'overgrown fossil' nature as Tanis did, but I will not be as gentle," Aleksei snarled at her, his eyes flashing brilliant silver in his ire.

"I think not, Aleksei . . ." Tanis's voice was frosty.

Gillian smiled at him gratefully, until he ended his sentence. ". . . because I will do it." His gaze was withering. Her smile faded abruptly.

Laughter interrupted. Anubis was doubling over. Apparently he thought this entire exchange was one of the funnier things he'd seen in his long life, and he was sharing that with them. How sweet. He obviously didn't get out much.

"Tanis, you have your hands full, but Aleksei . . ." He laughed again. When he could contain himself, he managed to finish. ". . . finally someone has gotten under that frigid skin of yours."

Straightening and wiping his eyes, which were shiny with pink-tinged tears, he looked at Gillian. "You are adorable. You have no idea how pleased I am that someone has finally chipped through the famous Rachlav family ice."

He extended his hands in a pleading gesture. "Forgive me, Gillian. I do not mean to make light of your attack. Khefre has indeed been plagued recently by Mummies since they opened the royal cemetery and mortuary temple.

"If any of us had known your intentions of exploring there, we would have warned you. I am truly glad, as I am sure Aleksei and Tanis are, that you were not harmed." It was a nice apology, except for the chortle that followed. "Oh, Tanis, if you could see your face just now."

Gillian found exactly none of this funny. Jerking away finally from both of them, only because they let her, she started for the door. Anubis stopped her with a gentle hand.

"Please, allow me to escort you, Gillian."

His eyes were dancing with mirth and she could feel his

unique power radiating outward. He wasn't a threat, just obnoxious. Lovely.

Glaring at Aleksei and Tanis, she accepted his offer. "That would be great, Anubis. If you have the time to spare."

An obnoxious Vampire escort was preferable to the chauvinistic musings of the Rachlav brothers at the moment.

"I always take time for a friend, little one."

Black eyes that were still warm with mirth smiled at her and the smile continued down to his lovely mouth. Flirtatious? Not really. He wasn't coming on to her, just enjoying himself immensely.

"We are leaving tomorrow night, Gillian. Be ready at twilight." Aleksei's tone was imperious and she ignored it.

Waving backward to the both of them, she waltzed off on Anubis's arm, listening to Tanis seethe. "This discussion has not ended, Gillian. Count on that."

Still angry but trying to manifest a smile, Gillian looked up at Anubis's profile as they strolled back to her room. "I suppose I should be flattered that they are so concerned for my welfare, but it does wear thin," she grumbled.

Reaching her door, Anubis leaned around her and opened it. The Vampire Elves had been at work again. She had food and drink on the carved table and there was an extra chair.

"Won't you come in for a moment?"

She didn't really want company, but she didn't want to run the risk of another confrontation with Aleksei or Tanis in case they dropped by.

Anubis regarded her for a moment, his obsidian eyes unreadable. "All right, Gillian. I would enjoy a few minutes in your company."

He waited until she sat, then joined her as she ate a light meal of cheese, fruit and the spectacular icy water she'd had earlier.

"So you have known the Rachlav brothers a long time, I gather?" Might was well dive right in, Gill thought.

"Yes. We all have. Tanis and I have been friends since we met. Osiris and Aleksei as well. They have great respect for each other. Aleksei, though nowhere near as old, is as honorable as our Lord Osiris."

Anubis was watching her closely, intrigued by her in some way.

"Have you always been a soldier, Gillian? I have been a

Vampire for thousands of years, but I remember how important women were to men. I have not forgotten completely what it was like to be Human." He managed to sound somewhat wistful. "We cherished our woman for so very long, it is difficult to conceive of sending such a precious being out into battle."

"Not you too." Gillian groaned. "I know you all are ancient. I understand you have wisdom and knowledge that I will never possess, but you all have really got to stop believing in the pampered-doll idea of a woman. She's a myth. I wasn't brought up to be in a gilded cage, I was brought up to take care of myself. I joined the Marine Corps because I wanted to know that I could handle myself in any situation. And now . . ." Her voice dropped off.

"And now," Anubis echoed, "you find yourself in the very position you wished to avoid, at the mercy of hopelessly antiquated males who believe in keeping you from harm, even subjecting you to their discipline, because you mean so much to them." Even gentle and teasing, his voice carried the weight and wisdom of all the centuries he'd lived.

"Gillian," he continued gently, "anyone can see that you are a being to be reckoned with. That is not in question. Do not judge Tanis nor Aleksei too harshly. They have never been in this position before, either. It has been a long time since either of them cared for anything but our common cause. Now, they have found a Human to care about. I am glad of this."

Gently he cupped her chin in his hand as he stood to leave, his obsidian eyes gleaming with life, yet she didn't see it, stubbornly looking away, not wanting to hear all of his truths right now. His fingertips were warm on her skin, but he wasn't forcing her to look at him, just maintaining the contact as he spoke.

His voice infiltrated her being, serene and calm. "It takes a monumental will to live for a Vampire to survive even a single century, Gillian. Most Face The Sun when they have isolated themselves so much that life no longer holds any joy. The evil ones like Dracula find entertainment in the fear and pain they inflict. But most, like us, learn to watch, love to learn and continue to look forward eagerly to the next step in Human development. We do not stop living simply because we have died in Human terms."

Lifting her eyes to his, she found compassion there. Nothing that she ever expected to find within a Vampire of his age. "Osiris told you: Humanity is nourishment for the soul of the

Vampire. Tanis has had his archeology. Aleksei has governed our people in his Country and he has his painting. Nourish them a little. Give them more of your fire and fury. Shake them to their stodgy foundations. But do not give up on them. They are not lost, but they are as near to hopeless as I have ever seen. I do not wish to attend the suicide of two such friends."

"So how come you are so contemporary in your thinking and they are stuck in the Renaissance?" It was an honest question, but it still came out more petulant than she would have liked.

"I am thousands of years older. I chose to learn to adapt long ago. Aleksei and Tanis are young to us. You are very, very young. Young and stubborn and full of the pride that Humans all seem to possess."

He leaned forward and pressed a chaste kiss on her forehead. "I look forward to knowing you, Gillian. Now you must forgive me, but the night grows old and my lady awaits me." Almost gliding, he moved to the door.

"Your lady?" Gillian wanted to know.

Anubis smiled. "Sekhmet. I believe you met her already. Goodnight, little sister. Sleep safely. You are under a Vampire Lord's protection." Just like that, he was gone.

Alone finally, she had time to think and to ponder. Anubis was right. So was Osiris. Working with Vampires and other Paramortals for so long she thought she'd understood them. She realized that she understood their problems, their frailties, but she knew very little about what they were like ordinarily. Chuckling at the thought of a Vampire or Werewolf as now being considered ordinary, when less than a decade ago they were still considered myths and monsters, she jumped when there was a knock at her door.

"Yes?" she called. "Who is it?"

"Tanis. May I have a word with you?"

Gillian started to say no, but went and opened the door anyway. "Did you come to yell at me again?"

His lovely face was unreadable, but he suddenly swept her up in his arms, nearly crushing her in the strength of his embrace. "*Dio, piccola*, you are supposed to be safe here. When you did not return . . . I thought . . . I thought . . ." His voice trailed off, and he took her mouth in a bruising kiss.

Gillian was surprised, amazed and shocked. She thought at the least he was there to lecture her on appropriate safety precautions against the undead when visiting ancient architecture.

The fact that he was kissing her and trembling as he held her was astonishing.

Pulling back to have a chance to breathe, Gillian searched his face. "Tanis, what is wrong? I ran into a Mummy; it scared the shit out of me, but I got away from it. I had no way to tell you where I was or that I needed help. I would have told you if I could have. Okay?"

Smiling gently at him she stroked his jaw. "I'm not that macho, and I'm not too proud to ask for help if I need it."

Realizing she was eye level with him, she added, "Now, put me down, please. I am sorry if you were afraid for me. It was not intentional, I assure you."

Tanis complied, but he didn't take his hands off her shoulders. "I know it was not intentional, *caressima,* and I apologize for being angry with you for something that was not your fault."

Golden eyes roamed over her, not in appraisal, but to assure himself that she truly was unhurt. Before she could reply, there was another knock, on the door jamb this time, and Aleksei's voice floated over her. "May I also apologize, Gillian?"

He walked in without waiting for consent. It wasn't Gillian's home or one that had been designated as such, so he had free entry. "My sincere apologies, little Captain. I was afraid for you and my temper got the better of me." His eyes were serious and she could feel he was sincere.

Having had an exciting day, then learning more truths than she'd wanted to know at the moment, Gillian needed companionship from familiar friends. Laughing, she hugged both of them; something melted in the region of her heart.

"I am breaking so many rules right now it's not even funny, but I really, really want you both to stay with me for awhile until I fall asleep." She moved to the bed, kicked her boots off and sat on the edge. "Now do you want to hear about my exciting adventure with the Mummy?"

The two males took a chair apiece and settled in to listen to her tale. Gillian's natural personality, unfettered by professionalism at the moment, soon had the three of them laughing as she relayed her unenviable situation. Both men were astonished while listening that she wasn't a sobbing mess, but both came away with a better appreciation and understanding of how far females had evolved since they'd taken notice.

Much later, when she yawned, Tanis took control. "Lay down, Gillian. You are exhausted." Too tired to argue, she did as he asked and crawled under the blankets. Tucking her in, he sat on the edge of the bed for a moment, stroking her hair. Aleksei watched from across the room. He ached to touch her, to comfort her as Tanis was free to do. Recognizing that his feelings were far transcending a doctor-patient relationship, Aleksei promised himself to keep his thoughts and desires firmly in check. They were a third of the way through his projected therapy time, and he didn't intend to alienate her.

"Good night, Gillian," he said softly and left without a word. Already sleeping, she didn't notice he'd left.

Tanis noticed. He leaned down and brushed a kiss across her brow. "*Bona sera, piccola*. Sleep well."

Wanting to stay but knowing he should leave, Tanis stood a moment longer, watching her breathing change to the deep, slow respirations of sleep. Jealousy flared for a brief moment. He knew Aleksei's feelings for Gillian had shifted. The brief displays of his brother's temper had been a warning. Tanis loved his brother, but he was growing to care for Gillian. The last thing he wanted was a rivalry when they couldn't afford it.

Aleksei would remain honorable. Until his therapy time ended and the compulsory waiting time expired, he could do no more than engage Gillian in polite conversation. Tanis didn't know where it was going between himself and Gillian, but he wanted to play it out. Turning from her and retiring to the chamber he shared with Aleksei when he wanted to wrap his arms around her was one of the more unpopular decisions he had ever made for his body. He ached to hold her, but now was not the time. Tomorrow night they would return to Romania and try to survive as best they could until this was all over.

CHAPTER
13

Back in Romania, Aleksei insisted everyone be lodged in the castle itself. Gillian grumbled about protocol and propriety but gave in after Tanis threatened to toss her over his shoulder and carry her there, personally. It was immense. Hell, the entire estate was huge. The castle rose between the pines and other old trees of the forest. Built of local gray stone, it shone almost silver in the moonlight. She was shown to an opulent room on the main floor while the Egyptian Vampires were shown to well-shielded quarters on the second floor. There were rooms below in the cellar close to the rejuvenating earth.

The room Aleksei gave her was amazing. Decorated in rich burgundy tones, all the fixtures were gilded, warming the room further. A massive four-poster bed occupied a great deal of the space, but the room was so big it wasn't overpowering. The bedspread was midnight blue velvet. A large silver *R* was in the center of it, embroidered with metallic threads that Gillian bet were real silver. An enormous modern bathroom, complete with both a tub and shower, was off to the left and more closet space than she could have ever dreamed of was off to the right.

Heavy furniture, a wardrobe, dresser, table, chair and nightstand, was carved from a dark wood that looked like mahogany. The castle was wired for electricity and modern plumbing, yet there were massive candelabras on either side of the dresser for aesthetic value, and the fireplace kept the room cozy and warm. Gill was beat and lay back on the huge bed to collect her thoughts.

Anubis and Sekhmet had accompanied them back along with three other Egyptian Vampires from Osiris's personal guard. Montu, named for the god of war, serious and unsmiling, his rich black hair braided in similar fashion to Anubis's; Noph, the other male, had been named for the ancient Egyptian capital known later as Memphis. He was inches taller than Montu, his hair cut shorter and unadorned like his Liege Lord's. He was an imposing male with a massive chest, tree-trunk legs and powerful arms; Maeti, the third guard, was female. Named for the goddess of truth, she was almost as lovely as Sekhmet. She was taller than her counterpart and clearly not fully Egyptian. She had sky-colored eyes and an easy laugh. Her hair was styled with bangs, straight and black. It was longer than any of the men's, the ends covered with tiny golden beads that tinkled gently when she walked. All five of the Egyptian Vampires had donned western-style clothing. It would be less of a shock to the locals than seeing Egyptian nobility strolling around the Rachlav estate.

Gillian was admiring the view from her window. The castle was situated up, and partly built into, the mountain. Flanked on two sides by the primordial forest, the back to the mountain, the front was a large meadow. The clearing glowed in the moonlight that shown from a velvety black sky, spangled with stars. From her vantage point, she could see the cabin and, further in the distance, the village of Sacele. There were isolated pockets of light, where other residences dwelt. The people of the region loved the earth and nestled their homes and villages harmoniously with the wild mountains.

A knock at the door startled her out of her musings. "Enter." It had to be someone she knew, so she didn't bother to turn around. Aleksei's deep beautiful voice stroked her mind.

"If you are settled in and find your room pleasing, I wondered if we might get a session in?"

Turning, she regarded him. He stood in the doorway, beautiful, sensual, Old-World romance, Paramortal power; completely off limits. "Certainly, Aleksei. I'll get my notes."

Waiting for her to retrieve pen and file, Aleksei was intrigued to discover something. Since the threat of war had emerged, he hadn't given thought to Elizabeta, nor succumbed to depression. Wondering if it was a fluke, he led Gillian down to the great hall. Sparsely decorated but elegant nonetheless, it wasn't as big as some that she'd seen in castles and manor houses in other countries like England, but was still massive and impressive. The room was a long rectangle seated against the main frame of the castle. On one end was a fireplace big enough to roast an entire steer in. The massive mantel above it held woodcuts, small painted portraits, antique glassware and a runner embroidered with the Rachlav colors of burgundy and midnight blue.

Above the mantel hung a portrait of the Rachlav family. Aleksei and Tanis were there, flanking an older couple that could only be their parents. All were dressed in garb reflecting the period of the sixteen hundreds, except the clothing was more Italian.

Seeing her puzzlement and guessing the reason, Aleksei explained. "My family has a home in Tuscany and we spent a great deal of time there. Mother was a trendsetter in her day and usually came home with trunks of the latest fashions. She insisted we look like Italian royalty instead of Romanian landowners." He chuckled. His mother had been a character, always bringing fun and life into the home and to his father's eyes.

Gillian watched him, saw his face shift. Glad that he'd had a good relationship with his family, sorry that he'd had to watch everyone he'd loved die, except Tanis. She moved to one of two huge couches positioned across from each other, near the fire, which was blazing merrily away, and curled up with her pad on her lap, waiting.

Realizing he'd been lost in thought, Aleksei seated himself next to her instead of across from her. Gillian watched him warily. Professional distance came down with almost an audible click.

"What did you want to start with, Aleksei?"

At first, she didn't think he'd heard her, he was so still. Then he spoke, and neither of them were sure it was a good thing. "I was not sure where I wanted to begin tonight." His voice was soft, a warm purr melting over her, and she repressed a shiver. "But watching you in your room just now I realized that I have not suffered the effects of my boredom nor my depression in the last few days. Could it be that I am finally healing?"

She had to think about that for a moment. Spontaneous remission was not unheard of, and while Aleksei hadn't been in a truly bad way when she'd first met him, now he fairly glowed with strength and power. Looking at him critically, she noticed his hair appeared thicker, blacker, longer and more luxuriant. His eyes were unwavering on her face, liquid silver lit from within. The sensual planes of his face and mouth were utterly masculine, yet his otherworldly beauty was almost heartbreaking.

Mentally shaking herself, Gill responded, noticing uncomfortably that Aleksei's kissable lips bore the lightest of smiles. "It is possible that you have had a breakthrough and didn't really recognize it." He looked puzzled, so she explained further. "Sometimes, life-or-death situations cancel out minor day-to-day annoyances and thoughts. You have had more important things to think about recently and not had time to dwell on your problems to any extent. Make sense?"

Raking a hand through his hair, he thought about it. "Yes, it does. I have been so consumed with thinking about what we were going to do and how we were all going to survive that I truly have not thought of the endless nights alone nor of the people I failed in my extended lifetime."

"Aleksei." She uncharacteristically put her hand on his arm where it rested on the chair. "I hope this is a major breakthrough with you, but I want to make sure that it is not a temporary rallying of your spirits. When this is all over, you will still have the life you had before. I don't want your fangxiety and depression to come roaring back at that point and for you to lose hope."

Ice-gray eyes looked into her own green ones. He didn't speak and the silence grew uncomfortable. Still she waited, knowing it was important for him to cycle through the thoughts that were flooding across his face.

"And why would that be a concern, Gillian?"

Uh-oh, the voice was a little chilly. Better tread lightly. Grinning, she went for lightening the mood a little. "Because I am a world-famous Paramortal shrink and it would damage my flawless reputation."

He wanted to be angry with her glib response, but found he could not. Her smile and natural sense of humor were contagious, and he returned it. It caught Gillian's breath as his smile blazed to life. He was astonishingly attractive in more ways than just the physical. She liked him. Really liked him as a person and a client and truly wanted him to feel whole again. It surprised her that she was having difficulty keeping this in perspective, but then life-threatening emergencies made for strange bedfellows. She pressed on.

"What was your depression based on?" At his quizzical look, she added, "Why were you feeling useless and hopeless?"

"Because I felt that I had little purpose in my life." Comprehension dawned. "So now that I have something to strive for again, I do not have time to wallow in my own self-pity."

Even Gillian winced when he came to that conclusion. That was a painful moment of self-discovery for him, and she said nothing, waiting. His eyes never left her face and she felt a blush creeping up her cheeks to her utter mortification.

"I do not know if my symptoms were due to simply existing, Gillian. Reconnecting with Osiris again made me realize that I need to develop more interests and more stamina to keep up with the waking world."

Keen silvery-gray eyes noticed her discomfiture instantly. Having her pack up and run because there was a latent attraction was not on his agenda. Trying to salvage the circumstance, he rose and stood before her, his hand out. "Will you not congratulate your patient for a significant, if not earth-shattering, breakthrough?"

Gillian did not want to hug him. Realizing that, she could have kicked herself. She was a physical woman. Hugging or touching her patients, no matter what their origin, came naturally to her. So many among the living were touch-starved; it was no less prevalent among the Reborn, undead or Fey. Why would Aleksei be any different? Why should he be different just because she was having a hard time with perception issues?

Steeling herself, she stood, put her pad aside and opened her arms to him. Instantly she was enfolded against his powerful chest, his arms locking around her and pulling her tightly against him. Too short to reach his neck, she encircled his waist, hugging him back for a moment.

Aleksei carefully kept his lower body away from her. He hadn't expected the intense reaction to having her in his arms if even for a brief moment. He bent his head, leaning down so that her arms would move up from his waist and around his shoulders to circle his neck. Blood surged through his body in an intense, molten inferno. The scent of her—clover meadow, snow and sunlight—hearing her pulse speed up to match his own, feeling the strength in her small body, all aroused him to a long-denied, aching need. He broke off the hug suddenly, reaching up to remove her arms from his neck gently, then stepping back, smiling softly down at her.

"I suppose for now we can terminate our therapeutic relationship, Gillian. If you are in agreement, of course."

"Um, sure, yeah. That would be fine, Aleksei."

Gillian cleared her throat, finding her wits and her voice. The hug had affected her too. Her hands involuntarily clenched after being deprived of his warm, rock-hard muscles.

"You seem to feel much better, and this was supposed to be brief therapy, so I'll write it up and we'll consider the matter closed." She turned to get her pad and pen. When she straightened, he was gone. *That's odd*, she thought. *I guess he had something to do.*

The something to do, was to get away from Gillian for awhile. Aleksei was outside and halfway up the mountain before Anubis caught him. "What troubles you, my friend?"

He spun to find Anubis in all his glory. "Nothing," he growled, not trusting himself to explain adequately.

"Not quite the truth is it, Aleksei?"

"It does not matter, Anubis. I wish I could have met her under different circumstances, but I did not. Now there must be a one-year waiting period before I can even broach the topic of getting to know her on a far more personal level."

"And Tanis moved first."

"That is part of it, yes." Aleksei sounded tired.

"What about Gillian's feelings? Does she have a say in the matter?" Anubis had few unspoken thoughts. Aleksei knew that he was teasing him, but it irritated him all the same.

"Yes, dammit, she has a choice, Anubis! Why in hell would she not have a choice? I have never forced my attentions on a woman in all my centuries and I do not intend to start now. I want her to be happy, that is all." He was pacing, raking his fingers through his hair.

"Great Amon, you do care for her."

Anubis was truly amazed. Aleksei had never dallied with any woman that he knew of. Elizabeta's selfish aspirations and death had haunted him, and he had been very careful to avoid any female entanglements. Now, faced with the one woman he could not have, she had become the one woman he wanted. The naked pain in Aleksei's face made him rethink his response.

"You are a Vampire, Aleksei. You have eternity to wait. Use your time wisely, my friend." Anubis vanished into thin air, leaving Aleksei to his thoughts.

A humorless smile curved his mouth. Yes, he did have time on his side. Gillian was worth waiting for.

Gillian wasn't waiting on anybody at the moment. Upon discovering that Aleksei had left her in front of the fireplace, she bolted up to her room and locked the door.

Shit, hell and damn, she swore to herself as she flopped unceremoniously on the bed, clutching her pad to her chest in an unconsciously defensive gesture.

Was she imagining it, or was the lovely Count Rachlav showing some untoward interest in her? She couldn't be *that* off her nut, could she? Her empathy was screaming at her while she was in his arms. He needed her, needed her comfort, her closeness and she had willingly given it . . . well, not willingly, but she had given it. She was struggling with her own sense of personal right versus professional wrong. If she'd bothered to be honest with herself, she'd have figured out that she was going against her nature to deny her feelings and attraction for this particular Vampire.

The legal pad came up to cover her face as she felt herself blushing again. *For fuck's sake!* she admonished herself. *He is a* client. Even if they just terminated their professional relationship, it was going to be a year before they could act on any possible attraction. That was assuming she was still in Romania in a year and that neither of them had found other attachments by then. One thing was for sure, she wouldn't be the one forming any sort of permanent attachment, now or later. Nope. That was out entirely. The nature of her dual career, her own quirky commitmentphobic personality. Definitely not her. Great Hathor's hells, her mind couldn't wrap around that concept.

CHAPTER
14

WAKING late in the afternoon the next day, Gillian checked her messages and her e-mail. Very bad news from the IPPA awaited her. The other therapist/operative (TO) they were worried about in the States had been found. Part of him in Texas and part in New Mexico. The forwarded report was graphic. *Torn apart* were the words used to describe the body. Another seven of their TOs who were currently in France, Switzerland, Italy, Hungary, China, India and California were being threatened and it wasn't looking good for the remaining thirteen of them.

Not only Paramortal psychologists were being targeted. Any Human-related business or profession that dealt primarily with Paramortal folk had received a threat of some sort. The IPPA only had specific information about the deaths and missing persons within its spectrum, but it was reasonable to assume that there were similar incidences across the board. *Shit, shit and double shit.* This was very, very bad.

An involuntary shiver ran up her spine at the next part. Several high-ranking Vampires and Lycanthropes with known affiliations to Osiris and Dionysus were dead or missing. One Vamp had also been of Dracula's line but, like Aleksei and Tanis, had allegiances with the other Lords.

The IPPA's instructions were clear and specific: Lay low;

take all necessary precautions; do not get killed. *Gee, that was helpful*, she thought, vastly aggravated. Going to the police would be redundant. The IPPA had already notified local magistrates and Interpol about the danger, with instructions to keep it out of the media as much as possible. Worldwide panic was not on anyone's agenda.

Paramortal legalization had been around for years but there were still undercurrents of prejudice. No one wanted the law-abiding Paramortals to suffer because of a disproportionate number of malcontents. Certainly no one wanted to go back to the dark ages of hunting and killing them. Most were productive, responsible citizens both in the Human world and in their own. "Live and let live" was very much in favor on both sides.

Swearing and still reeling from the latest headline news, Gillian found numerous e-mails from Arkady Boganskaya—Dante had been informed of her brief absence, but was clearly not happy with being ignored. He'd been wreaking havoc on the castle and the guests. Could Gillian come quickly please? Or at least as quickly as possible? Rolling her eyes, she dialed Arkady and told him she'd be right there, apologizing for her necessary absence. He was grateful and delighted to hear from her and, after hanging up, ran to Dante's hallway to inform the Ghost that Gillian was on her way.

She left a note for the Vampires in case it got late and she wasn't back, but chose not to share the other information from the IPPA at that point. The news was bad enough that she intended to deliver it in person, even though the thought made her cringe.

On the way to Dante, she mulled over in her mind the best way to diplomatically break the news. Pulling into the Boganskaya Castle parking lot, Gillian was hit by a sense of dread. Ghost fear, she realized. Not good. Not good at all. Dante was projecting his displeasure forcefully and it was spilling over into the great outdoors. A temperamental Ghost with an attitude she did not need right now. Slamming the door shut, she stalked up to the main doors and into the great hall. Arkady popped his head around a corner to thank her for coming, then vanished. He looked a little pale.

Gillian hit the stairs, cursing under her breath. Dante's hallway and the foyer in front of it was covered in blood. The stench made her gag and annoyed her to no end. Okay, she was getting angry. Diplomacy first. Then . . . find a rock.

"Dante!" she called out in her best concerned-therapist voice, which echoed through the castle. "I came as soon as I could!"

A hiss of breath behind her caused her heart to leap. Her pulse was already racing, sweat beading on her brow from the fear Dante was projecting in his ire. She spun to find Dante uncomfortably close, his blue eyes snapping in anger, his wounds visible and horrifying.

"You have been gone three days with no word." Dante wasn't a happy spirit.

"No, I left word with Arkady. He told you I had to leave unexpectedly."

Then she felt it. Empathy in her line of work was invaluable sometimes. Even if she hadn't been as gifted as she was in that area, she would have picked up on it. Fear. His fear and anxiety coupled with centuries-old trauma. Post-traumatic stress disorder in all its glory. He'd opened up after six hundred years of anguish, shared his experience. She'd understood him, listened to him, helped him come to terms with his feelings, then had left him hanging. Damn it. He'd been processing alone over the last three days and had needed to vent his long pent-up emotions.

Anger left her abruptly. It wasn't his fault. He had every right to be furious. He had no access to a support network or group, although the idea of a "Ghost Group for Shattered Spirits" struck her as a rather intriguing idea. Gillian was his only anchor at the moment, and she'd weighed anchor and left.

"Dante, you have my most sincere apology."

Searching his face, she thought she saw the lines of tension lessen a little. "I did not want to leave abruptly like that, but I had no choice." Okay, that brought an arched eyebrow and disapproving look. Time for truth.

"Dante I am being targeted. There is . . ." She paused over the word. ". . . an altercation going on between some groups of Vampires and those of us who have dealings with Paramortals or have you for clientele are being hunted and systematically slaughtered."

Dante's eyebrows shot up and something flickered in his too-blue eyes for a brief moment. "Truly, *dolcezza*? You are in danger?"

Her hands were grasped by a suddenly whole Dante, whose hands felt solid and warm. She tried not to jerk back at the unexpected feeling and touch. Ghosts just weren't supposed to do what he was doing.

"Yes, I am, but so are many others. We're trying to figure out what to do," she told him gently.

Damn, that almost sounded helpless. Damage control. "I don't want you to worry about me. I am perfectly safe. I just have to be extremely careful for awhile."

Squeezing his hands lightly, she let go and backed up. A little distance between them would be wise at the moment. He followed, crowding her. Rats.

"*Dolcezza*, you must not allow anything to happen to you. I am certain I am not your only patient who feels this way." His voice was too soft, too gentle, and Gillian was on alert.

"Look, Dante, I am your therapist and I will continue to be, but I am perfectly capable of taking care of myself. I have friends here who are protecting me to the best of their abilities."

"Friends, *cara mia*?" He'd backed her up into the hallway, an amused smirk on his generous mouth. "No, a man, I think. What manner of man is he that he can command your obedience and loyalty?" Jealousy dripped from every word. A firm line needed to be drawn.

"Dante, no offense, but my personal life has no bearing on your case. And no one *commands* my obedience. My loyalty is given freely or not at all."

He heard the crackle of anger in her voice. Interesting. So there was a man. Not Arkady, surely. He would have scented her on the man's clothing. Someone else and nearby, judging from the speed with which she'd gotten there after contacting Arkady. Dante's quick mind was rifling through what he knew of the area from listening for centuries. He'd figure it out soon enough.

Gillian hastily maneuvered around him and went to fetch her chair. Dante instantly moved the table next to her. "Thank you, now let's get started. If you want to talk about feeling angry with me and why, we can start there if you like." She sat and waited.

"No, Gillian. I am no longer angry."

I am furious, he thought. She needed a reminder of who should be foremost in her thoughts. Secretly glad of her help, he still had ulterior motives behind his continued association with the little blonde minx.

"I do not wish to dwell on your absence, *cara*; I would rather talk about my fears that you might never come back." Leaning against the stones in his customary way, ankles and arms crossed, he waited for her response.

He was lying, she was sure of that. The heat was off his anger but something else replaced it. Something dark and deep and as cold as the grave. It made her cautious.

"I understand. But I do want you to know that there might be more unavoidable absences in the future, so you don't get angry if I don't show up." Waiting a moment for that to sink in, she continued. "It isn't personal, Dante. I am not avoiding you. You are important as a client to me, but my life is important too."

"Of course, *dolcezza*. I give you my word that I will not 'take it personally' if you sometimes go away." Now he was patronizing her but she let it go.

"All right, then let's talk about your abandonment issues. Besides anger, how did you feel when Arkady told you I had to leave, and you had no one else to turn to?"

Focusing on her question, Dante thought for a moment then, sorting through his feelings, he told her: basically, as a narcissistic personality, he had felt betrayed and ignored. So, she helped him reason out, that had led to hurt, which led to anger—a much easier and more convenient emotion to deal with. "Si," he agreed. "It is much easier to show the horns than the heart."

"What?" Gillian laughed. "What does that mean?"

"When facing a threat, a bull will show his horns, not expose his heart to the peril. It is the same with men." Dante shrugged casually. "We do not expose ourselves to attack. Only by gentle persuasion can you persuade the beast to accept you as anything but an adversary."

Gillian had to think about that for a moment, then realized the ghostly Italian's characterization was right on. Men, at least the males she knew, were definitely like that.

Dante watched her. She was a student of Paramortal behavior, of direct observation and interpretation of mental disorders, but woefully lacking in the nuances of men and women. It would make his efforts all that much easier. Frowning, he realized that it disturbed him a little to think of violating her confidence in him, but not enough for him not to try.

Watching the frown flit across Dante's perfect features, his face partially shadowed by his thick auburn hair, Gillian wondered about him. What kind of man he had been. It would have a bearing on the Ghost he was. She knew what was in the file; facts cut and pasted onto the pages of what had been a man's life. In her prior dealings with Ghosts, none of them had demonstrated all the abilities Dante had shown her in their brief acquaintance. Either the other Ghosts had been holding out on her or Dante had picked up some metaphysical skills somewhere. Dead for six hundred years, he was still suave, sophisticated, intellectual, arrogant and very, very sensual. There was no doubt that he'd had his own personal fan club while alive. Gill wanted to know what he was thinking.

"Any conclusions?"

"Many, *dolcezza*. When I have thought them all through, I will share them with you." His enigmatic smile did nothing to lighten the quiet mood.

Now it was Gillian's turn to frown. Dante laughed. "You are a delight, *dolcezza*. So intelligent, so capable, yet a long-dead swordsman has you puzzled by his musings." He stepped forward, took her hand and kissed it. Gillian sighed. This was getting to be a habit. At least she wasn't twitching anymore from his warm touch.

Looking up at her, over the back of his hand, his eyes sparkled. "It grows late, Gillian. Go to your lover before he worries for you."

At her outraged look, he straightened, dropping her hand. "I will see what I can find out about this Vampire conflict, *cara*. I have what you might call *connections*." Blowing her a kiss, he vanished into the hallway.

Feeling petulant that the observation tables had been turned on her, Gillian gathered her things. The bad thing about dealing with beings that were centuries older was that they did have more life experience than Humans. It didn't make her ineffectual, just more transparent. She stopped in her tracks. *Transparent to a Ghost*. Giggling, she hurried down to her car.

It *was* getting late; the sun was nearly three quarters down as she sped along the now-familiar stretch of highway back to the estate. Twilight engulfed the landscape as she went deeper into the mountains, fear now riding her. The memory of the near attack in her car was painfully fresh in her mind. Taking the fork up to Rachlav Castle, she skidded the little car around the curves.

Suddenly the warmth and light contained in the gray stones and the company within seemed very alluring. So what if they were Vampires? They were at least Vampires who were her friends. A screech of tires brought her to a stop. Leaping out, she kicked the door shut, autolocking it, and bolted for the main entrance. Her heart nearly stopped when movement flashed in her peripheral vision and she stopped, dropping backpack and keys, her body instantly molded into a fighting stance.

Wolf. Correction: wolves. A fair number of them, in fact, who were absolutely fascinated by the appearance of a Human female in their forest, except for the fact that these wolves were *big*. Bigger than any wolf Gillian had ever seen. Wolves the size of ponies were sidling up to her on all sides, jaws agape, teeth sharp as daggers and gleaming white in the moonglow. Not. Natural. Wolves. A chill went down her spine and coalesced in her stomach. Nice doggy. And not a rock within reach.

Loup Garous. Lycanthropes. Werewolves. Shapeshifters or *Shifters* if going with the politically correct term. Gillian's mind was racing for a nonviolent solution. Something that wouldn't involve blowing a hole in one of the wolves or in her own abrupt dismemberment. What she very quickly ascertained via the solid brick wall of reality her rational mind just crashed into, being a rather bright woman, was that she had maybe three or four seconds left to live.

"Oh hell."

What to do, what to do? Run for the doors of the castle before they caught her and tore her to shreds, or stand, fight and be torn to shreds. These were the kind of decisions that tended to make her cranky.

CHAPTER
15

SLOWLY, she inched her hand toward the gun she carried in her pants pocket. It was loaded and had a round chambered. She'd not gotten around to unloading it after returning from Egypt. Trouble was, it had regular bullets in it. The Glock 22C was a powerful handgun. Loaded with .40-caliber rounds, it would stop a charging Werewolf or most of their Shifter friends. With a 9mm's velocity plus a .45-caliber's knockdown power, it would punch a fair-sized hole in a Werewolf, but unless she scored an exact head shot, it still wouldn't kill it. Not permanently anyway.

Note to self, get silver-capped ammunition, came the brief thought. *If I live through this*, came the next as she sidled toward the heavy oak doors. She might not live through it. After being shot, the theoretically holed Lycanthrope would be pissed off over having to heal a fist-sized flaw in its lovely fur, and its friends were certain to be disagreeable about their newly ventilated packmate.

She almost made it close enough to the main entrance to risk a sprint, except for the sizable beastie that grabbed her hand in jaws that would have made a shark proud. To her credit, she didn't scream or even whimper. Jerking her hand out of its mouth was definitely out. If she were even nicked by those razor sharp fangs, there was a strong possibility she'd wake up furry on the next full moon.

Kicking it in the face was a no-no also. Same problem. A boot to the face: teeth into her hand. Not acceptable. Faced with a no-win situation, Gillian did the only thing she could do under the circumstances: she froze. Offering absolutely no resistance to the massive creature that held her, watching her with intelligent green eyes that were still far too Human, despite being surrounded by a muzzle and a lot of fur.

The others loped up, surrounding her in a tightening circle of fangs and tails. Shit. Dying within ten feet of safety irritated her to no end. The wolf holding her hand released her and moved silkily back into the circle of lupine-based bone and muscle. Forcing herself to be still, Gillian's mind was trying to figure a way past them. Tactically, she was screwed. They could outmaneuver her without effort. Organized and relentless, a pack of Lycanthropes would terrify the most stalwart Human, and even some of the monsters.

Just when she thought it couldn't possibly get worse, she heard Aleksei's voice. "Do not move, Gillian. They are here at my request."

He must have given them some sort of signal—Gillian couldn't tell, since he was behind her—because they all backed off, opening a pathway to the door. Her muscles bunched involuntarily in preparation for a major haul-ass to the Vampire and safety. Wait . . . safe? A Vampire? Before she could wrap her mind around that, Aleksei's voice demanded her attention.

"Walk, do not run," he commanded her. "Straight to the door, Gillian. Now."

Doing as he ordered, she moved. Every instinct and nerve ending in her was having hysterical fits. They fired in mind-torquing unison, telling her to run like hell, get away, get away fast, even as the door was looming larger in her range of vision. Reaching it, she slowly put a hand out, opening it and pushing it in. Just. One. More. Step.

"Stop." Aleksei sounded closer. She turned slowly and watched him walking gracefully out of the darkness, heedless of the Fur Pack of Death lounging about on his front lawn. The Romanian nobleman strode unconcernedly toward her, frowning and looking like a six-foot, seven-inch thundercloud. Stepping closer to her than she would have chosen, he reached out to pull her beneath the shelter of his arm, then beckoned the wolves.

They came en masse and it was intimidating as hell, even for a seasoned soldier like herself. There were at least fifteen of them, now that she had a chance to count cold wet noses, exclusive of arguing with her internal abacus over whether it was a bright idea to tally up Werewolves while standing among them on a moonlit night. Reflexively she shrunk against Aleksei before she could stop herself, and he tightened his arm around her.

"Put out your hand again, slowly."

"Fuck that."

"Do it." It wasn't a request.

Hating to see her hand shaking, Gill did as he told her. The biggest one, the one who had grabbed her hand earlier, came forward. Sniffing her hand, which held not a single tooth indentation, he licked it finally and sat down in front of her, his jaws opening in a doggy smile and his pink tongue moving as he panted in the autumn air. The others all visibly relaxed and either sat or lay down.

Aleksei's voice rumbled, deep and pure, enchanting Gillian as she listened to him speak to the wolves. "She is under my protection and therefore under your protection. No harm is to come to her or those others who dwell within my walls."

He paused a moment, making sure they heard him clearly. "Guard her as you would your own mate. Do not fail me in this."

His voice took on a chilling note that Gillian had never heard before. She glanced up at him, but his face was expressionless as he regarded the pack.

The leader seemed to nod, then rising, gave a short series of barks to the rest. All rose and, with a flurry of tails, vanished into the night.

Gillian turned to Aleksei, still safely tucked under his arm. Looking up at him made her feel rather small and delicate. He was so much taller and his frame much more massive. Ignoring the feeling, she thanked him.

"I thought I was dead meat, Aleksei. Thanks for rescuing me."

Turning his head to look at her, his silvery eyes were angry. "Do not be out after dark again. The wolves are here for your protection, Gillian. They would have been introduced to you tonight regardless of this incident, but you ran a terrible risk."

His voice was deep and low and entirely too calm, but she wasn't paying attention to that after her near-death experience.

Sighing, she conceded, "I know and I am sorry. It got late at my other appointment . . ."

He grabbed her, shaking her just hard enough to frighten her a little. He was furious. "Dammit, you could have been torn apart!"

The look on his face and the heat of his anger spilling over her convinced her to shut up for once. "I cannot protect you if you insist on making yourself a target! Those are *my* wolves out there, but they could easily not have been. I do not own all the forests nor command the loyalty of every pack or Vampire in the area."

Releasing her, he spun, pacing away from her, then whirling back, his icy eyes pinning her. "I understand your position Gillian, truly I do. You have obligations which must be attended to. I do not expect you to obey my every whim and order without explanation, but disregarding obvious safety measures is inexcusable."

Gill fidgeted under his direct stare. She knew she'd screwed up. It was her responsibility to watch the time better. Feeling like a raw recruit being dressed down by her drill instructor, she unconsciously snapped to parade rest and met his eyes.

"I understand why you're mad at me. It won't happen again. I give you my word."

Aleksei swallowed the rest of the tirade he'd been ready to inflict on her. Truth was in her words. She meant it and that would have to be good enough. He was still shaking with anger and fear for her.

"Gillian, when I think about you, out there, alone . . . what might have happened . . ." He raked a hand through his thick hair, his voice hard with anger but full of something else she couldn't immediately identify. "Do not put yourself at risk again, Gillian. I will take action next time." Turning on his heel, he stalked off, anger radiating in his every movement.

"What the hell does that mean?" she muttered to herself as she turned to find the nearest bathroom and wash the lupine saliva off her hand. Realizing her keys were still outside, she went to the door, yanking it open. Searching the yard for the wolves, expanding her senses, she felt no threat.

"Do you think it would be better if you let me do that for you?" Tanis's unexpected voice made her jump.

"Goddammit, Tanis, don't sneak up on me like that!"

"If Aleksei returns to find you outside in the dark after his lecture, I will not be able to intervene, *caressima*." He stroked her hair softly as he passed her on his way out the door. "What am I looking for?"

"Keys, backpack. I dropped them out there when the wolves came up."

Tanis quickly retrieved the items, bringing them back to her. "Thanks, Tanis. I'm going to go find something to eat, assuming you have food in here somewhere, then take a shower."

"Take your shower, *piccola*. I will bring you food." Tanis headed for the kitchen before she had a chance to protest.

Tanis was also displeased. He'd heard the tone in Aleksei's voice and the reason for it. It took all his control not to reprimand Gillian for being careless, but Aleksei had done a good job of it. She didn't need both of them yelling at her.

It bothered him that he heard the notes of protective anger in his brother's voice, but there was nothing he could do to help him. It would be a long year for Aleksei to ponder his feelings. Being trapped in this situation with Gillian wasn't helping, but he would deal with it. Tanis didn't know what he wanted to do either. He could hardly blame his brother for being confused or for being very attracted to Gillian.

Once Gillian finished her shower, she returned to her room in a blue silken robe the management had evidently provided for her, since it had a large *R* embroidered on the lapel and was about thirteen sizes too big for her. She found a sandwich, soda, and Tanis waiting for her. He reclined on the bed while she ate, watching her with interest. When she'd finished, he was still watching her, golden eyes unreadable.

"What?" she said, exasperated. "You keep staring at me."

"I am wondering what propriety would dictate at the moment." The heat of his gaze was warming her from the inside out. Clearly he wasn't happy with her either. She wasn't in the mood for another lecture and cocked a bronze eyebrow at him expectantly.

"Propriety?" she echoed.

"I do not want to assume that you would want me in your bed, *piccola*. So I am thinking about how to ask you if I may stay, without sounding crass." Golden eyes crinkled just a bit at the corners as his mouth curved in a sensual grin.

Goddess, he had a magnificent smile. He hadn't touched her, but his voice was making her toes curl.

"Tanis, relationships don't work that way. You are welcome unless I tell you specifically that I want to be alone."

"And do you?"

"Do I what?" Gillian was getting tired of this. She did want his company, but wasn't sure how to ask. Tanis wasn't the only one with communication problems in Vampiric love situations.

"Want me, *piccola*. Do you want me tonight?" His voice had dropped an octave to a deep fuck-me-now purr. Watching her, sensing her desire for him, he waited.

Gillian was rooted where she was. Just seeing him lounging on her bed, listening to him, admiring his otherworldly beauty, caught her breath and made her pulse leap. Yes, she wanted him. And just for tonight, she would allow herself to need him a little. Nodding, unable to verbalize what she was feeling, she went to him. Tanis opened his arms and she fell gratefully into his embrace.

When his mouth took hers, he dropped whatever shielding he'd had, letting his emotions roll over her. She felt his worry, his anger, and something else. Jealousy? Tanis? No, not possible. Rolling her under him, blanketing her with his much larger frame, he kissed her deeply, his hands stoking the fire between them. Needing to hold her close, needing to feel her safe and alive beneath him. Gillian needed him too. She needed to feel safe for the moment and in his arms; for a brief time, she could feel as if the rest of the world had fallen away.

Soon the silky robe joined his clothing, littered on the floor in their haste. Hard and aching, he pressed her back into the feather mattress. Gillian moaned as he roamed down her body, leaving no part of her unkissed, untouched. Reaching her navel, his tongue swirled, making her giggle and curl up. Grinning wickedly, he slid a hand between her knees, pressing her thighs apart, then dipped his dark head to her golden bronze curls. Wedging his broad shoulders against her thighs, he pressed her back and open to his investigation. She gasped as his tongue lapped at her, arching up against his mouth.

Encouraged, Tanis slid two fingers inside, hardening to the point of pain from the slick, hot feel of her tight canal. Giving his attention to her every fold and valley, he enjoyed hearing the soft keening noises she made. Pulling back just a little, he whispered to her, "Let go, *cara mia*. I am here to catch you."

Continuing his ministrations, he felt the spiraling of her climax beginning. Wrapping his arm over her hips, holding her tight to his teasing mouth, he groaned audibly when she shattered for him, tasting the tangy salt of her orgasm, loving her crying out his name.

Fingers tightening in his hair, Gillian pulled him up. Still clenching and releasing from the first orgasm, she needed him inside her. "Come up here, Tanis. I want you in me."

Tanis made his way up her body, kissing and laving her breasts, her neck. His velvety-hard arousal brushed her thigh and urged her legs further apart. Gillian's head was back; he was gently nibbling her neck, his erect sex probing gently at her opening. He paused, raising his head to look down at her. "Open your eyes, *piccola*. Look at me as I fill you."

She did as he asked, watching the amber in his eyes glow gold as he pressed inside, slowly and inexorably. "Hurry, Tanis," she gasped, gritting her teeth against his slow penetration. Chuckling, he flexed his hips, filling her and seating himself completely.

"Better, *piccola*?" His voice was amused black velvet. When he began to move, a slow, deep, sexy rhythm, she breathed, "Yes," then pulled his head down to kiss him, their tongues dueling as their bodies merged.

Arching into him, her legs wrapped around him, holding him tightly, meeting each thrust. Tanis took his time, enjoying the tight velvet bands of slick roughness stroking over him, feeling how well he fit inside her. Gillian was writhing beneath him, needing him to hurry.

Letting her set the pace, Tanis moved with her. Soon both of them were covered in a light sheen of sweat, trembling from holding back. Wrapping his arm under her hips, he lifted her, increasing the depth of his strokes, lengthening her line, burying himself over and over. Begging him for release, Gillian dropped her hand between them, but Tanis got there first, shackling her wrists gently, pushing her arms above her head, his hips moving harder and faster, driving her to a burning ache.

Feeling her begin to crest, the deep ripple of her climax beginning, he breathed, "Now, *piccola* . . . together. Come, *mi amore*."

She bucked beneath him, drenching him with her liquid heat, her body tightening around him, milking him. Pressing deep at the apex of a thrust, he exploded in hot, thick jets against her core. A feral growl tore from deep in his chest. Gillian nipped his chest, prolonging his own shattering release.

Gathering her in his arms, he rolled them so their bodies stayed locked together but he wouldn't crush her with his weight. Passion was still in his kiss as he cradled her, stroking her hair.

"God, Tanis, that was incredible," she managed, when she got her breath back and their heartbeats slowed.

Male amusement filled his voice, "Only incredible? Then we need more practice."

Watching his eyes, she marveled at his sheer beauty. "Thank you for getting my mind off things." She snuggled against his hard chest. "This is still all a little unreal."

"I know, *piccola*. It is for me too." Beginning to harden again inside her but feeling her weariness, he tamped down his own needs and just held her. "Sleep, *cara*. I will stay with you until you sleep."

Too tired to argue, Gillian let him hold her and let herself be comforted. She had dreams that night. Dimly she realized Tanis had withdrawn from her and had gone, but her dreams were erotic, hot. It seemed that she made love over and over all night long. Once she thought she had a glimpse of light-colored eyes. Whether blue, green or gray, she couldn't tell, nor would she fully remember.

Awakening late in the day, she was amazed that the bed looked as though a hurricane had ravaged it. Looking in the mirror, her hair was tousled, her lips swollen. She looked like she'd done the entire Carpathian Olympic Team. After a shower to loosen her sore muscles, she headed off to visit Dante, leaving a note that if it got too late, she'd stay at the inn in Sacele or at the castle of her client. It was all she could do for now.

The next few weeks passed in much the same manner. Gillian continued to see Dante daily, always timing her visits so she could leave well before sunset. The Ghost was getting better. There had been no more incidents of frightened tourists and Arkady was pleased. Gillian told him Dante's prognosis was good and planned on discharging him soon.

More news came from the IPPA: the Paramortal operative in India was dead, the one in Hungary was missing, and the one in Italy, missing and presumed dead—her office had been found splashed with blood. A lot of blood. A dozen or more individuals who had dealings with Vampires and other Paramortal businesses or who administered services to the non-Humans were also dead or missing worldwide.

She hadn't shared the gloomy news with the Vampires. No sense in alarming everyone. Being edgy and paranoid herself was plenty. Getting to know the Egyptians was interesting. Anubis and Sekhmet were—dare she say it?—adorable. They set the stage for each evening's inevitable discussions, sharing humor, ancient intrigue, all while managing to remain close, always touching, clearly hopelessly in love even after centuries. It would have made Gillian gag if they weren't so completely sincere. She felt no deception from them; their love was real.

The male guards, Montu and Noph, held themselves a little apart. Eons of keeping themselves more separate was an ingrained habit. As personal guards to Osiris, they tended to use whatever leisure time they had more intensely. They worked hard but they relaxed and played hard as well. Availing themselves of Aleksei's vast library when they weren't patrolling the estate, keeping their agile minds stimulated and curious, they also made a trip or two into the surrounding villages for inspiring female companionship. Gillian made an effort to get to know the female, Maeti, better. The woman was cultured, poised, wise and, to Gillian's delight, hysterically funny.

Maeti shared her background with her. She'd been born in Egypt two thousand years prior to an Egyptian lord and a Greek mother. Falling in mutual love with a Vampire from Osiris's court, she'd been reborn and was happy until her mate had been killed after only a century together. Isis, whom Gillian hadn't met but who was Osiris's coruler and mate, had heard of the young female's plight before she could Face The Sun in her grief. Isis took her under her watchful eye, made her one of her own guard, restored her interest in life and her hope.

Maeti had grieved but knew her mate would have wanted her to continue. With Isis's help, she'd developed new interests and looked forward to each passing decade. The Vampiress had a quirky sense of humor that strayed into the bawdy range quite often and Gillian found her a wonderful friend and confidante.

Tanis and Aleksei both made short trips into the countryside, meeting with various leaders of the Lycanthrope, Vampire, and Sidhe communities who were either known affiliates of Osiris and Dionysus or definitely in opposition to Dracula. The Rachlavs hoped to strengthen their alliances and close their borders, keeping this section of Romania completely safe.

Dionysus sent a mated pair: a male Lycanthrope and a female Vampire, both of whom were calm and lovely, radiating none of the wildness that Aleksei said normally came with his Line. At first Aleksei was furious that he had not sent the guards promised by Osiris, but after learning they were specifically for spying in Immigration, he relented and sent thanks to the Greek lord for his generous help. Dionysus responded with a guarantee of safe passage anywhere he or his allied cells held sway and promising a visit to Romania soon.

Gillian was curious about how a Werewolf and a Vamp could be mated; Aleksei explained that it wasn't necessary to "turn" a Human or any other. Rebirth into a Vampire was not necessary for them to have a centuries-long relationship. The exchange of blood four times, in quantity, was required to create a Vampire. If lovers wanted to remain together but one did not wish the loss of their Humanity, three limited exchanges created a condition where the non-Vampire enjoyed the aspects of longevity, fast healing, resistance to diseases, heightened senses and a telepathic connection with their lover. According to Aleksei, it was actually a greater statement of love than merely turning the non-Vamp. More than a marriage, it was an eternal bond—or for as long as the Vampire survived.

Spending as much time as she was with Vampires on a casual level was affording her a monumental opportunity. Asking and receiving written consent from all of the immortals, Gillian took copious notes, intending to write a paper that would update the IPPA's and the Corps' information base on Vampires. Not only would it help other Paramortal psychologists, operatives and therapists, but it would ensure Vampire clients were treated based on knowledge from the most accurate information available.

The Lycanthrope pack made friends with her quickly. Cezar Jarek, the alpha male, impressed her with his ability to morph from man to wolf at will. He explained that it was what distinguished him from his pack. Astronomical control was required as well as stamina. Shifting was draining if done more than once a night. Contrary to popular belief, the full moon was not necessary for a Lycanthrope to shift. Need of any kind—hunger, sex, defense—was sufficient to allow the change.

During the weeks of waiting, Cezar introduced her to one of his dominant males. Pavel Miroslav was a mess. A young male in top form, his coat was a color Gillian had never seen on a wolf: Golden underfur, the heavy guard hairs of his pelt were a rich coppery color, shot with charcoal. It gave him a curious dimensional quality, and he could melt into the shadows or surrounding landscape unnervingly fast. Problem was, Pavel had developed a terrible allergy. Alone or around his packmates while in wolf form, his eyes streamed, his fur fell out in clumps, his nose ran and he had a hacking cough that Gillian didn't like the sound of.

Pavel had immigrated from Russia after being set upon by several mastiffs that belonged to a rural farmer. Said farmer had an attractive daughter whom Pavel had the hots for in Human form. Apparently he didn't like the idea of having a Lycanthrope for a son-in-law and had forbade the two to continue their relationship. Naturally the young lady and the young Werewolf weren't going to let dear old Dad spoil their fun. One bright night, Pavel had arrived to spirit her off so they could mate and marry, hopefully to raise little cubs together. The girl, Olga, unfortunately was a bit clumsy and made a clatter climbing out of her window.

Her father had awoken, guessed what was going on and had loosed the massive dogs from the home. Trained to defend his livestock from wolves, bears and assorted Paramortal beasties, the dogs voiced their approach in deep baying cries. Pavel had fled but not fast enough. Without time to shift and no weapon, he didn't have a chance. Built like a linebacker, standing six foot, four inches in his bare feet and weighing in at a lean, mean two hundred sixty-three pounds, Pavel was not a weakling. However, getting hit from all sides by five giant dogs that weighed between a hundred and fifty to two hundred pounds apiece would have felled an adult Kodiak bear. He went down under their rending jaws in chilling silence.

Olga's screaming had brought her father out to call them off. She swore she'd never see him again, only please, would he keep the dogs from killing him? Dad had complied; a sharp whistle and the huge canines dropped their prey. Only the good fortune of being a Lycanthrope had kept Pavel from bleeding to death in the field. Torn and aching, he had dragged himself into the forest and found a little cave where he could rest and heal. Lycanthrope healing is truly a miracle to behold. Shifters heal at a phenomenal rate—faster than Vampires, faster than anything known in the Human or non-Human world.

Lying there in the mud created from his own blood, Pavel reflected on his options. Realizing that Russia might not be the place to be, he'd lain there until the bleeding stopped and new skin formed over the vicious wounds, then painfully made his way back to his home. There he'd rested another day before packing his few belongings and heading south to Romania, where he heard of free-ranging packs and fewer mastiffs.

Now he'd joined Cezar's pack, proved himself brave and stalwart, despite his allergies. Cezar liked him and wanted to advance him within the ranks, but Pavel's constant coughing, shedding and sneezing made him useless for anything but an all-out fight. They had gone to Lycanthrope doctors and Human doctors; Pavel had endured dozens of shots, hundreds of pills, countless shampoos, ointments and salves. Nothing helped.

Cezar had a suspicion it wasn't a physical ailment and suggested gently that Pavel talk to Gillian, after learning from Aleksei who and what she was. He hoped that she would be able to help his young friend. Gillian said that she would try but she needed him in Human form. Cezar dismissed Pavel from his duties until something could be discovered.

Pavel slinked into the hall as a Human. He looked so sheepish that Gillian bit her lip not to giggle. Young and stunning, he couldn't have been more than twenty-five in Human years. Long, blonde hair shot with black and copper strands crowned his head, falling in waves down his back. His eyes were an intriguing deep, dark blue.

Handsome seemed to be a requirement for non-Humans and Pavel was no exception. Not as breathtaking as the Vampires, he and Cezar, who stood behind him, making sure that his young friend really stayed, were impressively attractive. Cezar was older, near fifty, Gillian guessed, but tall and heavily muscled. His hair, like his pelt, was charcoal with a pale cream undercoat. His eyes were brilliant green.

"I will leave you with the doctor, Pavel. You have nothing to fear, young one. Your place in my pack is secure." Cezar's voice was deep and affectionate.

He liked his packmembers and got along well with them. None wanted to be the wolf who tore out his throat when he grew too old and sick to run with them. He was a commanding presence, but Gillian stepped up and shook his hand anyway.

"I'll do my best, Cezar."

"I know you will, Doctor. His place is secure no matter what occurs." At that he left, shifting on the run to join the others guarding the estate.

Gillian took Pavel into the library where it was quiet and settled in for a full intake. Pavel turned out to be very sweet, very embarrassed, but very willing to try anything. He spoke in soft, low tones, explaining the beginning of his problem, which had been about four months after arrival, and the agony of having allergies tormenting his lupine senses. Shifters weren't supposed to have allergies. Like most Paramortals, werewolves didn't get sick from Human ailments or respond to Human medications. Gillian listened, took copious notes, then came up with an idea.

Pavel, like most Human and non-Human patients alike, was terrified that he was actually crazy, at least in his layman's idea of psychosis. He desperately wanted to know what was wrong with him and had been praying relentlessly since Cezar had suggested speaking with Gillian that she would determine what was wrong and how to fix it. He was slumped down in the chair across from the tiny blonde, watching her as she wrote, her brow furrowing a little in concentration. When she raised her eyes to his, there was triumph gleaming in them. For the first time in years, he felt something of a glimmer of hope.

CHAPTER
16

"PAVEL," Gillian began gently, "I think I have an idea of what's bothering you."

He looked so sweet and hopeful that she leaned forward and took his hands in hers, offering comfort through her empathy. She could feel his fears, read his need to know what was tormenting him, understand what was wrong. The antiquated Freudian notion that a patient didn't need to know what their disorder was or how to treat it, had been thankfully thrown out years before. An informed patient was a patient that would work toward battling their disorder rather than living in terror over what it might be in abstract terms.

"Yes? What can it be?" Afraid to hope, he waited.

"Your symptoms are that of post-traumatic stress disorder, probably as a result of the original attack which led to your conversion, then compounded with the mastiff attack which led you to move here. But Pavel . . ." She paused a moment, making sure his eyes were back on hers and that she had his attention for the bombshell she was about to drop on him. ". . . I think that your allergy is to fur. It's probably related back to the traumatic stress you've endured. Sort of like if you weren't a wolf, this last attack wouldn't have happened. If you hadn't been around a wolf, the original attack wouldn't have happened. I hope I'm making sense here. I'd like to find out, with your permission, and see if we can't alleviate this for you." She waited while that sunk in.

Pavel's hamster was doing overtime on his mental wheel. Click. Bluer-than-blue eyes widened with understanding. "You mean I am doing this to myself? The itching? The shedding? Am I mad, Gillian? Have I gone crazy?"

Gillian held his eyes with her own. "No, Pavel. It means that you lived through a life-threatening, nearly life-ending experience twice. Your first attacker was lupine. Your last mastiff attackers were canine. As a wolf, they are your distant cousins, animal or not."

Careful, she thought. *He's new to this.* Pushing warmth and compassion toward him with her empathy, she went on.

"So what happened is that at first, you were in shock, then numb. You went through your first transformation and I'm thinking it was scary. When your mind was ready to start processing what happened to you, you started having nightmares, flashbacks. The fact that your allergies did not respond to any known medical treatment and that you did not have them before all this occurred, suggests that it is taking place in your mind. Something with fur nearly killed you twice; now you're reacting to fur, even your own. Does that make sense?"

It did, but they discussed it for a while longer. Pavel noticed that her pheromones had shifted. She was projecting warmth and support to him. He hadn't known Humans could do that. Focusing on what she had said, he asked, "But I was bitten when I was changed. Why would I fear being bitten again?"

"When you were turned into a Lycanthrope, something with fur bit you. I don't know if that was during an attack or the throes of passion, traumatic or not, but the result is the same. Two near-death experiences happened to you which are related to furry beings."

Pavel visibly relaxed. "So this condition, can it be cured? Can you make it stop, Gillian? At least make it less bothersome?"

"I believe so. I would like to try something with you, if you agree." Flying blind now, she had no idea how well her suggestion would be received. She'd never tried anything like it on a Shifter. Pavel trusted her, hopefully enough for this to work.

His deep blue eyes focused on her. "What? Please help me, Doctor. I cannot live like this."

She noticed his return to her professional title and let it

stand. To remind himself of what she was obviously was comforting to him. "I would like to try hypnotism on you, Pavel. Go back through both those situations and see if we can alleviate your stress, help you come to terms with all of it. Would you trust me to do this?"

To her surprise he laughed. "Doctor, I am a simple peasant, but even I do not believe in this hocus-pocus. You are a very bad girl for trying to fool me in this way."

Grinning, not the least bit offended and glad he was reacting with genuine humor, she responded, "I didn't believe it either, Pavel, until I saw it done and received training in this method. Will you at least let me try? I am not an expert, but I know what I'm doing. The worst that can happen is that we fail. You will be no worse off."

While he thought about it for a moment, she thought about it too. She'd had success with a Vampire who kept dreaming about being staked and a tiny demi-Fey who had been tormented by a dryad with threats of pulling off her wings, but she'd never hypnotized a Lycanthrope. Patient and quiet, she let him make his decision.

"All right, Doctor. I will do it. Should I lie down?"

"Please call me Gillian, and no, you don't need to lie down. We don't even have to do this right now or even today if you're not comfortable."

"I am not comfortable, that is true," he agreed, but his eyes were anguished. "But if there is a chance, I will try it. I will even try magic if it will make it stop. I will think of what you do as a type of magic, Gillian. I want *you* to help me, not just anyone, I want your help because I believe you are sincere and not making jokes about the Russian peasant wolf."

"Pavel, I would never make fun of you or any patient's problems. I want to help you, not make you feel worse about it." Gillian's eyes were the warm green of a hot spring, her empathy and pheromones filling his senses with calmness. He could smell her anxiousness over him and his condition. She couldn't have been more sincere than if she'd taken a blood oath before him. He believed her, believed in her.

"What do I do?" he asked, his eyes earnest.

"Just sit back in your chair and watch me." She gave his hands a final squeeze, then pulled back to allow him to get situated.

He obeyed her and settled back in the large wing-backed chair. Gillian lifted her pen; it was diamond-cut metal and sparkled in the light. She twirled it between her fingers, giving him a forced focal point. "Focus on the pen, Pavel, and listen to my voice."

Softly, coaxingly, soothingly, she spoke to him. Assuring him to trust her, that all would be well. Counting him down into the half sleep of the beta level of his mind, her empathy wide open to him and his deep fear, she felt it when he went under, relaxing into her voice's suggestion.

Hoping and praying to whatever gods were listening that she was doing the right thing, Gillian tapped into him, focusing on the most recent attack first. Deeply under, his breathing heavy and slow, Pavel heard her.

Twilight came and the Vampires rose. Shielded within the castle stones, all windows covered with heavy tapestry drapery, they could move about before full dark fell. All of them were old enough and powerful enough to stand the last rays of sunlight and could move about freely during the day if it were heavily stormy and overcast or if they were out of direct sunlight. The library doors were shut and Aleksei could sense Gillian inside with someone. His senses told him it was Lycanthrope. He had his hand on the door, then stopped, not wanting to interrupt if it were a client.

Cezar entered the front door in Human form just as the Egyptian Vampires filed into the hallway. Tanis also paused at the library for a moment until Cezar spoke. "Your little doctor is helping one of my pack, Aleksei. I hope you do not mind."

"Of course not, Cezar, it is her job after—" He was interrupted by a horrific snarl that lifted into a blood-curdling howl, coming from the library.

Heart in his mouth, he and Tanis moved as one with blurring speed, reaching for the doors with the rest of the Vampires and Cezar crowding on their heels. Nearly ripping the doors off their hinges, they barreled into the room. The sight that greeted them froze Aleksei's blood.

Gillian was behind Aleksei's heavy desk, face white but determined. Her legs were braced and apart, her gun drawn and pointed at a pony-size blonde wolf who was stalking her in a classic attack position, growling low in his chest, ears forward, tail held in a flat line behind him. Pavel was crouching, growling, gathering himself for a lightening pounce. Gill had about four and a half pounds of pressure on a five-pound trigger. Any movement by Pavel was going to open a porthole in him. That she hadn't plugged him already was amazing. No one would have blamed her.

Visibly trembling, Gillian didn't glance over or acknowledge their entry, though the wolf's ear flicked momentarily toward them. He'd heard.

To her credit, her arms were rock steady but her hands were quivering. When he'd shifted less than five feet in front of her, she'd crawled backward up and out of the chair as he convulsed rapidly into the blonde beast before her. Never taking her eyes off him, gun drawn, she'd backed across the desk, putting as much furniture between her and the snarling Werewolf as possible.

Going for the door was out, so was yelling. Pavel would be on her if she so much as twitched. Also to her credit or her stupidity, Aleksei thought briefly, she hadn't made so much as a squeak in the face of impending death. Her fear was palpable in the room, but she looked death in the face and dealt with it.

Nobody stopped for questions. With blurring speed, Aleksei went for Gillian, imposing his large body between her and the nearly charging Werewolf, taking her gun arm down and away from him and the others, shoving her behind him. The Egyptians formed a wall between them and the drama unfolding scant feet away.

Tanis and Cezar went for Pavel, who was slavering in an openmouthed growl, his body turning to meet the new threat; haunches bunching for a leap that would take him into his alpha and the Vampire. Cezar's commanding bellow filled the room as Tanis blurred, grabbed the wolf in a deadly embrace, pulling him up on his hind legs, the Vampire's left arm across his chest, the other positioned to snap his neck if he did not obey his alpha.

"Pavel!"

By the time the authority in the leader's voice stopped echoing, everyone was shaking. The blonde wolf stopped struggling in Tanis's arms. They were well matched at about the same height on two legs, but the wolf outweighed Tanis by quite a bit. Still, proving that Vampire strength was more than legendary, Tanis held him and kept his balance, his arms like tempered steel that would crush the wolf's chest or snap his neck like a twig if he moved again.

Cezar grabbed Pavel's muzzle and forced him to look at

him. The alpha's power poured through the room and Cezar forced Pavel to shift. In moments, Tanis held a naked man in his arms who was bathed in sweat and semiconscious from the forced change. Taking his wolf in his arms, Cezar apologized profusely to Aleksei and to Gillian, who had come out from behind the Vampires and was looking at them with a querulous look on her pale face.

"No, it's all right, Cezar. I don't know what happened. He shifted on me while he was under hypnosis." Her voice shook a little. Anubis and Sekhmet flanked her instantly, effectively blocking Aleksei, who also tried to get to her side.

"I will speak to you later then." Cezar started out, carrying the naked Pavel, Montu and Noph following him closely in case more intervention was needed. Maeti ran to get the door.

"Please don't hurt him, Cezar." Gillian didn't want him harmed. "I don't know why he shifted. Please let me find out. I don't think he attacked me intentionally." She wasn't sure what happened, but she didn't think Pavel would really try to hurt her in his right mind.

"I will not punish him then, Gillian, until I hear from you or Aleksei." Then they were gone into the night. Maeti locked the door, and the three guards returned, falling into place by the library doors.

Aleksei was shaking. That had been too close and right under their noses. Tanis tried to lift Gillian in his arms but she struggled and he had to put her down or drop her. "Cut it out, Tanis. I'm all right." She wasn't, but damned if she'd let them know. It broke Aleksei's heart to see her so vulnerable and be unable to comfort her himself.

"What happened, little sister?" Anubis's gentle, rich voice was soft but compelling.

Sekhmet put an arm around her shoulders. "You must tell us, dearest. He is your client but his leader must know or he will execute him."

"I . . . I'm not sure."

Hell, might as well add "breaking confidentiality" to her list of blunders. She would tell Pavel later. If he wanted to report her, there was little she could do.

"I hypnotized him to get to the origins of a trauma. I went through two major incidents in his life, the most recent one first. He did very well. We walked through it easily. He was responding to my questions, my suggestions. This shouldn't have happened!"

She started to shake and Sekhmet squeezed her shoulders tightly. "Go on, love."

Nodding, she did. "We got to the earlier trauma, were right in the middle of it, and he shifted on me."

"What was the trauma, Gillian?" Aleksei asked softly, needing to know.

"When he was changed. We went over the first night he changed. Oh God!" Her eyes widened. "That must have been it. He was in a beta mental state—it's the state we dream in, can function in. He relived it, but he *really* relived it."

Turning to Aleksei, her eyes pleading, she said, "You have to tell Cezar! Don't let him kill Pavel, please! This wasn't his fault!"

Frantic to make him understand she started toward him, forgetting her legs were wobbly from the shock of nearly being lunch. She staggered against Sekhmet when they wouldn't hold her.

Aleksei moved instantly, brushing the others aside to get to her, unable to bear her fragile state a moment longer. Sweeping her up in his arms, he turned back to the room. "I am taking her to her room. I will be back shortly."

Gillian was still too shaken to argue, then realized she still held the Glock in her hand as Aleksei carried her from the library. Only Tanis noticed that she did not struggle this time.

"Christ, I forgot I had this. Thanks for not letting me shoot anyone." Looking up at his perfect profile, she smiled as his icy gray eyes turned to her. "I feel the shakes coming on again." Her teeth chattered helplessly.

"Shock," he said gruffly. "You are in shock, *piccola*. You need to rest, to eat something. I will send Maeti or Sekhmet to you. You do not need Tanis tonight."

Reaching her door, his voice held an authoritative note of finality as he opened it with a thought, taking her into her room and laying her on the bed. The gun went on the nightstand beside her. He looked down at her for a moment, raw heat in his silvery eyes. Every cell in his body demanding that he hold her, comfort her, love her. Dominant, protective, alpha instincts rose within him, demanding that he take her, make her his so he would have the right to shield her, keep her safe. His body became an imperious ache, his arousal a hard line against his thigh. If he stayed in this room . . . if she touched him now . . .

Gill reached up to take his hand in thanks and he jerked

back, not trusting himself for the moment. He had to turn away from her surprised and hurt expression so she wouldn't notice the reaction of his body to her need. She would misinterpret his desire for her as only sexual and that would destroy her trust in him.

"Forgive me, Gillian. You want Cezar to know what has happened. I will tell him. No harm will come to Pavel. You have my word."

Keeping his back to her and striding out of her room, shutting the door behind him, was the hardest thing he'd ever done. She could have died tonight—if he and the others had been seconds slower, Pavel would have torn out her throat.

Leaning on the wall outside her room, he got his raging emotions and protesting body under control. He couldn't get her small form out of his mind. She was so unbelievably fragile but so incredibly strong. Anyone else would have been curled in a sobbing heap on the floor. Even he was trembling.

"Does she know, Count Rachlav?" Maeti's soft voice was pitched only for Vampire ears to hear, and Aleksei spun at her words, staring at her incredulously. He'd been too distracted to hear her approach.

"Know what, Maeti?"

"Know how much you care for her?" There was a twinkle in her sky-blue eyes as she walked past him, and into Gillian's room without waiting for permission to enter.

Aleksei was astonished. Was he that obvious? Maeti barely knew him and she had guessed. Tanis knew, but he was his brother and shared blood and a relative bond. He needed to be careful or he would wind up compromising his own honor and Gillian's oath. Swiftly, he went outside to inform Cezar that he did not have to execute Pavel for violating the pact of protection for those under Aleksei's care.

Tanis was just as surprised by what had happened and by his brother's abrupt assertion. He'd started after them but had been stopped by Anubis. "Let him take her, Tanis. You may be her lover but sometimes a lover is not what is needed at the moment."

Grousing, he'd stayed put, letting himself be drawn into a conversation with the rest of them about the intricacies of Gillian's profession. Maeti stayed with Gillian, finally talking her into food and a hot bath.

Later, clean, relaxed and fed, Gillian pulled up her e-mail on the laptop. More festive news. The Italian therapist's remains had been located. More of her cadre were now going missing in various countries. Looking over Gillian's shoulder, Maeti quickly read the news, stunned by what she saw.

"Count Rachlav must know this, Gillian. It concerns your safety and ours," she lightly chastised her friend.

Sighing, Gillian disagreed. "I haven't told him for that very reason, Maeti. Everyone is half crazy trying to protect me. Don't you think these others had protection? It didn't help them . . . How will it make a difference if I add more worry into the mix?"

Maeti picked up a brush and attacked Gillian's wet hair, hoping to relax her more. "You do what you want, my friend, but when he does find out, and he will, you will be sorry you did not disclose this when you were able to."

"I know. That's what worries me."

CHAPTER

17

AFTER a night of rest, Gillian visited Dante, who informed her that the conflict was spreading. Apparently he did have connections. Ghosts in general were allying themselves with the Osiris and Dionysus camps. They had nothing to gain from Dracula's rule, nor from the others, but the majority of displaced spirits did not want to be exorcised, banished, ignored or avoided by causing a panic in Humans if they chose the wrong side. There was no need to declare allegiance to a leader who would clearly disregard them as insubstantial and unimportant.

Most of the Sidhe—Seelie, Unseelie and Mith-Seelie of the Light Court, Dark Court and Twilight Court, respectively, including Fairies, Elves, and their kin—were falling into a sort of neutral area. Where the Sluagh's loyalties lay was anybody's guess. Most definitely did not want to be under Dracula's banner, but nor did they wish to remain as fringe citizens in the current Paramortal/mortal world. Humans tended not to always take them seriously and there was a growing movement to bring legal injunctions for libelous depiction against the works of the Brothers Grimm; the makers of Keebler cookies; Kris Kringle d/b/a Santa Claus (a limited liability company), who insisted on depicting his workforce as indentured servants to a fat, bearded Nordic man in a red suit with a reindeer-drawn sleigh;

and the Walt Disney Corporation for their largely unflattering characterizations of magical folk such as demi-Fey Tinkerbell and Unseelie Maleficent.

J. R. R. Tolkien, in contrast, was a hero among the Fey, having brought Elves and others into the full glare of celebrity; as was TSR and related companies for Dungeons & Dragons and other role playing games, and author Laurell K. Hamilton with her Merry Gentry series. They rather liked mortals knowing that the Fey, Elves, Fairies, Dwarves and Hobbits could kick their asses on many levels—not all magical.

Osiris sent word through Anubis that envoys were needed to convince the Sidhe and their friends that he and Dionysus were trustworthy and that the Fey, all of them, were respected by Vampires and their kin. Dionysus was sending some representatives out, as was Osiris; hopefully they would bring back good news of treaties signed and sealed. Osiris asked Aleksei if he would like to be considered for one of the diplomatic envoy appointments. Since Count Rachlav was the head of the Romanian faction of Vampires and therefore a VIP in Fangdom, it would be an honor for any Fey to host him. Aleksei said he would give it some thought; then Anubis butted in, pointing out that it might not be a wise idea since Dracula was gunning for Aleksei in the first place.

Tanis, listening to the exchange, which began to get heated when Aleksei's sensibilities were offended by the suggestion that he hide out, offered to be one of the envoys instead of Aleksei. As the Count's brother, he held a high rank; he was also a target but not an obvious one, and therefore could leave and return will little fanfare, hoopla or attention being drawn to himself. Besides, he found he rather liked dealing with the Fey and their intricate societal practices, which Aleksei found tedious.

After much discussion and argument along with Osiris's rethought recommendation, Tanis was duly appointed and made preparations to leave. His first visit would be to Finland—home and Gateway of the Elves, then the United Kingdom. Ireland held a large population of Werewolves that might be persuaded to be on their side.

Gillian was not happy about this development. She and Tanis were not exactly a bonded couple, but he was her friend and she didn't like him out of the country and away from the protection he had there at the family castle. They had a discussion or two about it—one heated where they wound up in bed and one not so heated, where they also wound up in bed. In the end, Gillian backed off, recognizing male muleheadedness in the Reborn. Tanis was a big Vampire and could take care of himself very well. Those steel-corded muscles were capable of lifting a small car or stopping a charging bull; he didn't need a petite marine guard at his side.

She pondered their friendship, thinking about what her life would be like if he weren't in it. Liking him had come easily, despite his chauvinistic overtones. Caring about him had been harder. Gillian lived her life securely behind a professional coat of armor. As an empath, it was safer that way. She could care about her clients, keep a reasonable clinical distance and close the file when the case was done.

Tanis had been her lover and friend for months but, true to form, Gill still remained somewhat detached. Tanis knew it, she knew it. Problem was, neither was doing anything about it. They rarely discussed their relationship or emotions. It was one of the reasons that he was more unsure of his own feelings than he normally would have been at this stage of their relationship. He cared about her, as a friend, as a lover; had respected her skill and courage, but knew her heart wasn't fully *his*. It made him wary and to think that a break might do both of them good, perhaps give them a little perspective. Tanis wanted to understand her; he wasn't sure how to go about it.

Gillian wanted to understand *Gillian* too; Tanis's feelings were somewhat extraneous at this point. Having a gorgeous, hot man available in her life—okay, she could overlook the Vampire thing—was still scary as hell. Completely competent and totally capable, Gillian still had a major flaw in her character. She had no idea how to truly love someone. It bothered her occasionally, but not enough for her to work on it.

Commitment phobia ran so deeply within her, she had no idea how to even begin to combat it. Her knee-jerk reaction to closeness was making her argumentative and aggressive with Tanis. If she held him at bay, pushed him away hard enough, was enough of a hardass, he'd let him alone. It had worked for her in the past and she saw no reason to change. This break wasn't threatening to her at all. It gave her time to ignore the problem for a while rather than face it. If Tanis had forced her to confront it, he would get Gill at her worst: a first-class bully. Behind the bully was someone very frightened of belonging to someone else, of allowing her intrinsic vulnerability to surface. Sometimes being a bitch was all she had.

Aleksei was another matter. His reaction and response to her the night of Pavel's near attack had been puzzling. Maeti had tried to broach the topic of the tall, dark and devastating count, but Gillian refused to discuss either him as a patient or that he might have feelings for her. As far as she was concerned, she was in a difficult position just being there. Thinking about how Aleksei might or might not feel was damn scary and confusing. She couldn't afford to contemplate it just yet. After the year time frame was over, if she was still in the Country, maybe she'd think about it. Otherwise it might blow over on its own. Avoiding emotional confusion was another strategic defense tactic she did very well.

Aleksei was having thoughts and concerns of his own. *Issues* was too vague a term. Aleksei did not have *issues*. He knew exactly what was bothering him. Four hundred years of discovering his inner Vampire had given him tremendous insight, despite the fangxiety that had initially brought Gillian into his life.

His normally high tolerance was being strained at every turn. Gillian's proclivity for getting into hazardous situations was wearing thin as his newly evolving feelings for the little blonde shrink were growing more intense, despite his trying to avoid contact with her as much as possible. Agitation showed clearly in his manner and bearing. He was becoming increasingly isolated: taking long walks alone, staring out windows, perusing the Internet and pacing the corridors until Gillian lost patience and yelled at him. That earned her a sharp reprimand from Aleksei, who noted that Gillian was not the castle activities director and would she please shut the hell up if she wanted them to remain on speaking terms.

Gill figured Aleksei focusing on the big picture rather than on the short, sassy detail living under his roof was probably better for their long-term friendship anyway. Edgy and temperamental, everyone was soon giving him a wide berth and letting the Lord of the Manor climb his own pinnacle. Maeti noticed that the pinnacle was looking more and more like Gillian's lithe and lush form every night.

Tanis was too preoccupied with his own thoughts in the matter to notice and could not have focused if he'd had bifocals on his emotions. Sekhmet and Anubis exchanged many a knowing glance. People who are happy in their committed relationships tend to be monumental pains in the ass. They believe that everyone needed to be paired up and deliriously happy, just like them.

Gag me with a spoon, Gillian thought after the umpteenth time that Sekhmet tried to have a little "girl talk" with her, while extolling Anubis's virtues, prowess and circumference. That was just way too damn much information for Gillian to stomach about a four-thousand-year-old Egyptian Vampire. She liked Sekhmet but wanted to be able to remain in a room with Anubis without embarrassment.

Cezar and Pavel showed up with Cezar practically dragging the mortified Lycanthrope into the castle to speak to Gillian personally. Sitting together in the same library where the near attack had happened, Pavel stammered and colored to his discomfiture and Cezar's amusement, but managed to apologize. Gillian graciously explained that it had not been his fault and that she took full responsibility for the failure of the hypnotherapy.

Aleksei entered during their conversation, scenting the pack leader and budding alpha wolf. His own senses on full alert after the last visit by the lupine league, he strode in and perched on the arm of the couch next to where Gillian was seated. Cezar had the audacity to look amused at the veiled threat. Pavel simply looked terrified. Hearing the last bit of conversation, Aleksei groaned inwardly, watching Pavel and Cezar join the Gillian Key Admiration Society, as she smoothed over the entire incident.

Shaking hands with Gill and Aleksei, Cezar and Pavel took their leave, with promises to let Gillian come to a pack meeting and to run with them if she would like. Enthusiastic, she accepted their hospitable offer, much to Aleksei's irritation. There was no way in hell he was going to allow her out roaming the mountains with a pack of Lycanthropes—he didn't care who their Alpha was. He trusted Cezar implicitly, but wasn't up for Gillian cavorting about in the midst of all that teeth and fur.

Cezar shut the door a he exited and Aleksei was startled by a resounding thump on his upper arm. Turning, he looked down into Gillian's intense green eyes, which were snapping in anger. She had punched him.

"What in the hell is wrong with you? You come in here and hover over me, threatening that poor kid?" Gillian hopped up on her feet to face him directly, trying to feel at less of a disadvantage. Well, damn, it didn't work; even seated on the arm of the couch, Aleksei was taller than she was. Fine. She'd wing it.

An ebony brow arched elegantly over his silvery gray eyes. Eyes that were taking on a distinctive red cast as his temper began to simmer. He had gone perfectly still the way only a Vampire can manage. It was unnerving.

"Gillian . . . ," he began, in a warning tone.

"There is no excuse or reason for you to babysit me, Aleksei. I am a former soldier and an adult. If I want your goddamn help I'll ask for it." She was seething. The entire company of resident Vampires were on her like white on rice as if she were a delicate little flower. Drove her nuts.

Reading her thoughts easily, since she was broadcasting like AM radio, he managed a smirk. "You are delicate, *piccola*. Much more delicate than you can imagine."

Damn. Shit. And hell. His voice was still the most remarkable thing she'd ever heard. That and the fact that his inherent sensuality and breathtaking beauty were combined with that voice. And that he was seated less than two feet in front of her. Close enough to touch . . . rock hard, er . . . muscles. Yeah, muscles. To smell . . . cardamom and nutmeg. To kiss . . . jeez, those lips, that mouth . . . Oh goddess. Her mind was wandering where it shouldn't be.

Stop it! she yelled at herself. That was *not* good. He couldn't be attractive to her just yet. He just couldn't. Good thing he made her really mad seconds later.

"Delicate my happy ass! I did not survive battlefield conditions and conflict in Somalia and Bosnia by being delicate, you insufferable shithead! Don't you lecture me about being delicate or being female or being a target. I know exactly what I am doing. I am being careful. I am being mindful of my safety. It's not like any of you would let me forget about it anyway for Hell's sake!"

She practically spat the last at him, drawing herself up to her full five-foot, two-inch height and bracing herself for the coming explosion. Her hands were clenched in fists at her sides, knuckles white and trembling in her anger.

Far from exploding in fury, Aleksei regarded her with glacial calm, as the deep beautiful voice rumbled from his chest. "Perhaps it would drive home the point of just how vulnerable and easily overpowered you are if I demonstrate exactly what little effort will be required to put you over my knee."

To her horror, she reddened under his unwavering glare. Devious, chauvinistic bastard. How did he do that? She could feel the weight of his age and power pouring over her. His eyes held hers, two pools of mysterious silver metal, but no metal ever held that weight of intelligence and heat. Having had experience in this area, she had no doubt that he would make good on his threat if she didn't shut up. Her mouth, however, refused to obey her brain's directive.

"We are not living in the fucking seventeenth century! You can't just spank someone because they don't agree with you!" She snarled up at him, trying not to look nervous on top of her self-conscious blush.

The look he gave her wasn't friendly. "Whether you agree with me or not matters very little, Gillian. I am less concerned with you being angry than I am with you remaining alive. I am an Old-World man; if I must resort to direct methods of convincing you, I will. That you will be alive to hate me will be a small price to pay." That he meant every word, she had no doubt whatsoever.

It was the first time being with him that she felt anything remotely akin to fear. Empathy flared; she picked up his anger, his fear for her and something else she couldn't place right then. One thing for sure, he was deadly serious. Aleksei apparently had a hell of a temper hidden beneath that silky ruffled shirt. Gorgeous and chauvinistic. Interesting.

"Why does it matter to you so much, my remaining alive, I mean? I'm just your former therapist and now a forced guest in your home. I'm nothing to you, Aleksei; you don't have to remain responsible for me. So why do you care so much?" Nile-green eyes stared unflinchingly into his own shimmering gray ones.

If her tone had been anything other than one of an honest question, he would have jerked her across his lap and thoroughly tanned her lovely rear. Powerful emotions were surging through him; he knew it and he knew why. She did not. Her clear eyes were guileless, with no inkling of her effect on him. Her question wasn't meant to provoke him. She was just asking.

Mulling her words, forcing down his turbulent emotions, Aleksei's voice softened a little. Velvet over steel. "It matters, Gillian. *You* matter to me, *mia preziosa*."

He shackled both her upper arms in his elegant hands and shook her lightly. "You do not understand why or how you impact another life but you do, *bella piccola*. You do."

In retrospect, it would be a profound moment for both of

them. Gillian looked at him as a man for the first time. Not as a patient, not as a Vampire, not as a resource, but a man who was trying desperately to put her needs above his own even if he pissed her off doing it.

Aggressive, powerful and dominant, he was from another time, another way of thinking. An alpha male in all his Vampiric glory. He couldn't help being chauvinistic and bossy any more than Tanis could. Being Lord of the Manor in more ways than one had made him the way he was. Four hundred years of living one way was not going to evaporate due to a limited association with a New-World woman.

Right now he was hanging on to control by a thread. Gillian could feel it. Seething emotions were pulsing through his being. He cared about her as a woman and he let her see it, honestly and openly. It was in his eyes, in his remarkable beauty; in the way his hands were curved around her arms gently but firmly. His voice was pitched differently. Love. Sweet freaking Hathor. He was falling for her and hard. Shit, she so did not need this.

Aleksei felt her brachial pulse leap under his hands. All he could do was hold her still in front of him and try to remember to breathe evenly like a living man. He prayed she wouldn't move because if she touched him, if the slightest brush of her fingertips flicked across his erection, he knew his control would shatter and they would wind up making love on the couch heedless of the library door being unlocked. Standing as close as she was between his legs as he sat on the couch's arm, he felt the heat of her body over his chest and groin, smelled her snow-on-clover scent like a heady drug. Thank the gods she didn't look down. He was hard and aching for her despite his anger.

Gill knew Aleksei was honorable; that he knew she was also honor-bound not to break her own profession's ethics and he would not push her to do so. Desire and need from him was beating at her despite her shielding and his own. Violating her trust was something he would not do, but he wanted her. She knew it and respected him for keeping a lid on it.

What he didn't realize was she didn't have to look down to know how aroused he was by her closeness. Her empathy was broadcasting that to her on every possible channel. Goddess, he was so unbelievably beautiful, sensual, touch-starved and so rock hard that it bordered on physical pain. Electricity snaked between them in a sensual current and it was all Gillian could do to stand perfectly still and wait for him to release her. If she moved at all, she'd accidentally brush against his inner thighs or groin, as close as her hands were to him. At that point all bets would be off, because they'd wind up in a pile of tangled limbs on the couch and fuck each other's brains out. The only thing that saved them both was the phone ringing.

CHAPTER
18

SLOWLY Aleksei rose, taking Gillian with him as he turned toward the desk and the still-ringing phone. Tanis picked that moment to enter the library and Aleksei dropped Gillian's arm like she was suddenly molten rock. Trying to seem as though she weren't running for her life, she scooted around the desk, away from Aleksei, and practically ran to meet Tanis.

"I am leaving now, *piccola*. Do not worry. I will be in touch."

Tanis swept an arm around her, pulling her against him in a warm embrace. Forgetting Aleksei for the moment, Gillian turned her face upward and met Tanis's kiss with a brief one of her own. When they pulled apart, Tanis had a thousand questions in his golden eyes, none of which Gillian was in the mood to answer. There was something wrong, he could sense it. As he scanned her mind lightly, Aleksei was foremost in her thoughts and those thoughts were turbulent. Puzzled but knowing this was not the time, Tanis waved to his brother, who was still on the phone. Aleksei waved back in a dismissive gesture and sent along their private path:

"Be safe, Tanis. I need a living brother, not a statistic from Dracula."

"I will. I am relying on you to take care of Gillian while I am gone." Tanis's voice was firm and a little cool in his head. Aleksei

excused himself from the phone for a moment and gave Tanis his full attention. Golden and silvery eyes locked on each other.

"You know I will see to her safety in every way."

"Yes, but I want it clear, Aleksei. Take care of her. I charge you with her happiness and well-being."

Understanding what his brother meant, Aleksei nodded, then turned back to the phone as Gillian walked to the door with his now-diplomat brother. They said their brief good-byes. Last night had been the long good-bye. Gillian didn't want Tanis to feel badly about leaving and Tanis wanted her to know that the separation would be good for them to sort out their feelings. Whatever happened, they would remain friends. Close friends.

He left then in a swirl of cape and gleam of boots. She shut the door and leaned against it. When he left, Gillian felt a little bereft. Not because she was in love with him, but because she'd grown to care about him as a friend over the past few months and rather liked his company. Tanis had felt a little off as well, leaving Gillian behind, but where he was going, Humans were not necessarily welcome, and she would be a detriment rather than a help, not to mention her being safer right where she was.

Sorting through unfamiliar emotional territory in her mind, she knew she'd need time to think. There was a window seat nearby and she took it, drawing her legs up and waiting for the inevitable "Aleksei conversation" that she didn't want to have, leaning her head against the ancient stones and pondering the stars.

Aleksei was having a difficult conversation of his own on the phone. At the moment, he was struggling between absolute shock and absolute fury. Apparently Gillian had been careless about checking her e-mail. When one of her contacts at the IPPA noticed that no one had heard from Gillian for a few days, they became naturally concerned. Her cell phone also went unanswered. One of the board members, Helmut Gerhardt, placed a call to Count Aleksei Rachlav, inquiring as to the safety and continued health of their MIA therapist/operative.

Aleksei was happy to tell them that Gillian was alive, well and safe. Puzzled as to why they would call him instead of contacting her, he asked. Dr. Gerhardt gladly filled him in on the circumstances, including the confirmed death of the paradoc in Hungary. The body had been found drained. Gerhardt was summarily surprised that the Count had not been kept abreast of all the developments. So was Aleksei.

The IPPA assumed that since Count Rachlav was handling Romania, that he was aware of all the developments. Gillian neglected to tell them she hadn't shared information. That was a mistake. Hanging up, he slumped rather ungracefully into the large wing-backed chair and tried to absorb everything he'd just been told.

Anubis strolled into the room, took one look at Aleksei and knew somebody was going to be on the receiving end of a very angry Vampire tirade. "What is it, my friend? You look like a thundercloud."

"I am going to have a word with Gillian." Aleksei rose slowly, deliberately, every muscle rippling, temper near snapping. Moving around Anubis, who stood deliberately in his path, he stopped when the Egyptian Vampire put a hand on his arm.

"You are very angry, Aleksei. Do you think now is a good time to speak to our little warrior? Does she need to hear what you have to say right this moment?"

Anubis was genuinely concerned. He'd known Aleksei for centuries. The Vampire was always reserved, calm and in control of his emotions. He had never seen Aleksei really angry, nor heard the heated tones that were in that black velvet voice. Gillian was in a world of shit, she just didn't know it yet. Anubis was certain that if Aleksei got hold of her, someone was going to get hurt, and he was betting it would be Gillian.

"Speak to her? Anubis, she has withheld information that could endanger us all. Tanis is correct; she should be disciplined."

Filling in the Egyptian, Aleksei watched his friend's eyes harden perceptively as Anubis "got it." Gillian had been unforgivably lax in her communication with them. Her safety and theirs was possibly jeopardized. If they had known how close in proximity the killings were coming, known about the other Paramortal psychologists' deaths and the deaths of the other Humans, they could have prepared. Now there was no way of knowing how close Dracula was penetrating.

Anubis stepped away. "I will remain, Aleksei. I know you are angry. I know Gillian is deserving of a harsh reprimand, but now is not the time to alienate her or frighten her away."

"That is where our opinions differ, Anubis. I fully intend to frighten her." Cold fury swept thought the room as Aleksei went to the library door. Opening it, he saw Gillian across the foyer, in the window seat.

He called out softly, "Gillian. A word with you, please."

Something in the softly spoken words made a chill run up her spine. His face was an unreadable, lovely mask, but the purring voice held soft heat. She could feel his anger beating at her from where she sat. Hopping off the window seat she went to him. Aleksei held the door for her, allowing her to precede him.

Seeing Anubis there was comforting, and she greeted him. "Hi, where's Sekhmet?"

"She is with Maeti. Come in, Gillian. Aleksei and I would like to hear your explanation on something." He settled in the middle of the couch, his arms draped across the back, and waited.

Feeling Aleksei's arm snaking around her waist, Gillian would have jumped, but she didn't have time. Propelling her forward, he took her to the desk. Half sitting on it, he pressed her hips against his thigh, his hand in the small of her back, and reached for a notepad. "I have had a very enlightening conversation with Dr. Gerhardt, Gillian. Do you remember him, perhaps?"

Startled, she looked up at Aleksei. An ebony eyebrow arched, then she was treated to his perfect profile as he read to her some of the interesting facts that Dr. Gerhardt had shared with him. Facts about Vampires, killings, disappearances; facts that Gillian had known about for days, even weeks. One fact in particular he called her attention to. The fact that the missing Hungarian psychologist was dead. Very dead.

"Explain." One word. Just one. That he could send a ripple of apprehension through her with a single word frightened her more than if he'd started yelling.

"I didn't want to scare everyone to death, Aleksei. You all are so concerned about me all the time. There are whole villages, countries, hundreds, thousands of people who are at risk, and they have no idea of the danger they are in." She searched his face, hoping he understood her, knowing that he didn't.

"Nor apparently do you, *mia ragazza angela*." Heat washed over her from his power. It was flaring in conjunction with his anger.

"Yes, but I am safe. More than anyone else, I am safe here, with you, with Tanis, with all of you." Gill gestured toward Anubis.

He was rubbing her back gently, he realized. A lover's comforting touch. Aleksei jerked his hand back as if the contact burned him. At his sudden movement, Gillian half turned, beginning to drop into a defensive crouch, ready to fight. A deep growl sounded in his chest, the tones so low that they vibrated through her. The warning was unmistakable. Instantly, she was bent forward over his thigh, the iron muscles in his leg pressing against her abdomen, an elegant hand holding her down.

"Wait, Aleksei, let me up, I can explain!" Her voice sounded a little bit petulant and she cringed inwardly.

"No, *dolcezza*. Not this time. You have the courage to face down guns and monsters, you will have the courage to live through this. You lied to me, Gillian. I specifically told you what would happen if you ever lied to me again. Give me one good reason, *piccola*, why I should not reprimand you as you so richly deserve."

This was the second time she'd been over an ancient Vampire's knee. She didn't like it any better this time either. What flew through her mind in those few seconds was that when Tanis had spanked her, it had been in the middle of a fight. No holds barred in a fight; all was fair. He'd made her mad, but she couldn't really cry foul.

This was different. Aleksei was angry. No, mad as hell was more like it. He was also scared. Afraid that she'd inadvertently put them all at risk from her failure to communicate. She felt it all through her empathic gift, but her sensitivity was keyed higher than that. He loved her. She was someone he loved, she had been unconscionably negligent and he was damn well going to make it clear that it was not to happen again. Ever.

One swat landed. "I asked you a question." Pure steel in that quiet, level voice. No velvet this time. That one smack hurt her feelings more than Tanis ever could have. She'd forgotten that Anubis was looking on with interest, that the library door was open and anyone might walk by. Nothing occurred to her except she'd let Aleksei down. He cared for her, had taken her under his protection, into his home.

Now, draped over his thigh, she saw things with incredible clarity. She did care what he thought. She cared a lot. His respect and his feelings were important to her. She had liked him, been attracted to him from the moment they had met. When all else failed, either a gun or honesty had always gotten her through. Shooting him was definitely out. Even with the current state of affairs, putting a hole in that perfect reborn body over something this ludicrous didn't work for her. She went for honesty. He'd smell a lie in a second and then he would finish what he was starting. Lying was absolutely a bad idea.

"I can't, Aleksei." Her voice sounded fragile even to her. "I can't give you a single reason. I fucked up. I'd say I was sorry, but I know that won't help."

The next blow never connected. Hearing truth in her words and realizing that she was scared, he stood her upright. He didn't want her afraid of him. Putting her need for comfort above his own need to chastise her, he held her there, silvery eyes boring into her soul. Paling under his scrutiny, she tried to pull back, but he held on to her.

"You do not know what you put me through, *piccola guerriera*." He drew a deep breath. "You terrify me." His heartfelt admission choked her up.

The big bad Vampire was afraid that the little blonde marine was going to get herself very dead. Hell with decorum, hell with her pride. She threw her arms around his neck and hugged him tightly, inhaling his marvelous scent of cardamom and nutmeg mixed with pure male stud. Even half sitting on the desk he was much taller, his frame much larger; she felt very aware of the difference in their sizes and very female.

"I am so sorry. I meant to protect you. I didn't think that . . . hell, I didn't think," she whispered into his ear in a shaky voice. She'd hurt him, frightened him for no reason and she knew it. That didn't feel very good. Maybe the spanking would be less painful.

Aleksei's arms enfolded her like a cocoon, pulling her against him, wrapping her in his strength and warmth. "I know, *dolcezza*. I know," he whispered into her hair, smelling the familiar scent of sunlight, snow and clover on her.

Finally having her in his arms shook him to the core. She was so small. Power and muscle wrapped in a short, dynamic, blonde package. That he couldn't take her upstairs and make love to her broke his heart. For Gillian, that she wanted to make love to him at all, to know him as he knew her, terrified her.

There was a terrific pounding on the door. Anubis muttered that he would get it and left. They didn't notice him leave. Moments later, "Aleksei . . . Aleksei you must come." The urgency in Anubis's voice snapped them both back to reality.

Exchanging a glance, they disengaged from their embrace and hurried after him, Aleksei gently moving Gillian behind him as they ran to the door and outside. The pack was waiting. Montu held his arms out to stop them.

"My Lord," Montu began. He didn't finish the sentence.

Gillian couldn't make out what the wolves and Anubis were staring at. She felt Maeti's familiar presence behind her. Turning to look at Aleksei, she saw his face harden into granite. Noph was coming up the drive from the gates to the estate with something in his arms. Her eyes focused on it, but her brain didn't make sense of it at first.

It was a body. Not just a body. The body was of a young Lycanthrope. He had been impaled lengthwise on a thick wooden stake. Cezar snarled and the pack howled its fury. Noph lay the body gently down near Aleksei's feet. Carved into the chest of what had been a young Werewolf was the Romanian word *Voldevode*.

"What does that say?" Gillian's voice was a mere whisper.

"Warlord." Aleksei answered her. His voice dark and cold as the grave. "Dracula's personal calling card. He is here."

Mentally he reached for Tanis; his brother couldn't have gotten far yet, and they needed him here. Silence greeted him on the familiar path. Tanis simply wasn't there. Dracula was at their door, literally, and now there was a void where Tanis should be. Not realizing he did so, Aleksei reached for Gillian.

If she hadn't been so furious, her knees might have given out. As it was, she felt Maeti take her hand in the steady grip of a friend. Unconsciously, Aleksei moved his hand over the nape of Gillian's neck, pulling her under the security of his shoulder. Maeti stepped away as Gillian reflexively molded against him, her arm going around his waist.

"I cannot locate Tanis." No one moved. The gravity of what Aleksei had just said stilled all of them.

The fun was just beginning.

CHAPTER
19

T ANIS had been missing for weeks. Aleksei, Cezar, Anubis and Osiris checked every contact they knew nightly. Dionysus sent word that he too had his operatives searching for Tanis. No lead was ignored, no rumor neglected. Looking for Aleksei's golden-eyed brother consumed most of everyone's time. Gillian put her own feelers out. Dante and several of the other local clients she'd picked up were aware of the Vampire conflict but not the disappearance of Count Rachlav's brother.

During this time, Gillian realized two things: Part of her missed Tanis a great deal but, curiously, more as her friend than lover. Second, in her darkest secret heart, her commitment-phobic self was rather relieved that she had no decision to make as long as Tanis was gone. She wasn't proud of that, but there it was. She wanted his friendship; she just didn't know if she wanted him, not for eternity anyway. Just thinking about it made her stomach hurt and the relationship monster claw at her inner claustrophobic.

Aleksei tried repeatedly to raise his brother through their familial mental link. The rest of his time was spent in communication with Osiris, planning strategies and negotiations; coordinating meetings with the various local paranormal community leaders; traveling around the Transylvanian province near the estate and village of Sacele, investigating reported attacks and deaths. One death had occurred near the village itself.

A young girl had been found in a field, savaged by fang marks on all major arteries. The Mayor of Sacele had called Aleksei in, as the governing Vampire and Count of the realm. She'd been bled dry, but apparently in the throes of sexual ecstasy, judging from how her body was arranged when she was found.

Gillian had gone with him. Her expertise as a field operative and her background in criminal psychology would be useful. She'd seen bodies before, investigated crime scenes. Familiarity with various types and manners of death made her a good resource, though not everyone was pleased about it.

Reluctantly, Aleksei had taken her along. He watched her as she examined the girl's body. There was little blood left, but the scent of fresh death was heavy on the air. The long grasses around the body were flattened and crushed. The local magistrate, Ivan Jarek, was Cezar's brother, and had heard positive comments about Gillian from him. He was more than willing to let her take a look at the body.

Aleksei was furious. Gillian watched his entire body coil with anger as he reviewed the scene. The heat her empathy read from him was palpable, and she had to fight down panic as her own stomach roiled from the effects of his rage. Even a young Vampire could project emotion like a beacon, but one who was hundreds of years old, like Aleksei, was power personified on a good day. Now, with his raw, hot fury spilling over her aura, he was positively frightening. Children under eighteen years were forbidden to be considered as prey of any kind and certainly not meant as a lover for a Vampire or any Paramortal. The girl had been seventeen with a full life ahead of her. She should not have been Vampire fodder. When he discovered the beings responsible, there would be hell to pay.

There wasn't a lot Gillian could do in the field—she wasn't a crime scene investigator, didn't do lab work, wouldn't solve the crime; but she could do a down-and-dirty investigation on site and give her immediate impressions of the scene, the victim and probable cause. Her knowledge of sexual predators was informative to Ivan and raised more than a few eyebrows, including Aleksei's. Thinking about Gillian having to possibly face down a true monster who fed on fear, power and control, sent ice through his veins.

Watching her as she calmly and methodically explained

what she had determined after examining the body and why, he was taken in by her natural ability to command authority and respect. She was in her element, comfortable in the role she was filling. He admired her calm and assured presence. Gillian's gift made others feel at ease, and the local chauvinists responded. The region they were in was rather isolated, as were most of the villages in Romania. Old traditions, beliefs and customs rarely completely died out. Women and children were precious, to be protected, cherished, not sent out into the ugliness of either the Human world or the paranormal realm. And never, ever to be on the front lines of a conflict.

Being witness to the assertion of her naturally dynamic personality, watching as the police officer's faces went from skepticism to respect, brought pride in her to the forefront of his feelings. Mentally he shook himself. Capable or not, soldier or not, she was still deserving of his most diligent protection, and she would receive it. Like it or no. He could not pursue her as a lover for another six months; then he would no longer be deterred. The clock was ticking on Gillian's oath. She would be alive at the end of that time frame if he had to lock her in the castle tower. War or no war, they would see that particular situation through.

"Aleksei . . . *hey!* Phase back in will you?" Gillian's dulcet tones crackled through his consciousness.

She snapped her fingers irritably under his nose. Petre Florescu and Ivan Jarek were with her. "Tell them what you're going to do," she ordered him.

Imperious little thing. He gave her a look clearly designed to intimidate her. She glared right back, a slight frown creasing her perfect brow, not budging an inch. Brat.

Every effort would be made to find the perpetrators, Aleksei assured Mayor Petre Florescu. He would deal with them personally. Watching the expression in those cold, ice-gray eyes, the Mayor had no doubt that justice would be done. The village inhabitants would be as safe as Aleksei could keep them. Taking their leave, Aleksei kept Gillian with him and spoke personally to several of the Vampires in the community. All happily agreed to continue to keep watch and discretely obtain information. They would pass on the request to known affiliates of Aleksei and Tanis. None had any information about the rogue or group that had perpetrated the attack.

Establishing the local Vampires who answered to him as

guards had been necessary for several reasons. Aleksei didn't want any of them hunted down and killed by an overzealous populace. Along with the Lycanthropes, they were the first and best defense to guard against Dracula's infiltration and they needed the network.

With the staked Lycanthrope the night of Tanis's disappearance, and now the girl's death, came the removal of any false sense of security they all had held on to. Fortunately the village of Sacele was indebted many times over to the Rachlav clan and trusted Aleksei to do the best he could do.

Most of them knew that he and his brother had been reborn. That their governing Count was a Vampire did not dissuade them from trust. Neither Aleksei nor Tanis, or even the Egyptians, normally fed locally. With the new issues of Dracula being a very real and deadly presence, the village held a meeting that very night.

Mayor Florescu reminded them that their town had been safe, free of Nosferatu, rogue Lycanthropes or philandering Fey for centuries. Surely they owed the Rachlavs more than their loyalty. A vote was taken and the Mayor himself delivered a formal notice to Rachlav Castle the following evening.

Your family has kept us safe, well and prosperous for a very long time, yet you have never fed here. Our citizens work for you, yet you keep very little of what you earn. Instead, you invest most of what you could call your own back into our community.

You do much for us, Count Rachlav, you and your brother when he is here. Now we know that you are in trouble. We know that your family and friends are threatened, as we all are. With respect for your position as our beloved Count, we the citizens of Sacele wish to make you an offer.

Contained with this note is a list. The list is of men and women, all of age, that would willingly donate blood to you and your loyal friends. We do not make this offer in fear. We do not make it to encourage you to do more for us. We make it because you have been loyal and generous to us and our families through the years. We are in your debt and you have our gratitude. If you need, we will provide.

It was signed, "The citizens of Sacele," notarized by the Mayor, Chief of Police and the Village Council.

A single blood-tinged tear ran from Aleksei's eye, and he had to swallow past the lump in his throat. To say he was touched was an understatement.

Mayor Florescu waited patiently, not wanting to interrupt the Count's thoughts, but he knew Aleksei was humbled. Gillian stood next to him, the Glock now openly worn on her hip in its familiar holster and position. She was wondering what the document said. It was in Romanian, so she'd have to wait for Aleksei to translate. Turned out, she didn't wait long.

When he could trust his voice, he looked at the Mayor of his town, there alone, trusting him. Clearing his throat past the lump in it, he began. "Petre." He used the Mayor's first name intentionally.

The selfless gift the villagers offered warranted acknowledgement. "Please thank them for their offer. I am humbled and honored that you all think so highly of me and mine that you would make this gesture."

Petre Florescu had been nervous about coming to the castle alone, but watching Aleksei's extraordinarily handsome face suffused with emotion, he knew they had done the right thing. "We want nothing to happen to you, Lord Aleksei. If you cannot leave the area to feed, you will die. We do not wish to lose you or your brother. The village, they would not accept another count in your place. If you are at war, then so are we, whether we wish it or not."

"I am stunned by this document, Petre. I had no idea we were so well thought of. However, please tell them that unless the need is very dire, none who are loyal to me shall feed in this village." He extended his hand, which Petre took in a firm grip.

"They knew that you would refuse, so everyone listed is putting some form of wolf on their home or at their gate, to let you know you are welcome." He shook Aleksei's hand. "Good evening, Count Rachlav. I hope that we will see more of you in the village soon." Mayor Florescu took his leave. Aleksei mentally signaled Cezar, and a Lycanthrope shadowed Petre until he reached his home unharmed.

Aleksei tucked the document under the blotter on his desk. He wouldn't take advantage of its terms, but he couldn't bear to throw away something that came from the hearts of his people. He was still amazed at the courage and warmth it had taken for the largely Human village to make such an offer.

"Wow." Gillian's voice at his elbow interrupted his thoughts.

" 'Wow'? I do not understand, *piccola*." Aleksei's puzzlement was evident as he tilted his head to look down at her.

She ignored the fact that he was over a foot and a half taller than she was. That and broad-shouldered, heavily muscled, narrow-waisted, gorgeous eyes . . . yeesh. His scent from the close proximity touched her nostrils. Masculine, warm, spicy, comforting, like cardamom and nutmeg. It was all she could do not to reach out and run her hands down his corded arms, bury her face against his inviting chest.

"Yeah, 'wow.' I am duly impressed with the love and loyalty you command from your village, Aleksei. It takes a very special Vampire to hold that sort of loyalty. Hell, it would take a special Human. I'm impressed."

Her head was cocked to the side as she looked up at him. She was so small and adorable. A muleheaded pain in the ass, but adorable. And much too close. The mere nearness of her, her scent of sunlight, snow and clover meadow; the delicate touch of her empathy shimmering across his power made his heart slam in his chest and his body tighten in response.

Fangs pressed against the tissues of his mouth, trying to descend as his groin was beginning to swell; both areas demanding him to penetrate and sample her. Now was not yet the time. He straightened and stepped back, leaning against the desk and folding his arms across his broad chest, iron control in place once more.

A slight smile curved his sensual mouth. "I have impressed the *piccola capitana*. Now it is my turn to be impressed. I know that you are not easily influenced in your opinions, *piccola*." He was laughing at her, she just knew it. His ice-gray eyes were iridescent, sparkling in the light of the library, clearly amused.

"No, I'm not. But I am willing to concede when I discover something that is by its very nature astonishing. Humans just don't completely accept Vampires like that, no matter how open-minded they claim to be. I am impressed, Aleksei. It tells me a lot about you to see concrete proof of how well you are loved by these people."

A glimmer of awe had crept into her voice. She knew more about him than any other being on Earth but this did surprise her. Unconscious pride in him rose up and was hastily put down again. She couldn't afford to think of him in any way but as a protector and benefactor at the moment.

Catching her thoughts, and being touched by them, Aleksei

chuckled. "It might be better, *piccola guerriera*, if you think of me as your keeper for the time being. You need looking after."

His comment should have pissed her off, but it didn't. His smile was magical and his voice warm and full of teasing mirth.

"Shithead, stay the hell out of my mind until you're invited." She grinned as she took a halfhearted cuff at him, then went to find Maeti for fencing.

His rich laughter followed her down the hallway. The warmth she had felt being near him faded along with the sound of his voice the farther she went from the library.

CHAPTER
20

ALEKSEI was impressive on a lot of levels, Gill thought as she changed into quilted fencing jacket, tight pants and soft, pigskin thigh-high boots. She was impressed she hadn't killed him yet. He was Old-World elegance, mystique, intrigue and temperament in a very tall, muscular, breathtaking package. Bossy, domineering and chauvinistic too. Oh well, no one is perfect.

Having none of Tanis's arrogance made him rather attractive indeed. Aleksei didn't need to be arrogant. He was power personified. When he entered a room or brushed the edge of her senses, she noticed. Tingles went through her when he was near. Vampiric power of his caliber made her empathy flare but this was different. This was warm, stimulating power from him. Maybe it was just in response to her. *Nah.*

She also noticed that as enlightened as Aleksei and the Egyptian Vampires claimed to be, they were hundreds and thousands of years older than she was and had very strong opinions about a number of issues. The men treated Gillian as if she were a china doll, absolute in their determination to keep her safe and alive. Sekhmet and Maeti were almost as bad as the males. They tended to treat Gillian as a favored little sister. Drove her nuts.

Point blank, she simply was not as powerful, experienced nor invincible as she wanted to be under the circumstances. Time as a battle-hardened captain in the United States Marine Corps had honed her body; her doctorate in psychology and position as a field operative had honed her mind and attitude to an edge that none of the Vampires had ever encountered in a Human female. They simply didn't have much exposure to Humans except as prey. She was opening up new windows of understanding for them as well.

Gillian was a no-nonsense woman in a world of bullshit. Normally she kicked ass and took names. When she chose to become a professional psychologist, combining that career with being a field operative, she'd put a very firm leash on her inner beast, needing to keep her own dynamic personality clamped down in favor of her patients' needs and the clandestine requirements of her missions.

Every so often, her own deep-rooted need for independence and individuality reared its head. Tactically, in the Human realm and most paranormal situations, she could protect herself. In the Vampires' world, she had a target painted on her back and she resented the hell out of it. Her iron will and Aleksei's continued to clash over matters of her ability to protect herself. Gillian did not seek out danger or trouble; she wasn't stupid nor was she so determined to be right that she had to prove herself by flaunting caution. She knew her capabilities in Human terms. She was learning about them in the paranormal universe. No, Gillian didn't actively seek dangerous situations. She was a magnet for them.

One night, several weeks after Tanis's disappearance and the two murders, Gillian was feeling especially claustrophobic from the constant vigilance of the Vampires and slipped out alone. The pack patrolled the property, Aleksei's Vampires were about and she planned on staying within close proximity to the castle.

Needing alone time and to walk without an escort became central to her thoughts. Getting outside was easy; staying outside was another matter. If she got caught outside alone . . . well, she didn't want to dwell on that thought. Feeling like a naughty child, she skulked through the trees on her way to a peaceful waterfall near Rachlav Castle, staying on the grass or exposed earth of the forest floor, careful not to make noise.

Her breath clouded lightly in the air in front of her. It was still cool in Romania, even in the late spring. The forest was filled with the scents and sounds of the night. Owls hooted, far-away animals rustled, the pine and the rich forest loam assailed her senses, bringing a sense of wildness to her. Giving in to the feeling, she ran through the trees into the darkness.

The night was clear, lovely, and Gillian sat on a huge boulder under the shining moon, smoking. The Glock was on her hip, loaded with silver-tipped bullets. Downwind from the spray of the waterfall, the light mist settled on her hair and clothes, blanketing her in a sparkling shimmer from the light of the moon. It was a tranquil setting right out of a fairy tale. Listening to the rush of the water calmed her whirling thoughts. Used to being in control of herself and her environment, she chafed under the restrictions placed on her. She was a marine, dammit. She didn't need a keeper or a babysitter. It went against her grain.

Suddenly, the crystal-clear air was oppressive. She stiffened and broadened her spectrum of feeling to try to pinpoint whatever it was. Climbing off the boulder slowly, crushing out the cigarette and stuffing the butt in her pocket while keeping the mountain at her back, she drew the gun, which already had a shell jacked into the chamber. Edging slowly toward the waterfall, she shut her mind down to a perfect blank. The only thing registering in her thoughts was what she saw as she scanned with total calm and an icy resolve. It was a place she went to when she faced life-or-death situations. In kill or be killed, Gillian was the killer. She'd been trained as a sniper and had been good at it. Her ability to separate her emotions and thoughts had made her deadly at her craft. The air grew heavier—the only thing she could think of was evil. It felt evil. Something was hunting. It didn't have her on its radar yet, but it had felt her in the forest or smelled the smoke and was hunting her. What it didn't know was the tables were about to be turned.

She backed up to the water's edge and kept going, her eyes never leaving the area that her senses were pinpointing. The icy water filled her boots and her back was becoming soaked from the chilly falls, but she was too focused to notice. Gillian knew that most waterfalls had a depression or cave behind them, and that was where she was going. It would either be easily defended or a trap. She was betting on the easy-to-defend angle. The Glock was all but waterproof, one of the finest guns on the planet, so she didn't worry about it jamming. Step by careful step, she backed into the falls and, feeling behind her, found a deep enough depression to stand in fully. The waterfall curtained the opening completely. Whatever was out there was getting closer, but it still couldn't find her. Her presence was masked by the noise of the falls and the water itself.

It never occurred to her at that point to call for help. The thing was close, and she didn't want to risk anyone's life who might come to find her. She kept her mind blank except for what she could see. A shadow entered her field of vision near the edge of the pond and she stepped back into the falls to look through the crystal veil. Evil. The person, thing, whatever it was, felt evil. Fear started to crawl in her gut and she shoved it aside, replacing it again with icy calm. It may not be hunting her on a personal level, but it was hunting tonight.

The dark thing waited by the water's edge about twenty yards away. It seemed to be checking the very air, the edges of its outline curiously blurred. Its gait was wrong, the knees seemed to bend the wrong direction. It walked upright, though hunched over, but seemed neither Human nor animal. Gillian had no idea how long it stood there or how long she remained motionless with the cold water beating on her head and body. Finally it turned toward the location of the village and started off. Its path would take it within ten yards of her; Gillian leveled the gun at its head. Seconds ticked by and her finger tightened on the trigger.

She knew it wasn't Human; it felt wrong. It damn sure wasn't one of Aleksei's Vampires or wolves, she would have recognized them or they would have called out to her from recognition of her scent. Taking a shallow breath and letting it out, Gillian let her instincts take over. "No hurry, no worry," had been drilled into her by her sniper instructor. It turned its head, looking behind it, and its face was illuminated fully by the moon. A snub nose and glowing eyes were surrounded by fur; long, upright, tufted ears stood out in the fall of hair around its face. Wicked-looking fangs gleamed white in the moonlight. She recognized it for what it was then: Lycanthrope. It looked like a demonic lynx, except lynxes didn't get that big. Praying that the old legends were true and that a .40-caliber silver-point bullet would be enough, she continued to aim.

Nerves of iron held her from panic. Every instinct told her to run, but she knew she'd garner a personal appointment with death if she attracted its attention. It would be on her before she made it fifty yards. Dying wet and cold in the moonlight, shredded by those teeth, wasn't really on Gill's agenda at that moment, making her very determined to win this round.

The creature had scented her, wanted her fear, was projecting it, but she'd be damned and dead before she'd give the thing that satisfaction. Sighting down the barrel, she pinpointed a dark eye and finished the squeeze on the trigger with a release of her breath. The noise was titanic in the small depression as the powerful handgun went off, the bullet going straight into the eye and brain of the Werelynx and nearly deafening her. Gillian erupted out of the falls and put two more rounds in its head, exploding it like a melon before it hit the ground.

Only then did she send out a mental broadcast for help, hoping someone would hear her. Then she noticed how cold she was, standing there, soaked through in the chill air. She needed to make sure the damn thing wouldn't rejuvenate, though she doubted even a Lycanthrope could survive having its head exploded by .40-caliber silver bullets. She had a curious urge to throw one of those bullets on the ground near the body, a la the Lone Ranger, but thought better of it. Anything with her scent could be used to track her.

She watched the body warily. Having discovered so many "known facts" to be in error recently, she didn't want to take the chance that it might rise again. The body smelled feral, wild, the scent of blood almost overpowering this close.

Someone heard her all right. Powerful arms encircled her and swept her up. Startled, but feeling that whoever held her wasn't evil, she turned to gaze into the cerulean blue eyes of a gloriously attractive Vampire. Raven hair swirled around his face in the night wind, contrasting beautifully with the amazing eyes that still held her gaze. He had a single platinum earring in his left ear, she observed as her eyes traveled over his heartbreakingly beautiful face.

Gillian felt his power like an electric current flowing over her. It raised every hair on her body. Said Vampire held her easily in one arm, made a fist, opened it and a fireball shot from his fingers, hitting the Werelynx's body and incinerating it. Gillian was speechless. Regular Vampires couldn't do that. Did that make him irregular? Thinking too much again. Aleksei was going to kill her.

"I will return you to Aleksei, *deliciae*." He chuckled with an accent that sounded . . . Greek? "Killing you is not on his mind right now, I assure you."

Dammit, did they *all* have to sound like that? Not to mention that Studs "R" Us factor. The only other Vampire that she'd met that rivaled the beauty of the one now carrying her swiftly through the forest had been Osiris. He was almost god-like in his beauty. Greek. God. Uh-oh.

"Dionysus?" she asked tentatively, her teeth chattering from the cold.

The cerulean blue eyes rotated; he never broke stride. "Aleksei will introduce us, I am sure, but you are correct."

It was a statement. He was reading her easily. Gillian barely felt the brush of his mind on hers. His power was another matter, it was crawling over her and making her skin tingle despite being chilled to the bone. His scent was different from Aleksei's, sharper, crisper, an undertone of pine and ginger, but very masculine and warm.

"I can walk, you know," she groused.

"I am faster."

Touché, Dionysus. Okay, so she'd be carried to her sacrifice. Lines from Plutarch, "With your shield or on it," came to her mind. He laughed, deep and ebullient at her thought, following the mental path back to its origins.

"A little thing like you should not be wandering around unattended. For a former soldier, you are incredibly undisciplined." Gill flinched at the reprimand. Gods, she hated it when older Vampires read her so easily.

Any retort she had to that was silenced when he arched a brow at her as they entered the castle yard. Cezar walked up and greeted the Greek god. "It is good to see you, Dionysus. Far too long have you been away and silent."

Said amiably, but the admonishment was clear. She had to love Cezar. He was absolutely loyal to Aleksei. Speaking of whom, he was striding toward them; she could feel his displeasure from where they were. Dionysus had swung her down, setting her on her feet next to him, looking down at her from a monumental height. Yup, he was tall too.

Aleksei had greeted the Greek lord, then taken Gillian inside for a little heart-to-heart talk and to dry off in front of the massive fireplace. He produced a blanket from somewhere, wrapped it around Gillian's shivering shoulders and escorted her inside. There, the nobly born, iron-willed, genteel, chauvinistic, Old-World Vampire and the opinionated, liberated, feminist Marine were having issues with the subjective topic of

Gillian being able to handle a preternatural threat alone, or Sexism in Survival Situations 101.

He wasn't pleased with her little nocturnal adventure and said so. Gillian growled right back at him. Aleksei was growing firmer in his resolve to do something about her attitude and told her as much. He paced behind her angrily while she defrosted, his scent more comforting than Dionysus's, making her feel safe despite his male posturing.

She pointed out that she hadn't received a scratch and had used Human techniques for staying alive. The look he shot her would have melted metal and he bit back a sharp reprimand. Gillian had the decency to look contrite. Shivery and a little blue, but contrite.

Actually, Aleksei was impressed that she'd taken out a Were-lynx and not yelled for help. Lycanthropes were nothing to toy with. Faster than a Human, almost as fast as a Vampire, they could disembowel a careless hunter in the blink of an eye. Realistically, he was horrified by what could have happened. If she had missed on her first shot, she would be dead now. There was very little fear in her when she was directly threatened, and he was awed by her stalwart nature. He hoped it wouldn't get her killed.

Knowing that she was no worse for wear, Aleksei sank into his chair, rubbing his forehead with long, elegant fingers. He had beautiful, artistic hands, she noticed with a jolt as she watched his almost Human reaction to stress. Clean, trimmed nails, aristocratic hands, but carrying enough power to crush a coin in his fist, bend an I-bar like butter or lift a car like it was a bale of hay. He couldn't possibly have a headache, but watching him demonstrate what had to be a simple leftover Human habit was intriguing.

"Gillian," he said tiredly, "promise me that you will not go off without telling one of us again." She started to protest but he waved her off. "No, I will have your promise. You may wander anywhere you like, in or out of my home, but you must tell someone." Sitting up, he steepled his fingers and pinned her with his eyes. "I only ask for common courtesy, *piccola*."

"Fine." Gillian was being agreeable. That was a bad sign, he could tell already.

"I rejoice." His tone was just as flat, eliciting an arched eyebrow from her. His gaze shifted down her small, somewhat damp form and his breath hissed between his teeth. The chill had hardened her nipples, making them clearly defined against her tight sweater. He wanted to drag her against him, strip those wet clothes off and warm her on the bearskin rug with his body.

"Go change, you are still cold," he ordered her. He had to get her out of there before his desire overcame his good sense. The scent of her damp heat was radiating from the fire's warmth.

"Fine." She turned to leave, dropping the blanket behind her, giving Aleksei a view of her curvy bottom in the still damp, tight pants and the fact that there was no pantie line. He looked away quickly.

Heading for the door, she pulled up short at his voice. "I am very proud of you, Gillian. Not many Humans would have had the courage to do what you did. You are extraordinarily capable."

She paused for a heartbeat. "Thank you, Aleksei. I appreciate you noticing." His little admission warmed her heart. Maybe he was learning. Smart Vampire.

He watched her leave, the cold grip on his stomach easing a little but battling it out with the heat pooled in his groin. The intensity of his reaction to her surprised him every time. She pushed him to the edge of his control time and again with her independent nature. Modern women. He wasn't sure if he should be pleased or annoyed by Gillian's ability to avoid being an entrée for a rogue Werelynx. Learning to trust her judgment was going to age him centuries. Not locking her up for her own safety was warring with his desire to protect her. Maybe she didn't need him after all. Worse, maybe she didn't want him. Nah. He couldn't be that wrong.

CHAPTER
21

"SHE is a handful, Aleksei. I do not envy you." Dionysus laughed openly, drawing a groan from Aleksei and a bemused snort from Cezar. The Greek god strode in, seating himself on the couch. Cezar remained near the door, but was fully part of the conference.

Inexplicably feeling the need to defend Gillian, Aleksei's response was sharper than he intended. "She is remarkable, Dionysus. I know of no other Human that is as capable as she, nor as courageous."

Cerulean eyes widened. "My apologies, Aleksei. I did not realize you cared for her as well. I will refrain from further commentary except to state that you have the patience of a Christian saint. I would not be so forgiving. Your *piccola principessa* is spirited and lovely. I wish you well."

Listening to the exchange, Cezar was amused. Dionysus, if anything, was more opinionated than Aleksei, Tanis, Osiris or Anubis on the role of a young female, particularly *piccola principessa* Gillian. Aleksei was warring intellectually with every instinct he had.

Vampires mated for life, whether their love remained Human or was reborn, they were loyal and protective to their chosen. The non-Dracula variety, anyway. Predatory and inherently dangerous by nature, the males were overwhelmed with the enhanced emotions and increased physical sensations the change wrought in them. It took them years to assess and integrate their newfound passions. They loved wholly and completely when they loved, protecting their women and cherishing them. The younger males were more "modern" in their thinking but remained hopelessly snarly when it came to the safety of a female that was under their protection.

Their females, whether Human or Vampire, were quite capable of killing if necessary, in particular the reborn ones. There was no difference in being a predator between male or female. By virtue of size and sheer muscle mass alone, most of the males were unparalleled in strength, but were unfailingly gentle with those they cared for, whether family or friend. They were also completely unreasonable and resistant to changes in attitude and learned behavior. A Vampire tended to stubbornly retain the bias and beliefs of the age in which they had been created. Aleksei was no different.

The fact that Gillian had not raised Aleksei's ire more than she had already was nothing short of a miracle. Cezar had spoken with Aleksei on more than one occasion, listening to his friend as he vented about Gillian's feminist attitude and her former occupation as a soldier. Aleksei, like Tanis, thought in terms of race, age, gender and size. Gill was Human, she was young (to them), female and she was small. Those traits meant that she needed looking after and protecting.

Neither were above disciplining her if necessary, as Tanis had already proven and Aleksei had come close to enforcing. Cezar didn't want to be anywhere around if Gillian truly pushed Aleksei over whatever line would force him to take action. She would be in for an immediate and abrupt discourse in Vampire protective genetic traits. Aleksei would view it as necessary to get her attention. Gillian would view it as bullying. If it came to that, Aleksei had better disarm her first if he didn't want a ventilated ribcage, because she just might shoot him.

Gillian was of the unwavering opinion that while protection is sometimes necessary and comforting, she was capable and adaptive; not needing constant observation or coddling. Cooperating with this entire situation set her teeth on edge but she would do it. She'd given her word after all. Didn't mean she had to like it.

Keeping busy with a few new local clients served to keep Gillian and Aleksei out of each other's hair. Dante was ready for discharge, but he made her promise that she would check up on him occasionally. With his history of temper tantrums, Gillian arranged to have "maintenance visits" with him, once a month for the next four months, to make sure he didn't regress. Not knowing how long she'd be in the country, or how long she'd remain in danger, she decided it was a safe time frame. If all hell stopped breaking loose, she could leave and still return monthly to check on Dante.

She continued to have the strange and erotic dreams whenever she slept. Often waking with the sheets tousled and damp, her body clenching in the aftermath of an incredible orgasm, but feeling empty. She attributed it to missing the regular diet of fabulous sex she'd been getting from Tanis.

The younger Rachlav had not yet been found and hope was growing slim that he was still alive. No one had stopped searching or looking for him. Alive or truly dead, Aleksei was determined to discover the whereabouts or fate of his brother. Gillian wanted to do more investigating during the day, but Aleksei absolutely forbade it. Dracula was definitely a presence and they had no way of knowing who might be a Daywalker servant of his. Gillian would not be doing any investigating or anything else alone. End of discussion.

The IPPA and the Corps backed him up on that in a strongly worded e-mail to Gillian and a phone call from Dr. Gerhardt, her friend and mentor at the organization. Bastards. All of them.

As time and the weeks crawled by, Gillian and Maeti amused themselves by staging sword bouts. Gill had fenced in college, kept it up as a hobby and was damn good with a rapier, epée, side sword and foil. Being a personal guard to the Vampire Goddess Isis, Maeti had some skills of her own. She showed Gillian the finer points of Roman short-sword combat.

Both of them wound up bruised, sweating and laughing amid the clatter of blades and lack of protective equipment. The Vampiress didn't need a protective vest since there was little the Human could do to permanently damage her—Gill didn't wear one, trusting Maeti's skill not to vivisect her during a match, and to control herself should she manage to knick the Human accidentally. Maeti generally won. Vampires had unbelievable dexterity, rivaling Elves', and a Human really had little chance against one of them in a fight. Still, it honed Gillian's skill to fence with a Vampire, and she grew more adept as time passed from the nightly bouts.

Getting drawn into mindless routine is one of the fringe benefits of being under paranormal siege. Hating that she was becoming a person who was filling time, Gillian forced herself to change
her habitual pattern. She tried drinking decaffeinated coffee and
soda for a few days, thinking the stimulant had her nerves on
edge. After a week of feeling like she had mono, she gave that up,
appreciating the chemical benefits of imported French lattes in
the evening and upon arising. Smoking was still part of her
regime, though she noticed she was going through fewer ciga-
rettes than she normally would. Probably due to not being able to
just sit and relax in the proximity of pending doom.

When she woke late one afternoon, she had a message from
Arkady Boganskaya. Dante wanted to speak to her; it was urgent, would she please come? Notifying him she would and
leaving word with Pavel, the Werewolf of Cezar's pack that she
was seeing for his psychosomatic fur allergy and post-traumatic
stress disorder, she went to greet her ghostly patient.

Dante had news for her. He had learned that a high-ranking
Vampire named Tanis Rachlav had been kidnapped by Dracula's forces, rather than killed outright. He saw recognition of
the name in her eyes and jealousy flared in him, bright and hot.
So, that was the man who had been instrumental in distracting
her. Dante's eyes narrowed imperceptibly as he felt her aura
shift with concern for her lover.

The Ghost had discovered that, as he healed emotionally, he
was able to leave his place of haunting for brief periods. He had
followed her to both the cabin and castle where she'd been staying, visiting her in her dreams. Haunting her erotically, making
love to her as she slept, Dante had satisfied his own centuries of
need on her body, pleasuring her as well. She had no idea he
was the source of those dreams—she suspected they were of
her lover. They were, he thought. Her Italian Ghost lover.

Memory of those visits stirred him, bringing his form into
solid, hardened reality as he thought of sliding into creamy heat
while she slept. Gillian wasn't paying much attention. Dante
formed and dissolved in front of her frequently. Unobtrusively,
he lowered his hands, clasping them in front of his groin. The
lace cuffs on his shirt draped down over the front of his tight
pants, helping to hide the evidence of his arousal from her, not
that she was noticing at the moment.

"Where did they take him, Dante? Can you find out for me?
Please?" she added.

Letting none of his own emotion come through in his eyes, Dante readily agreed. "Of course, *dolcezza*. I will find out what I can and inform you soon."

"Thank you. I appreciate it and I know his family will as well." Gillian, for the first time, offered Dante her hand, rather than him simply taking it.

His eyes never left her face as he gently took her hand in both of his. They were firm and warm, but she was used to Dante's contradictions and it no longer spooked her.

Completely serious for once, he told her, "*Dolcezza* . . . Gillian, I will do what I can to find your lover. I appreciate and respect what you have done for me. I have found freedom as I have never known, thanks to you. It is the least I can do for you, *cara*. Perhaps I may assist in his recovery as well."

"Thank you, Dante. I will let you know." Hurrying off, she couldn't wait until Aleksei rose that night to tell him what she'd learned. It wouldn't occur to her until later that Dante had used the term *lover* in reference to Tanis and she hadn't contradicted him. The Ghost hadn't missed that point either, and it rankled him deeply.

Dante watched her practically run from the hallway, leaving her fresh fragrance behind her. He was hard, aching, furious and jealous. Let her tell whom she would. Whatever he found out, he would relay, to an extent. She would take on the task herself to find her lover, of that he was certain. It would be dangerous, that was also a certainty. What Gillian did not know and could not appreciate was that Dante wanted her: dead or alive. It didn't matter to a Ghost if his girlfriend had a pulse or not, or was a noncorporeal being. What mattered was that Dante was a special Ghost.

A special Ghost with a possessive, jealous streak who was obsessing over his lovely therapist. Dante Montefiore had been Human once; or at least posing as one. What he was, was part Fey. Dark Elf to be exact, known among themselves as the Grael. He was inherently magical and could do a number of things that Ghosts normally had trouble with: complete transubstantiation into a solid form for long periods of time being one of them.

Dante's auburn hair and creamy complexion were from his Human roots, but the stunning icy turquoise crystalline eyes were pure Grael, passed down in diluted blood to him from a great, great grandmother. Dante could not perform magic; Dante *was* magic. It flowed through his spirit as surely as it had flowed through his veins when he was alive. The phenomenal abilities he possessed as a swordsman were due to inherent Elf dexterity. He was unbeatable, because no Human could take even a part Elf in a fair fight where dexterity counted.

The Grael were the dark brethren of the Elf world. Feared, spoken of in whispers, if at all, they were the nightmare sorcerers and assassins of the Fey. Evil was too mild a word for what they were capable of if you pissed one off. Perversely, as bad a rep as the Grael had, they were one of the most extraordinarily beautiful of the all races of the Fey. They possessed skin the shades of which ranged from obsidian black that seemed to absorb any light, to shimmering moonlight silver, which glowed under the light of the stars, all beautiful like the Grael themselves. Their hair was typically crystalline white, flowing over their shoulders like silken ice; eyes either sparkling white or varying shades of frosty, glacial blue, faceted like gemstones and iridescent. Their tall, unearthly beauty was heartbreakingly lovely to both Humans or other Fey but was combined with a frigid, sometimes lawfully evil soul.

The Dark Elves were nothing to be trifled with. They could make the average serial killer look like a rank amateur when provoked. Other Fey avoided them almost pathologically, going miles out of their way to avoid a Grael-settled area. Skilled assassins, their abilities with lethal weapons were truly alarming. Their weapons of choice were the garrote—a nasty, thin, razor sharp wire that could strangle or decapitate—a recurved short bow and a curious blade that was a cross between a stiletto and throwing knife. All killed silently, as did the Grael. Serrated-edge swords were worn but rarely used, except in all-out war. Blades clanging made too much noise otherwise.

Those in their midst who chose the path of magic were revered as much as they were feared. Outcasts among their own kind, the Dark Elves formed small colonies, the males solitary and vicious, the females beguiling and nefarious; coming together only against a common enemy, otherwise keeping well away from each other except for breeding and ceremonial rights. Once in awhile, a male Grael might take an exceptional Human female as a paramour or concubine. Dante's distant relative had been such a female. Their blood had suffused his veins and cells. Their inbred magic had made him what he was: a dangerous, transubstantiated, egotistical, magical Ghost with a strong taste for the needs of the flesh and an ego to match. During his life-time, his astonishing natural beauty and charisma had kept the need to reach for his own magical essence at bay.

Death had brought him fully into touch with his Dark Elf side. Dante had very little morals while he lived. Honorable as he had been on the dueling field, he was conversely ruthless and obsessed in his personal life. When Dante had wanted a woman, he got her, used her, moved on. He had been a rake and a light-hearted rogue in life. Being murdered, traumatized and pissed off for six hundred years had made him into something else.

CHAPTER
22

GILLIAN was positively bouncing when Aleksei strode into
the room upon arising. Anubis, Sekhmet and Dionysus followed him in. "I have something marvelous to tell you, Aleksei!
I can't tell you where I got the information, but I can tell you
that Tanis was taken alive."

Silvery light shone from Aleksei's eyes as he spun toward
her, grasped her shoulders, searching her face to determine if
he'd heard her correctly. "Truly, *piccola*? My brother lives?"

"Yes!" Gillian shrieked, completely forgetting herself for a
moment and throwing her arms around his chest as that was as
high as she could reach.

As her arms contracted around his solid mass, her hands
rubbed his back gently, feeling the lean, powerfully corded
muscles there. Aleksei's heart slammed hard as her small body
pressed against him. He pulled her close, lowering his head to
kiss the top of her hair, inhaling the scent of sunlit, snow-
covered meadows and clover. She was alive and warm in his
arms. It made the hurt less that Gillian was terribly excited
about it too. If she and his brother truly loved each other, he
would not interfere.

"May I know where the information came from, little warrior?" Sekhmet's soft voice pried into their hearing.

Gillian pulled back from Aleksei a little reluctantly. "I can't tell you, Sekhmet. Truly I can't. I can tell you that I should have more information soon and that I will let you all know immediately."

Moving—no, *gliding*—across the floor, Dionysus came forward. "I do not understand why you cannot reveal your source, *deliciae*. We are your friends, after all. Why may we not know?"

The Greek Vampire Lord had been a sporadic visitor since his rescue of Gillian and had apparently just returned.

Aleksei tried to put his arm protectively over Gillian's shoulders, but she knocked his hand away. "I can't. You will just have to accept that." She could face this without Aleksei's help.

Temper, temper, brave but incredibly stupid piccola guerriera, Aleksei thought. Fortunately Gillian couldn't hear him unless he wished it as she faced down Dionysus without flinching.

He loomed over her, dwarfing her with his greater bulk, cerulean eyes boring into hers. "You are very brave and very demanding for such a little female. Aleksei may yet need to take you in hand." The reprimand was clear. Gillian drew a breath to verbally blast him, but was interrupted.

"She cannot tell you, Noble One, she is bound by honor and oath." Maeti swayed into the room, her black hair hanging free, sky-blue eyes piercing and stepped in front of Gillian.

Dionysus seemed to have forgotten how to breathe for a moment when she entered. With his abrupt comings and goings the Greek Vampire had not yet met all the residents of Rachlav Castle. Gillian watched his clear blue eyes rake Maeti's tall, slender form, his eyebrows rising appreciatively. Maeti blushed under his scrutiny, dropping her eyes for a moment, then lifting them to lock onto his penetrating gaze. Gillian didn't know Vampires could blush. *Well, damn. Learn something new every day.*

"Explain." It wasn't a request.

"She is a healer of the minds of our kind, noble Lord. She cannot reveal her source because it is one whom she helps. To do so would be to violate her oath of confidentiality. Gillian will tell more when she knows more." Her voice was sweet and beautiful and Dionysus was visibly affected.

Gillian watched, fascinated as Maeti turned the full power of Vampire seduction on one of her own kind. The raw sexuality in the room was palpable.

The Greek Lord's eyes glowed and he unconsciously reached for Maeti's hand. She did not disappoint him and allowed him to take it. Stepping forward, he lifted her knuckles to his mouth, his eyes never leaving her face. "How do you know this if she cannot say?"

"Because Gillian is honorable and would reveal who told her otherwise."

Damn, the girl was good. Not a shot fired and Dionysus was practically drooling at the Egyptian lady's feet. Gill would have shot him. Oh well. Everyone does things differently.

Later, Anubis and Cezar were deep in conference with Gillian over what to do with any further information she might bring them. Maeti and Dionysus had vanished into the night, still staring at each other, fingers laced together. Aleksei was pacing like a caged tiger, listening to the others talk. Montu and Noph tried to engage him in a game of dice, but he declined. Sekhmet finally grew tired of his pacing and drew him to sit on the couch next to her, patting his hand comfortingly.

Her voice was pitched only for Aleksei's ears, but Anubis heard her through their shared link. "You are worried, my friend, that if Tanis lives he and Gillian will still want each other; that you will have to step aside for your brother's happiness."

Anubis mentally intruded on her observations gently. *"My love, he is not ready to confront this truth you see."*

"He will hear me, because he wants a different truth than the one he is facing, beloved. Now, do be quiet and let me speak to him." She fluffed him off, hearing his warm laughter in her mind.

Harsh lines of worry etched the Count's beautiful face. "I do not wish to interfere with what they both desire and need, Sekhmet. I want my brother back, nonetheless."

Smiling, she brushed light fingers over the back of his hand. "It may be what they wanted for a time, Aleksei, but it is not what both of them need. Tanis's fate lies along a different path. Gillian should be yours and, in some ways, already is." Her black eyes were warm with understanding and she exuded gentleness and caring. Not a bad trick for the goddess of justice and vengeance. Still, she was his friend and trying to help.

"I wish it were true, Sekhmet. I mean no disrespect, but I cannot impose on Gillian now, whether Tanis is found or not." The weight of centuries was in his statement.

"Then do not break her oath, but be there, Aleksei. Stop avoiding her. Be her friend. She could use one, and so could you."

Giving his hand a final press, she rose gracefully in that boneless way only Vampires can and glided over to join her mate, leaving sandalwood and cinnabar in her wake. Anubis moved a muscular bronze arm around her waist and pulled her onto his lap. Sekhmet's arm went around his broad shoulder, and she nuzzled his hair. Watching them, Aleksei felt the void of the empty space next to him. He wanted Gillian's small form in it desperately, but to be her friend would have to do for now.

As if reading his thoughts, Gillian looked up, meeting his silvery eyes with her own green ones. She smiled, her face alit with hope and sheer loveliness, winking at him, making his pulse race, sharing in a wordless nod her hope that Tanis would be rescued. Aleksei sank back into the cushions of the couch, his hand raking through his hair in frustration. What kind of a man was he? His brother was missing—no, *kidnapped*—maybe tortured, maybe dying, and he couldn't get up just yet because watching Gillian smile at him had triggered an aching arousal that was all too obvious under the tight pants he wore.

Cezar bellowed suddenly, startling Aleksei, who had desperately been thinking of something *else* besides what making love with Gillian would feel like.

"Are you out of your mind, girl?" Cezar shoved his chair back and stood, whirling on Gillian, who had also leapt to her feet and was facing down the massive pack leader with a determined gleam in her eye.

Aleksei blurred over the back of the couch, interjecting his large frame between the irritated Werewolf and the obviously put-out Gillian. Anubis flanked him instantly. Cezar growled at both of them.

"You had better talk some sense into the little princess here, Aleksei, or she is going to get herself killed."

"Don't you lecture me, you overgrown rottweiler! You have nothing to say about it, and neither does Aleksei, for that matter. I am going to do something productive instead of sitting here waiting for Tanis's body to be recovered because we didn't get to him fast enough!" Cezar started for her at "rottweiler," but was walled in by several Vampires, as Montu and Noph had joined Aleksei and Anubis in their intervention efforts.

"What the hell is going on?" Silvery eyes pinned her where she stood. "Gillian?" Aleksei grasped her upper arm with his large hand, not allowing her to pull away from him.

"You do something about her, Aleksei. I will not have any of my pack held responsible if she is going to talk like a crazy woman." Cezar didn't bother masking the anger in his voice. The Vampire needed to know how serious his concern was.

Aleksei had never seen the alpha wolf this agitated. "What does he mean, *cara*?" His eyes narrowed dangerously and he stepped into her, crowding her. "Well?" Patience wearing very thin. Okay, she'd talk.

"I told him that when we find out where Tanis is being held, I can call in a friend or two from the service, take a couple of the wolves, maybe one of the Vamps, and we can rescue him fairly quickly." His eyebrows shot up, then down into an intimidating frown, so she hurriedly added, "We have done reconnaissance many times, Aleksei. I am good at what I do and I wouldn't suggest it otherwise. I do not have a death wish and I have no intention of sacrificing myself. This is about getting your brother back, not about grandstanding or my personal feelings in the matter."

Thoughts flew across Aleksei's face and the silvery gray eyes shifted into cold platinum discs, icy with anger. His sensual mouth tightened along with the grip on her upper arm. She felt his anger pour over her as he spoke, raising the hair on her arms and sending a hot tingle down her spine. Gillian didn't pull back because she couldn't pull away. His voice was low, deep, beautiful and full of heated reprimand.

"*No!* Gillian I will not risk you even to save my brother. Do not even think of doing such a thing."

Cezar smirked triumphantly and even Anubis raised a brow.

"*Virgo*, you cannot believe that you would be safe in such an endeavor. We will recover Tanis, but you are not to be risked." Anubis's normal lightheartedness was gone and his obsidian eyes were serious. "You have become our friend, Gillian, Sekhmet's and mine. There is no lesser evil here. You are not more important than Tanis, but neither are you less. This endeavor would be suicide. You cannot think to go."

"I have to think about it. Tanis is my friend as well as yours." Her eyes implored Aleksei but her voice was command-grade USMC, firm and resolved. "No one gets left behind, Aleksei. If Dracula is as bad as you say and he has Tanis, there is no way in hell I am going to stay here, locked in a castle like some helpless heroine in a novel. This is real life. I can help and I intend to. You can forbid me to go, even lock me up, but I will do this. I would rather do it with your help and approval, but I will do this."

It was Aleksei's turn to feel the warm tingle of her anger wash over him, the sheer force of nature that was Gillian Key. Easily reading her thoughts and feelings, he knew nothing would deter her. Fighting down his own fear, anger and instinctive dominance, he turned fully to her, taking her shoulders in both his hands. This close, he loomed above her. He was twice her size and pissed. It took all her intestinal fortitude not to tremble.

Aleksei held her eyes as firmly as he held her before him. She was worried and scared but her gaze never wavered on his and she held her ground. The rest of them drew a collective breath. Defying Aleksei outright was not a good idea. All of them knew the Vampire Count was falling for the little blonde. His instincts were honed by time and need. He'd been a Vampire far longer than he'd been Human and those instincts took precedence. Gillian was baiting a tiger. Everyone waited, Gillian was trying not to quiver from the force of their personalities colliding. Aleksei had gone completely still in a way only a powerful, older Vampire could.

Maybe honesty was way overrated, she thought as she watched his face. Standing in front of him, hearing and feeling the reactions of everyone in the room, discretion being the better part of valor occurred to her. Chess. This was chess, not poker. Bluffing was out. In chess, the best defense is a good offense. Offense was also not a good plan at the moment, seeing Aleksei's frame of mind, but she could work around that. All right, she'd play the cooperative psychologist—for now. Now, how to word it without lying. Lying was a very bad idea with this many older Vampires in the room. Aleksei looked positively thunderous, whether from fear for her or simple anger at her defiance, she couldn't tell.

Reaching a hand up, careful not to try pulling away from his grip, Gillian put her hand lightly on his broad chest, avoiding the open collar of lace and ties; his skin warm beneath the expensive linen. "I know you're only trying to protect me. I just don't want Tanis to die if something can be done." There. That was honest. And she hadn't said a thing.

Though the contact of her hand on his chest shot heat through him, he gave her a look that was not particularly friendly. "That is not the correct response. You will not be doing it, *piccola*." Shit. Smart Vampire. Why couldn't he be cute and stupid instead of gorgeous and intelligent?

"You will remain here, under my protection. You will not attempt to leave to rescue Tanis or there will be hell to pay. Is that clear?" His anger flared his power, ruffling his hair and hers and he shook her lightly. "Do not make me ask you again."

No way was she going to win this argument here right now. Chess later, discretion now. "Crystal clear. I will not leave in an attempt to rescue Tanis. Fine. Have it your way." There. That was almost diplomatic. Immediately, one hand dropped from her, but his eyes were on her face.

"Do not test me in this, Gillian. I will do whatever need be done to keep you safe. We will find my brother, but you will not be involved in the risk." Keeping a tight clamp on his fear and concern, he bit the words out between clenched teeth. She would obey him in this. Or else.

"Fine."

Dammit, she was up to something, he knew it. That was entirely too easy. "Gillian." His fingers tightened on her arm. The warning was clear.

"I said fine."

She spun on her heel and stalked off; he let her go, watching the aggressive way she moved, admiring her strength and spirit. There was a collective easing of tension when she left the room. Turning back, he met Cezar's eye.

"She is not through with this argument, Aleksei." The older alpha growled.

"If she leaves, she will not get far," came the response, chilling everyone's blood with the double meaning.

If Gillian left, she would be in danger from Dracula. Even if Aleksei found her first . . . well, she wouldn't want Aleksei to find her first. Sekhmet and Anubis exchanged a look. Aleksei was clueless as to how to deal with his little blonde problem. Used to leading, making decisions, giving orders and commanding loyalty, he was also stubborn, determined and infinitely more dangerous than the Human female could guess. Gillian was his equal in every way but physical strength and speed. A perfect complement to him with every bit as much determination and courage. Sekhmet had a feeling that the two iron wills and their owners were about to clash.

CHAPTER
23

GILLIAN stormed up to her room, booting the door shut behind her with a resounding hollow bang. She needed help and she needed it fast. The IPPA was out. Dr. Gerhardt would make sure no one assisted her leaving. As far as they were concerned, they were successfully protecting at least two of their people, Gillian and another therapist/operative in Britain, and they would not be amused to know that she was thinking of going on a covert mission. They could discipline her by sanctioning her license or jerking it completely. She didn't want that. Anything she did would have to be completely on her own.

The USMC was out too. Daed Aristophenes would have her head mounted on the wall behind his desk after he spent five or six hours kicking her ass himself. She was an operative with a blown cover—a sitting duck in their eyes. Rescue wasn't needed, but discretion was. As far as the Corps was concerned, she needed to keep her pretty ass right where it was, ride this out and they'd reassign her after everything blew up or blew over.

Maybe not completely. Hmm. Dante. She needed to talk to Dante. Checking her watch, she saw it was late but dialed Boganskaya Castle anyway. Arkady answered. No, it was not too late; they were having a party. Would she like to come? She started to say no, then thought better of it. All right, she'd be there within an hour.

Hanging up, she gathered what she'd need: her backpack, now stuffed with a changes of clothing, her gun, extra magazines of bullets, flashlight, garrote, throwing knife and spine sheath, cell phone and charger, extra battery and plug-in for her laptop and a tiny black book with entries in code. It contained information for contacts that she'd made while in the service. She hadn't used them in years and hoped some were still good.

Dressing and putting on makeup took longer. Gillian rarely dressed up and almost never wore makeup. It added to the illusion of her going to the party. Swiftly braiding her hair, she tossed it impatiently over her shoulder, where it fell in a golden rope down her back, secured by a leather tie. Looking at herself critically in the mirror, she thought she'd pass for an affluent American psychologist.

The dress was nearly sheer. A stunning deep emerald green, it shimmered with gold sparkles, the material light, soft and comfortable. It left her shoulders and arms bare, the sleeves slit from shoulder to wrist bands, the material hanging in a soft drape under her arms. The skirt was short, hitting her mid-thigh, loose enough to run in but tight enough so she wouldn't be embarrassed. On her feet were skimmer slippers dyed to match the dress. Her skin glowed with health and her eyes, ringed in kohl, shone even greener than normal as they reflected the color of the dress. Gods she looked idiotic. Rolling her eyes, at her reflection, she moved to leave.

Grabbing her laptop in its case, she gathered car keys and backpack and marched back to the library. Poking her head in, she called out to the group. "I've been invited to a party at Boganskaya Castle. I'll take one of the wolves with me, Cezar, if that's all right with you. Don't wait up." Backing out, she headed for the front door, trying not to run. She almost made it.

"Gillian." Aleksei's voice was a soft, deep purr, freezing her in her tracks, her back ramrod straight. He circled her like a shark coming around in front, his hand reaching out to almost but not quite skim down her golden braid. Moving around her, his pulse raced, his body clenched with desire and pulsed with raw need. She was an elfin beauty, delicate and winsome but regal and untouchable. He knew she could feel everything radiating from him even without her inherent empathy, and he made no effort to conceal his feelings or his arousal.

"You look lovely."

That voice sent a shiver up her spine and pooled heat in various regions of her body. He'd managed to make her wet and tingly with that one brief sentence. She had a clear, vivid sensation of cool sheets sliding over sensitive heated flesh, of large strong hands caressing, of a thick male arousal poised to penetrate, of bodies intimately intertwined and straining together as ultimate pleasure was achieved. A few more months, then she'd be able to explore everything that voice promised if the offer was still open and they were both still alive.

Goddess, she did not need this right now. His need was beating at her. Anger and desire, passion and heat all in that very tall, scrumptious package. Desperately keeping her eyes on his face and not letting them drift down to the thick, engorged outline laying against his thigh, very emphasized by the tight pants he wore, Gillian tried to keep it light. "Thank you, Aleksei." Her eyes sparkled mischievously. "I clean up all right."

"You are beautiful, *piccola*."

Shit. Damn. Hell. Those ice-gray, silvery eyes should have been cold but they burned with banked fires. Heat followed his gaze as he looked her up and down appreciatively. Breasts ached for his touch and she went creamy with need.

He could scent her desire. She was already wet and slick for him, making his body throb in response, hardening almost to the point of pain. Fangs burst forth inside his mouth as his traitorous body demanded her penetration and claiming. Their mutual need crackled with electricity between them, charging the air with raw sexuality.

She had to get out of there or she'd embarrass herself by leaping on him and riding him until they were both sweaty and exhausted right in the middle of the hallway. Reflexively her legs shifted further apart as he scrutinized her. Just thinking about the length and width of him, his proximity, his scent . . . cardamom and nutmeg . . . pine . . . and her body betrayed her with what it wanted: Aleksei, deep . . . hard . . . inside . . .

"Aleksei, I have to go. Arkady Boganskaya is having a little soiree and I need to show up. I'll be careful, I promise."

Head high, she swept past him and out the door, calling for Pavel as she headed for her car, trembling with passion and a need she couldn't name. The door slammed shut behind her and the young wolf with a hollow finality that echoed in more than just the castle's ancient stones.

Aleksei couldn't move from where she'd left him. If he tried, he would shatter to pieces. He'd watched her eyes dilate, the flush of desire coloring her cheeks, her tongue unconsciously moistening her lips. Her aroused scent hung heavy in the air. When she'd moved her legs apart a little in anticipation . . . her nipples pebbling . . . needing his penetration . . .

Putting out a hand, he leaned on the ancient stones, trying to slow his rioting pulse and calm his breathing. Thank God his pants were tight and held his erection down or he'd have a tenting problem that would not easily be explained to anyone who should find him there, panting against the wall. Moving was a very bad idea. Tight as his pants were, the material would shift over him . . . the slightest brush against his distended flesh right then and he would have exploded like a randy, untried youth in a tidal pulsing flood.

Where the hell was his iron control? He'd caught Gillian's thoughts. Only her honor and oath had kept her from crawling up him and wrapping herself around him like a coat. She'd wanted to ride him, mate with him right there in the hallway. Aleksei's teeth ground together, his hands clenched tightly into white-knuckle fists. He groaned in frustration as he took a few deep breaths, trying to keep himself from spilling inside his velvet pants. Never had he met a Human female with the raw sexuality to rival a Vampire.

So full and focused were his thoughts that he didn't startle at Anubis's voice. "Are you all right, Aleksei?"

"No."

Anubis left him to his torment, chuckling as he led Sekhmet off to relieve their own needs privately.

Pavel had joined Gillian at the car and rode in silence for a while as they drove to Boganskaya Castle. He noticed her aroused scent and knew her dilemma with Aleksei. They'd become friends since the night he'd tried to kill her while under hypnosis while dealing with his psychosomatic allergy to fur. He was young, fairly inexperienced but eager and had the potential to be an Alpha in his own pack one day. Cezar, the current Alpha, was grooming Pavel for that position should anything happen to him. He encouraged the young Lycanthrope's friendship with Gillian, knowing her military expertise would be helpful for the young male to learn from.

It was Gillian who broke the silence during the ride.

"Pavel, I know I can trust you, but I also know you're loyal to

Aleksei, Cezar and the pack. I do not want to ask you to violate any oath of fealty you have to them, so when we get to the castle, I want you to just walk away. Give me a two-hour head start before you go back to Rachlav and tell him that I took off. Okay?"

Enigmatic blue, blue eyes regarded her. "Lady Gillian, I am loyal, but I have sworn before my Alpha to protect you. Count Rachlav was completely serious when he said your safety came before all else. If you are to go, then I will go with you. My Alpha will not kill me or punish me for following an order that he supports wholly."

Reaching over, she squeezed his hand warmly and her eyes stung. Pavel was loyal and he would stand by her, no matter what. As long as he wouldn't pay for it later, she welcomed his help.

"All right, Pavel. I am more grateful than I can say. I could use the company. And for Hell's sake, call me Gillian." Her grin was infectious and he returned it, nodding in agreement.

They drove up and got out, Gill taking the computer and backpack with her. She and Pavel sprinted up the walk and entered. Quickly locating Arkady, she told him she had an emergency and asked if there were a place that she could have privacy and quiet that had outlets for the computer. He showed her to a private study where she unloaded her pack, hooked everything up, then sent her empathy out and called to Dante verbally.

The Ghost appeared moments later, thankfully not full of stab wounds, but glaring at Pavel who stood near Gillian, growling low in his throat as the fear Dante was generating flooded the room.

"What is it, *dolcezza*? Who is this with you?" The Ghost's hollow voice intoned.

Very aware that she was treading a thin line with confidentiality, she dodged around introductions. "Dante Montefiore, this is Pavel Miroslav. He's a Lycanthrope with the local pack, Dante, and my friend. Pavel, this is Dante, obviously a Ghost, but also a friend. Both of you, be nice. And Dante? Knock that shit off."

She glared at the Ghost for emphasis and the cold fear he was manifesting abruptly ceased. "I need to know what else you found out about Tanis Rachlav. It's a long story. I don't have time to go into it now, but I need to leave for a while."

Dante's eyebrows shot up at that. He didn't want her to leave but he had no reason for her to stay. They weren't scheduled for a visit until a month from then unless it was for exchanging information. "He was taken to Finland, Gillian. By whom or what I do not know. They drugged him somehow, then while he rested, spirited him away."

"Finland. Okay, let me think." The computer beeped its readiness and she typed a carefully worded e-mail:

Lugosi rises. Require stake. Availability now. Fellowship rejoined. Middle Earth?

Arkady popped his head in for a moment, making them jump. "Doctor, you have visitors. Shall I show them in?"

Gillian and Pavel exchanged a quick "Oh shit" look. Surely not. No one knew what they were planning yet. Any further speculation was halted when Dionysus and Maeti entered. Arkady shut the door and went back to his party. Gillian hesitated over the enter key on the computer, waiting to see if the axe was going to fall.

"Young warrior, you would test the patience of Hephaestus." Dionysus chuckled. "But I cannot fault your bravery and determination."

He knelt next to Gillian, looking briefly at the computer, admiration in his voice. "So this is more of the Human's communication devices. I do not indulge in technology; I am a simple man."

Looking at the stunningly beautiful Vampire god's profile, Gillian couldn't fathom how he could be thought of as simple. She looked up with questions in her eyes to Maeti, who had moved to stand behind the kneeling Vampire.

"Gillian, whatever you are planning, Dionysus and I will help you. Tanis is special to you, but you care for Aleksei more." Maeti's ice-blue eyes were warm with understanding. "You want Tanis back for him, more than for yourself, because you care about Aleksei's feelings more than you fear his anger."

Apparently Maeti had been paying attention in Get to the Point class, Gillian noted as she cringed at the Vampiress's words.

"And it frightens the life out of you, does it not, little Captain?" Dionysus's rich voice joined the discussion as he noted

Gillian's response. He rose to move his arm around Maeti and pull her close.

"For a brave woman, perhaps the bravest Human I have met personally, you are terrified of what your heart might wish for. The future is uncertain for us all, Gillian, even those of us who can claim near immortality. If we live through what you are about to pull us into, give Aleksei a chance." He glanced at Maeti, who was smiling up at him. "She is giving me that chance. I am willing to take it."

Gillian felt her heart lift in happiness for her friend, though she was a little miffed that they understood her better than she did herself. She was supposed to be a psychologist; all mysterious and unfathomable. Right.

Reaching out to grasp Maeti's hand in her own and wanting to change the subject, she said, "I am very happy for you both." She looked to Dionysus. "Maeti's waited eons for you. I hope it is the end of her waiting."

Dionysus touched Maeti's face with an infinitely gentle hand, his cerulean eyes glowing with more than desire. "I have waited eons for her. She waits no more." Turning serious, he looked back to Gillian. "Now, little sister, tell us what havoc you are about to cause."

Popping the enter button and flopping back in the chair, legs splayed, Gillian sent her message. "I'm calling in some old favors from friends I had in the service."

An *ahem* from Pavel made her remember she was wearing a very short skirt. Hastily she brought her legs together as a deep chuckle came from Dante, who had clearly enjoyed the view. Damn Ghost. She'd forgotten he was in the room and glared at him. He was totally unrepentant, his mouth curved in a sexy smile, and he winked at her. Gill rolled her eyes and explained to the assembled creatures what her plan was.

Within an hour, her computer signaled that she had e-mail. She opened it and read.

Bored to tears and need target practice. Hobbits and Elves meet in Rivendell.

Meanwhile Gillian was trying various numbers in her book, finally getting through on one of them. Whoever she needed to talk to did not have a phone, but the message would get through via a complicated chain of communication and protocol. Taking a breath, she collected her racing thoughts and focused on a language she hadn't heard or spoken in years and managed to be diplomatic.

Mord morne faeigli bridhone Mellion Tithen gothwin Maelthin finden, pedo eluen londe Bothil hall sereg Suuuth.

Her accent was awful, her grammar atrocious, but she received an affirmative response, said, *"Naamat,"* and clicked off the phone. Turning, she met a number of confused faces.

"What?"

"I know hundreds of languages, little Captain, but that is one I do not recognize." This from Dionysus who was looking at her as if she'd suddenly done something very interesting.

Gillian laughed. "I'm sorry, it's High Elvish. I have to relay a message through gods only know how many others to get to a particular individual. In Elvish, I know it will be repeated exactly and get to the right person. Very few outside the Fey know the language unless they know an Elf, very, very well. Therefore, if anyone taps into the phone frequency, they're not going to know what the hell I said."

"The message was: 'I request to speak to the tall, dark-haired warrior, the hero prince who is the friend of the gold-braided female soldier at the Elven home near the Bothil River regarding a hidden blood drinker.'"

"How is it you know Elvish, and a 'heroic warrior prince'?" Maeti's eyes twinkled. Vampires could be very nosy. Generally when you didn't want them to be.

"Long story," Gillian hedged. "He was under my command in the service. The United States Marine Corps does not discriminate. And you can stop looking at me like that; we were only friends." Glaring at all of them, she dared them to press for more. They didn't.

Dante spoke up then, making Gill jump, since he appeared behind her. When the hell had he moved? Stupid Ghost. "Why do you need the services of an Elf?"

"Because you said Tanis had been taken to Finland. That's where my Elf friend lives, or rather, where we can access him. He can find out what we can't, he has ties to all of the Fey, light and dark. By the time we get there, he will have information for us."

Dionysus looked incredulous. "He will understand this message? It will get to the right individual?"

"Oh, absolutely. Elves are highly intelligent and very literal. The fact that I contacted him at all constitutes an emergency. The subject of my request, well, let's just say there aren't many Vampires being secreted away into Finland. He will find out where and if Tanis is still in the country or he will find Tanis. It makes little difference to him. He owes me a favor."

Gillian's smirk was not particularly comforting, but they all believed in her and what she was trying to accomplish.

"There are very few dark-haired Elves, and even fewer who are royalty. It will get to him. I am sure of it."

Grabbing her backpack, Gillian went to the door. "Wait here for a few minutes. I need to change, then we'll get out of here."

She vanished to find Arkady and asked for a room to change in. He showed her a bathroom in his private suite. As soon as he left she stripped down, washed off the makeup, then redressed in her usual garb of cargo pants, black sweater, photographer's vest and hiking boots. She could purchase anything else she needed personally, like a coat and supplies. The Vampires didn't need to regulate their body temperature, nor did Pavel.

Rejoining the group, everyone realized they needed a plan for how to get out of the country and back in without tipping off any Dracula operatives. Dionysus, like Aleksei, had a private jet (being reborn apparently had its financial perks) and suggested that if they were making plans to leave the country, they needed to move faster. They could fly out of Brasov straight up to Helsinki. There, they would need a transport helicopter to take them to due north into the heart of Finland.

It was an area surrounded by lakes, mountains, rivers and deep, thick, unexplored forests. It was there that a particular clan of Elves had resided and watched over a doorway into their various worlds for millennia. Finland had over 160 airports, but only 73 with paved runways. The helicopter was their best bet and would not restrict them to governmental airspace.

Gillian made one more call to a friend still in the military, got clearances and waivers for entering and exiting the countries that would be ready within a matter of hours, and arranged for her requested supplies to coincide with their plane's arrival in Finland.

Thanking Arkady for his hospitality, they all piled into Gillian's Opal, drove to the village, gassed up, then headed for

Brasov. Gillian's stomach was in knots; she knew Aleksei
would be furious and hurt, but she was counting on him being
fabulously happy when they brought Tanis home. At least she
hoped he'd be, which might deter him from killing her.

CHAPTER
24

THEY made it to Brasov, then Helsinki without incident. Dawn was cresting, so the Vampires remained on the plane, safely tucked away in the cargo area while Gillian and Pavel disembarked to stretch their legs a little. The air was crisp and fresh, even on the tarmac of the airport. Since they were in a private jet, they were refueling at a hangar rather than one of the main gates. Gill checked on their helicopter—it would be there at sunset—and picked up a duffel bag that held a coat; field rations; mess kit; spade; a small but lethal crossbow with twenty wooden, twenty iron, and twenty silver-tipped bolts in a quiver; an ultraviolet flashlight; water purification tablets and a small packet of compartmentalized napalm. It would burn tinder no matter if it were dry or not, even in rain or snow.

Apprehension crawled through her. By now, Aleksei and the others would know that they'd gone, but not where. An involuntary shiver ran through her but she shrugged it off. She'd faced down horrors on the battlefield. One four-hundred-year-old Vampire was not going to intimidate her. Okay, maybe he did, but she wasn't going to let him see it.

Bitchy. Yeah, that was the ticket; she'd get bitchy and he'd leave her alone. She had never met a male she couldn't bully or intimidate. Aleksei had just caught her off guard before, a weak moment or two. That must be it.

Since lying to herself was getting her nowhere, she checked her e-mail to kill time, plugging into a port in the hangar. Pavel was off hunting—for what, Gillian didn't want to know. Sure enough, there was e-mail from the IPPA, warning her not to take chances, to stay in Romania and avoid conflict. Too bad she'd already taken matters into her own hands. She snorted derisively; they'd get over it. Dr. Gerhardt was used to her handling things on her own. Even if some of her activities occasionally gave him tension headaches and stirred up the ulcer he claimed to have. Gerhardt knew from experience that Gillian wasn't a thrill junky. He'd defend her if necessary if the board became angry with her current little endeavor.

Returning to the plane, Gillian stretched out on the closely placed seats, two abreast, and covered her eyes with her arm. She wanted to catch a nap before the evening. They'd be on foot for a while after the helicopter dropped them, depending on where the encampment she was looking for was located. She'd never been there, having only heard about it through elaborate description, and was going on a diagram that she'd drawn under the scrutiny of her advance scout, Lieutenant Mirrin Everwood, High Elf Clan. She hadn't seen him, talked to him or heard of him in years. Assuming he was still alive wasn't a stretch. Elves were highly gifted in many aspects, intellect and survival skills topping the list. Mirrin was no exception. He was one of a handful of people that she trusted implicitly.

Elves were extraordinarily honorable, even the Dark Grael were no exception. If any Elf said they were going to kill you, love you or stand loyal to you, they were honor bound to complete the deed. Mirrin was probably not thrilled to hear from her; they'd left things strained between them, but she hoped for the sake of loyalty and old times, he'd help.

As her mind wandered, she drifted gently into a light sleep. Soon her dreams began to develop into fantasy. Desire flooded through her. Penetration. Heat. Climax. Gillian woke gasping, her eyes locked with those of a snarling Werewolf in Human form. Pavel's deep-throated growl raised the hair on her arms.

"Do not move, Gillian." Pavel's order was imperious and final. She didn't move.

"Remove yourself from her, spirit."

That was delivered in the same flat monotone, followed by

another growl. Pavel started to shift, his face becoming longer, sharper, blue eyes unblinking and beginning to burn with an internal flame. He was staring at the empty air just above her prone form.

It took Gillian a moment to comprehend what he'd just said. Spirit? What the hell? All at once, understanding flooded her: horror, fury, disgust and pure unadulterated rage.

"Get. Off. Me. Dante."

Each word was enunciated clearly, with glacial calm, though she was quivering with anger. The pressure between her legs eased gradually, as did the unseen fingers that were gripping her hips. Gillian scooted off the chair and backward toward Pavel.

"What in the hell do you think you're doing?"

She was incredulous and furious . . . and talking to thin air. The Werewolf stepped in front of her, the upper half of his body had shifted. He looked like an upright wolf wearing a flannel shirt and jeans. That was the power that made him a candidate for Alpha. Partial shifting was not possible by but a few powerful individuals of werekind. Right now, he had imposed his body between her and a certain Ghost who had just taken advantage of her.

Dante shimmered into solidity, lacing his pants casually as if all was well. He could have solidified fully clothed if he'd wanted to; as it was he was taunting her, a smirk on that lovely mouth of his. Gillian murmured a quick binding spell for malicious spirits, pivoted around Pavel and punched Dante in the mouth. Since he was solid for the moment and her spell held him where he was, she connected fully and he went down, astonishment written over his aristocratic and lovely face.

"You son of a bitch!" If Dante hadn't already been dead, she would have shot him. Ghost fear flooded over her and Pavel, leaving their teeth chattering and both of them trembling. Gillian reached for Pavel's hand only to jerk back as the wolf-faced man snapped and snarled at her to take care; the Human tones muddled with his lupine muzzle. Looking down, she saw the thick claws that had erupted from his former fingertips. If she'd grabbed his paw, she might have been scratched.

"Thanks, Pavel," she whispered gratefully, knowing the Lycanthrope was near to panic from the level of fear clawing at her empathy and the slight foam forming at the corners of his mouth, but he stood his ground between her and the threat. So

was she for that matter—close to panic, that is. She could hear
his labored breathing and her own pounding heartbeat. The
wolf's eyes were dilated but burned with a hellish light. Turning
back to Dante, who was rising from the floor, fully solid and
looking murderous, she drew her gun anyway and leveled it at
him. It was a fruitless, stupid gesture, but it made her feel better.

"You! It was you all along, giving me those dreams!" Green
eyes snapping in fury, Gillian confronted her now former patient. Former indeed. There was no way in hell she was going to
revisit a therapeutic relationship with him now.

Dante laughed, his voice deep and cavernous. "What are you
complaining about, *dolcezza*? You enjoyed it. Every. Single.
Time."

That was a cheap shot. Fucking Ghost. Literally. Gillian
wasn't that easily provoked into fury. Keeping her temper had
saved her ass many times. Dante wasn't this far from his natural
haunting grounds without some magic being involved, that she
was sure of. What to do, what to do?

Sunset was still at least an hour away, and while Dionysus
might have something in the line of actual magic in his reper-
toire, she and Pavel wouldn't last that long in the midst of
Ghost-generated fear without succumbing to panic and fleeing
the plane into the darkening Finland evening. Dante certainly
wasn't going to suddenly get all repentant. There had to be a
way to tip the scales.

Ego. Dante was an egomaniac, and that was his Achilles
heel. "You dumb shit, you may have generated some sort of response, but you can't hold a candle to a warm, breathing male in
my bed. As far as I'm concerned you were only big enough to
generate a mild wet dream. Nothing spectacular, really."

Forcing her mouth into a taunting smile took some doing,
but she managed. "Were all your little conquests in the past vir-
gins? Didn't know what to expect? Or did they just start out
with very low expectations of you as a lover?"

Utter rage suffused Dante's remarkably handsome features.
Every wound on him opened up and he bled copiously. Tipping
his head back, giving Gillian and Pavel a marvelous view of his
slashed throat, he screamed his rage, spraying both of them
with wet, red spray. The fear intensified and even Gillian wondered if she'd be able to last the next few seconds. One more
turn of the "screw."

"Oh now *that* is really attractive. Every girl wants to fuck a drippy, butchered body," she chattered out between her jiggling teeth.

That elicited another furious shriek from the now-humiliated and enraged Ghost. Pavel chuckled but it came out more of a choking cough from his elongated lupine lips. Her binding spell picked that time to crumble. Dante's innate magic finally over-rode it and he crackled out of existence, taking his blood, gore and anger with him, his howl of rage echoing in the confined, tubular space of the plane.

Gillian and Pavel climbed over seats and very nearly each other in their haste to get off the plane and out into the still-bright sunlight. The chill from the Ghost's manifested fear had reached down to their bones. It took twenty minutes of standing in the sunlight and Pavel shifting back to Human form before they both felt calm, warm and strong enough to reenter the plane.

"That transparent, unearthly son of a bitch!"

Putting it mildly, Gillian was furious. Dante had a few sneaky-ass tricks up his lacy sleeve. How and what, she didn't know. At least her instincts had been right; he was far from the average Ghost.

Pavel was also not amused. "I will help find a way to destroy him. He assaulted you, Gillian." A low, deep growl came from his chest and his eyes glowed dark purple in his rancor.

She thought about that for a moment. Damn him, anyway; Dante was right. She had enjoyed it. Every. Single. Time. That pissed her off.

"No, he actually didn't, Pavel. In my dream state, I was not unwilling. It wasn't rape, but he did take advantage of the situation. Let's go back on the plane and figure out how the hell he's manifesting this far from his haunting."

Reluctantly, they mounted the stairs to the plane. Pavel went first, insisting that he face any threat ahead of her, Gillian close behind, nearly mirroring his steps in an effort to keep the big Lycanthrope as close to her as possible. She didn't bother to point out that neither of them had been effective against the Ghost.

There was no sign of Dante but the Vampires would rise soon and the chopper was on its way, so they had to hurry. A quick look through her backpack and laptop case delivered several small stones that Gillian couldn't remember being there. As her abilities extended to a minor amount of touch telepathy, Gill closed her eyes, held the stones tentatively, concentrating on them. The smell of blood crept into her nose and the impression of cold fear. She opened her eyes, finding Pavel crouched in front of her, looking very concerned.

"I know how he did it. Dammit, he has to be either part Fey or was a necromancer in life. These are part of his hallway. He must have put them in my bag when we were there last night. That's how he's manifesting this far away—transference through an object."

"So he followed you here?" Pavel asked, his voice a soft growl.

"Yes. I don't know why, but I'm going to put a stop to it."

The growl intensified. "I will take the stones far from the plane, Gillian. He will not trouble us again."

She chuckled. "As much as I'd love for you to do just that, Pavel, dissociating Dante totally from his haunt would be disastrous for him and for me."

Pavel looked confused, so she explained. "If we take away his 'anchor,' so to speak, it would be tantamount to murder in the Ghost domain. He's too far away to get back to the castle, so he would be a stranded spirit, unable to leave this place—or he'd simply dissipate into oblivion. Either way, I'd be responsible. He's an ass, but I can't just destroy him."

"What will you do then? You can't allow him his freedom, knowing what he has done to you." Pavel was angry. Retribution was a big concept in Lycanthrope society and Pavel definitely wanted retribution for the insult to Gillian.

"No, I can't." Gillian frowned, thinking. "Damn, I wish I had some sea salt to put the stones in to bind his ass; as it is I'll have to just cast another binding spell directly on the stones and hope it holds."

She wasn't a witch or a sorcerer but she could perform simple spells for specific purposes; some for helping her clients in her practice and a few for self-defense. Holding the stones, she murmured over them, concentrating on an impenetrable shield around them. Pavel rummaged around in the galley of the plane and managed to find a salt packet. Apparently, Dionysus kept a stocked larder for his Human servants. Gillian sprinkled some of it over the stones for good measure, then dumped the lot into a small plastic bag, also from the galley. Pocketing the stones, they were on the verge of being pleased with themselves for outsmarting Dante, when the Vampires rose, climbing out of the cargo area, looking stunning as ever.

"Have you been entertaining yourselves while we slept?" Maeti's eyes were bright and sparkled with laughter. Gillian glowered at her.

"Not hardly."

The tone in her voice and the scent of fear was enough to bring questions to the Vampiress's eyes and Dionysus's arm protectively around Maeti's shoulders.

"That Ghost followed us here," Pavel said for clarification. "He has been molesting Gillian."

"*What?*" There was no hint of laughter in Maeti's voice now and her eyes grew cold.

Gillian explained the situation, adding that Dante was now safely bound and would be dealt with later. Dionysus and Maeti exchanged a glance.

"We are remiss then, in keeping you safe young one, if this has occurred right under all of our collective noses." Dionysus was appropriately concerned and angry.

They hadn't done their jobs if the little Human had been violated in this manner. He knew Aleksei's fury would have another target when Dante's duplicity was exposed. Right now the other Vampire was justifiably incensed over Gillian's overt disobedience. Dionysus had been able to reach Aleksei through their link and assured the Romanian Count that Gillian was alive and well and being looked after.

To say that Aleksei was less than soothed was fitting. He would have come straight away, but Dionysus assured him that Aleksei was needed in Romania to keep the current Paramortal population somewhat united and safe and to assure that Dracula gained no further allies in his effort.

"The spirit is contained now?" Dionysus wanted to know.

"I think so. When we get where we're going, my friends might have some magic to throw on him to permanently put a stop to his shit. If not, he'll just have to remain bound until we get back to Romania." Gillian was annoyed and it showed, but she was also focused. Dante was a pain in the ass but he wasn't the threat at the moment. Her dignity was ruffled but she was basically unharmed.

The roar of the approaching helicopter interrupted her thoughts. All of them piled out of the plane to meet it. The airplane pilots, Human and loyal to Dionysus, would stay here until the rest of them got back. The chopper pilot was another USMC captain that Gillian had known. He was also a Vampire.

"Hey sexy!" He waved at her, shouting above the roar of the propeller blades.

"Hey Luis!" Gillian climbed aboard, taking the time to shake his hand as she scooted into the copilot's seat. "Luis, this is Dionysus, Maeti and Pavel . . . guys, this is Captain Luis Clemente. Best damn chopper pilot ever." Her grin was infectious and they all slid into their seats smiling.

Luis saluted Dionysus. "I am honored, my Lord. I am of your Line." Luis's dark eyes met the Greek Lord's.

Dionysus acknowledged him. "I am pleased to meet you as well. If Gillian trusts you, that is all I need to know, but I am honored that you are of my Line. This is my mate, Maeti."

Luis grinned, nodded to Maeti—"Ma'am"—and Pavel, then turned his attention back to the controls of the chopper. Gillian watched him as he took the machine airborne. Luis was a fairly young Vampire, only about eighty years old. He looked exactly the same as she remembered him, like a devastatingly handsome, tall Puerto Rican man. His black hair was a little long for the military but the Joint Chiefs of Staff were a little more lenient with their paranormal enlistees and officers than with their Human counterparts. His eyes were deep brown and intelligent, his features breathtaking and even. Luis had flown night reconnaissance flights for her in the past and his skill was impeccable. Gill trusted him with her life then and she did now. Reaching over, she patted his arm suddenly and was rewarded with a smile and questioning look.

Realizing he was curious about her unusual impulse, she answered the unspoken question. "Nothing, Luis. Just glad to see you again." Turning her attention to the blackness out the window, she fell silent, thinking about the meeting to come and trying to formulate her words into diplomatic Elvish.

CHAPTER
25

THE flight lasted about an hour. It seemed longer since they were flying with only running lights in the pitch black. Luis had typical Vampiric night vision and could see perfectly even without the red and blue lights that were flashing rhythmically on the nose and tail of the helicopter. Gill's night vision was stellar for a Human, but she wouldn't have been able to see a tree dead ahead in the darkness. The moon was but a silver sliver in the sky and while the stars turned the velvet black into a wonderland of sparkling fire, the landscape wasn't viewable.

"Landing now, per the coordinates you provided." Luis's voice was teasing. He had a good idea where she was headed and who they would meet there. Their unit had become a very close group in the service. Members of a Special Forces team specifically trained for rescue, diplomatic coups and assassinations, their bond had been forged on the first difficult mission they had been assigned. Diverse backgrounds and races had been welded together skillfully by Gillian and her amazing empathy. Okay, so maybe a little bit of it was from her unique style of command.

When two members of separate Elf races refused to cooperate with one another during a recovery mission and threatened to mutiny, Gill told them point blank that they would get along under her command or she'd shoot them herself before they ever got to court-martial. One of the Elves, a junior lieutenant Grael Elf, nicknamed Trocar, had laughed at her demeanor and audacity, verbalizing disbelief that a U.S. Marine, and a female at that, might employ such tactics. Gillian had calmly turned, drawn her Glock and shot him through the kneecap.

As he writhed on the ground before his shocked comrades, Gillian had put the heated muzzle of the gun against his temple and asked if he wanted to restate his opinion, her green eyes icy. He did. Grael respected subterfuge, illusion, honor, and shows of strength. Gillian's delicate appearance was illusion; he hadn't expected her reaction and now she had him at her mercy.

Trocar revised his opinion damn quick, said so, then with his knee magically healed by the efforts of their team, became one of Gillian's strongest advocates, following her blindly on many a mission. The other Elf, a Forest High Elf to be specific, was not impressed by the show. High Elves tended to be patient and occasionally condescending to Humans, considering them a youthful, impulsive species with great courage but little common sense and a devious nature.

Lord Mirrin Everwood, princeling of his people and the first to step into the modern Human era, looked down his aristocratic nose at his commanding officer's method and the motley crew he'd been assigned to. Fortunately he had enough sense not to mention it to her, preferring to watch and see how she truly led before casting judgment. Gillian impressed him eventually on several levels, showing phenomenal intuitive judgment, amazing stealth and dexterity that was bordering on a sixth sense in hand-to-hand combat. Mirrin followed her at first because he had agreed to be an "experiment" for his people. Later he followed her for the same reason they all did: respect, and more than a little love.

It was Mirrin she sought now. The princeling had returned to his people after his tour of duty was up. There had been administrative pressure to keep him in the service, but Gillian had managed to cut through more red tape than downtown New York during Christmas season. She got him out, honorably discharged, with accommodations for bravery above and beyond the call of duty. In the unspoken code of the Marines, he owed her. Mirrin was nothing if not honorable. He would help.

The helicopter touched down gently and Luis cut the power. The blades rotated to a halt and the group climbed out. Luis stayed with the chopper, waiting for Gillian's signal, which she gave moments later after hearing the rush of a river ahead and to the right. She had a flashlight, but would rely on the Vampire's vision and Pavel's senses to guide them forward. The stars above cast silvery shadows over the landscape. It was a faint light but still a light. The river was a wide black ribbon nearly obscured by the trees. The land was fairly flat, all gentle slopes before the thick forest that lined the river. Gillian knew that not too far in, the land became hillier as it became the mountains. That wasn't where they were headed.

What few knew outside of the Elven tribes was that J. R. R. Tolkien had been not so much a genius as he had been an observer and trusted friend. Having a heartfelt belief in every legend having a basis in fact, through exhaustive research, looking in precisely the right places at precisely the right times, a lot of luck, and demonstrating his trustworthiness, he had been allowed a view of a world that none knew in his time. Permission was given to him to record what he learned, saw and experienced, with the condition that none ever learn from his lips or those of his descendents where or how he'd come by the knowledge.

The professor had turned endless years of study and the cultivating of those friendships into the popular novel series *The Lord of the Rings*, a collection of seven books containing *The One Ring Trilogy* and *The Hobbit*. Middle Earth was real, only the names and places had been changed to protect the innocent and avoid undue persecution of the guilty.

It existed even now as a destination behind a shielded Doorway the Elves had constructed with the help of the Thralian Wizards to keep the encroaching Human world out and their beautiful but treacherous worlds within. If there were ever a need, the Gateway would be destroyed, sealing their various domanins forever behind unbreakable, magical fields.

Elves knew no boundaries of time and space. They could straddle the dimensions, the various worlds and the ages at will, though few did. As detailed as any books had been, they were far from complete. The Elves' world was complex, multilayered and would never be easily understood by any but those indigenous to it. The great man had remained an Elf friend for the rest of his life, his descendents watched over by a Guild that had been formed for just that purpose.

There was a doorway near his estate and he had crossed that doorway near the end of his life. Emerant, one of the Great Elf

Lords, had been fond of the man and had allowed him passage into the Lands of Solace, an area of neutral magic just inside the Doorway before the world of his stories was encountered. There he dwelt, happy and well, aging slowly with the beauty of the world he so loved and in the company of the Elves and his lovely wife whom he had adored above all other beings.

Gillian knew the stories, knew the legends that Mirrin had shared with her, comrade to comrade. The Gateway was along this river bank. She didn't intend to enter it, just to wait until it was opened from within. Mirrin was punctual; he'd be where and when she asked him to be or he would send a representative to state why he could not. All gathered on the river bank. The water was low and dark and it sang as it flowed over the ancient riverbed.

They stood together, waiting patiently. Pavel growled low as a shimmer began in the landscape before them. Like a curtain, the trees and river parted and Lord Mirrin Everwood stepped out of the veil, bow in hand, followed by three others, all cloaked and hooded. Two of them were Elves from the way they moved with incredible feline grace and the other, shorter person, was someone Gill had also requested to join them.

"Caen Brith, Mirrin an Everwood." Gillian spoke first and directly to Mirrin, holding her hand to her heart and bowing slightly in welcome.

His rank with his people demanded respect, even from her. To her surprise, Mirrin grasped her in a tight hug. Elves weren't really touchy-feely people, and she was astonished by his gesture.

Setting her on her feet, Mirrin looked down at the smaller Human. She looked tired and stressed, and her blood pressure was up, that much he could tell instantly. Elves were highly intuitive and had a sort of limited telepathy. Their hearing also was just as acute as legend told. His former commanding officer looked a little careworn to his sharp eyes, but now was not the time to speak with her about her health. Gillian wouldn't tolerate it with the urgency of her current mission.

Gillian watched him giving her the once-over. If he knew what was good for his stunningly handsome self, he'd keep his mouth shut. Mirrin was as she remembered: tall, elegant, heartbreakingly lovely, with black hair down to his waist tied back from the crown in a warrior's braid showing his caste and tribe, the front section left free to allow his aesthetically pointed ears to be clearly seen, his turquoise eyes glowing with their own light.

"Caen Brith, Gillian Mallen Findel." Mirrin's rich voice flowed over them all.

Even the Vampires noticed. He turned to indicate his companions, the smallest of which wasted no time in pouncing on Gillian and bearing her laughing to the ground. Pavel was on her in a moment, yanking the slight form off his friend, then standing in confusion while Gillian and the female he now held laughed hysterically.

"Kimber Whitecloud! Damn glad to see you!" Gillian climbed to her feet. "Put her down, Pavel, she's obnoxious, definitely not harmless, but she's not going to hurt me."

Pavel set the woman down and she turned to him, raking the hood off her head and regarding him with laughing eyes. His breath caught in his throat. Taller than Gillian but lighter built, Kimber Whitecloud was a glorious combination of several Human races to their highest compliments. Her hair was golden bronze and braided all over her head; it hung in plaits down her back, under the cloak. Grass green and golden hazel warred in the slanted eyes that were full of mirth and ringed with black lashes. Those remarkable eyes stared daringly into his own.

Her skin was silky bronze, a shade or two darker than her hair; her lips full and dark pink. No makeup adorned her but she was the loveliest thing Pavel had ever seen. Her scent was like a drug: warm, comforting, tantalizing . . . the scent of the loam of the forest and sparkling water. He wanted to tuck her under his arm and never let her go. He was sorry when she turned from him to clasp Gillian in a death grip that left the smaller woman gasping for air and laughing.

"Captain! Well met and well . . . merry!" Kimber laughed, then turned to the other, yet unintroduced Elves. "This is Hierlon."

The Elf she indicated raised a slender, elegant hand and removed his hood. Like all his fellows, he was beyond lovely. Platinum blonde hair shimmering with glints of gold and braided in a manner slightly different from Mirrin's framed a face that was both arrogant and breathtaking. His ears were bare as well, showing off their delicate points to their best advantage.

Hey, if you had aesthetically pleasing body parts, why not flaunt them? Gill thought. Dark eyebrows, starkly contrasting his bright hair, rose above steel-blue eyes. His mouth was full and kissable, though it wasn't smiling at the moment. Disapproval was in his look and in his stance but a heavy bow of the

Golden Elves was in his hand. The carvings on it indicated that he had status among his people and was a master archer. Nodding to Gillian with his hand over his heart respectfully, it was still clear he wasn't fond of the company she kept.

"Caen Brith, Gillian Mellion Mirrin." Hierlon spoke in a soft but commanding voice that brought to mind crisp, cold nights, warm lips and smoldering embraces.

Damn. Elves all had that silky, magical quality to their voices. Outside of the Vampires, they were also the most remarkably beautiful people Gillian had ever seen, even in her limited contact with them. Until she'd met Osiris, Aleksei, Tanis, and the rest of the Vampires, the Elves she knew had been the sole occupants in her Hall of Memories under "Legendary Beauty." Hierlon was arrogant but he addressed her respectfully and acknowledged her friendship to Mirrin. Gillian could overlook his attitude and not knock him on his ass.

"Caen Brith, Hierlon."

She returned the gesture with a little push to her glare which startled him from the brief flash in his blue eyes, then his expression hardened to a perfect mask. Fine. She'd not bother him further with idle chatter.

The third figure walked up without speaking, blackness in the depths of the hood. Gillian's empathy flared at his approach. Recognition clicked and she threw her arms wide to hug the tall, quiet figure who swept her up and spun her before setting her on her feet. She reached up and pushed back the hood.

"Trocar," she said a little breathlessly.

Crystalline white hair spilled in frothy waves out of the dark hood and glimmered in the starlight. Maeti's gasp brought a sharp look from Dionysus as the Elf's face was unveiled. Carved out of blackest obsidian, the Dark Elf's face was phenomenally, achingly lovely, putting even the Vampires to shame.

He was the arcane black of the darkest, starless depths of the deepest cavern in the Abyss. Silky ebony skin covered well-defined muscles on his tall form. His hair, eyebrows and eyes all seemed to be made of the finest white crystal. Like spun clear glass, his hair settled around his face and shoulders, barely moving in the light breeze. Trocar's eyes were devoid of a dominant color. Crystalline white like his hair and brows, they were iridescent, sparkling like faceted jewels, framed by equally shimmering, amazingly long lashes. The Grael were a beautiful, deadly people. They were also shunned by all other Elves and most of the Fey. Gillian was shocked to see him in the company of a Golden Elf. No wonder Hierlon was aggravated. He must have had tremendous respect for Mirrin to go along with being a guide to a Grael.

"Greetings, little Captain." Trocar's voice was no less alluring than Mirrin's or Hierlon's but Gillian knew the mind that fueled his speech and it had less effect.

At Gillian's confused look, Kimber volunteered: "I found Trocar here when I arrived. Mirrin and he have been looking for your friend. Hierlon has been our guide to the Gateway."

Leaning in and knowing full well the Elves could hear her perfectly, Kimber added in a whisper, "He's kind of an arrogant hardass but he's really got a good heart underneath."

Mirrin and Trocar laughed. Hierlon didn't. He stayed back from the rest of the group, on alert and watchful. Dionysus and Maeti remained also on watch and back from the group. Pavel was at Gillian's side, as always, but looking longingly at Kimber.

Werewolf in Love. The Saga Continues. Oh boy! Gill thought, noticing the initial attraction. Kimber was staring back at the tall, blue-eyed blonde wolf with an undisguised hunger on her face. Goddess, puppy love. They didn't have time for this.

"Well?" Gill inquired, returning her gaze to Mirrin's bemused face.

"I am sorry, Captain. We found traces of your friend's passage through our lands but he was spirited away from here   to England, we believe."

Mirrin had the decency to look annoyed. "Whoever had him was hard pressed to avoid Trocar's magic, so they remained only a little ahead. Unfortunately we were unable to prevent their departure."

Gill turned on Trocar, who actually stepped back at the smoldering look in her eyes. "Who the hell has the level of wizardclass magic in your realm to be able to force open this doorway?"

A thought clicked in her head. She advanced on the Dark Elf menacingly. "Trocar, I swear to the Goddess, if you had anything to do with this . . ."

Trocar was affronted, or at least so it seemed from what they could tell from his dark features in the night. "Captain, my Captain." His voice was silky and soothing. "Even I do not possess the knowledge to open the Gateway or any other alone. Only the Golden Elves and Darkenwood Clans can do this. We Grael, our High brethren and the Sea Clans cannot. The lord and lady of the realm do not hold us in as high esteem, apparently."

The bitterness in his voice was unmistakable. Hierlon and Mirrin looked on coolly as ever, unruffled by the Grael's resentment.

"Someone did!" Gillian snapped.

"In truth, I do not know," Trocar answered, his hands going out in a helpless gesture.

Her direct stare pinned both remaining Elves. "Well, goddammit, who knows?"

"I do not know. I do not even know the reason your friend was taken, Gillian. We only tried to find him and rescue him for you."

Mirrin spoke softly, not wanting to aggravate her further. Gillian threw up her hands and started pacing and swearing under her breath.

Kimber moved forward but didn't touch her. "Gilly, honey, you need to relax. We'll find your boyfriend. We've got a great team."

Her former captain whirled, grinding out "He. Is. Not. My. Boyfriend." between clenched teeth.

She paused, letting that sink in. "I know we have a great team, Kimber, that's why I called you all here. And I apologize, Mirrin; I know that you've done your best. You too, Trocar. I was unable to give you more information at the time."

Turning, she included Trocar and Mirrin in her visual line. "Tanis is a hostage in a very ugly war that has begun." Taking a deep breath, she expounded on the subject, "Dracula has started a war, enlisting aid from the nonliving, the Fey, the Lycanthropes and he will probably contact the wizards and the Elves. The purpose of this war is the enslavement of Humans by the paranormal world. We are nothing but cattle to him, to be used for food and amusement."

Kimber hissed at that. Mirrin's face darkened, even Trocar looked furious. "He means to make servants of us all then, Captain. One such as Dracula would not stop at ruling"—he paused for a heartbeat—"only the Human world. It offers nothing of power to his domain."

Seeing the look on Gillian's and Kimber's faces, he added, "I am sorry, my dear ladies, but it does not. There is simply not enough there to be of value except as a food supply. We of the Fey would be pawns and puppets, the muscle, if you will, serving the immortal Vampire reign. You Humans would be housed, fed, even cared for to provide nourishment for the overlords and chattel for the rest of us. Truly you would be only cattle or servants in a organized breeding program, the conditions of which we can only assume would be dismal."

Kimber started toward the Grael, a murderous look on her face. "You pointy-eared, arrow-twanging, cave-dwelling, arrogant son of a *munthridal*!!"

The term she used was Dwarvish and particularly vulgar. Trocar's look grew thunderous and he stiffened. Even Hierlon's eyes widened in surprise.

"Sorry, Hierlon," she tossed over her shoulder.

Mirrin gave an inelegant snort. He'd spent enough time with Humans and knew just how far they would go in anger.

Gillian stepped between Kimber and the Grael, who was trembling with anger. "Okay, enough. We don't have time for this. Kimber, he's right. That's exactly what Dracula would do and why. Let it go."

Leaning in toward Trocar, she whispered, "Try to be a little more diplomatic with your observations until everyone is used to the idea."

He nodded, but his crystalline eyes never left Kimber's defiant form, even as she turned and walked back toward the blonde Elf still patiently waiting by the river.

Chewing on her lower lip, Gillian thought for a moment. "Trocar, you're a full wizard now, right?" At his nod, she went on, "So even with your skill, they were hard to track."

Again, he nodded. "All right, so they used some form of Fey glamour combined with magic, which means an alliance has already formed or is forming. The power of a single wizard is not enough to breach that doorway. This was not a random kidnapping, nor was it accidental that they pulled him through the Gateway."

Trocar and Mirrin exchanged a glance. Mirrin spoke. "We knew you would have these questions when we discovered he had traveled through our domain. Trocar and I have remained in contact through the years, so I called upon him to find out what he could about any alliances forming among his own kind. Hierlon and I have also queried where we could.

"Unless the Dark Wizard has returned, or another one of his black robed order has come forth, we can find none who have helped them. The only possibility now is one of the older Fey who had possessed a godhead at some point in time or another true Vampire Lord."

Gillian thought that over for awhile and they all gave her room to pace and think. "If that's true, we may never find out who assisted in this little venture. The Fey aren't going to give up one of their own to anyone for any reason, and if it's one of Dracula's Vampires, we are at a dead end there too. They'll settle it themselves in their courts, eventually, particularly if our side wins."

There were nods and murmurs of agreement within the assembled. No one wanted to go up against Fey Court or have to do with their disciplinary practices. The matter was better left alone. The Elves would make sure that the Gateway was spelled better to prevent it from happening again.

"We need to focus on where Tanis was taken. England, right?" Trocar and Mirrin nodded. "Great. So we'll start there. I need to know who is available and wants to embark on this little adventure."

Mirrin gestured to Hierlon who stepped back through the veil to return with three packs. "I will accompany you, if you wish, Gillian."

She smiled fondly at him. "I know, Mirrin, but your lady will be most displeased with me if I get you killed out here. I don't want Dorian's arrows of doom pointed in my direction, thank you very much."

Mirrin's lady was a half-Elf with red hair and a bad temper. Gillian didn't know her personally, but Mirrin had bored her to tears with descriptions of his lady love during his tenure in the service and Gill knew more about her than she cared to. Funny thing was, she was sure she'd like her if they ever had occasion to meet. Dorian Leganth of Penmoor was a perfect grounding influence for Mirrin. Gill wanted him to be happy. He deserved it. Reluctantly, Mirrin nodded.

"I will go, Captain. You have my oath that I will assist you in whatever manner I can." Trocar's beautiful voice flowed like the finest syrup and there was a brief sparkle in the air as he spoke.

Elves, like one of the Fey or Sidhe, were inherently magical. When they took an oath or someone gave them one, the Magic that Was simply tweaked it into a binding contract. Gillian was surprised but pleased. The Dark Elf was like all his other fellows: dangerous, treacherous and deadly, but the Grael's evil wasn't extraneous as it was with Dracula.

Honorable and lawful were what some called them, despite their vicious nature. If a Grael said something, he meant it. If a Grael vowed something, it got done, even if it was in a most unpleasant manner. The end justified the means in their reality. Their reality was just really scary was all. Gillian thought having someone really scary on their side might just make a difference down the line.

"All right, Trocar, you're in. You know the rules. Piss me off and pay the consequences." But she patted his arm anyway and he smiled, his teeth glaringly white against the absolute black of his skin.

"That's why I'm here, princess." Kimber had gone and retrieved hers and Trocar's packs from Hierlon. "I need a little adventure."

She dropped everything at Gillian's feet with a large thud. The pack was stuffed and obviously weighed a great deal. Kimber grinned sheepishly at Gillian's raised eyebrow. "Just a few tools we might need later."

Gillian didn't want to know. Kimber had been a sniper in the USMC. She was an expert with primitive weaponry and not too shabby on a flamethrower either. Gillian trusted her to watch her back in all matters. Kimber looked jovial and harmless, but Gillian had seen what she could do when she was pissed off in a firefight. It wasn't pretty.

"Mirrin . . . I . . ." She turned back to the tall, dark-haired Elf. "I want to thank you—" He didn't let her finish.

"Unnecessary, Gillian. We are comrades and friends. My debt is not yet paid to you. If you need me, you may call." Mirrin hugged her. "I wish you well, Captain. In all things." He stepped away, saluted to her and Kimber, then moved back to Hierlon's side.

Gillian waved. "*Namaste*, Mirrin, and my thanks, Hierlon, for your assistance in guiding my friends."

The tall, blonde Elf bowed slightly, then turned and disappeared through the veil. With a final wave, Mirrin followed. The slit in the landscape disappeared as if it had never been.

"Will you be able to get back, Trocar?" Gill asked suddenly. Nothing like hindsight.

"Yes, of course. All dwellers of that domain know how to ask for admittance. It will be granted. I have committed no crime."

He added the last part for the Vampires. They'd said nothing, nor had Pavel during the conversation, but Dionysus had Maeti positioned behind him, with himself between her and the Grael. Trocar hadn't missed the gesture. He'd leave well enough alone for now.

"Let's move, then," Gillian ordered, already starting for the helicopter. Luis saw them coming and revved up the blades.

CHAPTER
26

THE attack was abrupt and silent. No one heard anything or scented anything due to the helicopter and river noise, the wind being against them and the relentless odor of gasoline and oil that comes with any machinery. Farther from the helicopter than the others, Maeti suddenly went down under a dozen black shapes, Dionysus racing to her, snarling and tossing bodies like cordwood. Pavel's silent leap landed him in front of Kimber and he took a Vampire to the face for his trouble. Kimber's Beretta 9mm turned the Vamp's jaw into hamburger and it screamed as it fell writhing.

"Thanks," Pavel growled at her, partially shifting, but she was already scanning the darkness for additional threats.

Gillian was flanked by Trocar as she drew her gun and moved toward Maeti and Dionysus, firing at the dark shapes as she ran. Luis was already out of the chopper, tossing his headphones to the seat and drawing his own sidearm, moving to help the fallen Vampiress. Dionysus yanked Maeti free and nearly threw her at Gillian and Trocar, who caught her easily, then turned and ran back to the helicopter. Gill hit several of the things, then was jerked back off her feet.

Finding herself on the ground underneath a Vampire, its lovely face contorted and fangs bared, Gillian fought to raise her gun but the thing was kneeling on her wrist. Silently she struggled, getting her left hand up and across her throat, sheer terror lending strength to her efforts.

Luis had holstered his gun and began swinging both fists locked together, knocking the Vampire that was using Gill for a cushion sideways. It snapped at him, growling. There was another yell, this time from Kimber as her arm was raked in an attack pass. An unholy howl came from Pavel as the Werewolf shifted fully, shouldering Kimber back and launching over four hundred pounds of muscle, bone, fur and fury at the Vampire. They rolled together, locked in a deadly embrace.

Dionysus was busy fighting off several Vampires in an effort to keep them from the others. Gillian had her own problems— Luis was raining blows on the Vamp that still sat on her chest. It had its legs locked to her sides, one hand in her hair, and was fending off Luis's attack with the other. Luis couldn't yank it off her for fear she'd be scalped or have her ribs crushed. Her hand was pinned so the gun was useless. Just fucking lovely.

There was a flash as two of the Vampires engaged in trying to dismember Dionysus erupted into flame. Nonliving torches, they still managed to shriek and run a few steps before imploding. Another fell to its knees, pressing its hands against its head before it jerked upright and wilted. Cerulean blue lights glowed from Dionysus's face.

This was the power that separated him, Osiris and, unfortunately, Dracula, from the Vampires under their lineage. He focused on another Vamp, a female, and she repeated the performance of the last, clutching at her temples before collapsing.

Kimber had exchanged her gun for her trusty flamethrower and was busy igniting another three. She'd nailed two that were far enough away from Dionysus not to set him alight. Pavel tore out the throat of the one he was fighting, then disemboweled it for good measure. Kimber finished off the remains with a blast from her veloci-candle.

Gillian, unfortunately, was still in trouble and getting nowhere fast. Her ribs were on the verge of breaking as the Vampire that sat on her tightened his grip. Luis was keeping up his rain of bone crushing blows. Already the creature's arm was shattered and raw from continually fending him off.

A shadow fell over her and Luis backed up, his eyes wide. Gillian, already arching back in an effort to get air into her strained lungs, looked up into the face of the Greek Lord. Dionysus reached in and forced the Vampire to look at him. In an instant the creature quailed, smearing blood on its face from its mangled arm and tipping over, dead. Dionysus pulled Gillian out from under the now truly dead corpse. He and Luis checked her over for injury.

Kimber had finished making crispy critters out of the last few bodies and waved happily to Gillian and the others. Dionysus moved so quickly to the helicopter that no one saw him take more than a single stride. Inside the craft, Trocar had bound Maeti's wounds. Dionysus stopped at the door, watching the Dark Elf as he leaned over his mate, ready to dismember him if it looked like Maeti was being harmed. The Elf wizard had magic but he also had the inherent healing ability of his kind. Chanting lightly and touching each cut and scratch, he helped Maeti's own ability to speed healing. After a few moments, he turned to Dionysus, whose eyes still glowed with a frightening luminescence.

"I have accelerated her body's own healing, dark one, but she has lost blood. You must replenish her." Trocar's voice was a beautiful lure, calming the Greek god.

"I thank you, Elf. There is a life between us." Dionysus's voice was no less beautiful but there was a faint sparkle in the air as a vow of truth was spoken before a Fey.

Climbing into the craft, Dionysus cradled Maeti to him, opening his shirt and lifting her mouth to his chest to feed her. She was awake but weak. He hissed in fury when he saw that she'd nearly been gutted on the initial attack and that a dozen bite marks marred her perfect skin. Even a Vampire can be killed by an attack of their own kind. Ancient as she was, Maeti was just as susceptible. Being an ancient was what had saved her. Her power was greater than those sent to assassinate them, but she had been drained.

Gillian poked her head in. "Everything okay, Maeti?"

Maeti's voice was thick with Dionysus's blood. "I will be fine, little sister." She smiled weakly.

"Gillian, give us a few moments, please."

Dionysus didn't need to say please, but he did, so Gillian backed out, joining Pavel, Kimber, Luis and Trocar in checking each other out. Trocar was healing Luis's hands and arms, which had been torn and battered from his defense of Gillian. Kimber was actually more bruised from Pavel knocking her out of the way, but the two of them were busy feeling each other up . . . er . . . checking for injuries. Gillian smirked at the two, then turned to thank Luis for his help.

The handsome Vampire was grimacing as Trocar worked his healing. Fey or Elf magic was closer to true healing than the necromancy or whatever it was that held Vampires together. It healed them, but it wasn't altogether pleasant. Gillian gripped Luis's shoulder as Trocar worked. "Thank you, my friend. I would have been toast if you hadn't stepped in."

"Who the hell were those guys, Gill?" Kimber wasn't shaken in the least. Had to love their resident near-sociopath.

"Guess," Gill snapped.

Kimber knew she wasn't mad at her, just frustrated that they'd all been caught so off guard. "Bad man with pointy teeth, Kemo Sabe, very bad man?" Kimber's humor rarely missed a beat.

"Thanks for torching them, Tonto," Gillian shot back, smiling.

The two of them had a friendship that transcended race or any disrespect. They'd been the Lone Ranger and Tonto in the field before, as well as a dozen other famous hero pairings. "Now we have to worry about what else these fuckers know, since obviously they knew we were coming here."

"Dante, perhaps, Lady Gillian?" Pavel asked. He remembered her telling him the Ghost was responsible for their destination.

Gillian shook her head. "No, he's an ass, but I don't think he would have deliberately misled us. Probably he was misled or used to plant information."

She turned back to the Dark Elf, who'd finished with Luis. "Trocar, thank you. For everything you've done."

The heartrendingly beautiful obsidian face smiled at her. "You are welcome, Gillian. I did give you my word."

Tapping her front teeth with the nail of her forefinger, Gillian thought for a moment. "Yes you did. Let me ask you something. I have a Ghost with some remarkable abilities locked up in rocks in my pocket—spelled with salt. Can you use divination or something and find out what the hell is going on and also keep him from attacking me?"

Trocar's brow furrowed briefly. "May I have the packet?"

She handed it to him without further ado. Closing his eyes, he ran his hands over it and the stones glowed for a moment. Trocar actually snarled and tossed the package to the ground.

"What?" Gillian asked.

"An abomination!" he said furiously. "These stones carry the essence of one of my own. This Ghost is Grael, Captain, make no mistake. That is why he can manifest upon these stones thusly."

"*Grael?* How in hell is an Italian mercenary swordsman a Grael?" Gillian practically bellowed at him.

"I have heard stories of this but have never seen it. What is this creature's name?" Trocar's tone was contemptuous.

"Dante. Dante Montefiore."

Trocar's breath drew in sharply. "He is Grael, Gillian. An abomination from a line of abominations."

Trocar was clearly incensed. "He is the result of the crossing of one of my people with one of yours. The resulting creature should have never been allowed to live. None of them. I had thought them all assassinated long ago."

Kimber stepped up. "Why is that an abomination, Trocar? Since when are you prejudiced?" She was a mix of a number of Human races and she wasn't smiling.

He reached for her but she stepped back, bringing the flamethrower up. "Don't."

Trocar laughed. "Little demon, we have been friends and lovers and still you believe the worst of me."

Gillian's eyebrows shot up at *that*. Lovers? Well, shit, who knew?

"Get to the point," Kimber spat.

"It is not an abomination to cross races, *layna*. It *is* an abomination to cross a Grael with any but another Fey. We are a harsh and violent people. We barely keep our own emotions in check. Elves have tremendous integrity and self-control, as you know, both light and dark. Think of the inherent power of one of my kind, unleashed into a Human with a Human's frail willpower."

Kimber got it. "A monster."

He nodded. "Not an obvious one, however." This time when he reached for her shoulder, she let him touch her. "Kimber, interbreeding between species is bound to happen. Elves and Humans have done it for millennia . . . but *not* with the Grael. There are reasons some of the legends are in place."

"That's where changelings come from then?" Gillian asked.

"Yes. If one of ours took a Human female, impregnated her, the resulting . . . infant would be taken, another left in its place. That kept your race and ours safe."

"What happened to the infant?"

"Mercifully killed. It was not its fault to be born."

Kimber and Gillian exchanged a look. Infanticide was appalling to them both, but it wasn't their place to judge the customs of another culture thousands of years older than theirs.

Elves called themselves the Dawn People. Existing before man, they had splintered off early, evolving into distinct cultures and groups. The Grael were just darker than any other Elvish group, both literally and figuratively. None of the others had the Grael's barbaric practices or their affinity with evil. Grael could be as civilized or as vicious as the situation demanded. Most of the Fey didn't want to find out where that line was drawn.

"I know our customs abhor you, Gillian. But such a child, if allowed to live, would eventually manifest into a thing such as this Ghost that you have trapped here. Even diluted Grael blood is dangerous." Trocar nudged the packet with his foot. "This will not hold him."

"Can you find out what we need to know without setting him loose?" Gillian was beginning to get exasperated.

"I believe I can. If nothing else, I can seal him within these stones so that he cannot trouble you again. When he is returned to his haunt, I can insure that he never leaves again."

Trocar paused a moment, staring at Gillian, who squirmed uncomfortably under his icy gaze. "Gillian . . . you said he attacked you. Tell me what you mean."

Gillian looked away, unwilling to embarrass herself to the tall Elf. Pavel stepped forward and spoke up. "He used her, Dark One. Many times."

A palpable chill emanated from the Dark Elf. "This is true?" His voice dropped lower, silky, soothing. "Gillian, tell me."

Putting an arm on her shoulders, he gently drew her to him. She shuddered but he knew it wasn't from his touch. "I apologize for this one of my race. Evil we may be, but we have no need to rape. That is not the manner of any Elf."

What he said was true. It was probably the only solid unwritten rule in all the Elf Clans. That and no Grael-Human crossings. No Elf had ever had to resort to rape. Their sheer unearthly beauty was enough to convince anyone to lay down with them. Even the Grael with their well-earned bad reputation could convince the most unwilling to comply.

"I will see justice done to this betrayer of my people, Gillian. This I promise you." Again, the sparkle in the air.

A vow of truth. Gillian didn't envy Dante if the Grael turned their sights on him. Whatever Trocar meant, it wouldn't be pleasant, that was for damn sure.

Luis revved the engines and they lifted off. He radioed ahead to see what kind of transport they could wrangle. They'd have to take what they could get since this wasn't an official mission . . . yet.

CHAPTER
27

Dionysus and Maeti boarded his jet at the Helsinki airport with a smile and a wave. The close call with Maeti's life had spooked the Greek Lord and he wished to take her away into the Wild for a time. Maeti wanted to stay with Gillian, but realized that she needed Dionysus as much as he needed her. She couldn't bear to see the fear in the eyes of her mate. Dionysus was well and truly in love. Gillian had become his second priority.

In truth, Gillian was relieved that Dionysus was leaving. Maeti she would miss; the female had become a close friend, but she understood on at least a surface level their commitment to each other. What it meant was Aleksei would no longer have eyes and ears tuned in on her every move and activity. She had known that Dionysus was reporting back to the Romanian Count, and didn't relish the thought of either Aleksei's worry or his anger.

The remaining group, Gillian, Kimber, Luis, Pavel and Trocar, watched as the plane lifted off on its southern journey toward Greece. They'd all meet back at Castle Rachlav soon, hopefully. As the strobe lights from the plane faded into the black of the night, Gill turned back to her friends.

"I want to thank you all for being here and coming with me. Other than Pavel, none of you know Tanis, but I can assure you this goes way beyond Tanis's kidnapping. We have to start knocking heads somewhere and this is as good a place as any."

With that, she locked eyes with Luis. "Captain? How are we getting to England?"

Luis smiled and pointed. There was an ancient C-130 Hercules cargo plane being fueled up at the end of the runway. Another pilot was jogging across the tarmac toward them. Human, from the lithe but heavy way he ran. Interesting how easily she could spot her own kind after so much time with the Vampires and Weres.

The man reached them, snapping a salute to her and to Luis, nodding to the others. "Captain Clemente? I'm Major Josiah Du Lac. I will be your day pilot."

Turning to Gillian, he flashed a brilliant smile and extended his hand. "Captain Key, I presume."

Du Lac was an attractive light-skinned black man with cover-model looks and a body to match. He was also a crack marine pilot who was tickled to be assigned to even a portion of the legendary team of Key and Company.

Gillian looked at the proffered hand and shook it warmly. "Thank you, Major. Rank acknowledgement isn't necessary since I am retired from active duty, but I appreciate the gesture."

"Once a marine, always a marine, Captain." Du Lac's personality was sparkling and Gill had to smile.

"Yeah, you're right. Now let's get this bucket in the air shall we?"

She moved off toward the C-130 Hercules with Trocar muttering to no one in particular, "Does anyone have any semblance of a plan in mind?" They all ignored him.

Everyone piled into the giant aircraft and secured themselves on the crew benches lining the inside walls of the plane. That is, everyone but Luis. Since it would be dawn by the time they reached London, the remaining Vampire was secured in a U.S. military regulation casket.

Pulling cargo netting over it, they affix it to the D-rings amidst huge crates of additional equipment and supplies bound for England. As a civilian, Gillian wasn't high enough on anyone's rung at the moment to commandeer an aircraft for her sole use; they'd gotten lucky.

Major Du Lac switched on the propellers and the massive engines roared to life. Gillian leaned back against the side of the aircraft as it began to taxi out, trying to figure out how to begin to look for Tanis when they reached Britain. After they were in the air, she and Kimber got as comfortable as they could to grab a little rest. The Elf and the Werewolf eyed each other warily but neither slept.

The huge plane landed after an uneventful flight, bouncing once before settling onto the tarmac as Du Lac hit the brakes to bring it to a halt some minutes later. After Du Lac shut off the engines, Gill and the others unstrapped and untangled Luis's casket from the netting. The Major went to find a gurney in a nearby supply shed. Trocar or Pavel would have been able to handle the casket alone, but no one wanted to draw undue attention to themselves at the moment.

Other personnel came to unload the rest of the cargo, hardly giving the small party of four and the silver casket a second glance. Gill thanked Du Lac earnestly for his help and discretion. He assured them he was available if they needed him for the return trip.

"I'll finagle it somehow, Captain, don't you worry." After a crisp mutual salute, he took his leave and the rest of them got the hell out of full view.

"Now what?" Kimber wanted to know as they moved inside an old hangar housing dusty World War II aircraft and a myriad of crates.

"I'm thinking!" Gill snapped, then realized she was being cranky. "Sorry Kimber, I am trying to figure out how the hell to even begin to locate Tanis."

A dark, silky voice softly suggested, "Perhaps finding the location of the Vampire community would be in order." Trocar was smiling, but it didn't reflect in his eyes.

Gillian regarded him for a moment. "That would make sense. I'm not thinking logically at the moment."

The tall Grael moved to her. "But think you must, Gillyflower." She grimaced at his old nickname for her as he continued. "This is not like you, Captain, to be so overcome with emotion that you allow yourself to be distracted." He lifted a crystalline brow.

She blushed. "I am not overcome with emotion, you lunatic! I am frustrated and uncertain of what our best course of action should be. I don't want to get everyone killed in the process of tracking down Tanis!"

"You should have thought of that before then, Kemo Sabe." That was from Kimber, who was glaring at her disdainfully, hands on hips. "Whatever it is, Cap'n, you need to snap out of it and get your shit together before we walk into something we can't handle."

Gillian went white. That pissed her off. They were right, but she'd forgotten they could be just as tactless as she could be. "Fine. Just give me a minute. I will get a handle on this."

Pacing, she tapped her front teeth with a fingernail as she launched a dozen plans in her mind and discarded each of them. The others left her alone, letting her decide what to do.

Kimber went with Pavel to track down food for the four of them. Luis would find his own meal when he rose in the evening. Trocar gave Gillian a wide berth, focusing on a book in his pack while his former captain paced the floor of the dusty hangar.

Gillian took the time to think and reflect. While in the service, she'd been selected for work in counterintelligence. The Marines had trained her in anticipation of her working for Special Forces; allowing her to work on a degree in forensic psychology, specializing in counterterrorism. When she made stellar exam marks, they fronted the bill for her PhD while she was still in the service. They'd fast tracked her and had not been sorry.

Captain Key, PhD, had run her crack Special Forces unit efficiently but quietly. Every mission had been a success, every hostage recovered, every assassination carried out with precision and daring. No lives had been lost, except for one hostage who had been killed within hours of his abduction; losses in her unit had been minimal. She'd officially retired early at twenty-six, with a chestful of medals, the respect of the top brass and the unswerving loyalty of her unit, then had gone right into Field Operations.

Now, two years out, she was in her prime, quietly and efficiently gaining professional acclaim within both groups she worked for. Right now, nothing was more important than rescuing her friend and keeping everyone alive while doing it. She hoped she didn't fuck it up.

What to do, what to do . . . ? she thought, tapping her teeth. Trocar was right; contacting the local Vampires would be logical, but it could also be the worst move they could make. She had no idea of who was allied with whom. A mistake at this point could be fatal for everyone, including Tanis. No, there had to be another way.

Gillian grabbed her laptop and plunked down on a dusty

crate. She had a satellite connection for backup and didn't need a cable or port at the moment. Searching the Net, she looked for any establishments in London and the surrounding areas that might be Vampire-owned or at least affiliated.

Her mind was racing endlessly, dividing her attention to focus on more than one issue at once. It was a trait that she had learned early on in her Marine Corps career and what had made her one of their exemplary commanders. It had also allowed her to look at the big picture while examining the details. Right now, she didn't like the conclusions she was beginning to come to. Being out of Romania and away from the shelter of her Vampire friends was giving full reign to her inherent cautiousness. She'd been lax in letting someone else call the shots and take care of her.

Since the world of the Paramortal had been known for thousands of years, going public twenty years ago for the many denizens had been fairly painless. Everyone romanticized the idea of Vampires, Elves, the many varieties of Fey and Ghosts in their midst, were a little more cautious about the Lycanthropes, Grael and true wizards, yet drew the line at very little about the activities of non-Humans. The Paramortal world had blended seamlessly into the world of the Human. Conflicts had been few and brief, generally settled in the councils or courts of the respective offender.

There were few communities who did not welcome their non-Human counterparts with at least a smile, still fewer who were holdouts to the "evil" of the non-Human. If Dracula was becoming more obvious and aggressive in his bid for power elsewhere as he was in Romania, Gillian felt the first glimmer of real fear that an all-out war just might erupt between Humans and the Paramortal world.

Humans would definitely come out on the short end of the deal. There was no way they could fight real magic from creatures that were inherently magic. It would be a proverbial and literal bloodbath and would accomplish Dracula's overall plan, whether he survived or not. In the brave new world, Humans would be the indentured race.

Those were not nice thoughts.

CHAPTER
28

SCRATCHING her head and trying not to think what she was thinking, Gillian noted some businesses, nightclubs, restaurants and events that might be owned or managed by a Vampire proprietor. They'd check those out tonight. Turning her attention to local and international news, she saw what she feared. There were more unexplained disappearances and violent deaths, besides the Paranormal psychologists that she already knew about, in various other occupations and industries.

Speculation was that there were a few rogue groups of werebeasts who were at fault. Authorities reported that the perpetrators would be hunted down and brought to justice in council. So far, public opinion hadn't shifted to the negative. But Dracula was reaching out further and preying on the unwary. It was only a matter of time before it became more obvious and all hell broke loose.

When Kimber and Pavel returned, Gillian shared with everyone what she was speculating as they ate. This led to some heated and excited discussion from Pavel about werebeasts taking the blame and Kimber figuring they ought to go out with guns blazing and kick everyone's asses. Trocar smiled in amusement, then, in a condescending tone, concurred with Gillian about the potential for a global problem between the two existing worlds, eliciting a heated debate with Kimber. Gill let them vent, sitting back and watching as they worked through it like they always did.

Pavel was the random factor at the moment. He was new and didn't quite understand that your fellow USMC buddies could want to rip your heart out in one moment yet walk through fire to rescue you the next. Trocar and Kimber gave him a briefing of their history and assured him that all hostility was only superficial . . . well, mostly. The blonde wolf shook his head and moved imperceptibly toward Kimber, eyeing the tall Elf with eyes that were lovely, blue and very chilly.

After Luis rose to feed and then returned, they got organized with their next move. Splitting up made the most sense. They could cover more ground and wouldn't be as obvious to any locals. Gill called for a taxi to meet them at the cargo entrance to the airfield, then had them dropped off in Soho to find some suitable clothing. The places they would be carousing had specific dress requirements. A lot of information could be gained from the denizens of the night, both Human and not.

The Soho district is a wonderful place in London. Full of every sort of funky, trendy, Goth, or sex shop anyone could imagine. Gill and Kimber decided to go with a trendy look and exited the dark little shop wearing what could only be described as something from Dial-a-Slut and Tawdry Togs for Tasty Trollops.

Kimber was in a black-and-puce leather miniskirt with a fuchsia strapless top edged along the entire top seam with marabou feathers dyed to match the material. Over it all was a Harley biker jacket with lots of zippers and snaps so that she sparkled with silver slashes and dots under the streetlamps.

She had on thigh-high black bitch boots and was carrying a purse that was as wide as she was tall. The fact that the purse concealed a lightweight aluminum crossbow, wooden bolts, miniflamethrower and an uzi was irrelevant—you couldn't see what was in it, anyway. The purse was made out of poofy purple parachute material, stuffed with batting that had been sewn in horizontal rings around the bag. It looked like she'd skinned the Michelin Man then dyed his hide to make a bag. Her Beretta Cougar 8000 9mm was strapped to the upper inside of her thigh. With her skirt as short as it was, she'd have no trouble accessing it.

Gillian's outfit was no better: black leather jacket with a pair of red-sequined, fanged lips embroidered on the back and scarlet-sequined fringe made her look as if the jacket were bleeding constantly. The shirt was a delicate shell pink tank top, with "Bite Me" in silver sequins over her generous chest. Her pants were faux leopard skin, tight but made of lycra and she had flat calf-high boots on in the same leopard print.

The backpack she wore instead of a purse resembled a large quiver and held a veritable arsenal as well. Mini phosphorus grenades and a cute little launcher for them; a dart gun with silver nitrate–loaded syringes; an identical crossbow to the one Kimber carried plus bolts; a sawed off .12-gauge shotgun; extra shells and a mini LED ultraviolet flashlight.

In addition, she had a small packet of salt, sandalwood incense, willow oil, basil, a copper dish, a lighter and flash powder that would allow her to bind any errant spirit that pestered them long enough for them to get away. Her trusty Glock 22C was strapped to her waist in back and a Walther PPK 7.65ml was in a belly band in front. It was a smaller, lighter gun than the Glock, but it still had a delivery like a brick through a plate glass window.

"Gillian?"

She turned at her name and stared openmouthed at the Vampire coming toward them. Luis looked hot. The tall Puerto Rican Vampire was dressed in a black silk shirt laced at his chest and wrists, very tight black linen pants, boots and a black cape lined with emerald green silk. Gillian rolled her eyes as Luis swept his cape back and bowed theatrically to her and Kimber.

Kimber curtsied, giggling, then launched into a full belly laugh. Gill and Luis followed the direction of her eyes and gasped before joining her in laughter. The elegant Dark Elf smiled and twirled, showing off his own red leather cape and outfit apparently from Red Riding Hood Does Bondage. The domination outfit, which covered his lithe six-foot, two-inch muscular form, encased him in screaming red leather from neck to feet. Trocar managed to look vaguely obscene since every ebony muscle was clearly defined—the leather was lightweight dragonet skin and clung to every chiseled bulge. Every bulge. Kimber gave a wolfish whistle at the Grael's endowments so lusciously displayed. Gillian could only laugh and point.

Pavel stepped around Trocar, looking vaguely annoyed in a skimpy loincloth and . . . collar? Yup. There it was. A rhinestone collar to which was attached to a violet leather leash, held by the Elf. The tall blonde wolf looked like a movie extra from

Gladiator via *Star Trek*. The loincloth that barely grazed his thighs was purple and sheer, held up by a twilight-pink Roman belt. Underneath the loincloth, fully visible through the sheer fabric, was a pale blue, shimmery thong that encased *his* dimensions, just barely.

Kimber's laugh faded and a glassy-eyed leer took its place. Pavel's stoic face cracked as he winked and also curtsied, sending Gill into another spasm of laughter, this time joined by Luis and Trocar, who were helplessly leaning on each other, tears streaking their faces as they eyed the women's gear.

Gillian wiped her eyes and straightened. They'd needed a little tension break and that was it. Now back to business. Trocar figured he and Pavel could cruise the seamier side of town via the sex clubs posing as a couple. Luis was off to a party in a classier neighborhood that the proprietor of the cape store had suggested. Local high grand pooh-bahs of all flavors would be in attendance and he might be able to garner some useful information, either directly or by eavesdropping.

Gillian and Kimber were off to the areas around the Tower of London and Highgate Cemetery. Melancholy members of both Human and Vampire races tended to haunt both after hours. If they got lucky, they might make a contact or two, and Gill had an idea.

Everyone had their respective assignments. Trocar promised to make arrangements at the Park International Hotel near Knightsbridge for the next few days. If they found Tanis they could always check out early; if not, they'd have to adjust their strategy. They'd all meet there at dawn. All except Luis. He'd find a place to rest in one of the many parks around the city. Vampires didn't need coffins to sleep if earth itself was available. Gill didn't like one of them being separated from the rest, but they didn't want to attract attention with asking for a coffin-safe room at the hotel.

Parting company, Gillian and Kimber hailed a cab and traveled to the Tower first. An imposing structure, the oldest part of which, the White Tower, built in 1078, replaced a wooden fortress built by William the Conqueror. The Tower had a dark and bloody history that made Gillian hesitant to step up to the main gates. Kimber noticed her reluctance. "What's up, boss?"

Gillian's eyes remained fixed on the imposing structure. "I'm an empath, remember?" Even from twenty yards away, she could feel it. Fear. Death. Age. Anguish. The buildings within were old and did not contain their secrets or their shame well.

"Oh, yeah," Kimber said, still looking at her. "Well, get your empathic ass in there so we can find some answers."

Jolted out of her thoughts by her former lieutenant's bluntness, Gill took a fortifying breath and walked forward. It was nine thirty PM, almost time for the Ceremony of the Keys, carried out at ten PM every night without fail for seven hundred years. She had managed to get tickets at the last minute by tipping a vendor rather handsomely.

Just walking through the main gate was impressive. Gill shielded instinctively. Good to know those defense mechanisms were still there when she needed them. She knew where she was and what she might encounter and her defenses had automatically snapped on. Sure enough, there were Ghosts aplenty here. The highest activity she could sense came from one area. Approaching one of the warders, the guards in the beefeater uniforms who lived and worked at the tower, Gillian inquired as to what lay in that area.

"That is where the Chapel of St. Peter ad Vincula is, miss. And beyond that is seven Tower Green." He responded in a lovely upper-class accent, pointing that way.

"What are those places?" Gill asked.

"The chapel is right next to the former place of the scaffold, where most of the prisoners who were executed are buried, miss. Seven Tower Green is the residence King Henry the Eighth built for Queen Anne Boleyn when they were first betrothed."

"Thank you," Gillian whispered, distracted.

She fixated on the direction he had pointed and moved a little to the side, hoping to be lost in the gathering crowd. Kimber followed, eyes and ears on full alert. Soon, they managed to slip into the shadows, and ran for the Chapel.

"Tell me again, Gillian, why are we going *here*?" Kimber wasn't nervous, she just wasn't overly fond of Ghosts.

Gill stopped in front of a small chapel with a brass plaque. "Because Ghosts know a lot more than people give them credit for. Now let me see if I can entice anyone to come talk to us."

"Oh yay!" Kimber said cheerfully, turning to watch the direction where they'd come from while Gillian pulled several items out of her backpack.

Putting a little pile of crystals on the copper dish from her pack and dousing them with willow oil, Gill flipped some flash

paper on it and lit it. There was a brilliant orange-white flare as
the paper lit and ignited the oil and incense. A handful of basil
was spread in a circle around herself and Kimber. Then, opening herself to the feelings of the place, Gillian sent out a soundless call. She wasn't specific; she didn't have a particular Ghost
in mind; there were so many that used this place for a haunt.

Age, the smell of old stones, ancient brickwork, sweat, steel,
the thick straw ... blood ... it all seeped into her nose and
senses. A chill crept over both of them. Kimber's teeth chattered and she backed up closer to Gillian. They could hear the
voices of the warders as they carried out the Ceremony of the
Keys, but the two of them were utterly alone amid the darkened
buildings. Almost.

Opening her eyes, Gillian could see the swirling whorls of
ectoplasm dancing through the air. There was a lot of them. Not
good. Maybe her call had been a little too effective. Ghosts
couldn't directly hurt a living person, but they could literally
scare them to death or make them run into walls or off a cliff if
one was handy. These Ghosts had a lot of reason to be pissed
off. Anger was one of the prevalent emotions Gillian was picking up. Annoyance was another.

"Why do you call us?"

A hollow, aristocratic and female voice asked, directly behind her. Gillian turned slowly. Showing fear at this point was
redundant. The inhabitants already knew she and Kimber were
scared from the amount of fear being projected at them. She
had to look up a little. The form that shimmered into solidity
was one of an older woman dressed in clothing from the fifteen
hundreds. Nobility by the looks of her: elegant, slender, refined,
and with a challenging look in her hollow eyes.

"I call you for wisdom and advice, Lady." Gillian was careful to keep her voice respectful.

One on one with a Ghost like Dante she could defend herself
pretty well, but there were too many of them here and shadowy
shapes were forming all around them. The Ghost cocked her
head, barely showing a faint line diagonally across but not tran-
secting the neck and traveling up the sharp, lined jaw. Gill
looked closer and saw a number of slashes in the woman's
clothing and on the visible parts of her skin.

Pale shadow lines and flaws on the luminescent visage as if
the woman had been viciously attacked by scores of sharp in-
struments. The scent of old death was all around them. Memory

stirred as Gill's British-history-recall brain cells went on over-drive to determine who this Ghost was that she was about to speak to. Something clicked and she knew.

"Countess Margaret Pole?"

The Ghost drew herself up proudly. "That was my name in life, yes."

"Countess, I am Gillian Key, a psychologist for those of your kind and I am seeking information about the Vampire Lord Dracula." Gillian didn't like using Dracula's name directly, but it would certainly expedite the situation if she cut to the chase.

The Ghost's eyes widened, then narrowed. "Why do you seek the knowledge from a Ghost and not a Vampire?"

Gill extended her hands, palm up, in a helpless gesture, "While I can determine age or power in a Vampire, I don't have the knowledge or the skill to always correctly determine an evil Vampire or a good one, Lady." That was honest. Maybe the Ghost would appreciate honesty for a change.

Countess Margaret Pole had been a noble, loyal to king and country. Her only crime had been to raise a son, Reginald, who wrote treason against King Henry the Eighth. Reginald, being a chickenshit as well as deemed a traitor, left England. Since Henry couldn't locate the son to bring to justice, he focused his attention on the old woman.

The seventy-year-old countess was imprisoned in the Tower for two years with no arrest or trial. One morning, her jailers arrived to announce that she was to be beheaded within the hour. They led her to the scaffold, where she refused to kneel in the thick straw and place her neck upon the block, knowing she was innocent.

Enraged, the novice executioner went after her, swinging his axe. Lady Margaret ran screaming as he pursued her, literally hacking the old woman to death as she ran, right in front of the horrified guards. Her death was violent, messy murder, pure and simple. Lady Margaret Pole was an angry Ghost and had lit-tle reason to feel the need to help the living.

Her eyes remained narrowed as she regarded the smaller blonde before her. "Many do not have the skill or knowledge to determine innocence or guilt, let alone evil or good, Human."

She paced around Gillian, who turned with her, never letting her out of her sight. The Ghost continued, "Why should I answer you? It is nothing to me."

"Margaret, stop being haughty and answer the young lady."

Gillian spun, hand going to her Walther at the sound of a resonant male voice that came from her right. A man was there, dressed in sixteenth-century clothing. He had been handsome in life, tall and slender. Unlike Margaret, there was a distinct line across his neck. Also unlike Margaret, he bowed formally to Gillian, who was backed up against Kimber, who also had her hand on a gun.

"Sir Walter Raleigh, m'lady," the Ghost intoned.

Gillian breathed a sigh of relief and returned his bow. Though executed unjustly as well, Raleigh had been a gentleman in life, and apparently remained a gentleman in death—but she wasn't after an ally, just information.

"Thank you, Sir Walter. I appreciate your kindness."

Gillian was careful not to let either formed Ghost out of her sight. Kimber was also doing her best to watch the swirling, partially formed ectoplasm to see who else might pop in.

"Dracula does not frequent here, ma'am." Raleigh's voice had a slight nasal quality that grated on Gill's nerves. "However, the Ghosts of the Tower have been asked to join with him to help establish Paramortal rule." Oops. That idea of hers about him still being a gentleman went right out the window. Raleigh's eyes glittered in the moonlight. His look wasn't friendly. "His request is being considered."

Oh, how festive, Gill thought, but she didn't interrupt.

"We have little reason to love mortals, you see." This was from Lady Margaret. "Mortals did little for us when we lived and have done nothing for us as noncorporeal beings."

The Ghosts were circling now, forming a tighter area around the two women. Gill felt Kimber's back tighten up—hell, they were both nearly paralyzed with fear.

This was getting out of hand. The ectoplasm was whirling faster and more figures were forming. Gillian knew, as did Kimber, that the Ghosts couldn't hurt them directly, but they could make sharp objects fall down on the women if they tried to get away. Here at the Tower there were way too many sharp objects on display. Icy hands were reaching out and touching the women with fleeting brushes. It was unnerving.

"We meant no offense to any of you," Gill said between chattering teeth.

"None taken," Raleigh replied, looming closer.

"Captain, let's leave." Kimber was done with this.

Gillian was too. She'd hoped to gain some useful information, but all they'd done was piss off the spirits. Slowly, back to back, they moved toward the front entrance of the Tower. Not surprising, the Ghosts followed, crowding closer.

"My apologies for whatever was done to you in life, but I had nothing to do with it," Gillian ground out, still moving slowly but surely toward light and people.

"All the living and the mortal are answerable to how our brethren are treated . . . m'lady." Raleigh's voice was colder and more nasal.

The collective Ghost fear that was being generated overcame the two former Marines. Gillian grabbed the salt and threw it at them, shouting an incantation of binding. There was no way in hell it would hold that many, but it would break their ranks for a moment. The Ghosts swooshed back, breaking ranks just enough for the two women to bolt through, then surged forward, shrieking, bleeding, carrying body parts and heads. Gill and Kimber ran flat out, Ghosts following, into the crowd of people witnessing the Ceremony of the Keys.

One look at the ectoplasmic horror approaching them and the crowd panicked. The resulting stampede carried Gillian and Kimber outside the Tower. White, horrible faces stared and screamed after them but they were free of the direct fear.

"Boss, remind me never to do that with you again," Kimber gasped.

She wasn't happy. Gill didn't blame her. She nodded, waiting for her heart to stop trying to come out of her chest and for her breathing to slow down. This was bad. The Tower Ghosts were powerful, old and very, very angry. If they'd thrown their alliance behind Dracula, things were about to get interesting. Though bound by the geography of their haunt, the Ghosts still could exercise influence on any Paramortal who happened through the gates. Since Gillian had just tipped her hand, someone was bound to find out there were mortals asking about Dracula.

"When you're writing your memoirs, is there a part where you say, 'And then we went to Highgate Cemetery?' " Kimber wanted to know. There was some of the spark back in her eyes.

"Yes." Gillian took a moment to collect herself and get her bearings.

They were outside the Tower, so they needed to go . . . northeast. It took a few minutes to hail a cab from the aftermath of mass desertion due to the tourists versus Ghosts incident.

Highgate was ten kilometers away. They could have jogged it easily but Gillian didn't want to arrive in another potentially hazardous place all sweaty and out of breath. There was plenty of time for being exhausted later.

The cab pulled down a one-way street and stopped before a formidable carved stone gate. "'Ere ya go."

The cabbie's accent was of the lower class but he'd been friendly and polite. They got out, Gill paid him and they went through the dark entrance.

"This is gonna suck too." Kimber muttered. She showed no pretense of being quiet but reached into her Michelin Man purse and pulled out her crossbow, clicking a bolt into place.

At Gillian's look, she said, "Do not even tell me to put it up. I've had enough bullshit for one night."

After a moment of thought, Gillian drew the Walther and cocked it, reflexively moving into a predatory stance as they moved into the darkness of Highgate.

The cemetery itself was legendary. The oldest section, the west side, had been built in 1839; the east followed in 1854. Both famous and infamous, common and noble lay here in their eternal sleep. Vampires and a variety of Reborn lived and skulked here. One of the tombs had even been the inspiration for Bram Stoker's vision of Dracula's resting place. The fictional Dracula, that is. The real Prince Dracula wouldn't be caught dead in a place like this, all broken down and overgrown. Gillian smirked at her humor as she continued down the cracked and crumbling footpath into the foreboding darkness.

If their nerves hadn't been on edge, she probably wouldn't have reacted as strongly; at least that was what she'd tell herself later. The cemetery was full of beings both living and dead. A shriek coming from her right raised Gill's hackles. There were loud voices and the sound of a blow being struck. Not bothering to look back at Kimber, whom she knew would follow, Gillian tore across the landscape, jumping over fallen and upright tombstones, splashing through standing water, narrowly avoiding breaking her ankle with the uneven terrain.

They were making a hell of a lot of noise but she didn't care. That scream had been Human and female. Bursting through a line of shrubs, Gill saw the Human girl backed up against a tree. She looked terrified and probably would have bolted at the sight of two people bursting from the undergrowth, except for the male Vampire who held her by the throat, pinning her against the large tree. The Vampire's hand glowed eerily in the moonlight—he was agitated but held her throat loosely to torment her.

Gillian didn't stop for small talk; her empathy told her that this was a young Vampire, maybe not newly dead but young and cocky. Gathering herself, she jumped and power-kicked him, knocking him away from the woman. It didn't knock him down; Vamps had reflexes like Elves. He spun, hissing, to glare at the business end of Kimber's crossbow, which he could see held wooden-shaft bolts, and the short blonde who had her gun pointed at his head.

The black robes of a Satanist adorned the Vampire, embroidered in red with a stylized image of the Horned God and various runes, which Gillian could tell at a glance made no sense; they were random and for decorative purposes only. He apparently was too stupid to know that the Horned God was pagan, a god of fertility, and the only blood that interested him was menstrual, from his female followers.

Lucifer, on the other hand, who the Satanists believed they worshipped, was a fallen angel—his countenance would be too beautiful and too terrible to be embroidered on a cheap robe, no matter how evil he was. Plus, as she'd learned while studying comparative religion in college, gods, goddesses and angels rarely condescended to involve themselves in petty Earthly matters.

Gillian had been born Jewish and raised in the Unitarian Universalist Church; she was not religious, but she was spiritual. She'd toyed with some Kabbalistic magic and theory during her youth and knew worshipping anything, good or evil, lent power to the being through the thoughts and intentions of the worshipper. Pagan, wiccan, however someone wanted to term her, Gill used magic occasionally, but it was herb or green magic, which required a respect and love of nature and living things. She respected and accepted a higher power, but had no particular creed, followed no dogma, so the symbols on the Vampire's cloak and apparent religion held no threat or fear for her.

Wiccans, pagans and even some misguided Satanists used Highgate for ceremonial worship frequently, due to the high spiritual activity and the seclusion. No one wanted to canvass the cemetery at night, so they had free rein to do what they wanted. The Vamp was young, his head shaved and a goatee in the most modern style graced his face. He also smelled musty, Gillian noted. A fanatic in life apparently, he was sleeping in the graveyard itself during the day.

Many younger Vampires who were Christian, Goths or Satanists in life chose to rest among the truly dead after their rebirth. Some did it for the shock value, others out of guilt for their choice. Most older Vampires, including most wiccan, agnostic, Goths, Jewish, pagan, even some of the more enlightened Christian-oriented wouldn't be caught dead in a real cemetery, especially the older or ancient ones. They tended to be fastidious and private, disdainful of theatrics.

"Bitch." The Vampire hissed again. "I shall feast on your sweet blood, then tear out your throat."

"And I shall fuck up your knee." Kimber suggested as she fired a bolt into the Vamp's left kneecap. He fell screaming and writhing. That hurt no matter what species you were.

Gillian moved and stood a little back but over him, her gun pointed at his head. "And I shall make your head explode like a melon, numbnuts."

Over her shoulder, she ordered the girl to get out. From the crackling in the bracken, the girl complied. The Vampire was heaping curses upon them as he snapped off the wooden shaft and drew it shakily out of his leg.

"I will heal, bitch, and I will find you."

Gill took the opportunity while he was down and busy to kick him in the face. Howling, he clutched his face and rolled back and forth on the ground.

She wasn't impressed. "Let me tell you something, asshole. I am your worst fucking nightmare. I have contacts all over the city and I will be all over your ass like the black plague if you abuse another Human."

To emphasize the point, she shot him in the face, the bullet going through the hand covering it, through and out the other hand and side. He was one of Dracula's progeny, there was no doubt. Osiris and Dionysus wouldn't stand for one of their Vampires taking up worship of either Satan or the dark arts.

"You tell your master to tell his master, that I am gunning for all of you." Gillian's voice was deceptively quiet but so full of menace that the Vamp stopped screeching long enough to stare at her, wide-eyed.

"The compact," he said, spitting broken teeth and blood. "You Humans cannot violate it!"

"Fuck the compact and fuck you," Kimber snapped, firing another bolt into his hip.

Gillian raised a delicate eyebrow as he clutched his newly wounded hip. "You are in violation right now, dumbass, for attacking that girl. I want you to spread the word so that your own master skins you and uses your guts for garters."

The Vamp paled even more, if that was possible. "No! She was willing!"

Gillian shot him again, this time in the shoulder, careful to only wound and not kill. "Liar."

"Stop! What do you want?" The Vampire was visibly cringing. Of course he had two bullet and two crossbow-bolt holes to contend with, so the women couldn't blame him for being a little skittish.

"I want you to tell me what you know about your master's orders."

He looked truly confused. "What fucking orders?"

Obviously he was a newly dead. Older Vamps were masters of perfect diction and rarely swore. The strongest English profanity Aleksei and Tanis had ever used were *hell* or *damn*—the Egyptians and Dionysus didn't swear at all. Hmm . . . a new angle to explore.

"The orders you all have from your dark prince, fucktard."

Gillian stepped closer and the Vamp scuttled back, still on the ground, growing even paler and now trembling. "Unless you want your rebirth to be one of the shortest on record, I suggest you start talking," she finished meaningfully.

"I don't know! I don't!" the Vamp wailed. "I am newly made, they don't tell me anything!"

Gillian moved up under Kimber's watchful eye and put the gun against his temple. "Wrong answer. Try again."

He tried to grab her and she kicked his elbow, bruising her foot but snapping the joint. He shrieked again and Gill swore, rubbing the top of her foot against her calf muscle. This time she put the gun against his forehead,

"I am going to ask what you know just once more."

"We are to cause panic, confusion . . . turn the Humans against our own kind." The Vamp managed to sound contrite and pathetic.

Gillian wasn't moved. "Why?"

"I don't know . . . ," he shrieked as her finger tightened on the trigger and Kimber moved closer. "Truly! I do not!"

He either didn't know or he had been frightened by something much bigger and badder than she was, so Gillian decided to drop it. Moving back but keeping the gun level on him, she said, "All right. Now, you remember what I told you: no more coerced, unwilling victims or I will track you, find you, then cut out your heart and feed it to the Lycanthropes."

Nodding, the Vamp tried to rise, but couldn't since both knees were damaged. He settled for crawling rapidly, like a giant, silk-covered spider off into the darkness.

Kimber lowered the crossbow. "That could have gone better."

Gill started to answer her, but there was an immense whirring overhead as though a plague of locusts was descending upon them. Both shared a glance. "That's a bad sound," Gill remarked, then took off at a dead run with Kimber peeling off in the opposite direction as the whirring got louder.

They didn't know what it was, but "divide the enemy, then kick its ass" had always been their motto. Hopefully whatever it was would split up and follow them both, giving them a better chance at escape or victory. They'd meet up after they circled around.

Mind racing as to what the hell it was, Gillian skidded up to a large moss-covered tomb and booted the chained wooden doors. The small confines of the tomb would limit access to her and give her a clear shot at whatever pursued. The wood was old and warped, so she kicked it again, hoping that it would give, but it creaked and held. She hadn't wanted to shoot the chains out of fear of alerting whatever was after her to her position. It turned out, her fears and the noise wouldn't have mattered.

Whatever was overhead and after her was closer and hot on her trail; it was clear now that she couldn't outrun it. The whirring grew louder and sounds like chirping and giggling were heard over the din.

What the hell? Gillian thought as she gave up on the door and turned to fight. Dropping to one knee, she aimed at the blackness overhead, trying to fix on a target, fishing one-handed in her bag for the ultraviolet flashlight. Directly over her something whooshed by. She ducked and it slammed into the old tomb. Gill spun and leveled her gun at a small lavender colored . . . Pixie?!?

"Oh Baldour's balls!" she snarled as the small, winged creature shook its head to clear it, getting to its tiny feet and staggering around for a moment, seemingly dazed.

Gill aimed a vicious kick and sent it spinning off into the bracken. The rest of the multicolored flock descended on her in that moment of distraction. The battle was brief, violent and mostly silent on Gillian's part; the Pixies kept shrieking their glee and chittering among themselves. She didn't waste energy screaming or heaping curses on the little winged menaces. Batting at them, getting off a shot or two, kicking several, Gillian fought to the best of her ability, but there were just too many of them.

Pixies. Cronus on a cracker, she hated Pixies. They were sort of a mangled cross between their distant cousins the demi-Fey, Imps, and true Fairies. They were also a pain in the ass. Traveling in flocks, the little terrors were the cannon fodder of the Fey world. Typically they were sent out to antagonize or capture an adversary deemed either too dangerous or too inconsequential. They died by the hundreds on their missions, but always accomplished their task. As stupid as they were determined, once set on a course, Pixies would cross land or sea, endure snow or fire to obtain their objective. They needed no provisions, needed no further instructions; they just did their job.

Historically they were used by all denizens of the Paramortal world who held a pact with the Fey. Gillian's mind was racing as she tried to fight them off. Who had sent them, why, and were she and Kimber really the targets? whirled through her mind. They could have been told to bring back two women walking together from Highgate and would do just that. It wouldn't matter if it were the wrong two women. Pixies were just that stupid.

Gillian had managed to shove the Walther PPK back into her pocket and out of sight as she realized she might not win this fight. Like the Glock, it had safety features built in, but she didn't want to risk the Pixies getting hold of a loaded gun, particularly with herself in close proximity.

"Ow! Shit!" She jumped as the teeth from a lime green one sank into her wrist.

Not good. Not good at all. Pixies' saliva was venomous. It wouldn't kill her, but it had a narcotic, hallucinogenic effect if enough of it got into her system. The little creature smirked at her through bloodstained teeth and Gill took that moment to punch it in the face, sending it flying into a nearby tree where it crumpled and was still. The rest of them paid no attention to their fallen comrade and continued the assault.

Soon, despite her best efforts, Gillian was trussed up like Gulliver by hundreds of silky cords and had been bitten several more times. Her vision shifted, the dark landscape whirled and Gillian relaxed in her captor's nets. The Pixies chattered excitedly, picked up Gillian's bag and Gillian then zoomed away into the night.

CHAPTER
29

THE darkly handsome Vampire surveyed his prey with eyes of glacial pale green, crystalline and icy. Even trussed up like a Christmas goose, the woman was attractive; her friend as well. Prince Dracula smiled to himself as he imagined the fun he would have with these two. Bringing Rachlav to his knees and under his thumb would be a delight before he killed them all.

With Aleksei out of the way, the Romanian Vampires would be his again. Dracula would again command all of Eastern Europe's blood drinkers and their allies. With the lot of them at his back, he would move against Osiris. The Greek Lord, Dionysus, was a wild card and would pose no real threat. His followers weren't organized enough to launch a serious hazard, and Dracula could afford to be selective in his war effort.

Selective he would be in how he dealt with Rachlav. The Romanian Count was strong; powerful enough to challenge him for control. Dracula had made sure Aleksei was at all times surrounded by those who could dampen his powers. Some of the Dark Fey had been allied to the *voldevode* and had blanketed Aleksei's lands with spells to ensure that he did not come to full power while Dracula was indisposed. Now that Dracula had made his intentions known, the Fey were reconsidering their positions.

Blood was blood. Whether it came from a Human or Paramortal source mattered little to a Vampire. They would be either cooperative conquerors in Dracula's brave new world or take their places with the Human cattle. Most of the Fey resented the implication that they would be, at best, no more than a lovely token populace within that world with the Vampires owning the full power.

Now, without Dracula's knowledge or intent, some of those spells he had ordered as a dampening field around Romania were weakening, crumbling and not being replaced. The local Fey were growing divided in their loyalties; realizing that this particular Vampire, whose magical strength they'd been ordered to quell, might be powerful enough to challenge the Dark Prince, they allowed the spells to corrupt and fade. As the vast metaphysical portals clanged open, Aleksei's world suddenly began to hum with ancient magic once again.

Aleksei felt it. It was like the surge of a thousand generators switching on. Tingling from head to foot, Aleksei looked at the darkened Romanian skies. What the hell? It felt as he did when he first rose reborn: suffused with energy and power, more power than he'd ever felt. His questing thought was answered . . . in more than one manner.

"You are coming into your own, my friend. Take what is yours and use it." Osiris's mind contact was always staggering to Aleksei, but not this time.

This time he felt invigorated by contact from the Egyptian Lord. Almost as if he were becoming . . . *"More powerful, yes,"* again the reverberation on his mind and psyche. *"You can be as Dionysus and I are. Use it, Aleksei. Save those you love."*

He turned away from the stars, back to the castle, ready to arrange a flight, find Tanis—and Gillian. Then, a whisper. A ghost within his mind. The voice of his beloved brother, now nearly shattered with defeat, touched his thoughts.

"England."

Silver eyes glittered and hardened to icy platinum as every muscle tightened with rage. Tanis was near death. The fact that he had managed contact with Aleksei, via the newfound powers, was nothing short of miraculous. Those responsible would pay for whatever damage had been done, and pay with their lives if Tanis met true death.

Gillian. Despite wanting to choke her at the moment, Aleksei prayed that she would find Tanis, and prayed that she wouldn't. Any being that had the ability to reduce his powerful brother to such a state could snuff out the Human's life easily. He knew the former Marine could take care of herself under normal circumstances with artillery and a battalion at her back, but as far as he knew, she was loose with nothing but a lone Werewolf for a companion; and these circumstances were far from normal.

After the damage done to Maeti that Dionysus had reported to him, Aleksei was afraid to hope that the brave little Human would still be alive. Dionysus had sent word that very night that he and Maeti were in Greece—to stay, it would seem. At least for now.

That left one option. He would follow them to England and bring them back. Walking swiftly, he headed for the warm lights of his ancestral home, farther up the mountain. Anubis and the rest of the Egyptians would hold the fort here. Cezar and his wolves would continue to patrol the borders. Pavel would not be held accountable for following orders to protect Gillian, no matter where she went.

They'd discovered the young wolf's disappearance the same night Gillian didn't return to Castle Rachlav. Cezar was proud that Pavel was doing his job and sticking with Gillian. Aleksei was furious that Gillian would risk herself and a pack member, but Cezar had suggested that was the least of their problems at the moment. Besides, Gillian was better off with even one known ally rather than facing danger alone.

When Aleksei entered the castle, Sekhmet noticed instantly that the Romanian Vampire was drawn taut as a piano wire. Mentally calling her mate, Anubis, she followed at a discreet distance to the library. Aleksei didn't waste time explaining what had happened to him. What was apparently happening to Tanis and where Gillian and Pavel were was more important. Besides, Anubis, Sekhmet and the other Egyptian Vampires had been informed by Osiris that Aleksei was more than prepared to handle this crisis.

"Then you must go to them, my friend," Anubis's beautiful voice echoed all their thoughts. "Find them, Aleksei, but do not judge her too harshly. She has only her courage and her honor. You are lucky to have such a friend, as is Tanis."

"I know," Aleksei said resignedly. "I am furious with her for her foolish act, but I am proud of her too. No other Human would have risked so much to save a Vampire they were not bound to." He left to prepare for his travel.

Sekhmet and Anubis exchanged a glance. Neither thought that Aleksei had noticed the time frame on Gillian's oath had lapsed during the last week. Now there was nothing to stop them from exploring the possibilities in their friendship. "He will remember when it is time," Anubis chuckled, pulling Sekhmet to him for a cuddle.

"We will pray to our gods for them," Sekhmet replied, then let him take her mouth for a smoldering kiss.

Back in London at the hotel, Trocar and Pavel were growing concerned. Gillian, Kimber and Luis had failed to return for their rendezvous. Electing to give the women and Luis a bit more time before panicking, Pavel lounged on the elegantly covered couch in the ornate suite.

"Where could they be?" Pavel growled, inspecting the actual flimsiness of his kilt.

Trocar was pacing, nervously running a hand through his silken, frothy hair. "I do not know. Since they went to separate destinations, we cannot assume that harm has befallen all of them." He stopped a moment. "Still . . . how long, wolf, would it take you to track the Captain and Lieutenant Whitecloud?"

Pavel sat up, ignoring the question for the moment. "You still address them by their military rank?" He realized that he was jealous of the Elf's prior relationship with both Gillian and Kimber. Especially Kimber.

Trocar smiled and it was wondrous. "Habit." He laughed. "It pains me to admit it, but I do have a great deal of respect for them both. Captain Key is a formidable leader, for a Human. Kimber, is . . . well, Kimber." There was no malice in his tone so Pavel quelled his irritation at the Grael's obvious affinity for Kimber.

Catching the Werewolf's almost imperceptible stiffening, Trocar assured him. "We were lovers once, but the time for us to have been together is past. I am not a rival, wolf. Do as you will. Now, however, please tell me, can you track them?"

"You may call me by my name, Elf. And yes, I can track them, even in Human form."

"Very well, then let us go to where we last met. Time works against us in this game, Pavel."

The Werewolf relaxed visibly at the soothing tone in the Grael's voice. The Elf was beautiful by any standard and the effect wasn't lost on the young wolf. Trocar knew exactly how he affected others and used it to his advantage. Pavel was stressed and Trocar needed him calm. He gestured gracefully to the door, watching as Pavel rose and came forward, sheepishly handing the Elf the end of the leash still attached to his collar.

Trocar took it with bemusement. "It will be worth the charade, my friend, if we find them alive."

Together, the leather dom-clad Grael and pseudosubmissive Werewolf left the room, the hotel, and caught a cab to the little Soho shop to begin their search. It would provide the beginning of the scent trail for Pavel's tracking abilities.

In the annals of history there are few recorded individuals with the depravity of Dracula. His crimes against invaders and visitors were only surpassed by his crimes against his own people, even against his own family. Legends of his dining amidst a forest of twenty thousand of his impaled victims, both dead and dying, abounded. It was said that he dipped his bread in the blood of those executed.

Another oft-repeated story was that he sliced his mistress open from sternum to pelvis when she dared to lie to him about a pregnancy. She had hoped to cheer him up by telling him she bore the fruit of his love. Dracula opened her up like a melon, demanding to know where his child was. There were other stories. Stories of him nailing the hats to the heads of Turkish ambassadors who refused to remove them in his presence; executing babies born out of wedlock and their mothers; flaying nobles who ignored their responsibility to their lands and lord.

Once he took vengeance upon the poor and infirm of his own city. He had invited the lot of them to a feast in a church. Astonished by their ruler's generosity, the unfortunate came to the feast. Dracula fed them well, then ordered the church doors and windows nailed shut. Dracula himself watched as tinder was stacked against the building and set alight. He then bragged that his city held no poor, no sick, no beggars; that only prosperity bloomed under his rule. The legends were true. Transylvania had a monster for a prince.

Dracula was a monster before his rebirth. The power of the Vampire only added to his twisted mentality. Now he was unparalleled in his viciousness and paranoia. Those close to him were there due to demonstrations of unswerving loyalty and blind obedience. His lieutenants possessed intellect as well. Dracula wanted orders followed to the letter, but also carried out in the spirit of the deed.

Watching as the women began to shake off the effects of the Pixie venom, Dracula sent out a silent call before moving to the stairs, leading up from the basement of the elaborate estate. He didn't want his identity or his presence known just yet. By the time the women were under his subordinate's thrall, he would be far away, using his time to plan his move against Rachlav.

The estate itself belonged to one of his trusted entourage: Mr. Oscar Gray, Esquire. He was a fairly young Vampire, but had sought out the dark prince in his mortal days, eager to be of service in exchange for immortality. Dracula's thoughts flickered briefly to his protégé.

Oscar Gray, who at the moment was lounging his six-foot, two-inch gorgeous body by a crackling fire in the upstairs library, had posed under the name of Wilde, a writer. One of his works, *The Portrait of Dorian Gray,* had been a shocking best seller. The story of an ageless immortal who had made a deal with the devil. Dracula found that little plot twist particularly amusing.

In the story, the character, Dorian, had a portrait painted of himself. The portrait, hidden away in a secret room, carried with it all the depravity, disease, debauchery of its owner—aging and morphing into a hideous caricature of its owner while Dorian himself stayed young and beautiful.

The story wasn't exactly fiction. Oscar had led a very checkered lifestyle. Upon contracting syphilis, he had sought and found Dracula, offering his own "soul" as it were, for the Vampire's kiss. Dracula had been only too happy to oblige. Oscar was a particularly juicy coup.

Bright, blond, blue-eyed, beautiful and wholly without a conscience, Oscar was simply charming, winning over mortals and Paramortals alike, a trait Dracula found endearing. His legal expertise was essential to circumvent immigration, acquire property, a dozen different identities, and as bait: a perfect lure for anyone, male or female since he was bisexual and didn't discriminate. Oscar owned the home they were in at the moment, but Dracula's call had gone to another. Someone he wanted to personally take care of Rachlav's little tart. Someone whose proclivity for twisted evil rivaled his master's and was much, much more obvious.

Over one hundred-fifty years before, this someone had become legend. That legend, like him, had never died. Moving through the stately hallways and corridors to pass his master on the stairs with an graceful nod, the Vampire was almost ordinary next to Dracula's dark, compelling beauty. Not particularly tall, about five feet, nine inches, of medium build and frame, his face was rather handsome, but in an almost ordinary, Human way.

Dark brown, wavy hair framed that face and curled gently about the ears. Eyes that were a peculiar shade of reddish brown, almost a rust color, took in the scene as he reached the basement of the estate. Two women, scantily clad and bound, lay before him. The ordinarily handsome face suddenly became fascinating with otherworldly beauty as the Vampire smiled. It would have made him lovely except for the deadly cold malice in his eyes.

Kimber was stirring. The Pixie venom had worked its way through her system, leaving her muddled, bleary-eyed and groggy. Peering out through golden-green eyes, she could see that they weren't alone. She instantly began to assess their situation as her vision cleared. Gillian lay near her but not close enough and didn't seem to have come to yet.

It was a dimly lit, windowless area, damp and dank. Probably a basement. The lone man who faced them was dark, not very tall, handsome but unremarkable. Then he smiled and that smile chilled her more than any threat from any enemy she'd ever faced. Instinct told her to scream, run, get away. Years of training and an iron stubbornness to overcome all obstacles fought a brief internal battle.

"Kemo Sabe," she whispered through a throat that was dry from the effects of the Pixie venom. "We have company."

Dimly, Gillian heard Kimber's whisper. Strange. She felt hungover but without the headache. Opening her eyes tentatively, she saw her friend lying nearby. Their eyes met. It seeped in what Kimber had just said. Shit, now what?

Turning her head slightly, her vision clearing rapidly, Gillian focused on the newcomer. Dark hair, what color eyes—rusty brown?—good looking, but . . . Jesus. She caught the smile that made him beautiful, then her empathy caught the soul and her blood turned to ice. Handsome yes, then suddenly strikingly fascinating and coldly malicious. Vampire. And a crazy fucker at that. No doubt in her mind about it at all. He was practically leaking evil and psychosis.

The voice was deep and inviting, clipped and pure upper-crust British. "My Prince wanted me to welcome you personally, Gillian Key."

He didn't move a muscle, just stood there like a mannequin, but Gillian was scared out of her mind. Pure undiluted evil seemed to radiate from every pore. The more she looked at him, the more it seemed the edges of his silhouette blurred just a little and his face seemed to shift. When she looked away, she couldn't remember exactly what his face looked like. The Pixie venom apparently had lingering effects. It was like coming off a bad acid trip.

"Tell your Prince to go fuck himself," she snapped and was rewarded by a flicker of pure malice in those rust-colored eyes.

"Such language from such a lovely mouth."

The stranger's tone never changed, but Gillian could hear Kimber's teeth chattering. Or was it hers?

"Let's skip the niceties and get to the point. What does your master want?" Gill deliberately used the term *master*. This one didn't look as though he'd enjoy being anyone's servant.

Laughter. He simply laughed, harshly, bitingly. It rolled like broken glass through her mind. "My 'master', as you call him, has entrusted me with . . . your care."

Now his voice was a purring suggestion. She could guess the nature of that suggestion.

"Just fucking lovely." Gillian sighed as she lay back on the damp floor, mentally shaking herself to scrape the Pixie-venom film off her thought processes. "Since you seem to know my name, you have me at a disadvantage, as I don't recall us being introduced."

The Vampire looked at her as though she were a slow student in his class. She could feel his power radiating from him. It wasn't as strong as Aleksei's or Tanis's but it was thick with depravity. He wasn't very old. Maybe a century, not much more. That she could tell. Old or not, his answer made her stomach churn.

"I left my true name long ago, Dr. Key. But my Prince, and history, have named me Jack."

That smile again. *Ew!*

"Perhaps you have heard of me and my particular talents from your history books," he added smugly.

"I'm not sure, is there a special category for sociopathic assholes in fangland?" Gillian smirked while still steadily gazing up at him from her floor-level vantage point. She'd felt him clearly—he was making no effort to conceal what he was, and he was one psychotic son of a bitch by anybody's yardstick.

He hissed at that, and his power surged. Kimber managed to swing her legs around and kick Gillian in the butt. "Shut up!" her partner snarled. "I know we're not supposed to show fear, but pissing him off is not a good plan right *now*!"

"Hey, it couldn't get much worse," Gillian bit back.

"I beg to differ, Dr. Key. It most certainly could be much worse. Just as it was for those lovely ladies in Whitechapel." Now it was the Vampire's turn to smirk as realization dawned in Gill's mind.

CHAPTER

30

SHE paled as realization clicked on, her thoughts picking that particular moment to rally and make sense of what he was saying. Whitechapel, London . . . ladies . . . worse things . . . his apparent age . . . the thoughts were muddled but lining up in a very unfortunate manner. If she were right about who and what stood before her . . . she and Kimber were in deeper shit than they'd ever been in before, without a prayer of getting out of this alive and in one piece. Ideally she was still under the hallucinating influence of Pixie-venom nightmares and would wake up cold and uncomfortable in some random Vampire's basement without the possibility of running into *this* particular Vampire.

Gods above, just this one time, let me be wrong, she prayed silently.

"Whitechapel?" Her mouth was dry and she cleared her throat. "Are suggesting that you are . . ."

"Not suggesting, Dr. Key, just stating a fact." He interrupted her smoothly, dropping his gaze to admire the nails on his left hand.

Kimber, who had also been paying attention and had read some of Gillian's deviant behavior textbooks, was drawing her own conclusions and had an opinion. "Oh *shit*."

"Jack," Gillian began, ignoring Kimber for the moment and

still desperately hoping that she was wrong. She shifted onto her hip and shoulder, raising her head higher to meet his eyes.

"Just Jack?"

She shivered involuntarily in memory of the faded autopsy photos she'd committed to memory, displayed prominently in a textbook on serial killers and their signatures. Wrapping her mind around this was difficult with the Pixie venom, and she really, really didn't want to come to the conclusion she'd already arrived upon.

Being a Vampire would explain how he vanished into history's pages of infamy, never having been caught, his identity to remain a mystery for all time. The most infamous serial killer in history, though his actual body count was fairly low . . . but known for the silent ferocity, the viciousness of his attacks . . . all against women. The things he had done to those women . . .

That chilling smile again. "Saucy Jack."

"Shit."

"Or in more conventional circles, Jack the Ripper."

He smiled more broadly as he watched terror enter the eyes of the two women. They were all the same no matter what century they were in. All of them were in need of guidance and purification from a strong male, especially these modern ones who dressed and acted like men. Sluts. He would see to it that they were properly prepared for his Prince's expectations.

What he didn't count on was that Gillian was just as determined that they would live through this. She was also rapidly formulating a plan to put him to rest once and for all, if she had to come back to England eventually to do it.

Kimber was struggling with her bonds in near panic. Gillian didn't bother, though she was close to the same panic. The Pixies, nimble-fingered little bastards that they were, had done a stellar job of immobilizing them. Until someone untied them or they were given an opportunity to help each other, they would remain tied up.

Talking might be a bad idea, but it was all she had at the moment. Proud of herself that she was able to keep her voice from shaking, she went for it. They were worth more alive than dead or they already would have been gutted and bled out; of that she was certain.

"All right, but I have to assume that even if you are Jack the Ripper, that your boss has told you to keep us alive, or we would already be dead."

Jack laughed. "You may assume that, yes. However, there is no guarantee that you will remain alive, Doctor. At least not in the Human sense." His eyes glittered at them but he still made no move.

Kimber interjected at that point. "But you're a serial killer, even if you are a Vampire. So that would eliminate you, er, feeding on us."

It was Gill's turn to swing around and kick her. "Shut up! Do not help me with making instructive observations, okay?"

After that moment's inattention, he was right beside them, a scalpel in his left hand. Both women flinched back as far as they could in their bindings. They knew his history and his manner of killing. He crouched, careful not to touch either of them directly, and stared at Kimber.

"You are correct. But I am more than that term you use—*serial killer*—my dear. I am what your Dr. Key would term a sexual sadist. Is that not correct, Dr. Key?"

At her surprised look, he added, "I am not illiterate, Doctor. I do read and I do keep up with your world's current events and terms."

"Great. I am impressed that you know your own pathology and diagnosis, you sick twist. Is this the part where you taunt us, then carve us up?" Gill was scared.

Kimber was torn between giving Gillian "atta girl" points for having brass cajones in certain-death situations, and choking her for being a smartass to a serial killer. She settled for squeaking in an inarticulate, unmarinelike manner. "Okay!"

"No, my dear Dr. Key. I am here merely as an incentive for you to cooperate." Jack's voice was soothing, neutral, as he ignored her comment. "If the Prince wanted you dead, he would have sent Bruno."

"And Bruno is worse than you?" she asked incredulously.

"Infinitely. The man has no finesse."

Jack twirled the scalpel in the dim light, studying its razor-sharp edge. Great. Wasn't that just fucking comforting?

Gill let that go. "Cooperate in what?"

"I will let Prince Dracula tell you in his own time. I am what awaits you should you decide to not be agreeable to his suggestions."

He rose. "I must leave you now, but shall return later. At some point I will send down food, drink and"—his gaze raked them both—"more suitable clothing."

With that, he turned to leave. Gillian didn't think—she kicked out with both legs, catching him off guard. As he fell, she bucked again, delivering a two-footed kick directly between his legs. Even a Vampire will notice a direct assault to his gonads and, with a groan, Jack folded like a bad poker hand.

Both women stared in stunned horror as Jack the Ripper assumed the writhing-lotus position on the floor, dangerously close to both of them. Gillian managed to get her shoulders up against Kimber's legs and shoved the other woman further back, away from the thrashing Vampire. Struggling mightily, Gill managed to get her knees under her and tried to get to Kimber, who was nearly bent double, fighting against her bonds.

Abruptly Gillian's head was jerked backward, her alarmed eyes meeting a pair of rust-brown orbs as Jack's fingers wrapped in her hair, pulling her backward, exposing her throat. Fangs slammed down as his mouth opened and his eyes blazed inches from her face.

"You pathetic little slut!" Jack hissed in her ear, twisting her neck painfully.

"Sick twist!" Gillian gasped out, refusing to give him any more of her fear than she already had.

"Oh fuck," moaned Kimber, watching the unfortunate exchange playing out in front of her.

Gillian figured she'd had it. This was a rather incongruous way to die, with Jack the Ripper's fangs in her throat. Silently she began her funeral prayer: *Cast not me down for I have done no evil . . .* —it was all she could do. He had her positioned so she couldn't move. Her strength against his was paltry at best. If she couldn't die fighting, she'd do it with dignity.

"If not for my Prince's order, I would open you like a melon." Jack's voice wasn't getting any better. He had the purring silk of any Vampire, but overlaid on it was maliciousness and hatred so thick she could have cut it with his scalpel.

Scalpel! Where was it? He'd dropped it on the floor, she was sure, or it would now be buried in her throat. Out of the corner of her eye, she saw a glint of silver. Fluttering her eyes shut, she went boneless in his hands. The unexpected collapse of his captive made Jack reflexively let go as she stopped resisting him and Gillian crumpled to the floor. She managed to fall on top of the surgical instrument, praying like hell that the Vampire wouldn't notice it was missing.

"There will be little time for fainting theatrics later, girl."

The Vampire got to his feet, glaring down at the little blonde curled on the floor. Kimber noticed that he wiped the hand he'd held her with on his trouser leg, then kept it out from his body, touching nothing with it. He whirled, gliding up the stairs and out of the room, his image blurring as he moved away from them. The door slammed forcefully behind him.

Once he was gone and they were alone, Gillian rolled toward Kimber. "Well, shit, let's get out of these strings and figure out how to get out of here." She moved to reveal the scalpel beneath her.

"And go where? We don't even know where *here* is!" Kimber pointed out helpfully.

"That's not the point. We can't just sit here and wait for whatever they have in store for us." Gill scooted and kicked the scalpel to her friend. "Here, cut me loose, then I'll do you."

Kimber and her dexterous fingers went to work, scraping the blade off the floor and trying not to slice Gillian's wrists or amputate a finger accidentally.

"Is that guy really Jack the Ripper?" she asked, still shaky.

"I think so," Gill answered. "His clothing was not quite period, but close enough to the nineteenth century. Did you notice how unobtrusive he was? Even now I can't remember what the hell he looked like."

"Yeah, I see what you mean, he's like an 'anybody.' No wonder he was never identified. No one would remember what he looked like," Kimber agreed.

"No one except his victims. He's like a chameleon. He blends into his background," Gillian said as Kimber successfully cut through the right strand and the bindings started to loosen.

That mitigated silence while Kimber fussed with Gillian's remaining bonds. It took awhile, but she got one of her former captain's wrists free.

"There!" Gill declared as she slid her hand free and took the scalpel from her friend. After that, it was only moments before she finished freeing herself and then Kimber.

Free but still trapped. Going up the stairs after Jack was completely out of the question. Who knew what was outside the upper door? They didn't even know what time it was. Damn. What to do, what to do? Gillian remembered her guns; one was still in her pocket, the other still at her back. The Pixies were stupid; they'd missed the weapons. A brief check and Kimber confirmed that she also had her gun. Both drew them out, Gillian deciding to keep the Glock and reholster the Walther.

Kimber whistled lightly. "This gonna help us, boss?"

"I don't know, but maybe we can bluff our way out."

Eyes searching the room, Gillian paced the perimeter, Kimber going the other way at a different height. Kimber was muttering to herself. Gill had to ask.

"What?"

Kimber turned, anger in her shining green-gold eyes. "Some fucking therapist you are, pissing off a sick bastard like that. As an operative, you know better than that! What the hell is wrong with you?" She was angry and let Gillian see it.

Gill stiffened a minute then slumped a little. "You're right, I shouldn't have baited him. But he's not my patient, Kimber, and he's Jack the Ripper. They're going to kill us. When I'm faced with a deal like that, I get snippy. I shouldn't have done it with you here and at risk too. Maybe the Pixie venom was fueling my fire, but it was stupid. I'm sorry."

Her own eyes searched her friend's. "We've been in tight spots before, but never like this, Kimmy. I don't know if I can get us out of this one."

Gill was the only person in the world who could call Kimber "Kimmy" and not be shot. It got through. Kimber grinned, despite her irritation. "Okay, Kemo Sabe, bad Vampire come back soon. What we do?"

Grinning, Gill said, "Well, Tonto, you go get the horses and I'll shoot off the lock, leaving a silver condom behind to remind others of truth, justice and the USMC way."

They laughed briefly, relieving tension. They were still in a world of shit and they knew it. The search of the room continued as they got back to the business of being marines on a rescue mission.

Soon Gillian found a false wall behind the stairs that transected the northeast corner of the room. A little prying and they popped it free. A door lay beneath the drywall. No one squeaked or squealed at their discovery since that might bring more unwanted company. Surprisingly, both of their bags lay in the room with them. Not surprisingly, the weapons they had carried in them were missing.

Kimber pulled a six-inch miniature crossbow out of her cleavage and holstered her gun. It had just one tiny bolt in it. At

Gillian's look, Kimber grinned. "Hey it may not look like much but it's accurate as hell at close range."

"Yeah well, newsflash, I don't *want* to be at close range to use it. Now help me get this door open."

Together, sweating, they managed to pry open the door. It gave suddenly, sliding back wide enough to get them and their purses through. What. The. Hell. Was. That. Smell? Both of them blanched and gagged at the uniquely horrid and sweetish odor that wafted out from the door. Gillian shrugged her leather jacket off and pressed it to her nose and mouth. Kimber followed suit with her poofy purse. Cautiously, they peered into the dank foulness.

Bodies were strewn over the floor, heedlessly thrown upon one another, rotting, decaying, smelling. They looked like women, but from the level of decay it was hard to tell. Gingerly picking their way into the room, Gill led the way. Something wasn't right. Peering closer at a nearby corpse dressed in what used to be a red dress with bleached blonde hair still affixed to its peeling skull, Gillian had a sudden thought and lifted the skirt up with the muzzle of her gun.

"What the hell are you doing?" Kimber squeaked, then wished she hadn't breathed as the fumes entered her mouth.

"Look!" Gill snapped, gagging as well.

Kimber looked. Under the skirt, instead of panties, was a thong barely containing male genitalia that were swollen and putrid from decay. The body had been eviscerated.

A quick perusal of a few of the others told the same story. Transvestite streetwalkers. Some looked as though they had been very feminine looking in life. There must have been fifty or more slaughtered bodies in that room. There were indeed a number of female bodies as well, but the ones with the most damage to them, however, were the males. Wondering who had a beef with the local tranny hookers, Gill jumped when Kimber poked her and pointed up.

There was a small basement window about ten feet up. Cupping her hands, Gillian waited for Kimber's foot. She stepped into the proffered hands and Gill tossed her up to grab the small ledge. Kimber didn't fool around; she smashed the window with her elbow, protected by the poofy purse, and pulled herself up and through. Turning, placing the poofy purse across the sill in case there was residual glass, she lay flat and extended her hand down to pull Gillian up. By some miracle she didn't scream when powerful hands grabbed her by the waist and yanked her back and away.

Gillian was climbing on top of the corpses, trying not to slip in putrefying bodily fluids when the back of her shirt was grabbed and she was hauled straight up and through the window. She found herself on her feet, facing a familiar concerned pitch-black face.

"Trocar!" Impulsively, she hugged him then was taken aback when he pushed her back, holding her at arms length to give her a once-over with his eyes.

"You are undamaged I scc, but there is an unpleasant odor which clings to your hair and skin." The elegant Elf wrinkled his nose and held her where she was, discouraging any further physical contact.

"How did you find us?" Gillian asked, ignoring his commentary about eau de corpse.

Trocar nodded toward Pavel, who was hugging Kimber and wrinkling his own nose. "Ah, Pavel, the famous search-and-rescue Werewolf."

Pavel growled at her. "It is not an activity I enjoy, Gillian, particularly now when you both smell like an open graveyard."

"That's exactly what's down there. At least fifty bodies, some of them male transvestites. There are female ones as well, but it's hard to determine exact numbers, if you know what I mean."

"Do you think it has anything to do with Jack?" Kimber inquired.

Gillian looked hard at her for a moment. "I think that's exactly who it concerns. Whether or not those murders are Dracula's idea or Jack's I can't say, but those people are dead and one of them is directly involved. He hasn't changed. He's still targeting hookers. Probably pissed him off no end to find some of them were not of the correct gender; that's why their bodies are so much more badly mutilated than the females."

She glanced at the horizon, which was beginning to pale. "We're nearly safe; it's almost dawn, but I'm betting our resident psychopaths have these grounds protected during the day too."

On cue, there was a snuffling from the side of the estate and a Revenant came lurching toward them. They were in an open field ringed by trees on three sides, the estate house itself on the other.

"Goddammit!"

Gillian was at the end of her tolerance, so she fired, popping the creature's head like a melon. The reverberation of the gun was extraordinary in the quiet dawn. Trocar flinched, covering his sensitive ears, and Pavel actually yelped.

"I am so sick of this . . ."

"Quiet!" Trocar cocked his head, palm held toward Gillian for silence.

She watched him as he turned slowly and moved back toward the basement window. Pavel let go of Kimber and went to the Elf, nostrils flaring.

"There is something alive in there," Trocar stated, then looked at Gillian. "It is not Human, but it is wounded." Pavel nodded to her to confirm.

While Gill didn't relish the thought of going back into that hellhole, she didn't want to leave anything sentient behind if it too was to be a victim of the Impaler or the Ripper.

"Shit. All right. I'll go back down. One of you two come with me since I'll need your ears or nose to track it down." She put her jacket back on to avoid the rough edges of the broken window.

Trocar braced himself and lowered her back down, then leapt lightly in after her, Pavel right behind him. Kimber was lowered into the morass of ooze by the Werewolf's strong arms.

Gill looked at them incredulously. "You all don't have to come."

"Course we do, Captain; we're a team." Kimber's irrepressible smile was back. Of course she was holding Pavel's hand, but the bounce was definitely there.

"Fine." Gillian pushed Trocar. "Go on; you heard it, you find it."

He moved forward but angled back to the far end of the basement, kicking bodies unemotionally out of his way. Stopping by the wall, he felt for a few moments with slender, nimble fingers. There was a popping creak and part of the wall separated and slid out. Behind it, covered in chains, manacled with wrist and leg irons to the foundation of the house itself, was a tall figure.

Matted, long black hair obscured the face, the clothes were torn, ragged and bore evidence of hundreds of bite marks. Hands that looked as if they were once powerful drooped lifelessly in the shackles, thin and emaciated as was the body. Little more than skin and bones were beneath the ragged clothing. Black boots that had once been shiny were scuffed, stained and . . . belonged to Tanis.

"Great Goddess!" Gillian stifled a scream. In spite of her years of combat, all the horror she'd ever seen, this truly shook her. Tanis. They'd found Tanis. Or what was left of him. "Get him the hell out of there."

Trocar and Pavel quickly snapped the chains, lifting the light, nearly bloodless form from the wall. Tanis hung limp in their arms. Gillian blinked away tears as she pushed the thickly matted hair from his face. He didn't respond.

"He's nearly drained dry but he seems to still be alive. Just barely."

"How can you tell?" Kimber asked.

No one had an opportunity to answer her. A horrendous shrieking filled the small space and fear swelled over all of them. *"Get away from him!"*

Materializing from out of the ceiling, a Ghost in all her open-mouthed, spectral glory flew at them. *"Drop him! Drop him!"*

She aimed for Trocar, shedding fear and panic with her screeches and flapping in the nonexistent breeze like a runaway handkerchief. *"You must not hurt him any more!"*

If Gillian had anything to aim at, she would have shot the damn thing. After Dante and the spirits at the Tower, Ghosts weren't big on her favorite-entities list at the moment. Trocar, however, had it covered. Whispering a few magical words in his language caused the Ghost to flutter to Earth like a Raid-sprayed butterfly. She continued shrieking, however, forcing Gillian to focus her empathy for just a moment before she ordered Trocar to send the damn thing into the Abyss.

"Shhh, it's all right. We're his friends. We want to rescue him. Do you understand me? We want to help him. He is dying."

Gillian's voice sounded surprisingly soothing, even to her own ears. The others stared at her as she attempted to placate the Ghost. "If you keep screaming, you'll bring the whole household down on us. Let us get him out of here," she said, focusing her warmest, fuzziest thoughts on the finally quieting Ghost.

Forming a little more, the Ghost shimmered and faded in her dismay, voice soft and shivery. "You . . . you won't hurt him? Truly, miss?"

Oh hell. The accent was pure lower-class English. Not cockney but servant class from about a hundred years ago. Gillian forced a smile and reached out a hand, the one not holding the gun, toward the incorporeal creature.

"No, hurting him is not what we want. Tanis is a dear friend. We only want to take him home. The best you can do is help us to help him. We need a way out other than that window." Gillian crouched down, closer, hand still out. "Tell me your name."

Her commanding but gentle attitude had the desired effect, and the Ghost responded. "Grace, miss. My name is Grace, if you please."

Grace formed a little more fully. She couldn't move as yet; Trocar's spell had her anchored where she was.

Looking her over, Gillian saw a plainly pretty girl with huge, haunted eyes, long brown hair that was twisted back in a knot and a rosebud mouth. The clothing was a skirt and bodice that hung simple, brown and modestly on the Ghost's thin frame.

"Well, Grace? Do you know how we can get him out?"

Grace nodded, paling even more, if that was possible. "Yes miss, I do." She inclined her head toward the opposite door. "But that one man, he's a bad one, he is. Don't let him see you. You might wind up like me." Her face crumbled and she started to cry, a lonely forlorn sound that Gillian tried frantically to hush.

"Shhh! You have to stop. Get hold of yourself, Grace, or you will get us all killed!"

The Ghost valiantly tried to stop and wound up hiccuping. Gillian dragged her free hand across her face in exasperation, turning back to the others. "Terrific, just terrific."

No one noticed the faint movement of Tanis's head at the sound of Grace's cries. Another voice intruded on their frustration. "I strongly suggest that you stop what you are doing and step away from the Vampire."

It would have been commanding coming from Gill or a deep male voice. What it sounded like was tiny musical bells. Grace gasped—no easy feat for a Ghost—and shrank back against the sticky floor. What the hell could cause fear in a Ghost? That was the question on everyone's mind as all eyes but Tanis's turned to see the source of the sound.

It took a moment, but through the door came a perfect vision of Fey beauty. Golden-brown hair, wide cornflower-blue eyes, perfectly shaped body encased in a tight, black body suit, commanding bearing and no-nonsense attitude. All together, she would have been impressive if she hadn't been six inches high.

The demi-Fey fluttered in on golden wings and hovered in the doorway, taking note of the lack of movement from the group assembled before her.

"Was I not clear? Drop him, drop any weapons you have, step away from him and line up against the wall," the musical voice demanded.

"Fuck off, Tinkerbell."

That was from Gillian, who was torn between laughing her ass off at the thought of using a demi-Fey as a guard for a Vampire and swatting the little twerp against the wall. She did neither.

"We're a little busy here and I'm not going to debate what we should do with a being the size of Peter Pan's wiener."

Turning toward the door, she swung her arm in a gesture meant to incite the others to follow her and started out. "Let's go. Tanis isn't going to last much longer."

"Tinkerbell" hissed, her wings making an angry buzzing noise. Gillian shooed her away from her face. "I said, fuck off!"

"Gillian, do not." A raspy warning from Tanis made her stop.

That moment of hesitation nearly got her killed. The demi-Fey spun in midair, expanding in seconds to full size. A fully formed adult female Fey stood in Gillian's path. Tall, blonde and very pissed off, from the way those wings were fanning behind her.

Gill barely had time to react as Trocar jerked her back a millisecond before the edge of the Fey's hand chopped in a perfect arced movement across her windpipe, throwing her the rest of the way back into Trocar and making it impossible to breathe. The blow hadn't fully landed because both the hyoid bone in her throat and her trachea were intact but bruised. As it was, she crumpled to the sticky, smelly, nauseating floor and found herself face to face with one of the murdered bodies.

"Gillian!"

Tanis struggled weakly against Pavel's and Trocar's steadying hands. Then, reaching for Gillian, who was still crumpled at their feet, he fell flat against her, shielding her with his large, wasted frame.

"Release Grace, Elf." The once beautiful voice was as battered as Tanis was, but Trocar complied.

Grace sprang up shrieking again and flew at the Fey. The Fairy simply ignored her and started for Gillian, who was now under Tanis's body for safekeeping. Drawing a stiletto from a sheath on the calf of her boot, the Fey moved in.

Kimber stepped in front of Gillian and got slashed for her trouble. She cradled the injured arm and, with a look of grim determination, started toward the Fey again, calmly flicking her own stiletto from up her sleeve into her hand. Pavel's warning snarl shook the chamber, and nobody noticed Trocar move.

Suddenly the Fey was on her back, the Grael's hands at her throat. She stabbed at him but he knocked the knife away. There was a muffled snap and the Fey went still under him, neck and wings broken. Grace squeaked and wrapped her transparent form around Tanis's waist while Pavel, Kimber and Trocar went to Gillian, who was still trying to remember how to draw air through her bruised windpipe. Kimber was bleeding from the slash down her arm, so Pavel fashioned a bandage with material from his skimpy lavender kilt, making it even skimpier than before.

Tanis's eyes went red for a moment at the scent of fresh blood as he pushed himself into a sitting position. "Get her away from me," he rasped, as fangs descended through his shriveled gum line.

Pavel moved Kimber behind him and faced the Vampire, ready to defend the woman if necessary. Trocar pulled her back farther, closer to the door, blocking the Vampire's view with his body as well. Tanis could still smell the blood but now didn't have the additional visual torment.

"Gillian?"

Strong, familiar fingers lifted her chin and she found herself staring into Tanis's eyes, now shifting back to golden again. Eyes that were almost shrunken in a face that resembled a skull, the skin was pulled so tight and thin. She managed a nod, still gasping and wincing with pain as she forced air through her throbbing trachea. Reaching up, she patted Tanis's shoulder in what she hoped was a comforting gesture.

"Allow me, Captain." Trocar eased gentle, warm hands around her throat, sparing a brief glance at the skinny, wretched Vampire who was glaring daggers at him.

"Do not exert yourself, blood drinker. I mean only to heal her."

Focusing his attention on Gillian, the Dark Elf concentrated his considerable power. She felt her throat heat up in a flare of warmth, then subside. Drawing air deep into starved lungs, Gillian patted Trocar's hand.

"That's great, Trocar. Thanks. I can breathe again."

To Tanis, she said, "I'm okay. Yeah he's a Grael, but he's

also a healer. We'll talk later; let's get out of here." As she struggled to her feet, the Ghost wailed softly.

"Please! Please don't leave me!"

Gillian didn't stop getting up or helping Tanis up. "Fine, come with us. Just shut up right now."

Tanis's skeletal hand on her arm stopped her. "They have another, Gillian. I heard his screams." His voice was weaker than before, she observed. He sure couldn't look any worse.

"Well, that's great. Look, we are not stopping to rescue everyone that could possibly be held captive in this palatial shithole. Now get moving and let's get out of here before something else happens." Her face held firm resolve that she wanted to be the hell out of there with everyone in one piece.

Pavel had finished with bandaging Kimber's arm and was sniffing the air. It was unnerving to watch him in Human form, doing such an obviously doggy thing. Moving out of the corpse-strewn room and into the original chamber where the women had been held, Pavel scented the stairs. "Here. It is faint, but his scent is up there."

"Whose scent for Crissakes?" Gillian was completely out of patience.

"Your friend, Luis."

"Goddammit!"

CHAPTER
31

RULE number one in the United States Marine Corps was that you left no one behind. Living or dead, your team, group, platoon or friends, you did not leave without them. Luis technically fell between two categories, being a Vampire, but it made no difference to his comrades. They were going to pull him out or they would all go down together. The party began to move toward the stairs when Tanis balked.

"*No*. Not without Grace."

"Tanis, look, I appreciate your loyalty, as I am sure Grace does, but we really need to get the hell out of here." Gillian reached over Pavel and tugged at her former lover's arm, but Tanis was implacable.

"*No.*"

"Shit." Gillian snarled, "*Grace!*"

They'd abandoned all pretense of not making noise. Sure as shit, something else would be coming after them soon, so it made little difference if they were discreet or not. The demi-Fey was only the beginning, of that she was sure. Jack the Ripper and Goddess knew who else were right upstairs—most likely comatose, with dawn breaking—but upstairs anyway, probably with guards. No one stopped to think why Tanis wasn't affected by the rising sun.

The Ghost fluttered over. "I cannot come with you, m'Lord Tanis. I only gave you what comfort I could here. You need a real lover, not a vapor."

"Grace, you have helped me survive. You must come with us." Tanis's voice was still raspy, but getting weaker.

"Don't argue with him right now. It will keep him calm if you're with us." Gillian and Trocar exchanged a glance. Apparently the Ghost had been a source of comfort for Tanis during his imprisonment. She'd find out all the details later; now was not the time.

Trocar cleared his throat. "If the young lady would prefer"—he let go of Tanis with one hand to indicate the fallen Fey assassin—"that one lives still, but just barely; if she would enter the body as the other's spirit leaves, she could become corporeal again."

Tanis struggled to lift his head and look at Trocar, then at Gillian for confirmation—she shrugged—and back to Trocar. "This is possible?"

Grace caught on and squeaked happily, twisting around Tanis's emaciated form. "I would do it for you if you want me to be real again."

Tanis's voice was growing weaker. "Yes. Be alive again, Grace, if that is your wish."

The Ghost blurred over to the body of the Fey and hovered. Trocar helpfully provided instructions. "Wait, little one. Not much longer." He listened intently. "Now."

Grace propelled herself into the Fey's lifeless body. There was a shimmering fountain effect as she pressed herself through flesh and bone. Trocar murmured a few words. The Fey jerked, back arching and bowing as the possession occurred, then lay still. The lips moved and the tinkling bells of the Fey's voice were heard. "I can't move! Tanis, help me!"

The Grael was already moving, propping Tanis against Pavel and Gillian, to attend to the newly embodied Ghost. He crouched beside her, his hands splayed around her broken neck and concentrated. There was another muffled pop, then the body jerked and seemed to shrink a little before poofing into the pint-sized, six-inch body of the Fairy standing amidst the corpse sludge of the basement. Wings, neck, everything was intact and working. She was a tiny perfect person with adorable wings that fluttered as she struggled to be airborne.

"I'm alive! Tanis, I am alive!"

"Sorry to interrupt this happy little moment, but we still need to find Luis and get the hell out of here." Kimber had been mostly silent, nursing her arm, but was regrouping well.

She'd been outraged and a little frightened by the speed with which the Fey had wounded her. Now she was pissed off and ready to fight. Trocar took a moment to heal the worst of the damage to her arm to prevent any incident with Tanis.

They mounted the stairs gingerly, letting Pavel's nose and Trocar's ears guide them. Grace was experimenting with her newfound wings and discovering that she'd forgotten that walls and people were solid objects, after she nearly broke her nose on Gillian's gun hand, then careened into the wall. Everyone but Tanis ignored her. He reached out and plucked her from the air, settling her into his shirt pocket for safekeeping.

"Tanis?" Grace whispered, her tiny voice trembling. "I don't think I can change back to full-sized form."

"We will worry about that later," Tanis whispered, smiling down at the tiny beauty and stumbling uncharacteristically on the stairs.

"Careful," Trocar reprimanded him as they continued on.

It didn't take long to find Luis in the estate. The smell of blood drew Tanis and Pavel like a beacon. He was unguarded, in one of the lower rooms that had been modified into a torture chamber. Fortunately, the rest of their weapons were in the same room, neatly laid out on a table, and they repossessed them.

Since Luis had been in Dracula's clutches only one night, he wasn't as badly off as Tanis was. Still, the damage was extensive. They'd staked him to a table in several very lethal areas, puncturing the arteries in his arms, legs and abdomen. It was meant to kill him, but slowly. Now with the lethargy of dawn, Luis was senseless and unresponsive. Luckily for him, Vampire daytime torpor had stopped his bleeding, or he would have bled out by now. He was still a fairly young Vampire and couldn't stay awake during the hours of full daylight.

Tanis, unhappily, was fully conscious and suffering. Luckily for everyone, he was so near death that he couldn't react to the amount of Luis's blood on the table and floor. As it was, his eyes blazed red and his fangs snapped down, driving through his lower lip with need. Writhing in Trocar's and Pavel's hands, even weak as he was, it took the combined strength of the Werewolf and Dark Elf to keep his teeth away from them. He required blood, and fast, before he went truly mad and killed one of his rescuers.

Gillian and Kimber pulled him out of the room, away from Luis, while Pavel freed the other Vampire and Trocar helped hold Tanis. Seeing how badly the Vampire was trembling, a bloody froth forming on his torn lips, Gill was desperate enough to offer herself as a donor.

Tanis graciously refused with a snarl. "No, *piccola*. In my current state, I might truly harm you, and that I will not do. Find a donor quickly, then I will go to ground."

See, that was the problem. Quickly. Quickly didn't look like it was happening . . . well, quickly. Kimber searched around while the other two held Tanis and Pavel appeared, carrying Luis wrapped in heavy velvet curtains. Soon, she found a way out of the estate that deposited them in back of the manor.

As she led them out, Gillian noticed the disturbing lack of guards of any kind. It was a little unnerving. The place was too damn quiet. There should have been some Human servants around, just breathing, walking. Some kind of noise in the large estate would have been apparent to at least the non-Humans. Gillian and Kimber exchanged a look that spoke volumes. Something was very wrong, but they couldn't pinpoint it yet.

Everyone was quiet, even Grace, as Trocar covered Tanis as best he could with his cape. Since the Elf and the Werewolf were the two strongest beings currently still fully functional, they decided to carry the Vampires into the forest and hope for a cave or other hiding place away from the sun's rays, which were beginning to stream over the huge house.

They discovered they were on the western side of the estate. That side of the mansion, the meadow and the forest beyond was still in enough shadow that they didn't risk the Vampires bursting into roman candles on the way across. Tanis was slung over Trocar's shoulder, Grace perched on his butt. Pavel had Luis in a fireman's carry as they all ran like hell to the shelter and safety of the thick trees.

Reaching the thicket, they paused in the most shadowy place they could find. Trocar gently lowered Tanis to the earth, sheltering him with his own body and vast leather cape. The Vampire looked quizzically at him, then flicked his gaze to Gillian, a thousand questions in his eyes.

Chuckling, Trocar reassured him. "We are close, but not in the manner which you believe, Vampire."

He rolled back his leather sleeve, exposing a sleekly muscled obsidian arm. "Take but a little to sustain you until we can attract prey. My blood is powerful and will invigorate you."

Gillian watched with Kimber and Pavel. It wasn't like the Grael to be too helpful without a damn good reason. He was her friend and she trusted him, but he was a Grael; he always had ulterior motives. Still, she didn't interfere as Tanis grasped the proffered arm and bit down. Trocar hissed at the sudden pain.

Unexpectedly, Tanis jerked back, nearly gagging. "Almighty hells!"

His voice was clearer and he abruptly looked more inflated. Grace fluttered excitedly around his head, squeaking. Tanis batted her impatiently away and she lit on a nearby log, sulking.

"Elf blood is powerful, but very disagreeable in flavor," Trocar helpfully provided. "That is one of many reasons why you will never see a Vampire Elf."

Wiping his arm free of blood and Vampire saliva with the edge of the cape, he rose, towering over them. He looked toward Luis, still curled beneath the coats and purses.

"That one will not survive if we do not get him out of daylight."

Tanis was on his knees and spitting unhappily into the fallen leaves. "Can't get the taste out."

"Anyone know where the hell we are?" Gillian asked.

"I can guide us back to the hotel, but Luis will not survive," Pavel stated.

"Bury him here," Tanis rasped, shakily getting to his feet. Kimber and Gillian reached to steady him. "Tanis is right, Luis will do fine if we leave him and come back later."

"How much later?" Kimber asked. "I don't want to be back here at night, thank you very fucking much."

"At least by dusk, plus Tanis has to go to ground too, very soon," Gillian stated, looking intently at her former lover. He looked really awful and she worried that he might not make it.

With Tanis too weak to open the earth, Pavel speedily dug a hole and lay Luis in it, packed his wounds with earth to help his own blood heal him, then covered him with earth and leaves. He'd be all right until nightfall, when Tanis would be rejuvenated enough to help him fully recover. The tall Vampire was looking paler instead of gray, which Gill took as a good sign; the Elf's blood had revived him a bit.

"I do not want to seem ungrateful, Gillian, but why did you

come after me? I cannot imagine Aleksei allowing such a thing, *piccola*." Tanis's voice was nearly back to its former glory after the light infusion of Elf juice.

When Gillian glared at him and a light blush hit her cheeks, he chuckled. "Aleksei will have much to say to you in this matter when he arrives."

"What?" Gillian blushed again. "Why is he coming here?"

"To rescue you, of course, little Captain, should you fail to rescue me." Tanis smiled at his former lover.

He knew it was over from the time he left. Gillian and he weren't suited for a long-term relationship but he didn't begrudge his brother from trying to win her. His brow furrowed.

"Which brings me to an unsettling question. Why did they allow us to escape?"

"I've been thinking about that too, but right now, we need to either bury you or get you a victim." Gillian was looking around to see if any movement stirred in the woods.

"Prey, please, Gillian. Only Dracula and his kind take victims." Tanis was offended but too weak to continue the argument.

Trocar shook and fluffed his crystalline hair out, then flapped his cape to straighten it after being rumpled by desiccated Vampire. He looked absolutely stunning and there wasn't one speck of corpse goo on him.

"You look like that when you were in the same places we were. It's just not fucking fair," Kimber muttered, much to the Elf's amusement.

"It is a gift." He smiled. "I will find Tanis some sustenance."

He melted into the trees. No small trick for a six-foot, two-inch Elf wearing a red leather slutsuit. Tanis sat heavily on the log where Grace perched. His skin was still taut but his eyes were clearer. Gillian sat next to him, ignoring the Fairy's indignant squeak. Dawn was fully upon them and Tanis was growing weaker even with the Elf blood infusion.

"Let me cover you, Tanis. The sun is getting higher," Gillian offered, holding her jacket up to shield him as much as possible. "Aleksei will never forgive me if you turn into a crispy critter now that you're out."

"Why are we out, Gillian? You just slithered into Oscar Gray's estate, rescued me, your friend Luis, then were allowed to escape. Why?" Tanis asked.

Kimber stepped up, eyeing Grace. "Because they knew we'd take a spy with us."

Tanis glared at her and Grace recoiled in horror as Kimber leveled the flamethrower at her. "Grace has been one of the reasons that I am still alive, Human. Do not threaten her before me."

To her credit, Kimber didn't move, but Pavel stepped closer to her, watching the Vampire closely. Kimber wasn't impressed with Tanis's warning. "Nope. It's too convenient. Dracula would have never let us out so easily."

She looked at Gillian. "It's either her or it's Luis. I don't think this one," indicating Tanis, "would just roll over for Dracula and turn traitor. At least not from what you've told me."

Considering Kimber's revelation, Gillian frowned. "Tanis, I don't doubt you for a minute and I've known Luis too long to not trust him at my back, even injured or tortured, but Grace is the wild card."

"No! I helped Tanis! I kept him alive!" Grace shrieked, flitting around the Vampire's head.

"I don't think so, and Kimber, get that away from Tanis." Gillian pushed the business end of the flamethrower in another direction.

A soft call turned their attention. Trocar was leading a pair of glassy-eyed female joggers toward them. The women were clearly enthralled, whether by being Elfstruck or magically enhanced by the Grael. He positioned them on their knees in front of Tanis, who looked pointedly at Gillian and Kimber.

"Oh, sorry." Gill turned away.

Vampires didn't like to be stared at when they fed any more than Humans did, but she watched him from the corner of her eye. Even starved as he was, Tanis fed only a little from each of the women and he took it from the wrist each time.

Neck feeding was rather intimate and required either a desire to create an erotic sensation or a deliberate intent to kill. A little blood from these two people would serve his purpose for the moment. Taking as much as he needed right now would potentially kill both of these women, so he fed lightly. Their blood also served to get the taste of the Elf's blood out of his mouth. When he was done with each one, he nicked his own tongue and laved his blood over the wounds. The pinpricks sealed instantly. No mark or bruise remained to testify that a Vampire had just given them wrist hickeys.

While Trocar was taking the women back to where he'd found them, Tanis used his once more superior Vampire powers to open the earth. The small amount of Grael and Human blood would keep him alive until nightfall when he could hunt for prey himself.

Lying down, he reassured the assembled group. "I will be fine. Let me rest for the day here. The sun is too high for me to remain awake much longer outdoors."

"We'll be back for you Tanis. You are part of our little family." Gillian assured him. "Marines never leave one of their own behind."

He nodded from his grave. "I am glad to have such friends." Then closing his eyes, Tanis waved his hand, closing the earth and giving himself up to the oblivion of Vampiric sleep.

"He isn't yours, miss, not any longer," Grace squeaked, inches from Gillian's face.

"What the hell does that mean?" Kimber wanted to know, snatching Grace out of the air and pulling her close enough so that she was cross-eyed.

The tiny demi-Fey shrieked and kicked at Kimber's nose. "I love him!"

Great Jolly Green Giant balls. Gillian rolled her eyes. "And you would do anything for him, right? Anything to save him?"

"Yes! Anything!"

"What did you promise Dracula?"

The tiny Fey body trembled and Grace burst into tears in Kimber's hand. "It was an exchange, miss!"

"Go on."

Sobbing, she continued. "He has my murderer as his servant. I promised to help keep the Vampire alive, to give him hope until Dracula could get his brother here so he wouldn't despair and Face The Sun, but I fell in love with him. Dracula was supposed to destroy the one who killed me if I managed to do this!" She wiped her nose on Kimber's thumb.

"*Ew!* Gross!" Kimber nearly threw her.

Gill stopped her with a hand on her arm. "So you traded your vengeance for his brother's life?"

Kimber raised her eyebrows at the tone. Even Pavel stepped closer. Gillian's voice was chatty, almost pleasant. "You were willing to condemn a man you don't know to death? For revenge?"

The former Ghost nodded miserably. She was noticeably less attractive with snot on her upper lip. Forlorn and pathetic, she wilted in Kimber's fist. She snapped to attention when Gillian grabbed her wings and extracted her from the fist.

"No! No!" Grace yelled, realizing that her size was just right for being flung into a tree, a rock . . . a pile of dog doo, which was what Gillian was now dangling her over.

"I ought to pull your wings off, you little bitch!"

No mercy was in Gillian's Nile-green eyes. "You set my friend up, you used his brother, you used us. Tell me why I shouldn't twist your tiny little head off."

"I cannot!" Grace wailed, covering her face with her hands and waiting for the inevitable.

"Then change back to normal size so I can kick your ass," Gill snarled. "At least that way it would be a fair fight."

"I cannot do that either! I do not know how!" Grace sobbed again.

"She's stuck, Kemo." Kimber smirked.

"Great. Well, she's coming with us," Gill snapped, then bellowed to the Dark Elf. "Trocar!"

He appeared at her elbow. "You screamed?"

"Bind her," she ordered him.

The Dark Elf murmured a few words and the Fairy wilted, this time into silence. "How the hell did you do that?" Kimber gaped.

"She is still a Ghost. Inhabiting the body of that Fey does not make her something different. She responds to binding magic like any Ghost." Trocar took Grace from Gillian and popped her into a pouch he materialized from somewhere on his Red Riding Hood Stud outfit.

"Let's get back to the hotel, change, and figure out our next move." Gillian and Pavel gathered their things. Pavel noted where they were by scent, then lead the group of Daywalkers back to their temporary digs.

CHAPTER
32

WHILE Gillian and the gang were having their adventures, Aleksei was en route from Romania. Emotions he had suppressed roared through his tall, muscular frame. He was furious with Gillian and heart-wrenchingly proud of her too. Tanis's relief at seeing Gillian had flowed through their blood bond earlier, and he knew his brother was safe. Safe because a little blonde ex-marine, too delicate looking to be a soldier, had rescued him.

He knew also that his brother slept now as he himself soon would on the plane. Aleksei and Tanis's rebirth were separated by only a few months and, up until very recently, their abilities as Masters had been fairly equal. Now that Aleksei had come into his own true level of power, only Tanis would still be termed a Master. Aleksei's newfound power was closer to legend.

Vampirism was a fickle gift. It blessed all who received it with extraordinary abilities. Most Reborn received only a modicum of what the Masters received. The Masters themselves received the ability to create more of their kind, in addition to higher, more significant levels of inherent skill. The difference in power between an average Vampire and a Master was like comparing a chihuahua to a rottweiler. Unfortunately, no one could be certain of the level of gift they would receive or bestow. It was a crapshoot and only a few won the Reborn lottery.

Then there were a few . . . a very, very few, that it blessed with almost godlike power. Those gifts took time to manifest over the centuries. The rottweiler would suddenly evolve into a Tyrannosaurus Rex, becoming a true Vampire Lord. So far, the ages had only seen the creation of four such individuals, at least that were known to all the others: Osiris, Dionysus, Dracula and now Lord Aleksei Rachlav.

Aleksei hadn't known the measure of his own power until recently when the dampening screens Dracula had maintained around his homeland and habitat had begun to fail. Now he had their power but had no idea how to utilize it to save his people. That, combined with Gillian's abdication, made him a trifle bit cranky.

The sun was up, dawn was upon him, yet the familiar torpor had not taken him yet. It waited while he safely moved about the shielded and curtained interior of the plane until he lay within an ornate box, lined with Romanian earth. He'd brought it mainly for transporting Tanis, knowing that his brother would be injured and in need of rejuvenation.

It was there, waiting like a heavy veil to draw over his mind, while he contemplated what he would do, could do, once he found their little party. Aleksei held it at bay like a gentle sleepiness as he closed his eyes, resting for the next few hours until he could rise and hold those he loved close again. His last thoughts were of a pair of Nile-green eyes in a delicate face surrounded by shimmering gold hair as his consciousness shut down.

Arriving back at the hotel, Gillian and the rest opted for food, showers and bed, in that order. They needed to process what they'd seen and what had happened.

"What the hell was with all those bodies?"

Kimber wasn't shy, she started stripping off the minute the hotel door closed, much to Pavel's amazement. He stared at her then seemed to realize that Trocar was in the room and moved to stand in front of her. The Grael smiled, moving to the bedroom to remove his tight, red leather jumpsuit.

Gillian was already in the bathroom divesting herself of the stained, smelly clothing and yelled back, "I think the Ripper had taken a turn in his pathology."

Silence was her reward, so she poked her head out of the door. Everyone was staring at her. "What I mean is, the main streetwalkers in Jack's time period were women. Now that's changed. He's targeting what in his mind is worse than a woman selling her body. A lot of those bodies were trannies. He must have a real beef against men masquerading as women."

"He's also still got his problem with women," Kimber interjected. "You didn't see him wipe off his hand after he had it in your hair. It was like you got cooties on him or something."

Gill lost her balance trying to remove a boot and fell against the sink. "Shit!"

There was a *clomp* as she tossed the offending boot against the wall. "The difference is that like most serial killers, he is adapting and getting better. It's harder to hide a body these days, so he's taking advantage of a convenient drop spot. And it doesn't surprise me that he wiped off his hand after touching me. Jack's female victims were all sexually assaulted all right, but with a knife, not his penis. He's got issues that have to do with more than just sex."

"Even Vampires are sensitive to the odor of death, *mellian*," Trocar's lovely voice interjected, changing the subject slightly. "Why would the others allow this travesty to continue within their resting place?"

Gillian thought about that for a moment from her floor seat. "Obviously Jack, or whoever he is, is an important piece in Dracula's scheming, so he tolerates more than he normally would."

"Or Dracula considers Jack sort of a thug or muscle for him. Like an enforcer. Jack does the dirty work and Dracula continues to look like the strong ruler who never gets his hands dirty," Kimber said helpfully, smiling up at Pavel and his protective stance in front of her.

The Werewolf certainly was handsome and . . . her eyes flicked down for a brief instant . . . hung like the proverbial horse. Pavel blushed under her appraisal, causing Kimber's generous mouth to widen more. She winked at him and he shivered. *Oh yeah, Gillian, mission . . . right.*

"Or that Dracula is a worse monster than the Ripper could ever be and he's just ignoring it for now," she finished finally.

That thought sobered everyone's mood right up. "I'm taking a shower."

Gillian snapped the door shut and lost herself to hot water and shampoo for a few minutes. She emerged to find Trocar draped artistically across the bed, clad only in a loose robe with a tray of fruit and cheese set out.

"Where's Kimber and Pavel?"

"I believe they mentioned a Jacuzzi."

"Terrific," Gill muttered, completely conscious of the fact that she was wearing only a towel and had a gorgeous hunk of hot male Elf on her bed.

She skirted around him and went to her bag to dig out something, anything, to wear so she didn't feel so damn exposed. Trocar couldn't help smiling. He was in a more accessible position this time and she knew it. Before, in the Marine Corps, she had been his superior officer and fraternization had been completely impossible. Now the situation was much different. She was still the leader of this mission but she needed him more, relied on him to an extent. It made her vulnerable in a way, something his predatory nature found very attractive.

"Stop staring at my ass before I knock your lights out," Gillian growled as she felt his eyes sweeping over her.

Her empathy had been on hold for a while, but like any natural talent, it wouldn't be denied for long. Being near her friends, people she cared about, made it impossible to keep shielding. Trocar desired her. He'd never shied away from that, unlike herself. Before as his commander, she couldn't afford the luxury of considering it, but now . . . now was *not* a good time. Plus there was Aleksei to consider.

Shit. That was someone she didn't want to think about right now. He was going to be pissed about all this but happy that Tanis was alive, er, still Reborn and functional. She gave herself a mental shake as she pulled her clothes free of the backpack. Thinking about Aleksei right now was not a good idea. The time period between him being her patient had expired but they were in the midst of a turf war and she couldn't afford to spare her concentration.

"Keep your eyes averted, Lieutenant," she snapped.

Trocar laughed musically. "We are far from a real battlefield, my former Captain. But I will allow you to shield yourself with your clothing while I take a shower."

The door closed as she turned and she was treated to a gleaming ebony length of thigh and curved buttock as the Elf abandoned his robe outside the bathroom. Rolling her eyes, she finished dressing in her turtleneck and a pair of shorts she'd forgotten were stuffed at the bottom of her pack. Yanking the laptop out of the pack, she snapped on the wireless router-adapter and fluffed the pillows on the bed so she could lay against them.

Pausing, she pulled her shorts farther down over her thighs. No use in giving Trocar a show when he came out when nothing was going to happen between them.

Pulling up her e-mail, Gillian wasn't surprised to find a number of urgent, then frantic, then vaguely threatening e-mails from her friend at the IPPA, Helmut Gerhardt. Figuring direct contact was better than answering a dozen e-mails, she dialed his private number, munching on the fruit and cheese as she waited.

Dr. Gerhardt was understandably worried after not hearing from her for several days. He kindly filled her in on current events in Fang & Fairyland. They weren't good. The mainstream press and authorities were starting to notice that a higher percentage of Humans were having disagreeable experiences with the denizens of the Paramortal. Cautionary reports abounded and some communities were jacking up curfew times for Humans which was causing a hell of a hue and cry.

Bodies were being discovered daily and more people were going missing nightly. Apparently the effects were being seen on a global scale. There wasn't a country that hadn't had at least ten or twelve violent and mysterious deaths in recent months. Modern-day forensics were only helpful if you had data to compare. Vampire, Fey and Lycanthrope DNA was being collected almost hourly, but with no central database, it was difficult to track down a specific subject. Especially if all their pals were going out of their way to make them remain invisible.

Each branch of law enforcement, particularly in major metropolises, had Paranormal officers, detectives and administrators. Some had been added after legalization, some had just come out of the proverbial wardrobe to the surprise of their colleagues. They were familiar enough with their own kind to know where to look and whom to ask, but they were just as hampered as their Human counterparts by simply being employed with Human agencies or working with Humans. The occasional Paranormal private investigator often wound up another statistic since they had no buffering employer who would miss them if they didn't show up at a briefing.

Gerhardt was adamant that Gill be extremely careful and get back to Count Rachlav's relative protection as soon as possible. Gillian snorted at that, reminding him that she and her group had rescued the other Rachlav from almost certain death.

There was a pregnant pause in the conversation as Gerhardt considered. "Very well, Schatzi, I trust your skills and your judgment, but there are those here who prefer to err on the side of caution. No one will sanction you for what you're doing, but there is a point, Gillian, where you must look to your own safety. You are not a police officer."

"Helmut, I'm not leaving my friends to hide in relative safety. This whole thing is a turf war. No, I'm not a cop but I am a soldier and at the moment, you're paying me to be both a psychologist and a field operative. I'm trained in warfare—okay, Human warfare—but this isn't much different. It's more subtle, mind you, and there is a lot less property destruction, but it's warfare."

Gillian's voice had a hard edge that Gerhardt recognized as her no-nonsense commanding voice. "As a psychologist, I know what kind of a psychopath we're up against, Helmut, and it's bad. Dracula is not your run-of-the-mill fanged menace and he's got Jack the Ripper as his new best friend and playmate. Which reminds me, the Ripper has switched vics on us—he's doing women and transvestites now." She let that sink in.

"Gillian, if the Ripper is still alive and has shifted his perspective, then he is evolving as a killer and a sexual sadist. Be careful and do not confront him—be a soldier and kill him if you have to, but do not, under any circumstances, take him on alone." Gerhardt was absolutely determined.

"Rehabilitating him is not on my agenda, Helmut," Gillian stressed. "I rather like the shoot now, ask questions later approach, myself."

"I understand, my dear, I truly do." He sighed. "But you have been such a positive force for our profession, whether you realize it or not, and most of us forget that you are also a decorated soldier. I know you can handle yourself."

Gerhardt was the closest thing to a parent figure she had and Gillian appreciated him. He continued. "In the Human and Paramortal worlds there are good individuals, bad individuals and very bad individuals. Not all Paramortals fall into the worst catagory, but that's the way Humans are going to see them again very soon. It was not long ago that Vampires, Ghosts and Lycanthropes were used as threats in stories and film to frighten people; the Fey were not held in high esteem either. There is a thin line we are all treading, Gillian. Psychologically, there is still help we can provide, but can't, if the tide is turned again."

It was Gillian's turn to sigh. "I know. It's idiotic. I'm doing the best I can, Helmut. Aleksei took good care of me but now it's my turn to start helping out. I'm a soldier first, no matter how much I hide behind my diplomas and medals for propriety's sake and my profession. Fighting on this level is something I'm learning. I don't want to wind up dead either, at least not in the manner I've seen. I'll be careful. Just hold down the fort, be ready with bail money and I promise to check in more often."

He realized that was as good as he was going to get, so he acknowledged her. "Think of the paper you can write after all your field work there."

There was a smile behind the voice, and Gillian felt warmed. He also failed to tease her about addressing Count Rachlav by his given name. Some things are better left untaunted.

"Thanks Helmut. I'll have you proofread it for me."

They said their good-byes and hung up. Just in time for Gillian to watch Trocar glide out of the bathroom, dressed in a towel.

Gillian felt her mouth go dry. Trocar was a vision of solid, glossy, black perfection. Gracefully in that manner that only an Elf of any sort could pull off, he doffed the towel and slid into a luscious-looking robe and pants made from spider's silk. That he did it without treating her to any more Grael eye candy was amazing. She watched him warily as he approached the bed.

"Don't even think it, Trocar. I'm not in the mood for your bullshit tonight." She glared at him as he slid into bed next to her, smiling and lovely.

"Think what, Gillyflower?"

Gill cringed at the nickname and under his intense, iridescent gaze. "Stop it."

"Stop what? I am not touching you."

He wasn't. He was just uncomfortably close. Gill refused to give him the satisfaction of seeing her nervousness by shifting away from him. Shit and double shit. He smelled of the crisp, icy woods when the first snows fell. Clean, refreshing, light snow and icy pine–scented Elf. His iridescent eyes sparkled like faceted jewels and his jet-black skin gleamed with a shimmery blue cast.

She would have gulped, but she didn't have any saliva at the moment. Chuckling, Trocar settled himself on his back, crystalline hair fanned out on the bed beneath him, one arm pillowing his head, the other artfully positioned on his chest.

"I do not intend to seduce you, Gillian. If you come to me, I want it to be willingly and without coercion."

"You're Grael; don't give me that crap. I know what you're like," she snorted.

"You know what I have allowed you to see and what you have read in your little books, Captain." His voice was extraordinarily beautiful in her ears.

Faceted eyes were on her, pinning her where she sat. "You only know a competent, loyal officer who once served with you. You have no idea what I am capable of."

Damn. He was right. She didn't know. She only trusted him based on past experience. They both weren't in the military now, she was not his commanding officer and he wasn't bound by anything other than their friendship. Did the Grael really maintain Human friends? As if reading her mind, he replied to her unspoken question.

"Yes, we can and do have lifelong Human friends. Yes, we are called evil, but lawfully so. I have followed you in the past as I follow you now: out of loyalty, admiration and a certain fondness for you, Gillian. We could never be a mated pair, but I do profess to a definite sexual attraction. You are a very desirable female." His voice had wandered into the I-am-currently-hard-as-a-crowbar timbre, making her shiver.

Her eyebrows shot up at that and she glared at him. Trocar ignored her heated expression and continued. "You and Kimber are lovely, as are a great many humans, but you are women who have so much more depth to you than most. Human females generally manage to become simpering, clinging fools around an Elf's beauty. That you do not, makes you particularly attractive."

Trocar was speaking completely without ego. He knew his race's attributes and was simply stating fact. "You are loyal, intelligent, persistent and utterly ruthless when need be. I admire those qualities in a female and am proud to be called your friend."

Sweet, suffering Hera, his smile was lethal. Gillian was uncomfortable to say the least, but she rallied. "Thanks Trocar. If things weren't so complicated right now, I might consider taking you up on your offer. As it is, I can't, so don't push it. I am glad we're friends though, and I appreciate you being here to help me and be supportive."

"Despite that, do not forget what I am, Gillyflower."

"What is that?"

"Grael."

He turned his back to her and settled in to sleep, leaving

Gillian to ponder what that meant. Trouble was, she did know. He was bad; an opportunist at the very core of his being, no matter how nicely the package was wrapped. Trocar followed her for the exact reason he had said: he admired her and this was exciting for him. If she gave him no reason to distrust her, he would continue to be on her team. He wouldn't overtly betray her to anyone or leave her side unless it was to his distinct advantage. Even then, he'd have the courtesy to tell her that he was out of the game before vanishing into whatever oblivion he went to when he wasn't with her.

Ordering those thoughts out of her mind, she settled down next to him on the bed, leaving the light on. She was drifting at the edge of slumber when she felt herself pulled against a hard, warm chest and her eyes flew open.

"Shhh, Gillyflower, just relax and let me give you comfort this night. I will do you no harm. My word on it."

Hell with it, she thought. Trocar was warm and strong, plus he smelled nice. Black-robed mage that he was, he was a healer and a healer was a healer no matter what color their robes. She relaxed against him and allowed him to hold her while she slept. Nothing would get past a Dark Elf set on "protect."

The aforementioned Grael enjoyed holding his former commander. She was attractive and he would absolutely take advantage of the situation if she wanted it, but he wouldn't force himself on her. Some of his personal characteristics set him apart from his brethren. Trocar had a certain morality that he twisted to fit his own worldview, something that puzzled even him.

Gillian had earned his respect long ago, the first Human to ever do so. He owed it to her to keep her safe and not violate her trust. It was somewhat irksome to take the proverbial high road, so he contented himself with cupping her breast while he shifted closer, then slept himself, his senses on alert for anyone but the Werewolf or the other Human female coming through the door.

Gillian's first two thoughts as she jolted awake later that day were, *Shit!* and *He's holding my boob!*

The first was because a deep, melodious, Romanian voice

had just stated, "This is very interesting, Dr. Key. Have you been searching for my brother in this diligent a fashion all along, or do you normally take Grael Elves as bed partners when things get . . . tense?"

The second was because Trocar's ebony hand was still gently cradling her breast, though he was awake and amused at her predicament. All this before she could focus her eyes, down any coffee, shoot Trocar out of principle or hit the censor button on her mouth.

Bolting upright, she managed to shove Trocar off the bed, gain her feet and spring up underneath Aleksei's nose sputtering, "What . . . who let you in here? Tanis is safe. We rescued him yesterday, you judgmental prick!"

She stood nearly chest to abdomen with the tall Vampire Count, glaring up at him, her Nile-green eyes throwing sparks of fury. Aleksei's own eyes went from shimmering pools of mercury to icy-hard platinum beneath raised brows. His sensual mouth tightened in aggravation at the little blonde before him.

Before he could reply, Gillian was off again. "Why the hell are you here? In this room? In this country?" She started pacing while Trocar eased around the bed, watching her, giving the pair wide berth as he moved from the room.

"Why aren't you back minding the store where you're supposed to be? I took care of finding Tanis; in fact we're about to go get him. Now you come barging in here, making fuckwitted assumptions about what I'm doing in bed with an Elf . . ."

The alarm clock on the nightstand picked that moment to go off loudly. Everyone jumped: Aleksei, Gillian and Trocar, even Kimber and Pavel in the next room. Gillian spun on reflex and kicked it with a roundhouse blow that sent it smashing against the wall. It broke her concentration long enough for her to realize she'd been rambling.

Shoving her hands through her hair, she took a deep breath, then exhaled, matching him glare for glare. "Look Aleksei, nothing happened. We're going to go get Tanis. If you want to come, fine, if not then stay here, but either way, stay out of my way." She grabbed her pants, boots and pack, then stomped into the bathroom, slamming the door harder than necessary.

Kimber appeared at Aleksei's elbow. "I told you when we let you in that you wouldn't like it if you came in here."

He spared her a chilly glance, his eyes hardening more as

Pavel the wistful Werewolf appeared at her side, draping his arm over her protectively while Kimber grinned and kept going.

"Count Rachlav, you are just like any other man who has tried to guess what our beloved Captain might do to gain information or to rescue a fellow team member; deals with Ghosts, sex with Elves, friendship with Vampires, where will it end?"

She turned, looping her arm around Pavel's waist. "Yes indeed, and you've been cut off at the knees just like the rest of them," she finished happily.

Hands tightening into fists, Aleksei sat stiff-backed on the bed, a fury that he'd never known almost overwhelming him. Jealousy. Over that damned Elf and Gillian. On cue, the bathroom door opened and Gillian, now fully dressed, started out, halting as she noticed him sitting there completely still. Still as only a well-seasoned Master Vampire could.

Briefly, their eyes met. Aleksei's were full of anger and something else, something deeper and more heated. Gillian's were cold and defiant. She didn't need the distraction right now. Right now, they needed to get back to Tanis and make sure that he had risen before Dracula's pals found him.

"You coming or going?" Gillian asked sharply, then headed out the door without waiting for an answer.

"Lead the way, Doctor," Aleksei replied, his voice clipped but still beautiful, rising to follow her with the unparalleled grace of an angry Vampire.

She moved off, strapping her holsters on, sheathing guns and knives. Kimber and Pavel were helping each other on with their equipment, sniggering. A glare from Gillian shut them up. Trocar, dark, elegant and lovely, was waiting at the door, fully dressed, equipped and bemused. Gillian shook her head at him to remind him to keep his mouth shut. He said nothing, just opened the door for her and the rest of the party.

Gillian led them downstairs in silence. They stopped at the front desk to drop off the room keycards, when the desk clerk gestured to them.

"There are some detectives looking for you, Dr. Key." He indicated a couple seated nearby.

The man looked like he fell off a Viking recruitment poster—naturally blonde, blue-eyed, tall and handsome. His dark eyebrows were in sharp contrast to the golden hair, clipped ever so properly in a longish style. Gillian vaguely wondered if he knew he probably had Elf or Fey blood. The dark eyebrows with the platinum hair were a dead giveaway.

The woman was tall but very slender, her hair was darker than the man's and looked as though it had been frosted with gold. Her eyes, even from where they stood, were a golden brown. Something about her was odd and Gill couldn't place it until she moved.

The pair had seen the exchange with the clerk and rose to come to Gillian and her little party. The woman had an eerie grace that offset her more heavy-footed colleague. Lycanthrope of some kind, Gillian figured.

"Dr. Key?" The man said hesitantly. "I am Inspector Brant McNeill, Scotland Yard, and this is Inspector Claire Jardin."

"What can I do for you?" Gill said bluntly.

"We were contacted by Dr. Helmut Gerhardt of the International Paramortal Psychology Association. He suggested that you might need assistance regarding rescue of your friends and some knowledge of whom is behind the murder of a number of known transvestite and female prostitutes." This was from the woman, who spoke with a light French accent.

"Oh Jesus." Gillian was annoyed. Gerhardt meant well, but he had just complicated their lives tremendously. "I am sorry if you were inconvenienced, but I really don't have anything to tell you. Dr. Gerhardt is my mentor and friend and he worries sometimes."

She made her smile friendly and pleasant, her gaze direct, and avoided looking at Aleksei, who was staring at her incredulously as she blatantly lied. Everyone else had a poker face on and were giving the police no indication that it wasn't the absolute truth.

"Dr. Key," Inspector McNeill said. "If you have any knowledge of these crimes, I must ask you to cooperate and provide us with the information." He gazed at her with a rather stuffy expression.

Gill was beginning not to like Inspector McNeill. When she didn't answer right away, he added, "We can detain you, Dr. Key; you and your friends."

Shit. Yes, he could.

"You know, Inspector, you can do anything you damn well please, but while we're languishing in your interview room having crumpets, more people are going to die."

That took him aback for a moment. "People dying are what we are trying to avoid, Dr. Key."

"Then let us go and find our friends first, so they don't die." Gillian deliberately kept the anger out of her voice. No sense in pissing him off more than need be. "After that, we could meet and see if we can assist each other. If Scotland Yard has no objections, of course."

The others stared at her. Gillian had no intention of sharing anything with the local authorities if it could be avoided. With any luck, they'd be long gone before explanations would be necessary.

Apparently Inspector Brant wasn't buying it either. "Dr. Key, withholding information about a murder, or in this case several murders, is against the law here. I need your cooperation— voluntarily would be preferable, but we can detain you until you provide what you know."

It was official; she didn't like Brant McNeill. "You get our friends hurt or killed with this delay and I will go straight to the media with Scotland Yard's helpful attitude in this matter."

Gillian worked at suppressing a smirk. No law enforcement agency likes bad press. What she didn't add was that, if anything happened to Tanis or Luis, she'd track down the good inspector herself for an unpleasant chat.

Fortunately, Inspector Claire intervened. "Surely, Inspector McNeill, we can agree to wait for Dr. Key to find her friends, then speak with us." Claire put her hand lightly on McNeill's arm. "I am sure she is reasonable when she is not worried. Correct, Dr. Key?"

Point for Inspector Jardin. "I am much more cooperative when I am not concerned about people I care for." Gillian remained with feet apart and braced, arms crossed, in front of Brant McNeill, who looked as though he wanted to drag her to the Tower dungeons for some persuasion.

McNeill didn't like this one bit. He was a "by the book" cop, which left little room for compromise. He was also not stupid, and could see that threatening Dr. Key was not going to work. "Very well."

His eyes flicked to the little party. "I am certain, though, that you do not need everyone to attend you." He pointed toward their little group. "You"—he indicated Kimber and Pavel— "will remain with us, answer a few questions, while Dr. Key and"—he waved absently at Aleksei and Trocar—"these others go after whom she is trying to find."

"Fine," Gillian snapped. Jerking her arm toward the hotel entrance, she indicated for the others to follow her and left the two inspectors without a word.

CHAPTER
33

TROCAR fortunately remembered how he and Pavel had located Gill and Kimber in the first place and was able to lead them back to the shaded grove behind Oscar Gray's estate. Aleksei glided alongside Gillian. Tall, silent and broadcasting his emotions like a beacon.

Gillian stopped short and grabbed his arm. "Look, you are spilling anger and worry out all over me . . . me empath, you Master Vampire, remember? I can't think clearly if I've got to wade through your emotional havoc, so tone it down a little, will you?"

She didn't wait for a response, just plowed on behind Trocar, trying to focus on where Tanis and Luis were, missing the dangerous gleam in Aleksei's silvery gray eyes as he watched her ahead of him. Trocar held up a hand palm out and Gillian stopped instantly, feeling Aleksei mirror her just behind and left. Two ebony fingers flashed up, then the hand turned and slashed across once. Trocar was using the hand-signal code they had developed during their time in the service together. He signaled, two ahead, no weapons, then melted into the trees ahead. Not good, that meant "they" were badass enough not to need weapons. She was under no such illusions.

Easing the Glock out of her pocket where it had been hidden

in the loose-fitting material, Gill thanked the gods her preferred firearm didn't require cocking and held it two-handed in front of her, pointed down. Her mind went to her calm, empty place and her breathing slowed as she waited, senses and empathy on full alert. Trocar knew his job and she trusted him to either take out whomever was stalking them or alert her as to how to fight it. Her focus was complete and she nearly jumped out of her skin when she felt a large, warm hand softly touch her shoulder.

Only years of training kept her from pulling the trigger as she whirled and leveled the gun at—Aleksei? What the . . . ?!

"Goddammit, Aleksei . . ." Gill hissed, but never got the rest of the sentence out. She felt rather than heard the disturbance in the very air around her and put out a hand to shove Aleksei back while she calmly turned to fire one-handed at whatever was about to pounce.

Grabbing her extended arm, Aleksei jerked her behind him, stepping between her and the Vampire, which launched itself silently. There was a sudden roar of flame, a shriek, and a crunchy thud before Gillian elbowed her way around Aleksei's larger frame to see what the hell had just happened. Aleksei was staring at his hand, silvery eyes wide and a charred vampire about five feet in front of him.

Before Gillian could open her mouth she heard a distinctive laugh. "That was great! Click! Whoosh! Foom!" Somewhat maniacal laughter followed as a tall brunette with streaks of fire-engine red and gold in her hair stepped out of the bracken.

"Jenna? What the hell?" Gillian was rather surprised to see her former arsonist, or rather demolitions expert, Jenna Blaise brushing twigs off her black-on-black outfit and slinging her pet flamethrower, "Flicker," back over her shoulder before embracing Gillian in a hug.

"Umph!" Gillian managed as she was squished in the taller woman's embrace. She looked up into Jenna's lovely sparkling brown eyes. "What are you doing here?"

"Hey, I heard you were organizing a little slash-and-destroy mission, so I thought I'd pop in to lend a hand." Jenna grinned madly, then turned her attention to Aleksei, who was still looking rather dazed. "Wow, he's a tall one. Yummy looking, too. Good thing you pulled her back; it helped me differentiate you from the other bloodsucker." Jenna never was one for tact when bluntness would do just as well.

Gillian stepped back between Jenna and Aleksei just to make

sure no one got torched who wasn't supposed to. "How did you find us?"

"The nice police officers at Scotland Yard heard about a certain famous parapsychologist being in town, so I went to your hotel. Kimber and that gorgeous hunk of Werewolf filled me in, so I hoofed it over this way. Lucky I caught up with you when I did." Jenna was her chatty, charming self and Gill did feel better not being the only nonmagical being at the moment.

"Shit—Trocar!" Gillian yelled, realizing one of their rescue party was missing.

There was no point in being quiet, the bushes around them were still crackling and smoldering. Quiet and stealthy was a vague memory. Trocar appeared on cue with blood on his tunic, followed by Tanis, who after his rest and evidently finding adequate prey, looked filled out and droolworthy again. A dusty Luis tagged along behind. Aleksei stepped up to embrace his brother.

"You screamed, fair one?" Trocar said dryly then gave a rather undignified "hmph" as Jenna pounced on him, squeezing the air rather forcefully from his lungs.

Recovering, he held her at arm's length. "Blaise, it is good to see you," he said, his face splitting into a wide grin. Other than Gillian and Kimber, Jenna was a Human whom Trocar trusted and appreciated being on their side.

While the Dark Elf disentangled himself from Jenna's multilimbed assault, Gillian asked him, "You took care of the other problem?"

"Exactly." Trocar stated, flinching a little as Jenna yelled close to his sensitive ears.

Jenna squeaked and grabbed the newly arrived Luis in a bearhug, eliciting poofs of dust from his clothing as the Vampire smiled weakly and patted her in return. "Clemente! You're out of the earth and the closet!" she exclaimed happily, admiring his bedraggled clothing.

Jenna detached herself from Luis, then froze in openmouthed wonder as her gaze locked with the golden-eyed Tanis, who had turned back from greeting Aleksei. The Vampire returned the look with an intensity that made the brunette bombshell pale then blush furiously.

Aleksei seemed to come out of his astonishment and looked at Gill. "Gillian, there is something . . ."

"Later, Aleksei. Right now, let's get back and collect the rest of our ragged band and get the hell out of here." Gillian shuddered at the sound of his voice trailing down her back like warm fur. "You OK, Luis?"

He nodded and brushed at the gray dirt and blood clumps still clinging to his clothing. He wasn't all right; Vampires were fastidious about their appearance, but they'd find him more prey soon and he'd be back to his spit and polish self.

"Okay, boss," Jenna quipped, linking arms with a startled Tanis who, ever the gentleman, escorted her from the woods as though it were down a runway with flashbulbs snapping.

The Vampire appeared to be caught by the sparkle in Jenna's warm brown eyes. Gill shook her head. She'd seen the show before; Jenna, with all her pyromaniac tendencies, was lovely and a magnet for any Vampire nursing a bruised heart and ego.

Getting back to the hotel was easy, as was stashing Jenna's flamethrower outside the building. They agreed not to share the circumstances of Tanis's and Luis's recovery with Inspectors Brandt and Jardin. Gillian wanted to get everyone out of there and back to Romania, where Aleksei's people could protect them. For once, she and Aleksei were in complete agreement.

Gillian's palm slapped the lobby doors open without breaking stride and headed toward their waiting group with a few brief but choice words on her lips for Inspector Hardass in the event he wanted statements taken right now, then froze so suddenly that Aleksei was hard-pressed not to step on her. Only preternatural Vampire's grace kept him from plowing into the small form in front of him, but he managed to make the near stumble look elegant.

"Hi, pumpkin," said the gravelly, slightly Southern-accented voice issuing from the generous mouth in the oh-so-handsome face of Daedalus Aristophenes, MD, PhD, Major, USMC.

He rose from his position in one of the high-backed lobby chairs and moved effortlessly in front of Inspectors Brandt and Jardin. Clasping Gillian's hand lightly, he winked at her. "Guess what Uncle Sam has in mind for us, starting tonight?"

"I'm retired, Daed. That's the official word, remember?" Gillian jerked her hand back and shoved him in the chest hard enough to stagger him a little. Aleksei moved up to flank her, unsure about what his next move should be and why this man was still alive, having just addressed Gillian as *pumpkin*.

"You're recalled, Marine; Reservist Clause. You're still a field operative, but your rank and benefits have been reinstated with back pay." Major Aristophenes smirked a little more than necessary as he delivered the news.

Tossing a newspaper to her across the table, he continued.

"You keeping up with the news lately? That Russian earthquake? With all the deaths and confusion, suddenly there's a child-trafficking problem going on with so many orphans and children, apparently abandoned by whatever families they had left. Guess whose crack unit has been volunteered to go in and put a stop to it?"

Watching Gillian's eyes harden, he hastily added, "The Feds, the Corps, the Joint Chiefs and Interpol are concerned about the bad PR that Paramortals are getting lately with all the deaths and kidnappings. It looks like some sort of a turf war is going on, wouldn't you say? It will be bad for the economy if folks start revoking the new laws and taking the PMs out of the global economic pool.

"You were suggested, being as high profile as you are in the IPPA, not to mention someone I personally trust, Gillian." Daed paused for a moment but her expression didn't change.

His eyes narrowed a little. "You're recalled tonight, Captain. Gather who you can, hire additional mercenaries if you have to. Just make sure they're PMs or used to working with PMs. We leave in three hours. I'll be in the bar."

Daed winked at her again, flicked a salute and tossed a dossier onto the chair he'd vacated. Turning all six feet, two scrumptious inches and two hundred pounds of his Greek-American bulk away, he sauntered toward the hotel bar to wait for her to organize her group. Damn, he looked good from the back. Gill wanted to plant her boot squarely in his sculpted ass.

Kimber stepped into Gillian's line of fire . . . or rather . . . *vision*, as her friend was fingering the grip of the gun in her pocket. "Holy Zorba, Batman, I did not expect to see him here."

"Yeah, me neither, and this just sucks." Gillian flipped open the papers and scanned them quickly. "Shit. It's all in order."

She looked at her team. To their credit, not one of them had bolted out the door during Major Daed's announcement. They were looking at her expectantly.

"You guys ready to rumble?"

"*Ooorah!*" shouted Kimber, Trocar, Luis and Jenna collectively, all suddenly grinning like hell and snapping salutes her way.

Inspector McNeill huffed, rising from his seat in ill-concealed irritation. "You have questions to answer for our department before you go anywhere, Dr. Key."

"'Fraid not, McNeill." It was Gillian's turn to smirk. "United States Marine Corps trumps Scotland Yard; don't like it, file a complaint with the US State Department, but my team and I are leaving *now*. You having nothing legal with which to hold me or any of us, so it's been real nice meeting you."

Turning on her heel, she stalked off after the Major, putting just enough sashay into her walk to be a bitch. Kimber, Luis and Jenna fell in smartly behind her out of habit. Aleksei, Pavel and Tanis brought up the rear in amazed silence.

The two speechless inspectors were left with contact information from the IPPA, Major Aristophenes's cell phone number and a lot of unanswered questions.

Major Daed, as Gillian used to call him to his face, was lounging with a beer, watching his little crew approach. His warm, black eyes sparkled as he watched her. Gillian gave great poker face. He couldn't tell if she was delighted or pissed.

She sat opposite him, taking his beer from his hand, swigging it, casually tossing her leg up on the table, then drawing and lighting a cigarette all in one motion—it was pissed, he determined, definitely pissed. She blew smoke in his face and he coughed.

Turning slightly, he noted those with her, rising to greet the tall vampires. "I am Major Aristophenes, Captain Key's commanding officer."

His handshake in Aleksei's and Tanis's hands was firm. "I understand you gentlemen may need transport back to Romania; we will be happy to provide that for you." Daed was at his worst: charming, intriguing and just plain overbearing.

"Cut the shit, Daed." Kimber was losing her sense of humor rapidly. "I don't know how you pulled off getting us all recalled, but I intend to shoot you before we're through with this mission or whatever the hell it is."

"Torched . . . first torched, then shot," Jenna said flatly.

Silence. Even Daed paled a little at that suggestion. "Look, this wasn't my idea. Brass wants a crack unit in there. Pumpkin, it's not my fault you keep popping up in international news. You're a celebrity! It was logical to think of you."

Gillian twirled the bottle she held against her knee and took a long drag from her cigarette. "See, Daed, the thing is, I am officially retired. These are all my people, not yours, and they're all retired too. You can wave dossiers and orders till the Vampires return to their earth, but nobody here will make a move without my say so.

"Whether we decide to cooperate or disappear, it will be my choice and theirs. Not yours. Not anybody else's. I've lived under your radar for a long time, as have all these folks. Do not presume that we can't and won't do it again, just to piss you off."

Dropping her leg and chair to the floor, she deliberately set the bottle down between them, insubordination dripping from her voice as she pinned him with very cold green eyes. "Let me enlighten you on a couple of things here, *Daed*. If you are full of shit on this, if this is just another one of your half-assed publicity stunts to maneuver you into some sort of promotion or position, you will not come back alive from this mission. I will see to that personally. And call me *Pumpkin* one more time and I will bronze your testicles for earrings. Am I making myself clear, *Major*?"

"Crystal." Daedalus knew better than to push her too far.

He wasn't high on Gillian's list of favorite people for a lot of reasons. The biggest reason being that Daed had a habit of volunteering "his team" for missions, then getting yanked out at the last minute. They took the risks, he wound up looking good. Gillian hated his guts and the rest of the team were not about to go against the opinion of their commanding officer.

"Good. Now give us the briefing and we'll tell you what we're going to do," she ordered him, after making sure he looked nervous enough.

They all sat back to listen. Aleksei and Tanis were allowed to remain under protest. When Daed initially objected to their presence, Gillian got up to leave and her entire team mirrored her. He settled for having the Vampires at the party.

By the time he was finished with the sordid tale of child trafficking in third-world countries, there was an outraged silence around the table. Interestingly, it was Aleksei who broke it. "I will offer all resources at my disposal if it will help you accomplish your goal of delivering these children, Gillian."

She shot him a grateful look. "Thanks, Aleksei; it would help if you could take Tanis and organize some sort of a grassroots campaign back in Romania. Make the people aware that even Humans they know can be monsters."

"And they're worse, because you can't tell the Human monsters from the Human heroes, anymore than you can tell the true monsters from the monsters who are on our side." Jenna was waxing philosophic, but every once in awhile, she had an offhanded idea. Possibly a result of all the chemicals soaking into her brain from her constantly changing hair color.

"That is an excellent point, *signorina*," Aleksei stated. "I will contact Osiris and determine if there is way that we can better establish who is 'on our side,' as you say."

Gillian beamed at him. He had all the qualities of a spectacular leader: intellect, compassion, honor, power that he did not squander in petty displays and some very powerful friends. Combined with the fact that he was simply gorgeous and it was enough to warm her opinion of him down to her toes. Tanis watched as his former lover and his brother exchanged a glance. Gillian was Aleksei's perfect complement if she could get her commitment-phobic self under control long enough to let him try to win her. Sometimes everyone needed a little push.

"Gillian." Tanis strode to her and practically lifted her into his arms. "This is only a temporary good-bye, *dolcezza*."

He kissed both her cheeks, hugged her quickly, then turned her and propelled her toward Aleksei. "You two say your farewells; I will assist Trocar and the Major in getting your things down to the street. I am very tired and wish to return to my homeland as quickly as possible."

That earned him a look from Gillian that said she knew he was full of shit. Tanis was rehydrated with borrowed corpuscles and was no more tired than she was.

In his brother's mind, Tanis added quickly, *"NOW would be the time for a poignant good-bye with the* piccola guerriera. *As the Humans say, do not blow it, brother."*

Her thoughts were interrupted by Aleksei gently taking her hand and looping it through his arm. "I would very much like a private word, Gillian, before you depart."

"We'll be waiting downstairs—all night!" Kimber hollered after them as Aleksei took her out a side door in the pub into a darkened alleyway amid the snickerings of her team.

Detaching herself from Aleksei, Gillian opted for distance and leaned against the damp brick wall of the outer building. Arms crossed, one leg propped behind her, she waited patiently while the Romanian Vampire paced uncomfortably. She'd never seen him so nervous. What the hell?

"That word, Aleksei?" Gillian finally asked. They needed to

get this over with and get going. His power was crawling over her, raising the hair on her arms and ruffling at her neck.

He stopped pacing and turned to face her. A kind of surreal peace stole over him. They were free of her oath, free of time constraints and yet now there was no time. If he wanted her to know anything, it would have to be now. Anything might happen between now and their next meeting. The strong attraction was still there. Gillian was just avoiding it and him like the plague since he'd found her.

Only geography, Gillian's professional oath and their combined honor and had kept them apart thus far. Her clear, Nile-green eyes regarded him warily, her posture closed and defensive. It irritated him that she was putting up walls now, but he wasn't about to let his temper get in the way, not this time.

Closing the distance, he placed a hand on the wall by her head, the other tipping her chin up to look at him, trapping her with his larger frame. "I expect you to return to me in one piece, Gillian. There is much we need to discuss upon your return."

Gillian watched him, not moving a muscle, wary, and on edge. "I have no intention of getting myself killed, Aleksei."

Goddess, he smelled good. That familiar warm scent of him, cardamom and nutmeg, hints of pine and fresh forest loam stirred her blood and she swayed ever so minutely toward him. His voice was a sultry beacon to her senses. She felt herself growing warmer, damper. Dammit, he was too close, crowding her. She could have stepped out from under his arm if she'd wanted to. Problem was, she didn't think she wanted to.

Tanis was over and done with; Dante was a bad taste in her mouth. Aleksei was a lot of things, she just wasn't sure if she wanted to start something right now. Good thing he was decisive, even if she was hesitant.

Two long, elegant fingers gently urged her chin and mouth up further, his other hand coming off the wall to lightly play down her hair and over her shoulder. "I want you to know something, Gillian, I have watched you, waited for you so you would not be foresworn on your oath. In my waiting, I have discovered that I was what you named me: chauvinistic, not recognizing your own innate gifts and abilities, believing you fragile and in need of guidance. In my desire and need to keep you safe, I may have pushed you away."

Shit, now he really was too close. Her brain was trying to

register what he was saying but his lips were against her temple, his scent warm and comforting.

"We both may have done or said some things that were regretful, Aleksei," she admitted, more to herself than to him. Unconsciously, she shifted a little, standing straighter and almost but not quite leaning into him.

"You have my respect, Gillian Key." His breath was simmering on her cheek and neck.

"Think on this one thing, *piccola*, while you are away fighting real monsters." His mouth paused over hers, his silvery eyes searching her own, questions in them. He leaned closer, his mouth closing the gap with hers with infinite grace and elegance until she stopped him with a hand against his spectacular chest.

"What one thing?"

Oh, for Goddess's sake, quit with the breathy voice, she scolded herself. "Think on what?" There. That was steadier.

For an answer, he sealed her mouth with his own. His lips warm silk, his tongue a hot wetness flicking over her mouth so that she opened to his explorations. It was tantalizing as he drew her against him, pressing her close, closer.

Damn, he is tall, she thought as she let him draw her into the deep kiss and powerful embrace. Her hands climbed around his slender waist and up his back of their own volition. She felt him tremble as she stroked back down the iron-hard muscles to cup his chiseled rear and press him against her body, molding them together until there was absolutely no space between them. The warm, firm heat of his right hand alternately teased her breasts into excited peaks, and slid over her bottom to tantalize her more. His left hand was woven into her hair, cupping her head, tilting her into his kiss.

Aleksei was almost afraid to move, afraid that if he disturbed their global explorations of each other that he would break the magical shell around them, shattering them both into pieces that would never quite be whole again. Senses already on overload felt her response, scented her heat as she came alive under his touch. Her hands roaming over his body, lightly at first, then with more strength, more demand, coiled his inner beast like a serpent ready to strike.

His own body had welded to hers, fitting perfectly against her despite their difference in height. There wasn't time to express all the pent-up emotion and passion in that kiss; he wouldn't sully the moment by taking her against the wall like an animal. Her liquid heat pooling in her pelvis and rushing through her veins called to him. Fangs exploded from the elastic tissue in his mouth, demanding that he take her and take her now. Shuddering with need, he fought not to crush her to him, fought against his instincts to sink his fangs into her neck.

Gillian's empathy was wide open; she felt his turmoil, then she felt the razor points of his fangs with her tongue an before she nicked herself on one. There was a guttural groan, whether from Aleksei or herself she couldn't be sure, and a powerful arm snaked under her thighs, lifting her in that heartbeat space of time before she tasted blood.

Aleksei's hips wedged between hers, opening her to the press of his sex as he pushed her against the wall of the alley. She felt him squarely between her legs. He was rock hard, large, thick, aggressive, his blood surging to completely fill the erectile tissue in time with their rioting pulses. Wrapping her legs around his waist, she let it happen, let her own passion and his need drive them both. Small, strong hands tangled in his thick wavy hair, pale digits in a sea of black, pulling him tighter to her mouth as she ground against him.

Through the tight linen pants he wore, he felt her damp heat, was helpless as she pressed rhythmically against his shaft, separated only by their clothing. Some flicker of sanity left in him kept him from crushing her against the bricks or tearing off their clothing to sink his raging erection deep inside the lovely body that was riding against his own. Aleksei held her with infinite gentleness, tenderly, gathering his power and pressing against the silken veil of her mind. Her blood was in his mouth from the nick on her tongue and he savored it, the sweet hot spice of her.

"*Open for me,* cara mia. *Open your mind and your heart. Let me in, Gillian.*"

She felt his deep, urgent whisper in her mind like an erotic wind. He could strip away her defenses, lay her bare to his power, but he didn't. He asked. Opening her eyes, she looked into pools of molten mercury. It was a request, not a demand. Right then, she wanted to give him what he wanted. To find out what that voice, those eyes, his power and his body promised. Gently she parted the curtain, cautious but trusting him.

Aleksei flowed into her mind like warm honey, fed her passion with his own, then effortlessly tipped her over the edge of a shining orgasm that shook her to the core. He felt her lower body react, felt her come against him, shuddering; heard her deep moan of gratification against his mouth. Large hands cupped her buttocks and pulled her tightly against him, never breaking the kiss, never shying away from her need as she pressed her contracting body tighter against his burgeoning erection.

As she trembled with aftershocks in his arms, Aleksei turned to rest her on his body, his own back against the rough bricks, and tried to remember how to breathe. Ending the kiss as softly as he had begun it, his raging body still hard and hot, he trailed his knuckles gently down her cheek, pressing his lips to her forehead, still holding her tightly but tenderly and calming his own racing heartbeat.

"Holy smokes, Aleksei." Gillian's voice was breathy, full of surprise and wonderment. "Do you always kiss like that?"

A deep chuckle answered her, "Only you, *carissima*."

"Well, damn." She shifted a little in his arms and he lowered her slowly, then wrapped his arm around her shoulders, bracing her as she got her sea legs back again. Looking down at him, she could see that he was in the same aroused state of moments ago.

"My turn." She moved in front of him, gently caressing the engorged outline as she began unfastening his trousers.

Aleksei's breath left him in a hiss. He caught her hand gently but firmly. "Save it for when you come back to me, *angelica*."

Green eyes widened. "I can't leave you like this, it's not right." She was stunned that he would ask her such a thing.

Bending, he kissed her mouth tenderly as it started to curve into an outraged bow and wrapped her captured hand around his waist. He stroked her hair, then cupped her chin again as he pulled away.

"I am fine, Gillian. I wanted to give something to you before you left. Something for you to think about while we are apart. I can wait for your return. There is not enough time now for me to make love to you properly. When we meet again, there will be time."

A golden eyebrow arched and her eyes narrowed a little. "Pretty sure of yourself, aren't you?"

"No. I am sure of you." Aleksei took her hand and led her back to the door leading back into the pub. Opening it, he gestured for her to proceed him, a smoky smile on his breathtaking face, his eyes still blazing desire down at her.

"Men. Jesus. I will never understand men," Gillian groused,

shaking her head as she moved through the door. Aleksei's rich laughter followed her inside, making her shiver with anticipation. She was still shivering at the memory two hours later as she boarded the plane for her team's next mission.

Explore the outer reaches of imagination with Ace and Roc—don't miss these authors of dark fantasy and urban noir that take you to the edge and beyond.

Patricia Briggs	Karen Chance	Anne Bishop
Simon R. Green	Caitlin Kiernan	Janine Cross
Jim Butcher	Rachel Caine	Sarah Monette
Kat Richardson	Glen Cook	Doug Clegg

THE ULTIMATE IN FANTASY!

From magical tales of distant worlds to stories of those with abilities beyond the ordinary, Ace and Roc have everything you need to stretch your imagination to its limits.

Marion Zimmer Bradley/Diana Paxon

Guy Gavriel Kaye

Dennis McKiernan

Patricia McKillip

Robin McKinley

Sharon Shinn

Katherine Kurtz

Barb and J. C. Hendees

Elizabeth Bear

T. A. Barron

Brian Jacques

Robert Asprin

penguin.com